S0-AAE-711

8/18

DATE DUE

09-08-18		

Blue Magic

A Novel

Debby Bloch

ISBN-13: 9781542343848
ISBN-10: 1542343844

To Martin Bloch, my husband and reader extraordinaire

Give me leave
To tell you once again that at my birth
The front of heaven was full of fiery shapes,
The goats ran from the mountains, and the herds
Were strangely clamorous to the frighted fields.
These signs have mark'd me extraordinary.

William Shakespeare
Henry Iv, Part I
Owen Glendower

CHAPTER 1

Sunday Morning

EDWYNA GLENDOWER SCOFFED at all those who thought she had magical powers. Whenever anyone said how lucky she was to have her work or find her condo or even just get a parking space, she bristled. Sometimes it seemed it wasn't just her mother who thought she was tuned into some mystical other world. Maybe, she thought, it was because she was so tall. Exactly six feet on her two bare feet, as she liked to say. Or because her hair, raven black and streaked with shimmering silver, hung straight down around her face and beyond her shoulders. It might have been her clothes, she surmised. She favored flowing garments in varying shades of blue—periwinkle, aquamarine, cerulean—decorated with embroidered objects which she said were not celestial symbols, although they did resemble stars and the moon. Whatever others thought, Edwyna knew she was perfectly ordinary. She was a woman who possessed the usual powers of a woman who knew her own mind and had been getting what she wanted for more than forty years. Forty-eight, almost forty-nine years, to be precise.

Edwyna slipped out of bed and into her indigo silk dressing gown. She looked back at the six feet of lump remaining under the duvet. Nick was still sleeping peacefully, unaware of the sun or her movements. He gave a gentle snort, turned over, and sank more deeply under the covers.

He was okay, Edwyna thought, but just okay. His carefully cropped grey hair with the always perfectly squared-off barber line at the back of his neck, his toned calves, his flat stomach—all showed he took good care of himself.

That was the problem. He took care of himself, not of her. She couldn't put her finger on it. When they were together he was attentive, took her hand or arm—almost in an old-fashioned way—when they walked in the street. Chose films she'd expressed an interest in, or made reservations at a restaurant she'd mentioned she liked. But there was something robotic about the way he did it. She remembered reading that society hostesses kept diaries of their dinner parties including guests and menus so that they never served the same dish twice to any guest. Maybe he had a file in which he entered the likes and dislikes of every woman he dated. She knew she wasn't the only one he dated, but that wasn't what bothered her. It was just that he never seemed fully present.

True, they made love after each of their biweekly dates. Making love was his saving grace. Edwyna mentally replayed the lovemaking of the previous evening. Just thinking about their lovemaking made her want him again.

Edwyna had felt the pulsing down to her toes and up into her throat. The feeling returned almost as if the sleeping Nick were awake, that he was doing what he'd done eight hours earlier. Edwyna allowed herself to close her eyes and remember his lovemaking, moment by moment.

As Nick carefully circled the areola of her left breast with his tongue, she longed for him to reach the nipple and take it fully into his mouth. But she wasn't speaking, just moaning, just catching her breath and holding it. He ignored the silent plea of her nipple and moved his mouth to her right breast. He rose above her and clasped both of her breasts in his hands, then rubbed them with his thumbs. Of course that did not bring the relief that Edwyna sought. It simply made the demands of her body more insistent. Nick released her breasts and moved his mouth, his tongue, the curls of his moustache down the center of her body. He stopped at her navel and paid as much attention to that single spot as an artist seeking to capture the beauty of a sunrise might pay to a single ray of light. The feeling was exquisite and unbearable. Then his mouth was on her. It was wonderful and terrible. Too much and not enough. He stopped. Sat back on his haunches. Looked into Edwyna's eyes, held them in his gaze as he slowly entered her. Edwyna tried to raise her hips to set a rhythm, to catch him in her rhythm. He held her hips steady as he slowly moved his engorged penis in and out, in and out, until Edwyna gave in to his rhythm, made it her own, and felt her climax shudder through her. Then he increased his pace until he, too, climaxed with an exultant cry. For a moment Nick lay, heavy on Edwyna. She reached around him to hold him to her, but he was ready, as always, to roll to the other side of the bed.

That was it. As engaged as he'd been with her, as into her—in every sense—until he came, once he came, he was gone. Edwyna knew from all their previous dates that there would be no repeat of the lovemaking.

Edwyna slid her feet into her slippers, slippers that perfectly matched the blue of her robe. That moment of donning robe and slippers always satisfied her. She felt regal. Nick slept on. She walked quietly across the burgundy carpet of her spacious bedroom and glanced at her reflection in the gold-rimmed mirror above the bureau. She bent at the waist to free her long, dark hair from its bedtime disarray. Then stood and looked in the mirror again.

"Up already?" Nick sat up and the comforter slid down his chest.

Edwyna didn't turn, but watched Nick's reflection in the mirror.

"What time is it? I hope I didn't oversleep," he said.

That's what she meant. How could you oversleep on a Sunday?

He swung his legs over the side of the bed. "I'd better get going."

She turned to face him. "Would you like some breakfast?" Edwyna didn't worry about having fresh croissants or fruit to serve because she knew the answer before she asked.

"Thanks. Just some coffee would be great. I'd like to get to the gym by ten and it's after nine already. I'll take a quick shower and be out of your hair."

He never asked what she would be doing. It was outside the boundaries of their twice monthly meetings.

Shower, coffee, gone.

Edwyna made herself a latte and settled down with the *San Francisco Chronicle.* There was hardly ever news about the Inner Sunset, the neighborhood in which she lived. It was quiet, almost suburban, with its one-family and small multifamily homes. Edwyna appreciated its mix of ethnicities and ages. On her block alone, there were two elderly Chinese couples; a Pakistani family of granny, mom, dad, and two teenagers; and a young couple, both of whom appeared to be medical students or interns at the nearby hospital complex of UCSF—the University of California in San Francisco. Irving Street, just two blocks north of Edwyna's home, held a number of small local shops, an excellent supermarket, and many eating places, ranging from a Jamba Juice to one of the best sushi restaurants in town. Golden Gate Park was one block beyond Irving. Lincoln, the street that bordered the park, led right to the Pacific Ocean, less than three miles west of Edwyna's home.

Edwyna turned to the real estate section. Although she wasn't in the market for a new condo and was happy in the one she owned, her business instincts kicked in as she watched the rising and falling home values—mostly falling since the market crash that began with Lehman Brothers' bankruptcy in September, about six months earlier.

That afternoon, Edwyna phoned her parents. This was part of her own Sunday routine, a part she always—almost always—enjoyed. Her mother and father still lived in the Petaluma home in which Edwyna had grown up. It was a two-story, white clapboard home complete with center hall, dormer bedrooms, and a front porch. The front porch even held a swing-for-two suspended from the porch ceiling by sturdy chains. The home was surrounded by life. A well-mowed front lawn yielded to birches that stood sentinel between the sides of the house and the neighbors' properties. The trees, in turn, gave way to Edwyna's father's prized rose bushes, the crowning glory of the backyard.

"Hello?"

"Hi, Dad," Edwyna answered.

"It's my girl!" Edwyna heard him call out to her mother. "Freddy, it's our girl on the phone. Wait for your mom, sweetheart."

Edwyna loved it when her father answered the phone. Every time she called, his response was as joyous and surprised as if she didn't call every Sunday and sometimes in between. And she

loved that he immediately called to her mother. Her parents—
Edward and Winifred or, as she liked to call them, Eddy and
Freddy—were as perfectly matched as their names suggested.
And calling her "his girl" and "our girl." Terrific! She knew other
friends might object to what they would consider being infan-
tilized. She read it for what it was—love. She might be in her
forties, but when she spoke to her father, she was a girl again.

After a few moments, Edwyna heard her mother's quickened
breathing as she picked up the extension. "I could not control
that dog," her mother said. "She got it into her addled brain that
there was some danger lurking in the rose bushes and she would
not stop barking or—it doesn't matter—here I am now."

"Hi, Mom," Edwyna said and smiled to herself as she pictured
Athena, barking at the rose bush roots, undoubtedly finding life
that no one else in the family could see. Despite her substantial
size, Athena—part bull mastiff, part foxhound—never seemed
to outgrow her puppy state of mind.

The usual Sunday morning conversations followed. Her father wanted to know everything that had happened during the
week, every detail of her accounting practice, everyone she'd
seen, each meal she'd eaten. It was only after he was satisfied
with the detailed history that the more probing conversation her
mother preferred could begin.

"What's the matter, sweetheart?"

"Nothing. Not anything. Just . . ." Edwyna didn't finish her
sentence.

"I'm just saying that the longer you spoke to your dad, the
quieter . . ."

"I guess that recitation of the week, I don't know . . ."

"Did anything happen that . . . ?"

"I guess it's what did and didn't happen. Nick . . ." Edwyna's voice trailed off.

Winifred waited a moment, then said, "He seems nice enough."

"Mom, that's just it. He's 'nice,' but not enough. I want someone I can really . . . Someone who . . ." Edwyna's voice trailed off again.

"Someone who—who what?" Winifred asked.

"I don't know how to describe it, but what I want is what you and Dad . . ."

"We don't always get along as perfectly as . . ."

"I know that. Remember, it's me. I heard some of your arguments."

"And not only arguments. There were the times . . . ," Winifred began.

"I remember some of the stony silences, too. But I always knew . . ."

"Knew what?"

"That deep down you two were—are—so in love with each other. And that's what I want. To feel that love and be loved."

"If you can figure out what you really want. You can have it. You always get what you want. Sometimes when you were younger, I thought . . ."

Edwyna tried not to let her annoyance show in her voice. "Please don't even start that idea. Please."

"Remember the doll you wanted? You'd already gotten all your birthday presents. But there was that doll in the window and you just wouldn't let go. Maybe I should have given in, but I didn't want to spoil you. And then, the next day, in the mail . . ."

"That was a coincidence."

"Still . . ."

"Mom, please. All my friends talk about how their mothers press their buttons. And I feel so great that we don't have that problem, but this idea that . . . We have been over this ground a thousand times. I know you want me to be special in some way. Believe me, if I had a magic wand and could wave it to bring the perfect man to me, I would do it. But wishes and wands don't add up to real life."

"And you're an accountant so you know what adds and what doesn't. I give up."

Edwyna imagined her mother raising her hands in surrender. "Mom, how about some practical advice."

"I wish I was the one with magical powers. I'd give you the man you want."

"Can you get away from the magic?"

"You've always gotten plenty of attention from men. Maybe you need to figure out exactly what you really want, put it into words."

"I could try to do that. Then what?"

"When I tell you what has always worked for you, you . . ."

"Right. I think we've gone in the same circle too many times today. I'll call next Sunday."

"Or before if you'd like," Winifred concluded.

The story of the doll that Winifred liked to repeat was true. Edwyna remembered wanting that doll so badly. It was right after her fourth birthday. She'd already gotten lots of birthday presents and had a dozen or more dolls, both new and familiar. But this doll sat in the toy store window, dressed gloriously in all blue—already Edwyna's favorite color. Usually the girl dolls came dressed in pink or yellow, but this Magic Doll, as Edwyna thought of it, had a blue dress that came just below its dolly knees, blue socks, tiny yellow shoes, and a blue sunbonnet with yellow daisies.

Maybe the doll remained so fixed in both their memories because it was the doll that had started what was probably the first argument they'd had. Edwyna remembered standing in front of the window, staring at the doll and insisting that she must have it.

"Mommy, please. That doll, I want that doll." Edwyna was sure that's what she'd said.

"You just got a new doll for your birthday." She was equally sure that had been her mother's response.

As Edwyna thought about the doll, she could almost feel the cold of the store window on the palms of her hands. She looked down at her now long, tapered fingers and remembered being little. In her memory the argument went on for some time and ended with her being pulled away from the window, her hand balled into a fist inside her mother's larger hand, her shoes scraping on the sidewalk.

The doll in the window arrived the next day by parcel post. Its little arms seemed to reach out to Edwyna from within the cardboard box. It was wearing its perfect outfit of blue and yellow. Edwyna bent down to the doll. "What's your name?" she asked it. And she heard it murmur, "Inanna."

"This is my magic doll," Edwyna had told her mother. "I got it by magic."

"You got it from Aunt Flora. In the mail."

However the doll, Inanna, had come into her life, Edwyna admitted that when she was young—six or so—she really did believe it had magic powers. She told Inanna all her problems and asked her to solve them.

The biggest one was school. Not long after she began first grade, Edwyna regularly got into trouble for wiggling, giggling, and chatting to the kids around her. As soon as she finished her work, while everyone else was still laboriously spelling, she liked to get the others to laugh by making silly faces and sounds. When, in the middle of a term she was moved from first grade to second grade, she was sure it was Inanna who had intervened on her behalf. After all, she had whispered over and over to Inanna, "I wish, I wish I could be in second grade." When she came home from school the day that Mrs. Berlin, her teacher, had moved her into the second grade classroom, she went to her room and thanked Inanna.

That evening at dinner, she told her parents about the move. "I wished and wished and wished it. I told Inanna. And then it happened. Today. I came home and said 'thank you' to Inanna. I gave her a big hug, too."

"I think you have to thank Mrs. Berlin," Edward said.

"Yes," Winifred agreed. "She was the one who noticed how bored you were and figured out that you were ready for second grade."

"But it was Inanna who told Mrs. Berlin I was bored," Edwyna insisted.

Of course, Edwyna thought, her parents had been correct when she was a child. All the special events that Edwyna had attributed to Inanna had perfectly rational explanations ranging from adult—not occult—manipulations or simply coincidence. But—and here was the irony—

as Edwyna grew out of the period she thought of as her "magic phase," her mother began to believe that Edwyna did have special powers. So that now there was hardly a problem or issue Edwyna could bring up that did not prompt her mother to suggest that she rely on those powers. Much as she would have liked to wish her life into perfection, to rely on a magic doll, potions, signs, or portents, she could not.

She did wish that she could stop revisiting these childhood memories, but every time her mother alluded to the doll or so-called magic events, the thoughts would flood her mind. Surely if she had magic powers, she would be able to control her own thoughts.

CHAPTER 2

What She Wants

ALL AFTERNOON, EDWYNA kept coming back to the conversation with her mother. While her mother had really gone overboard about the magic stuff, she did have a point when she said that Edwyna had to figure out what she wanted. Edwyna realized that all the success she'd had in life came from knowing precisely what she sought and then seeking it in an organized way.

That evening, Edwyna sat at her desk, an old-fashioned table with a top of well-worn green leather supported by gently curving legs. Edwyna had found it several years earlier, wandering around through one of the many impromptu garage sales in her neighborhood, the Inner Sunset of San Francisco. And at another similar sale, she'd found the perfect older oak armchair. She was not an antiques aficionado, so she didn't know if the chair and desk matched in period or style, but the not-too-worn patina of the chair seemed to speak the same language as the desk. While she liked the desk and chair, Edwyna's favorite piece, across the room from the desk, was the large wing chair that sat in perfect alignment with a corner of her bay window. That was her place for reflection and dreaming. The desk, on the other hand, was her place for work. Although most of her accounting practice took place in her downtown office, she kept the current *U.S. Master Tax Guide* on a bookshelf near the desk for late night or other urgent work. And she intended to get to work. She would figure out what she wanted, put it into words, and develop a plan of action.

Edwyna knew she wanted a man. But what else? What could she say about the man she wanted? She couldn't describe his features or physique, his age or tastes. It wasn't just a man she wanted. It was a lover. No, Edwyna thought, she'd had plenty of lovers—and she wasn't going to reveal the number to anyone, certainly not to a new lover. Something more. She wanted to be someone's beloved. And she wouldn't mind if he were her beloved as well. Now, as she neared her forty-ninth birthday, she worried that it might be too late. And if forty-nine came, could fifty be far behind? She knew she looked great, and she didn't feel at all different, not inside, not where it counted. And maybe the fact of almost forty-nine was the perfect motivation to change how she'd lived, or more precisely, how she'd loved.

However she'd accomplished it—"luck" as her friends said, or "magic" as her mother said, or just knowing people and the world as she herself thought—she'd had plenty of men in her life, but none of them had given her that feeling she'd read about, seen in films, heard in songs. The closest she came to recognizing what love would be was seeing a man take a woman's face between his hands as he kissed her. Even seeing those movie scenes sent chills through Edwyna's body. That feeling was enthralling, complete, different from the sexiest scene of touching, clinching, or ripping clothes from each other's body.

Her lovers had done all of that. They loved her breasts— rubbed them through her clothes, cupped them in their hands, kissed her nipples, licked and sucked. Edwyna couldn't help but smile to herself as she pictured all the men she knew lined up at her breasts, taking turns with them. She had been crushed against a man's chest and pulled in with hands on her butt so that they were pelvis to pelvis. And she'd been in that rip-our-clothes-off-this minute-before-we-really-get-the-front-door closed scenario as well. All that heat! Where did it go?

There must be some law of physics, exchange of matter and energy, some rule that would explain where the heat went. Edwyna didn't mean just the heat of the moment, she meant the heat that seemed to dissipate with the length of the relationship. Maybe there was a formula. She tried to work it out. $(HNew)(-T)=HEend$. The heat of a new relationship multiplied by the negative of the number of days or weeks or months of the relationship gave you the heat at the end. Less than zero! If she were honest with herself, she'd have to admit that she was the one who ended a relationship as often, if not more often, than the men with whom she'd been involved. She'd never had the patience to see if there was more than met the eye.

No one, not one of them, had ever put his hands on her face and held her still in a long kiss.

She wanted to feel that way about a man, too. She wanted to be in love. What would that look like? Movie scenes flitted across her mind. Black and white films. The ones she watched on television on TCM. She'd put her arms around his neck, twining her hands together, stand on tiptoe or raise one leg. That was romantic but still not quite the same feeling as she would have when her true love held her face. What would make a man feel as loved as she wanted to feel?

She'd have to ask Howard. Howard was Edwyna's neighbor, the closest she had to a best friend. He lived alone in the other condo in the two-family building. The design of the building was a familiar one in San Francisco. From the street, a flight of stairs led to a landing, common to both apartments. At the landing level, the front door on the right opened to Howard's apartment, which was on the first floor. Edwyna's door, on the left, opened to a flight of stairs to her second-floor apartment.

Edwyna had never had one best friend. And just as she'd had, and still had, many boyfriends—now man friends, or as they now said friends with benefits—she'd also had any number of women friends, but none of them that one true friend. She heard other women talk about the one woman in their life to whom they could tell everything, the person who could call them up short when they said, "I never felt that way before." The friend who would say, "Yes you did. Don't you remember when . . . ?" Well, never mind, it wasn't a best friend Edwyna sought.

Edwyna looked around the room as if the answer were hidden somewhere in her furniture or its walls. She studied her plush red sofa and the long glass table in front of it. She stared at the fireplace. Unfortunately she couldn't light a fire—another "spare the air" day in San Francisco meant no wood-burning fireplaces. Nevertheless she stared at the lightless logs, looking for a way to find love. She wished people were right when they thought she had magic powers. She'd just "abracadabra" and presto, a man would drop down through the chimney. Not Santa Claus, she hoped. Not even Edmund Gwenn, who'd played her favorite movie Santa Claus. Although she wouldn't mind someone like John Payne who believed in SC and convinced Natalie Wood and Maureen O'Hara that there was a Kris Kringle. She knew her mind was wandering whenever she began mentally to replay favorite films.

She knew what she had to do. She had to write down what she wanted. Did she dare to say something that seemed so simple yet also so romantic, so movie-like? What the hell, she thought and reached for a blue pencil from the box that always stood ready on her desk. The desk's single drawer held a dozen or so sheets of linen paper and a leather-bound notebook. She drew a sheet of paper from the top of the pile and wrote: "I want a man who loves me and who I can love." She stopped. Should the second *who* be *whom*? She realized that question could keep her going all evening and that would not be productive. But she was also reluctant to write the next sentence. She closed her eyes for a moment, then opened them and gripped the pencil. "I will know he is the right man when he takes my face between his hands as he kisses me."

Edwyna sat back, relieved. She read what she'd written, folded the sheet of paper, and slipped it into the drawer under the blank sheets and as far back as it would go.

Now what? If there was no magic, then she'd just have to take action. She'd make a list of what to do. Her list-making dated back at least to junior high school. The first list she could recall was designed to get friends.

In junior high school, there were lots of new girls, girls who didn't know how different she'd been in elementary school where she'd sat in the back of the classroom, a loner, her eyes always in a book, her mind far away in realms where the powers of children made a difference. *Dandelion Wine*; *The Lion, the Witch and the Wardrobe*; all the Narnia books, one after another, straight through to *The Last Battle*. Then *Over Sea Under Stone*—how she'd wished she had a brother like Simon or Barney, a brother for mysterious and magical adventures, but she only had Donald, her very ordinary, very annoying younger brother.

In junior high school, she put aside the books long enough to watch the other girls and make a list.

1. Wear plaid skirts, blouses with round collars, and sweaters with buttons down the front.

2. Giggle a lot!
3. Eat only tuna fish sandwiches for school lunch, and if my mother includes a banana, say, "Eehew."
4. Never bring a thermos of chocolate milk (even though I love it). Buy a drink in a cardboard container.

She remembered that after wanting girlfriends—and she did become popular within just a matter of weeks—she'd also discovered boys in junior high school. She wanted them to like her too. She'd made a list then. What was on that list? All she could remember was that it included licking her lips, sticking out her chest, laughing at their jokes, and not answering math questions before they did. That had worked in junior high school, and it still seemed to work, even though all the men she now met were past junior high age, at least chronologically.

She had to admit, if only to herself, that in junior high school, she'd not only made the lists that led to her rapid success, but she'd also told Inanna what she wanted. "Girlfriends, girlfriends," she'd whispered over and over in Inanna's small plastic ear. Then later, "A boy. A special boy. A boyfriend," became her secret message to Inanna. Edwyna smiled as she thought of those simpler times, her simpler self. Of course it had been the analysis and action that brought her friends, not the silly whispering.

Edwyna wasn't sure what had put thoughts of her childhood into her mind. It had probably been the conversation with her mother. Her mother could implant an unshakeable train of thought with just a word or two.

Edwyna still held the blue pencil in her hand, a pencil that brought back another flood of memories. High school and the blue pencils. If you didn't understand the beginnings of algebra, you just went to Edwyna's house. She sat down with you on her bedroom floor and, using her blue pencil, showed you how to find X. If your English composition seemed to be decomposing before your very eyes, Edwyna's blue pencil helped you move sentences and paragraphs around until the whole essay made sense. Maybe that was the start of everyone in school talking about Edwyna's magic. Everyone called it "E's Magic Blue Pencil."

Edwyna knew it was just an editor's pencil that Edward had given her from his office. She'd visited his office—he was a newspaper editor—and had so loved the blue pencils that he'd given her a dozen on the spot. She kept them in a special canister that she'd covered with blue contact paper. Without any conversation about it, her father refilled the canister whenever it was almost empty. Edwyna loved that about her dad.

Edwyna didn't love the idea that her pencil was magic. That suggested the same idea her mother now wanted to talk about, about how she got whatever she wanted through some sort of magic. She was able to ignore her mother—all the girls ignored their mothers—but not her friends. When her friends didn't stop calling them "E's magic blue pencils," Edwyna felt a combination of pride and discomfort. Pride in helping her friends and discomfort with the thought she had access to . . . to something otherworldly. That's when the withdrawing started. Now, when anyone suggested that there was something out of the ordinary about Edwyna, something that made her special or different, she stopped seeing them.

Although high school time was the beginning of her refusal to accept any magic in herself or her life, when she went to college, she still brought Inanna with her, kept her propped up on pillows on her bed, and whispered to her from time to time.

It was her first year in college and she could not have been happier. She was flying, floating. Even as she enjoyed the required

core subjects, she looked forward to the reading, the performing, the total involvement in the production of the plays that
she would study as a theater major, a performance major. Even
better, she and Karen, her roommate, had become instant buddies. They not only shared the disorder of their small room, the
crunch of clothes in their miniscule closet, the fug of sleeping
air above their beds, but also as much of every waking moment
as they could. Karen was her complete opposite. Not just in
looks. Where Edwyna was outgoing and instantly likable, Karen
took longer to get to know. Edwyna was naturally invited to every
event on campus, those that were planned some time in advance
and those that sprang up spontaneously. Pretty soon people
knew that inviting Edwyna meant that Karen would be there as
well.

That togetherness even applied for the time Edwyna spent
with Richard. Most of the time, anyway. Edwyna had met Richard
just a month after her first term began when she went to watch
tryouts for a student-written play about the civil rights movement.
She saw him as soon as she entered the room. He was standing
in front of the stage, slightly to one side, completely engrossed in
the action on the stage. Edwyna had come to the auditions to see
how she'd fare against any college competition, to see if she'd
be as successful in getting roles as she'd been in high school.
But she was barely aware of the readings, as she could not stop
herself from staring at him. He was gorgeous. Tall. Long blonde
hair. A beard. A junior. She felt so lucky when he came up to her
at the end of the tryouts.

"Why didn't you audition?" he asked as if they'd known each
other forever.

"I just wanted to see what it was like. Besides . . ."

"Is this your first year?"

"Freshman. Yes."

"Of course, otherwise I would already know you. And you would be mine!" He wiggled his eyebrows suggestively.

Edwyna knew he was right. She would be his.

"Let's go," he said. He took her arm and linked it through his in a theatrically old-fashioned gesture.

They went right to his room. It looked just like her room except that his corner laundry pile had briefs and T-shirts where hers and Karen's had panties and bras. She was glad she'd worn her new bikini that day because she was pretty sure she knew where the day would end, how it would end.

He sat on his bed, his legs folded, almost in a lotus position, in front of him and patted the spot opposite him. Edwyna sat down, imitated his posture, and looked at him, waiting for the next move.

He just sat there, looking at her. Finally he said, "I've never met anyone as beautiful as you. Where did you come from?"

Edwyna giggled nervously. She shrugged.

"I mean it. Where do you come from?" That ordinary question began a conversation that lasted through what might have been dinner time until late that night. They talked about their families, their first pets, their favorite books, the music they liked, the foods they hated, their best friends since first grade— and their worst.

At that time, when the sky was the darkest and the light seemed to want to break through, their conversation turned to yawns and they lay down next to each other. Richard pulled the comforter off the floor over both their bodies and they fell asleep.

They didn't even kiss until morning. The kiss was perfect, although Edwyna worried about having morning mouth. When he kept kissing her, she guessed her breath was clean. His was fine.

When she returned to her room in time to grab her books for her first class that day, Edwyna stopped to blow Inanna a kiss. "Thank you," she whispered, although there was no one in the room to hear her.

That was the beginning of Richard and Edwyna's time together, and it seemed to get better and better. They were quickly known as a couple on campus and then, with Karen, as a threesome, except for the special times when Edwyna and Richard were alone together in his room. Those times were wonderful. Edwyna was sure they would be together for the rest of their lives. They had so much in common, not just love-making, although that was incredible. Their shared interest in theater, their strong feelings about politics. Just everything.

After the winter break, early in the spring term, Edwyna began to feel something was wrong. First Richard didn't seem to want to spend as much time alone with her in his room.

"I have a cold," he said. "No energy."

"Working on the play. Middle of tech rehearsals," he said. "Just not enough time in the day."

"Too many damn papers due," he said.

When Edwyna asked him what was happening, he grew annoyed. "I told you. I'm busy. I can't just have sex whenever you want it."

When she looked as if she was about to cry, he put his arms around her. "I'm sorry," he said. "I'm just overwhelmed with work. Wait until you're a junior. You'll see how tough the classes become." He kissed her, and they made love after all. But even that makeup sex didn't seem as good as it had been. To Edwyna it seemed as if he wasn't there despite all the evidence of his body.

Edwyna thought she really had to talk to him about what she felt. After all, they could talk about anything, everything. She'd even told him about Inanna and the blue pencils and the magic or whatever it was. One afternoon when they were ostensibly studying together, she began to talk about her feelings. "What's wrong between us?" she asked after a long windup.

"I keep telling you, there's nothing wrong. Don't worry. It's your imagination. Just your imagination." That was his answer.

However, it wasn't her imagination. Cynthia, another theater major, helped her see what was right in front of her.

"Where were you yesterday?" Cynthia asked.

"Yesterday. I don't know. Class. Here. There. What was yesterday?"

"Yesterday at the student union, the rally against apartheid. I saw your buddies. The killing of Stephen Biko, probably by the police, was just too . . ."

"Buddies?" Edwyna asked, not wanting to know the answer.

"Richard. Richard and the quiet one, the blonde, you know who I mean."

"Karen?"

"Right. It's always the three of you."

Edwyna wanted to ask how they looked together. But she didn't ask. She knew.

That evening, Edwyna waited for Karen to return to the room. She waited in vain. As the evening passed into night, Edwyna lay in her bed, covers over her head, trying to still her heart, her body. She knew what the expression "jumping out of her skin" meant. That's what it felt like, like all of her was going to explode.

Karen would have to return sooner or later. Clothes, makeup, books. Something would bring her back to the room. Edwyna waited.

Finally, about five in the afternoon of the following day, Karen returned to the room. "Late. No time to talk. Gotta run," she said, dashing about the small room, throwing clothes down, picking others up.

"What's your hurry?" Edwyna said.

"Just gotta go," Karen said.

"Not yet." Edwyna got up from her bed and sat on the floor in front of the door, her long legs stretched in front of her. "Heard you were at the anti-apartheid rally yesterday."

"Yeah. South Africa. Terrible," Karen said, continuing to pick up, put down, pick up stuff.

"With Richard."

"Ran into him."

"Just ran into him. Hope you didn't get hurt."

"Get hurt? What do you mean 'get hurt'?"

"He's a pretty big guy to run into."

"What are you getting at?"

"You know what I'm asking you. Just answer me. Answer me straight."

"Okay. Yes. Richard and I are—whatever you want to call it—whatever you were doing. Everything you were doing, we are doing. Get it? Now get out of my way."

"Why? Why Richard? You're supposed to be my best friend."

"Your best friend? You think you're so special dragging me to one event after another. I didn't want to be your friend, no less your best friend. But no. When you wanted me to go with you, there was no stopping you. You only *think* you have friends. You just have that stupid doll. You think I don't hear you whispering to her at night. You think you're so great. Imagine what everyone will say when I tell them you still sleep with a doll. You think you have some kind of magical powers. Richard told me that. Magic! What a bunch of hooey! Well, Edwyna—and what kind of stupid name is Edwyna—the magic, if there is such a thing, is mine now. Get up and let me out of here. I'm late to meet Richard."

Edwyna could not have moved from the floor even if she wanted to. Richard and Karen. Whispering to the doll. Richard telling Karen her secrets.

"Get up this minute or your precious doll will be toast." Karen grabbed Inanna from the bed.

Edwyna got up. "I thought you were my friend," she said.

"Shows how much you know," Karen said over her shoulder as she left the room.

The rest of that semester, Edwyna avoided most people, especially those who had been her friends just a few months earlier. She didn't know whether Karen or Richard had ever told anyone about Inanna or about the magic. Really she'd always said *maybe* it was magic. How could Richard have told Karen so much about her? All the secrets she shared with him? Every time she saw people standing together speaking quietly, she felt they were whispering about her. She was miserable, alone and miserable. Karen had moved in with Richard, taking all her stuff with her. Only one soiled T-shirt remained in a corner of the room. When Karen had scooped up her pile of laundry, it had fallen, unseen, to the floor.

Alone in her room, Edwyna made up her mind. No one would make her feel this way again, so betrayed, so foolish. She didn't know which was worse, losing Richard or feeling everyone was laughing at her. She made up her mind. She didn't believe in magic at all. If there was magic and she had the power, Richard would still be with her. She took Inanna from the bed and threw her on the closet floor amid a bunch of papers she'd written, papers she couldn't decide to keep or discard.

By the end of the term, she made up her mind about something else. Even the courses she'd enjoyed seemed boring. She began to study the college catalogue. The courses in theater no longer seemed interesting. They were so wishy-washy. A description of the capstone course sealed the deal:

Complete your major project by fully entering the magic of theatrical production as you select a play . . .

The "magic of theatrical production." No magic for her. For weeks she thumbed through the catalogue, reading course descriptions, trying to find a major that would suit the new Edwyna. Sociology almost made it, but she didn't want to study about people. She didn't even like people anymore. Psychology the same. She wanted a major that dealt with the real world. Nothing mushy like literature or romance languages. She toyed with the idea of majoring in physics or chem, but lab work was not her strength. Then she found what she was looking for. Accounting.

Accounting, the college catalogue said was "the language of business," and it "prepared you directly for work." She liked the sound of that phrase, "prepared you directly for work." It was real. There was nothing magical about it. The course titles were solid. She'd begin with Introduction to Financial Accounting and Introduction to Managerial Accounting. That would be followed by Intermediate Accounting, Cost Accounting, and Advanced Accounting. There were more courses, courses about taxation and auditing. As Edwyna read the names of the courses, she pictured large ledgers with grey cloth covers, ledgers that opened to neatly ruled pages, pages filled with precisely aligned columns of numbers. Perfect. Without even talking to her parents about it, Edwyna saw her advisor and switched her major.

"Of course, you can feel free to major in whichever program suits you best," the advisor said. "But I see so many students who want to go in the other direction. Leave a business-oriented major for theater or something in the arts."

"Shows how little they know," Edwyna thought but did not say.

Enough of past mistakes, of lost love, lost friends. Edwyna knew she was no longer that silly girl. She got up from her desk. Walked across the room. Looked out the window at nothing in particular except the darkness of night. She'd have to get started with the list. She picked up her pencil and retrieved another sheet of vellum from her desk.

1. Ask the married women I know how they met their true loves.

Does that mean their husbands are their true loves? And what about the group of friends who were married for the third time? She had a whole gaggle of them. They said they were a club, all married for the third time and all to men younger than they were. In fact, they were a club, all members of the same book club as well as the thrice-married club. Had those men ever held their wives' faces between their hands? Did they still do that? She had to rethink Item 1.

2. Put a personal ad on the best websites.

That led to thoughts of a sublist. Edwyna always liked it when she could divide a list into subcategories. She tapped the blue pencil against her teeth and thought about a heading for the list. It bothered Edwyna's accountant's mind to have a list without a heading. "Ten Ways to Find a Lover" did not quite say it. She didn't want another lover, and what if there were more or fewer than ten ways. "Finding Men" was too general. She reached into the desk, took out the leather notebook, and opened it to a blank page, marked by a blue ribbon. She wrote, "Finding Love," because that was what she wanted to do, wanted to happen.

She copied the first item on the list, changing it a bit, and then the second. She was ready for subcategories:

1. Ask married women how they met their true loves
2. Put personal ads on websites
   RomeoandJulietMatch.com
   Craigslist
   JDate
   Others?
3. Put an ad in *The New York Review of Books*
4. Find and attend events for singles
5. Read my horoscope
6. Let friends—book club ladies?—know that I'm looking for love.

The book club would be meeting in a few days. Edwyna wasn't sure how she'd ask the women about meeting their true loves.

Maybe she could research that in some other way. But most difficult of all would be telling friends about what she sought. What friends did she mean? Howard? The book club ladies? She tried to create what people called an "elevator speech," a quick spiel about her desires, but she couldn't even begin. Then she pictured herself asking Lila or Carolyn—two of the book club ladies—to lunch. Maybe coffee or tea was better. She imagined how she'd lean across the table and say quietly, "I need your help with . . ." At this point her ability to focus on the conversation failed. Instead her imagination opened the scene.

They were in some crowded coffee shop. People were lined up to place their orders and they stood behind Edwyna's table. The barista was calling out names and coffee drinks. "Mike, cappuccino, extra foam." "Lucy, decaf, soy macchiato." Edwyna decided to delay this course of action.

Edwyna looked over the list. Maybe RomeoandJulietMatch.com would do. She'd have to look into it. Craigslist she'd heard might be sleazy, attract the wrong kind of person, whatever that meant. JDate was certainly a stretch since she wasn't even Jewish, but she'd heard that Jewish men made the best husbands. Did that mean that they also were the best lovers? Scratch "best lovers"; insert "most loving." And *The New York Review of Books*—that was where the Round-Heeled Woman had placed her ad. She had gotten a number of lovers, which was what she wanted, as well as a published book.

Edwyna doubted that she would really read her horoscope. Certainly nothing there could help her. It was as silly as accepting that she had magic powers. She didn't erase Item 5, but she thought of something else. She could put herself on a social networking site and see where that led. She hoped she didn't get too many weirdoes, but maybe that's how she could learn what gave men that feeling of being loved. She added two items:

7. Start a social networking page
8. Research how men feel loved—interview and Internet

Edwyna left the ribbon on the page of lists, closed the notebook, and put it into her desk, then crumpled her first draft and discarded it. She leaned back and let her mind drift to the idea of someone holding her face. She remembered a meditation she'd learned from a guru. She rubbed her hands together until they felt warm, and then placed them so that her palms covered her cheeks and her fingers closed her eyes. Not exactly the same thing, but lovely.

CHAPTER 3

The Book Club

CAROLYN OPENED THE book club discussion. "Enough chit-chat. Overall impressions, a scene that stands out or a character you'd like to talk about."

Edwyna looked at Carolyn, at the three other women in the club, and then back at Diane, in whose home they were meeting. Diane's living room exuded comfort with its cushy sofa and chairs upholstered in the colors of the southwest desert. The most outstanding feature of her living room was the collection of kachina dolls that lined the walls. The kachinas ranged from a simple piece of tree root with the barest representation of features, to elaborate constructions with movable arms and colorful decorations. Some seemed to be made sturdily enough for children to hold and play with. Others—with full figures—looked almost like small humans. Their round eyes seemed to stare out at Edwyna although she could not imagine what sound might come through their beaklike mouths. The kachinas were decorated with feathers or dried flowers, rattles, bows and arrows, and other objects that Edwyna could not identify. Although the discussion had started, Edwyna was distracted by the dolls. She could not keep her eyes off them.

Edwyna could not imagine amassing so large a collection of dolls, in fact of anything. She wondered about them, almost asked Diane about their origin or what they meant to her, but stayed silent. They were in the middle of the discussion of the book. After all, Edwyna knew people who collected penguins and others who had owls. And she'd heard of one woman whose last name was Fox. She had foxes everywhere you looked in her home and even a foxy necklace.

Edwyna tried to focus on the conversation, but her thoughts continued to wander. This was the first meeting of the group outside the book store where they'd begun. She'd had the idea of joining a book club because it would be a nice change from her often solitary work as an accountant but wouldn't require any superficial socializing—the kind where each woman felt the need to tell all. Telling all—or even a part of all—just wasn't her thing. Also, she was at one of the stages in her life where she'd deliberately dropped several women friends and let some others drift away. She thought she'd be safe when she joined a club at her local bookstore, The Ink Stand. But the group had fizzled, as often happens with such groups. Someone moved, another had a baby, a third a divorce. When there were only five stalwarts left, Maggie, the owner of The Ink Stand, had told them they were too few to sustain the club. She'd been warm and polite. Still it was bye-bye bookstore and hello Diane's house with its strange dolls.

Edwyna tore her eyes from the dolls and realized that Carolyn's leadership had led to a spirited discussion about *State of Wonder* by Ann Patchett. The novel was about a woman scientist who followed her lab partner to the Amazon jungle when she learned he suddenly died. It was no wonder that Carolyn, herself a biologist, had chosen this novel, which dealt not only with love and fidelity but with a discovery that might enable women to bear children throughout their lives.

The conversation continued through its usual hour although, unlike the conversations at the bookstore, this was lubricated with some crisp white wine. No one drank to excess, but the group was more relaxed. What Edwyna liked about the club—besides the books chosen and discussed—was that she would not have otherwise known these women.

They had all celebrated their host Carolyn's sixty-fifth birthday a few months earlier at a bookstore meeting. She'd regaled them with tales of biological lab mishaps, events the public never got to see or hear about. Edwyna's favorite was about the time a lab assistant fed some mice to newly arrived snakes, only to learn later that the mice were at the heart of what had at the time seemed a most promising line of inquiry.

There was, however, one strange coincidence in the group. All four of the other women, everyone except Edwyna, had been married multiple times, in fact three times each. None of them seemed embittered by whatever life experiences had caused the turmoil, turmoil that must have ensued between each marriage. After all, there had to have been deaths or divorces. They simply accepted those times in their lives, even laughed about them.

Once in a while, one of the women would reveal a detail about her earlier marriage. It was usually a passing comment. Edwyna didn't even remember how she'd learned that Carolyn's first husband was from Canada, like Carolyn. All Carolyn would ever say about him was that he "was left out in the cold." Or "he just left me cold."

Once Lila, with a perfectly straight face asked, "Do you mean like the Eskimos put their elderly out on an ice floe at the end?"

Carolyn just smiled, held up her glass as if to toast Lila, and rattled the ice cubes in it.

The question was so Lila, a brash transplant from New York City. The same age as Carolyn, she'd long retired from her job as a high school principal. But she hadn't stayed away from adolescents for long and now worked as a volunteer with teen patients at St. Mary's Hospital. A slim five-foot-five, she'd moved to San Francisco with Alan, her third, about fifteen years earlier.

Early in the group's life, when they were still meeting at The Ink Stand, someone had asked her why a native New Yorker, complete with accent and attitude, had given up her work and friends and moved to San Francisco. Lila answered, "I have two words for you." There seemed to be a collective intake of breath as if they all expected the "F" word or something similar. After all, could you trust a New Yorker to behave in the laid-back California style? Looking around, meeting each person eyeball to eyeball, Lila extended the moment. Then she smiled and said, "David. Jeffrey. Do you want to see their photos?" And while everyone gave a relieved laugh, she reached into her handbag, pulled out her iPhone, and clicked on the home screen—a photo of her grandsons, David and Jeffrey. "And," she continued, taking the phone back for a moment, "here's a photo of my current husband, Alan." No one said anything about *current*, but some raised their eyebrows and several women looked at each other, smirked, and nodded. None of the eyebrow raisers or the smirkers were in the newly constituted book club.

The matriarch of the group, the oldest, was Diane. A few months earlier, she'd celebrated her seventy-fifth birthday by climbing Half Dome, the iconic peak in Yosemite. She was probably in better shape than the three sixty-plus-year-olds, and Edwyna thought she herself wouldn't want to enter a physical contest with Diane. Diane had spent a few years in Russia and now worked with Russian émigrés helping them not only to master English but also to navigate life in San Francisco. At the right moments Diane would speak at length about Mark One, Mark Two, and Mark Now. No one could believe that she'd really married three men with the same name.

The first time someone had asked Diane about it, she'd quoted an old Miss Manners newspaper response. "This is what I remember," she said. "Miss Manners was asked: 'What do I do when I call my current boyfriend by my former boyfriend's name?' And Miss Manners had answered, 'That's why the word *darling* was invented.' I figured," Diane continued, "I'd finesse the whole problem of forgetfulness or talking in my sleep. I'd circumnavigate the issue by choosing men with the same first name. All I can add is that I'm glad Mark One was not named Algernon. Imagine how narrow a field I would have had to find Algernon Two and Algernon Three. I'm a lucky ducky."

While Diane was quite willing to talk about the Marks—One, Two, and Now—she would never say much about her time spent in Russia. It was clear from her conversations about her work with the current crop of Russian transplants—many of whom were making great strides in engineering technologies in nearby Silicon Valley—that she was fluent in Russian. Every now and then, Lila would tease her about being a Cold War spy or, as Lila would say, "A cold warrior." Diane just smiled. While they all knew that Dorothy was from Louisiana—nothing could quite eradicate the remnants of her N'awlins drawl—and that Edwyna was a native Californian, Carolyn a Canadian, and Lila a New Yorker, no one could quite identify where Diane was from. "Oh, all over," she would say, with a wave of her hand, when asked. Or, "Did I ever tell you about the time Mark One and I . . ." And she'd be off and running on a tale so fascinating, so exotic, that no one even remembered the question.

As the conversation about the book drew to a close, Lila stood to refill the wine glasses and said, "Now that we've finished the serious literary discussion, I have a question. Do you think Marina should have relinquished Anders to his wife? I don't know if I could be that self-sacrificing, that good."

"I thought about that too," Dorothy said. "But she is going to have the baby."

Comments from the others followed swiftly, one upon the other. "Do we know that for certain?"

"Well, that was what the drugs were for, and she ate the fruit of the tree."

"Ah yes, the good old fruit of the tree. Remind you of any other story?"

"Why does it always come back to women being good?"

"Or being blamed for badness?"

Dorothy said, "Well, you know the old joke: Said the good little girl to the bad little girl, 'Gee, but it's hard to be good.' Said the bad little girl to the good little girl . . ."

Diane, Carolyn, and Lila groaned in unison, and then all four said perfectly in chorus, as if it had been rehearsed, "It's got to be hard to be good."

Edwyna could not believe that these supposedly mature women were still caught up in sixth-grade jokes, but she also could not keep herself from joining in the laughter, indeed giggling, that followed.

"Ladies, ladies," Carolyn said as she tried to regain control of the conversation. But she still had to wait a few moments for the last laughs to subside.

"Let's come back to the book. Diane raised a great question. Is this the same old story? Is Marina's eating from the tree of fertility the same as Eve in the Garden of Eden?"

"Well, tree of fertility could be thought of as the tree of life," Edwyna said.

"And we could extend that metaphor to the Tree of Knowledge," Diane agreed.

"It's the women in this novel—Karen, the professor, and the native women—who really know what's important, what's going on." Edwyna felt on safer ground now that she had managed to avoid staring at the dolls.

"Generally true?" Dorothy asked.

"Yes. Women are wise. Wiser than men," Carolyn said.

"In so many ways," Lila agreed.

"Wise Women, I propose that we name our new group: Wise Women," Diane said.

"All in favor?" Carolyn asked.

Four hands went up as the women nodded. Edwyna hesitated. She'd enjoyed this meeting, but she was so much younger than the others. She didn't want to spend even one evening a month listening to everyone talk about husbands or children—or worse—grandchildren. And what if the group then descended—that's how she thought of it—descended into making gourmet dinners or home-baked desserts for each other? True, none of this had happened at this meeting, but . . .

"C'mon," Carolyn said, almost as if she could read Edwyna's mind. "We need a youngster in our group. If you don't join, we might think it's ageism."

"No, not at all, just wondering if . . ."

"Stop wondering. Just join us. You can be our baby," Dorothy chimed in.

Edwyna was quiet for a moment while her mind raced, looking for ways to decline the invitation, to scotch their enthusiasm.

Then Diane said to Dorothy, "Don't be ridiculous. Not our baby, our little sister." And she turned to Edwyna with a smile so warm that Edwyna felt her face and body glow as she nodded yes without any further thought.

"And do you agree to our name, to being Wise Women?" Carolyn asked.

Again feeling Diane's warm smile encouraging her, Edwyna nodded and raised her hand in agreement. She wasn't sure what had happened. Why had the women all smiled so happily over what seemed like such a small thing? Who cared what the group called itself? And why had there been that soft chuckle—almost a cackle from someone's throat? Lila's? Dorothy's? Edwyna couldn't quite tell.

More important was the next book to be read. "How about *Practical Magic*? Hoffman, I think," Edwyna suggested, although she didn't know why that book had come to mind.

"Too obvious," Diane dismissed it.

"On the Internet, I looked over the best 100 book lists for the last couple of years," Dorothy said. "You know, each year there are far more novels by men than women?"

"Nothing like that surprises me," Carolyn said. "We burned our bras, and now young women are wearing girdles. Just call them something different. Body shapers."

"Do you mean Spanx?" Edwyna asked.

"Even the name is degrading," Diane said. "So S&M. But back to books. We don't have to rely on bestseller lists. How about a terrific writer from the 1950s, Barbara Pym? She had some early success as a writer but didn't even come into her own until she was 'rediscovered,' as they say, by two 'important,' as they say, male critics. How about her last book, *A Few Green Leaves?*"

A few final words of agreement and good-byes ended the meeting.

The Wise Women barely disturbed the evening fog as they walked quickly toward their cars.

CHAPTER 4

Vlad

EDWYNA PULLED THE diaphanous curtain aside and watched the fog swirl past her window. She liked to sit in her favorite blue velvet wing chair and watch the fog from the corner of her eye. She'd placed her chair so that it looked into the room, its side to the window, for just that reason. The movement of the fog caught obliquely and intermittently gave her the sensation she was sailing—sailing to some unknown port. But tonight she was on a different journey—her first date in the new program to find her one true love.

It was about two weeks since she'd placed her ad in *The New York Review of Books*, the morning immediately after the meeting of the Wise Women. When she left that meeting, she'd felt happy until she realized that she was the only one with no one waiting at home. She didn't know the state of the marriages of any of the others, but if there was no one, no one waiting at home, there couldn't possibly be a true love. "Duh!" she'd muttered to herself. It was time to put her list into action. She mentally reviewed the options she'd outlined. None seemed attractive. Maybe she should give it up. Settle for a capable orgasmic evening with Nick every two weeks and fill the rest of her time with films and books. Books—*The New York Review of Books*. Okay, she'd taken one chance and put an ad in that venerable publication's "Personals" section.

She knew she'd stacked the cards against herself, choosing a New York publication when she lived in San Francisco. On the other hand, she reasoned the *Review* drew readers nationally, even internationally. She read the ads in several back issues, ads that were now conveniently online as well as in print, and she decided on two principles. First, her ad would be as brief as possible. Second, she would be modest—not "fabulous," "passionate," "brilliant," or "gorgeous." She'd written:

> **SAN FRANCISCO WOMAN**—*single, tall, forties, self-sufficient seeks male partner for romance.*

When she showed the ad to Howard, he'd groaned and said, "This is absolutely the least attractive ad I've ever seen. You say you want romance but your wording is so prosaic, so businesslike, that I can't believe anyone will even consider answering."

She had the choice of including her email address or telephone number but avoided even that invitation to close the distance between herself and whoever might answer. She selected instead the option of having *The New York Review of Books* assign her a box number. All—or any—interested readers would have to write to that box number. And she had to wait, in turn, for the mail to be forwarded to her. Howard was right, no one had answered her ad, but when she read the ads of others, one had stood out.

> **INTERESTED IN A BRIEF ENCOUNTER** *that might bring A Man and A Woman to True Love? I am a single man, 50 +, 6 feet +, in good shape Every Which Way. If you're interested and in San Francisco, please write.*

All those film titles caught her eye, and he too had chosen to have a NYR box number assigned. She saw that as a signal that they might think alike, might move at the same pace. She worked hard on her answer, keeping it brief and matter-of-fact. She worked in just one movie title, *An Affair to Remember,* even though that wasn't what she wanted at all. She was sure they were bonding on their love of old movies—and the fact that they were both tall.

Edwyna jumped when her doorbell rang. It was too early. She was ready, dressed in blue, but it was only six o'clock. She didn't expect *him* for another hour. However, it wasn't *him.* It was only Howard.

"Twirl around, girl, and let he see how fine you look."

Brooklyn-born and raised, Howard had moved to San Francisco for its allegiance to the Rainbow Flag. He and Edwyna had been neighbors for the past fifteen years or so. Edwyna figured from various references that Howard was sixty or more, and he looked it. Almost bald but for a tonsorial fringe, drooping wattles that his on-again, off-again beard didn't hide. He hadn't cultivated the requisite San Francisco buff. Not at all. Edwyna had estimated that his pudginess was due in equal parts to his love of old movies which he would watch, sometimes with Edwyna, for many uninterrupted hours, to unfortunate genes for short and chubby, and to a love of what he called *bubbelukshen*—chicken noodle soup—noodle casseroles both savory and sweet, slow-cooked veal paprikash served over nockerl, a crinkly Hungarian pasta. Howard had explained that *bubbe* was not *Bubba* as in *Forest Gump,* but *grandmother* as in sweetest, dearest woman who ever cooked for me. He hadn't explained the rest of the word, but when Edwyna benefitted from Howard's offerings of *bubbelukshen*, she didn't care. Howard had even declared that *pho*, the popular Vietnamese soup was *bubbelukshen*, and he'd learned to make his variation rich in cilantro and chicken.

"When is Vladimir expected?" Howard repeated the name and sounded out each syllable separately, "Vlad-ee-mir!"

"Just Vlad will do," Edwyna said.

"Ah, Vlad the Impaler." He wiggled his bushy grey eyebrows in a poor imitation of Groucho Marx. "Which kind of impaling . . ."

"There will be no impaling of any kind," Edwyna answered. "Do I pass inspection?"

Howard nodded emphatically.

"Then off you go." She took Howard by the shoulders and turned him back toward her apartment door.

"Vlad Johnson," Edwyna murmured to herself. Certainly an unusual combination of names. Maybe his mother was Russian and his father English. Or maybe he had changed his last name to conceal Romanian ancestry. Wasn't Romania the home of the original Vlad the Impaler? And wasn't he the inspiration for Dracula? Edwyna caught herself, stopped her mind from wandering into even stranger areas. It was Howard's fault that she had even started in that unprofitable line of thought.

Edwyna looked at herself in the mirror once more and then went back to the window. The fog had really come in. Not a star could be seen and the moon was completely obscured. Better take a warm wrap, she thought, and gave a bit of a shiver at the expectation of the cold and damp of a San Francisco evening. She was ready for Vlad, ready for love.

The bell rang and Edwyna pulled the lever that opened the front door. She stood at the top of the stairs eagerly awaiting her first sight of Vlad. He might have been Romanian or

Russian, but that wasn't the first thing Edwyna noticed. He was not six-foot-three as he'd written, probably closer to five-three. And if by being in shape every which way meant that there was as much of him around as there was vertically, he certainly measured up. He'd said he was fifty-plus, and that plus part was certainly true as he huffed his way up the stairs to Edwyna's flat.

"Hi ya, sugar," Vlad said. "Boy-oh-boy, you are certainly one long drink of water." He gave a drawn-out wolf whistle.

Edwyna didn't think anyone had made that sound in several decades.

"Ya got some climb here." Vlad stood at the top of the stairs, fanning himself with the Kangol cap he'd been wearing. "Bet it keeps those long legs of yours in great shape. I like that in a woman. Plenty of her. Plenty of you and all in great shape. I'm just gonna sit here for a minute, hope you don't mind, and look over the landscape." With those words, Vlad sat down heavily on the sofa, which emitted a complaining puff of air. "Come on over. Sit next to me." He patted the cushion.

"Would you like a drink of water, some white wine?" Edwyna ignored Vlad's invitation.

"Wine. That would be terrific. You got anything stronger?" Vlad waited for an answer, but Edwyna had already slipped through the arch of the living room and the swinging door to her kitchen. She looked at the bottle of MacRostie chardonnay she'd chilled earlier, then put it back in the fridge. Instead she poured two glasses of wine from her open bottle of cooking chardonnay, known familiarly as Two Buck Chuck because of its price. This would indeed be a brief encounter.

Edwyna handed Vlad a glass of wine, and ignoring his repeated patting of the sofa cushion, she moved to her blue velvet chair.

"Playing hard to get," Vlad said. "That's okay for now. I can see you're a lady. But lady, you'll find out, I know what ladies like." And Vlad took a hearty swallow of the wine.

"That was such an interesting notice you put in the *Review*," Edwyna said. "What caught my eye were the references to old movies. I love movies, old and new, romances, dramas, comedies, anything but suspense. I think my favorite is *Sabrina*, the original one of course. How about you?"

"Yeah, sometimes I'll go to a movie. Not like when I was younger and the back row of the balcony was your only hidey hole, if you know what I mean."

Edwyna knew what he meant, but she suppressed the image it conjured up. She soldiered on. "I recently realized how much I like the work of Kurosawa. Do you have a favorite director? Actor?"

"I don't like guys. I'm a guy, you know what I mean, so I like actresses, girls. Marilyn Monroe, now that was some star. And the other one, the one who lost her head in some freak accident. Jane something or other. They were great. Really built."

Edwyna sipped her wine in silence. She could not quite decide where to take this conversation next. Vlad had already finished his wine. He held out his glass and patted that damned seat cushion again. Edwyna looked out the window. God it was dark out there. And then back at Vlad.

"Tell me," she said, "you don't really seem to like movies, at least not a whole lot, but you put all those movie names into your ad in the *Review*. Could I ask why or how did you come to do that?"

"What is this *Review* you're talking about?"

"*The New York Review of Books?* The personals column?" Edwyna found all her statements were turning into questions. Had she let the wrong person into her home?

"A book review. Why would I want that? I don't read books so much that I need to read something about books." Vlad paused, looking at Edwyna through narrowed eyes. "Listen, you look like a nice girl. So I'm going to level with you. Not beat around the bush, if you know what I mean. Because I'd really like things to work out between you and I. Here's what happened. My friend, Sid, he said to me one day, 'You need to meet a better class of girl. Let me help you get some numbers, some possibilities. Okay?' I figured, you know how it is, what do they say, 'Nothing vented, nothing gained.' So I told Sid to go ahead. And here I am. The rest, as they say, is the story." Vlad, if that was his name, held out his two hands, palms up, as if he had now explained how he had shrunk almost a foot and gained a decade from the man who'd placed the ad and answered her response. Vlad continued, "I gave him a few bucks. I want you to know, honey, I always pay my own way. And I can be very generous, too. I hope you get to see that side of me." Vlad smiled.

Edwyna said, "Let me be honest too. I told you—or anyway I told Sid—that I was single. But that's because I can't stand my husband. I want to meet someone who will marry me and support me so I can leave that lousy bastard. And I thought tonight would be a good night to meet because . . ." Edwyna paused and then was inspired ". . . it's his bowling night, but just before you got here, he called. Arnold called. And they cancelled the games because too many of the men were sick from—from getting flu shots. I'm not . . ."

Vlad was already getting up. "Is he tall—like you?" he asked.

"Well, sure. A little taller. And bigger, you know." She made a muscle, holding up and clenching her right fist.

"Well, doll, it's been . . ." Vlad was too far down the stairs too quickly for Edwyna to know exactly what it had been for him. But she knew what it had been for her. She took the two glasses into the kitchen, put Vlad's in the dishwasher, poured out the remains of her Two Buck Chuck, and refilled her glass with the MacRostie. She dialed Howard's number. "You've got to come up, right now."

"Are you choking?" Howard asked. "Are you all right? I'll kill that bastard Vlad if . . ."

"I'm not choking. I'm laughing. Get your butt up here. I've opened a bottle of the MacRostie and need you here so I don't drink it all by myself. And you will love this one. Let me just say there was no chance of any impaling, although I did consider defenestration for a moment. But then he left of his own accord."

While she waited for Howard, she thought of telling the story of Vlad at the next Wise Women's meeting, but no. It was too personal, not the kind of thing she'd bring up easily.

CHAPTER 5

Birthday Dinner

HOWARD HELD UP his glass of Prosecco. "To you. On your birthday. I hope this year brings you all that you want."

Edwyna clinked her glass against his. "To all," she echoed. "Although you know that for me 'all' means just 'one,' the right one. I love celebrating my birthday, but I wish that somehow I could have birthdays without getting older. Especially this year. I'm forty-nine. You know the number that follows this one. Even worse, all those articles about thirty-somethings being unable to find the men of their dreams. Where does that leave me?"

"It leaves you ahead of the pack. First of all, the statistics in those studies are really questionable. You see . . ."

"Anyway, I may get a teeny bit older, but hope springs eternal. Who said that anyway?"

"You've got it. Amendment to the toast—to THE ONE," Howard pronounced definitively. And they clicked again.

Edwyna unfolded her white linen napkin and smoothed it over her dark blue skirt. It was a little longer and little fuller than was strictly in fashion. But she so much preferred the sense of freedom it gave her hips and thighs compared to the Hillary Clinton pantsuits—black, sometimes grey—that she wore to work. Her silvery blouse—long, full sleeves, low-draped bodice—caught the lights above the table and sent them shimmering into the room. Howard was the perfect foil for her looks, she thought. He was elegantly dressed, or as elegantly as a short, round man could be, all in shades of brown—dark slacks, dark shirt, her-ringbone jacket—with a bright yellow silk pocket square. Edwyna liked the notion that she was the bird in full plumage against her solid dark branch.

With a nudge, Edwyna encouraged Howard to look at the tables displayed before them—a tableau for their pleasure. "San Francisco courting rituals," Edwyna began. "Look at those two over there. I know exactly what's happening."

"Do you know them? I mean, have you met them?"

"No. Of course not. But I can tell you that this is their first night together and that the relationship will not last much beyond tonight unless she is as hot as she looks. Then I give it a month. No maybe a week."

"C'mon. You can't know . . ."

"Look at her outfit. Tell me what you see."

"I can only see above the waist."

"Don't be boring or obvious. Of course that's all. They're sitting . . ."

"First thing I see," Howard said, "she's got really big knock-ers, breasts, tit . . ."

"Are you admiring them? That's not your . . ."

"Well, I may not want them, but I can't help seeing them. Not the way she's dressed in that absolutely pure white jersey top stretched so completely creaselessly across them and then the lovely curves, the two lovely curves spilling..."

"Are you sure you're still gay?"

"I do go to museums, you know. And I can admire the Naked Maja without wanting to do anything about it. This is the same."

"Get off the boobies. What else?"

"She has very long, I mean extremely long blonde hair and red lips, and she's smiling."

"Right. Now watch her mouth for a few minutes," Edwyna instructed. "And just keep reporting about her mouth."

"She's smiling. She's smiling. She's still smiling," Howard said, and then again, "She's still smiling."

"And notice that all this time we've been watching her, she just keeps smiling. She doesn't speak."

'Let me get this straight," Howard said. "Because she has a well-developed chest, long blonde hair, a smiling mouth, and she doesn't speak much . . ."

"Doesn't speak at all."

"You are convinced that she is here for the first time with the man opposite her and that they will go to bed in a relationship that will be short-lived."

"Right."

"Let's order. I need some sustenance. I need to consume calories, carbs, proteins to follow your line of thinking." Howard signaled to the waiter, placed their orders, and sat back. "Let's just enjoy this wine for now." He poured more bubbles into each of their glasses.

"This is such a perfect way to spend my birthday," Edwyna said. "You always pick just the right restaurant."

"This is your fave!"

"And you know why?"

"I know you love the food and the ambiance. The wine. And we're always so relaxed." As if to emphasize his last points, he leaned back against the tufted leather and raised his glass once more to Edwyna.

"And I love watching the people. For example, take the guy we've been looking at," Edwyna continued.

"Is he your kind of guy? He sort of resembles Vlad. I know how much . . ."

"How could you even think . . . ?"

Edwyna paused as the waiter put their plates of steaming pasta before them.

"Can I take that as a no?" Howard carefully twirled the strands around his fork, using the spoon to support his expert action. He concentrated on his pappardelle, rich in a beef ragu, as he waited for Edwyna's response.

"Look how smug he is. Leaning back in his chair. Almost tilting it back on its hind legs."

"The chair's hind legs or his?"

"The only thing I can say for him is that he's not bald. Nice head of hair. I wonder if he dyes it. It's very dark."

"Why didn't you ask that about the woman?"

"Ask what?"

"About dying her hair?"

"Well, first of all, she looks really young. And second, women coloring their hair is . . ."

"Don't tell me you're going to say 'normal.' And how come he 'dyes' his hair and she 'colors' . . . ?"

"Is this my birthday party? I'm not going to tell you the story if you keep getting off track."

"I think this is the track. Look how you've judged this innocent couple by a few physical details."

"Are you saying I can't find the right guy because I'm . . ." Edwyna stared at Howard, daring him to continue. This was forbidden territory for a birthday dinner.

"Right. His hair is too dark and too full. Definitely shows evil tendencies."

"Now you've got it. He is using his power to seduce this much younger woman who has fallen under the spell of his assurance and money." Edwyna slipped right back into the story.

"And you see the assurance by . . ."

"Remember how she just smiled and smiled. Look at his mouth. He doesn't stop talking."

"But you can't know what he's saying," Howard argued.

"I heard him order. Very imperious. Didn't ask her anything about what she wanted. Just, 'We'll have . . .' and then, 'We'll have . . .' and, 'Then bring us . . .'"

"You couldn't have heard all . . ."

"I did. And look. He's kissing her hand. I'm not going to watch." Edwyna looked down at the table as if searching for a missing fork or spoon. "Tell me if he nibbles her fingers or worse."

"What could be worse?"

"Never mind." Edwyna had pictured him putting one finger after another into his mouth and slowly sucking on them.

"You can look up now," Howard said. "Our next course has arrived and so has theirs."

"Look, he's cutting up her food as if she's a baby, his baby."

"Now you are definitely wrong. They're just sharing some salad. We often do the same thing. But you are right, he does keep talking and she does keep on smiling."

"Did you hear his accent?"

"How can I hear an accent from someone two—no three—tables away from us?"

"Just listen, under the other voices. His voice is very deep. Watch his lips. You can tell when the sound you hear matches the words on his lips. You'll know it's him speaking."

Howard paused. Tilted his head as if to free an ear. "Mid-western? Maybe Michigan?"

"Wrong, wrong, wrong."

"Wrong?"

"It's Russian."

"Russian? Not Polish? Or Czech?"

"Yes, I'm sure."

"Maybe you're into some Russian fantasy because of your un-requited love for Vlad."

Edwyna ignored Howard's comment. "And that completes the picture," she said.

"What picture?"

"He is a Russian oligarch."

"So not only Russian, but an oligarch—who have you been reading? Le Carré? Cruz Smith?"

"Oligarch! The *Wall Street Journal* tells it all. You know they are all crooked, although they have front businesses. So he has some business here. And she's an administrative assistant or not even that, maybe just the girl who gets coffee and Xeroxes and . . . just someone at the bottom of his totem pole."

"I don't think Russian oligarchs—or any other Russians—have totem poles."

"Don't be so literal."

"Maybe you were thinking of some other kinds of . . ."

Edwyna continued as if Howard had not spoken. "He asked her to help him at the end of the day, offered her dinner to make up for the work, and now he has other tasks in mind. He's taking advantage of that poor girl who is just wowed by his ap-pearance of wealth and power."

"I don't hear his accent. And my story is that the poor guy is probably some shlub head over heels with the girl who's having her way with him. But this is your birthday. So I'll buy your story. Eat your veal before it gets cold and before they bring dessert."

"Dessert! Did you order something special?"

"Is this your birthday?"

Edwyna knew she had the story, the right story. Howard had obviously backed off when he told her to eat her veal. But she did want to enjoy the incredible mix of the veal, the perfect sauce, the tiny shrimp, the pieces of crab, and the unexpected addition of artichoke.

Howard had indeed ordered their dessert when he'd made the reservations. A perfect mound of soft chocolate cake surrounded a molten chocolate center. "Happy Birthday, Edwyna," written in dark chocolate frosting outlined the cake, which was more than big enough for the two.

They sipped their coffee and slowly ate the cake, the gooey center, and even the icing around the perimeter of the plate. Edwyna savored each bite. Each time she closed her eyes, not wanting any sense other than taste and feel to be engaged by distractions around her. A sip of coffee, a bite of cake, a sigh of delight.

Edwyna had almost forgotten about the Russian oligarch and his inamorata when she realized they were no longer at the table. "I guess he's taken the poor thing to his lair," she said to Howard, expecting him to follow her thoughts.

"Do you mean the couple you invented? I guess you were too involved in your chocolate indulgence to hear the exchange as they got up to leave."

"I thought you couldn't hear them."

"Well, I heard this. Just as he stood, someone came over and shook his hand. And I distinctly heard him say, as he gestured to the blonde-haired, red-lipped, ever-smiling, well-endowed woman, 'I'd like you to meet my wife,' although I couldn't hear her name."

"Howard, you are my best friend, and I am so grateful to you for this scrumptious dinner, but you are also a fibber. You heard no such thing."

Howard held up his hand in protest. "Nuh-uh. It's the truth."

Edwyna reached for her coat and patted his arm. "Nice try," she said.

"Edwyna, this time you are wrong. I really heard him introduce her as his wife. Over there. Look. The man in the grey suit. That's the man he introduced her to. I'm pretty sure he's the maitre d' or maybe even the owner. He'll confirm . . ."

Howard turned toward the grey-suited man and raised his arm, beginning the universal restaurant gesture for attention. Edwyna quickly pulled it down.

"Don't spoil my fun. I'll stipulate that he's not a Russian oligarch. Well, at least not an oligarch. But I'm telling you I can read that relationship. Besides, never let the facts get in the way of a good theory."

"Keep the story if it satisfies you. Consider it part of your birthday present."

Later that evening, Edwyna was still chuckling to herself over the story she'd invented. It didn't even matter if she or Howard had been right about the couple. It was the camaraderie of agreeing and arguing, the warmth of friendship.

Edwyna took off her celebratory outfit and hung it carefully in the closet. Why couldn't she find that warmth with a man? Of course, Howard was a man, but that wasn't what she meant. She meant a man who might turn out to be her One True Love.

Edwyna emptied the contents of her evening purse onto the bureau. Maybe there wasn't such a thing as One True Love. Maybe, like her story of the Russian oligarch, it was just made up.

Edwyna reached into her closet, onto her shelf of bags, searching for the soft bag in which she kept her evening purse. As she jostled the bags on the shelf, a tote slipped from its place and landed on the closet floor with a bang. It was her favorite book tote, a black bag with portraits of famous women writers on the front and back. The bag, which should have been empty, had some heft. Probably she'd left the book from the Wise Women meeting in it. There was no book, but a folder, dark blue, almost black, tied with a ribbon of the same color. Edwyna slipped the bow on the ribbon and opened the folder. It contained a sheaf of papers that seemed to be newspaper articles. She skimmed the first one.

The New York Times
> July 13, 1977
> Mom and Babe Saved
> Fireman Delivers

New York City—Sean O'Hanlon, a New York City firefighter, delivered Ruth Reynolds' baby during yesterday's blackout.

At 9:15 PM, last evening, Ruth Reynolds, 26, of 444 East 82nd Street felt her water break and knew her labor had begun. Her husband Gary Reynolds, also 26, left to hail a cab, taking the elevator down the thirty floors of their apartment building.

Interviewed today, Mrs. Reynolds said, "I was only a few minutes behind him." However, it was a few minutes too late. The blackout stopped the elevator between the thirtieth and twenty-ninth floors.

"I was so scared," Mrs. Reynolds said. "I thought I was going to have the baby in the dark, all by myself. I banged and banged on the elevator doors. I think I was screaming." Apparently, as reported by Mrs. Reynolds, one or more neighbors must have heard her cries for help as she thought they were trying to open the elevator doors.

Mrs. Reynolds could not explain why the elevator suddenly began to move, although the building remained in darkness. The doors opened to admit Sean O'Hanlon, the firefighter Mr. Reynolds had somehow found in the darkened streets.

Firefighter O'Hanlon said, "This was the first baby I delivered. I'm glad he's healthy and the mother is okay too."

No one in the offices of the building management were available for comment on the operation of the elevator.

When asked what she thought had happened, Mrs. Reynolds said, "The elevator took off on its own. The door opened, and there was my husband and the hero he'd found. I don't know how it happened. It was a miracle."

The news clipping had no name on it, nor did the folder. It probably belonged to one of the Wise Women. She put the tote back on the shelf. She'd deal with it later. Right now she just wanted to think about the possibility of one true love versus a world of Russian oligarchs.

CHAPTER 6

Soup

EDWYNA PUSHED THE supermarket cart down the soup aisle. The weather was cold for San Francisco, and she wanted the comfort of a big bowl of soup. But she didn't feel like cooking, and she certainly didn't feel like going out. She was still too full from last night's delicious birthday dinner to want another major restaurant meal or even a multicourse meal at home. Maybe she could find some of Howard's *bubbelukshen* in a can. But she doubted it. She picked up one brand of noodle soup after another. The label on one featured "no salt." Another touted "no fat." A third had neither fat nor salt. And a fourth had no salt, no fat, and "low carbs." None of them celebrated richness, excellent—or even good—flavors. If she wanted a warm liquid without any substance, she could just go home and drink a cup of warm water.

"Do you know which of these is good?" She heard the disembodied voice over her shoulder.

"Not really," she answered without turning around. "I have the same question."

"Frankly, they all sound pretty dreary."

"Exactly what I was thinking." Edwyna turned around. She held two cans of soup in her hands, reading the labels. When she looked up from the long lists of ingredients, she saw a nice-looking man, about her own age, she thought. Nice looking but nothing outstanding, she thought. Of course he was dressed in jeans. So was she. So was probably everyone else in the market. But he did have incredibly blue eyes. In an instant, she took all of this in, so quickly she didn't miss a beat between turning and hearing his question.

"How are you going to choose? I'll just get whatever you get. What's worse—cooking for one or eating this canned food?"

"Maybe this one will be good. It says 'Old-Fashioned Goodness,' all in caps, so I guess it's true," Edwyna replied. She smiled.

"Eating alone is really a bummer. But you don't look like you ever have to eat alone."

Edwyna felt an unexpected blush—or was it a hot flash?

"And shopping for one is even worse. But I guess I'll have to get used to it." The stranger in the soup aisle sighed.

Edwyna looked up from her scrutiny of the cans. Why was this guy sending her such personal messages? A pickup line? He was tall enough. As soon as she thought "enough," Edwyna knew she was sizing him up as a potential . . . well, just sizing him up. Because the *enough* meant she could walk next to him without stooping. He was thin. Kind of pale. And he had the day-old stubble that meant he was either careless about his appearance, hadn't shaved, or was too careful about his appearance and was cultivating the supposedly testosterone-laden "no sooner do I shave than my beard just grows right back" look made popular on TV shows about macho guys. He did look kind of forlorn. But she wasn't going to fall for it.

"You may not want to follow my choice," Edwyna said. "I have no idea of what I'm doing."

"Why not? I thought maybe we could shop together. You could be the leader and I your loyal follower."

"I guess canned soup is just not my thing." Edwyna wasn't quite sure how to respond.

"You mean you usually make your own or . . ."

Why the inquisition? Edwyna thought. Maybe the guy just wanted to talk about soup.

"Can't really say. But here's the one I'm taking." Edwyna decided to leave the soup choice to fate and reached for the nearest can.

Tall, thin guy took the one right next to it. "Now we have twin soups. Thanks." He pushed his cart down the aisle and waved back at her over his shoulder.

"Strange," Edwyna murmured to herself but didn't allow herself to quite finish. "I thought . . ." What was her problem? Glomming on to every stranger who came her way. Couldn't she just have a passing supermarket conversation without thinking about the guy as a possibility? Still, he had started her thinking by talking about shopping and eating alone as being a new thing. Of course, her mind had gone to divorce. Or maybe he was a rich guy who never shopped for himself or who did it all online. Or maybe he hadn't left a woman—or been left by one—maybe he'd just gotten out of jail. Or maybe his wife had died tragically a few months earlier. "Okay, Ms. Glendower," Edwyna admonished herself. And she knew that whenever she addressed herself formally, she was fed up with her own extended line of thinking—if she could even call it thinking. "And maybe he just came from another planet." Edwyna pushed the cart so fiercely to rid herself of her own thoughts that she nearly ran into the rump of a short, plump woman who'd been bending over to look at the canned tomatoes in the adjacent section of the aisle.

With a cart full of groceries, Edwyna surveyed the checkout lines. She moved toward the shortest line and then realized this would put her right behind Soup Man. She hesitated. Looked around. All the other lines were much longer and everyone on those lines had full carts. If she pulled her cart up behind him, would he think . . . ? Why should he think anything? After all, the whole scenario had only been in her mind. It was the shortest line.

Edwyna steered her cart behind his. Suddenly it seemed her cart had a mind of its own as it gave his cart a not-so-gentle bump. She knew she had not pushed her cart into his on purpose. Without looking around, he put his hand on the side of the cart to steady it. Her cart rolled forward again. And once again, he steadied his cart as it was nudged by hers.

"Sorry," she said to his back.

This time he turned toward her. "Oh, that's okay."

"I guess my soup is looking for its twin," Edwyna said.

"Pardon me?" Soup Man or the tall-thin-slightly-bearded-visitor-from-another-planet guy said.

He smiled the kind of smile that said, "I guess you know what you mean but I don't have a clue, and furthermore I couldn't care less." Which Edwyna realized was a lot to get into a smile.

"The soup. The cans of soup. Back there." Edwyna pointed in the general direction of the soup aisle.

"Oh yes. You're the nice lady who helped me choose a soup." He raised the can of soup in a toast: "Here's to good souping." And he turned back away to move his purchases from the cart to the conveyer belt. Only his back was facing Edwyna when she heard him say, "I hope I've chosen the right one. I'm not used to shopping for myself."

Edwyna realized he was not speaking to her at all but to the cashier, a young woman he seemed to be checking out at the same time as she checked out his groceries.

Edwyna moved the foods from the grocery bag to her kitchen counter, separating the perishables from the shelvables, when she heard Howard's signature ring.

"One moment," she called. Boy was she happy to see him. "Howard, I had the strangest experience today. I thought . . . well, I thought I might have . . ." Edwyna continued to pile vegetables into the fridge as she spoke.

"Spit it out. Good? Bad? Animal, mineral, or vegetable? If animal, human or nonhuman? Robotic? Did you meet a robotic being? Can a robot be considered a being? That's a really interesting . . ."

"Hush! See this can of soup?" Edwyna held the can of soup toward Howard. "I needed some sustenance and was looking for your granny's kind of soup, the food you call . . ."

"Yess . . ." Howard drew out the word. "I'm offended. There's no finding *bubbelukshen* in a can. I'm concerned about your sanity if you think you are able . . ."

"So, I was in the soup aisle. And this guy, a man, comes along and starts asking me about soups, about how to choose soup."

"Don't tell me you thought this was a pickup. Did you read some women's magazine that told you about finding true love in usual yet unexpected places?"

"Yes. I mean, no. I didn't read anything like that, but I did think he was coming on to me. He made a big deal of how he was shopping alone and eating alone. And then how he wanted to eat exactly what I wanted to eat." Edwyna told the events in a breathless rush.

"And then?"

"And then I saw him again at the checkout line."

"And then?"

"Nothing. He acted like he'd never seen me before. I even had to hold up the soup can to remind him of . . ."

"This is the worst I've ever seen you. Seriously," Howard said.

"Do you think I'll see him again?"

"You could just camp out in the supermarket."

"Be serious," Edwyna said.

"I am being serious," Howard continued, "or trying to reach you by exaggeration. You have taken a wisp of nothingness and tried to turn it into something."

"But what if I do see him again? San Francisco is a small town. I'm always running into people I know or met somewhere else."

"Why would you even want to run into him again?" Howard asked. "And you can put that soup can in the cabinet now. Stop brandishing it like some holy relic."

"What if he's the one? And it's destiny. But we didn't know it. And now I have to find him. Even my cart reached out to him."

"Say again. Your cart?"

"My cart kept bumping his cart. And I swear I wasn't moving it."

"You are making so little sense. First you have maintained all along that the world is a rational place, not influenced by forces beyond our mental control."

"I'm not suggesting that there is something magic in how we met or that I can make him reappear in my life. It's just a 'what if' kind of question."

"I can't believe what you're suggesting. If I had to give you a motto, it would be 'The fault, dear Brutus, is not in our stars, but in ourselves.'"

Edwyna replied, "I could answer that with another one: 'There are more things in heaven and earth, Horatio, than are dreamt of in your philosophy.'"

"Which one is it?"

"You know me too well."

"Then why have you gone all *Sleepless in Seattle* or *You've Got Mail?*"

"You think I'm not going to have a happy ending. Edwyna banged the can on the counter. "Some friend you are."

"I didn't say that. I know you want a different kind of relationship than you've been having. You want love, not lust. But truly, I don't know what will happen."

"I wish I could know." She held the can between two hands as if the can alone, not its contents, could warm her. "I wish I could know what's in store for me after I go through all this effort of online stuff and blind dates and whatever else."

"Calm down. Sit down," Howard said. "Give me the can." Howard took the can from Edwyna's hands, rummaged in the drawer for the opener, opened the can, then lifted a pot to the stove.

When Edwyna began to say something, Howard said, "Ssh. Wait."

And when she began to speak again, he put his finger across his lips in the universal gesture for silence.

Edwyna obediently watched him bring the soup to the simmering point and pour it into two bowls.

"Sit down. Here's a spoon," he said. "Eat."

When they were both eating, Howard said, "If you're willing to have some fun with trying to find out what's in store for you—for both of us—I have an idea."

"I need soup," Edwyna said and continued eating.

"Just listen. Friends of mine told me about a great tarot reader. On Market, near Castro. The name of the place is—get this—The Crystal Palace of Love."

"Puh-lease!"

"Just a lark. We could go for a lark. The name itself is so luscious. Just say it: 'The Crystal Palace of Love.' I picture a dark room with crystals, like stalactites hanging from the ceiling, reflecting the light from spinning chandeliers."

"Is this some retro disco fantasy?"

"No. It's," Howard's voice deepened as he said again, "The Crystal Palace of Love. Dependent crystal hangings, spinning chandelier, lots of red velvet, red velvet couches against the walls. A very Madame Récamier chaise, also red velvet, with a fringed shawl."

"You don't think I might run into Soup Man simply by accident, or by coincidence, but you believe that someone can tell us the future. Really? Mr. Engineer. Or should I call you 'Your High Techiness?' Really!"

"Of course I don't believe that we'll learn anything. Get you out of your doldrums. An amusement. We can laugh about it at dinner afterward. I heard of a terrific new place nearby."

"Do you know the reader's name?"

"I think my friend said 'Tanya,'" Howard answered.

"And the reader," Edwyna said, caught up in Howard's fantasy of red velvet and fringes,

"Tanya—a dark woman, her long, black hair caught up in several glittering combs, wearing a long, red floral skirt; black lace-up boots; an embroidered, off-the shoulder peasant blouse. And the smell—incense and burning candles. Very Russian!"

"You and your Russians. I knew you'd go!" Howard pumped his arm in victory. "I'll make an appointment for us one evening next week."

Edwyna didn't know why she'd been so taken with the idea of a chance encounter leading to romance or why she'd consented

to go with Howard to—what had he called it—The Love Palace—
something like that. True she wanted love, but she had a perfectly good relationship with Nick. Well, not perfect. But good. In
fact, she was seeing him the next Saturday night.

The idea of things Russian had not left Edwyna's mind. When
Nick had asked her where she wanted to go on their next date,
without hesitation, she'd said, "How about a Russian restaurant?"

Nick had chosen The Little Hermitage. As soon as they entered
the restaurant, Edwyna felt it was indeed all things Russian. Of
course, she'd never been to Russia, so she couldn't be sure, but
it was definitely her image of Russia, complete with murals of
onion-domed buildings and waiters in ballooning pants and
brightly colored shirts.

"Would you like to start with a soup?" the waiter asked.

Edwyna definitely did not want soup. She had had enough
of soup.

The waiter continued with a description of pelmeni, little
meat dumplings, and other specialties that were unfamiliar to
Edwyna. She looked at Nick, who seemed completely engaged in
the waiter's long descriptions.

Finally the waiter finished his recitation, and Edwyna and
Nick decided on starters. Fried pelmeni for Edwyna and cucum-
ber salad for Nick.

"This is delicious," Edwyna said after she bit into her first of
the piping hot dumplings. She could not resist offering Nick a
taste, although she knew that he never accepted and never offered tastes from his own plates.

"This salad is excellent," Nick said. "So cooling. So fresh."

As they were almost through their main courses, rabbit stew for Edwyna and sautéed fish filet for Nick, a band complete with accordion and balalaika began to play, and several couples immediately took to the small dance floor.

Edwyna looked at Nick.

He shook his head. "I don't think I'd be any good at this kind of dancing. Let's enjoy the music and the show."

Edwyna found the music irresistible. Her feet tapped of their own accord. She clapped with enthusiasm.

By the time they were eating their dessert crepes filled with poppy seed and jam, Nick was clapping along. They stayed until the band stopped for a break.

"What fun," he said as he helped her on with her coat and led her to his car.

At home, Nick declined any more coffee, then yawned and stretched. Edwyna took the cue and walked toward her bedroom.

As Edwyna sat on the edge of her bed and bent to remove her black kitten-heeled pumps, she saw Nick's long bare feet in front of her. She raised her eyes and saw that he was ready for her before she had touched him. He stood in front of her, clearly aroused and clearly still clothed. He held out his hand to Edwyna and she rose from the bed. He pulled her close to him, so close she felt he could almost enter her through the double layers of their clothing. Then he moved slightly back, just far enough so that he could put Edwyna's hand on his erection. He directed her hand to the zipper on his slacks and she opened it, then his belt, and the button on his pants. Nick stepped out of his slacks, removed Edwyna's, and pulled Edwyna to him again. Slowly he ground himself against her until she thought they would both climax through their underclothes. Just as she thought she could not hold back for one second more, Nick stepped back. He pulled off her black lace thong, his own black briefs, and pushed her gently but definitely onto the bed. He straddled her head and she took him into her mouth as he reached behind himself to thumb her clitoris. Despite all previous experiences with Nick, to the extent that Edwyna could think between the spasms of delight, she thought this was going to be quick. Too aroused to stop. Too far gone into it. No more foreplay. Who needs foreplay? Then, without climaxing, Nick removed his throbbing penis from her mouth and his hand from her vagina. He lay down next to her, side-by-side, and began kissing her as if they were at the very beginning. His mouth lingered on hers, his tongue flicked in and out. A snake. A beautiful shining wet snake. One hand fully captured a breast, cupped it, soothed it, and excited it at the same time. The other hand, the other breast. All of the movements were slow. Excruciatingly slow. Nick rolled onto his back and pulled Edwyna on top of him. She guided his penis into her and began the slow dance of love. As she moved to her own rhythm on top of him, he raised his head and licked her breasts. The multiple sensations were too much for Edwyna. She increased her pace. Nick ignored her breasts and reached to touch her clitoris, but Edwyna had already found a rhythm and a posture that gave her all she needed. She rode him until she felt an overwhelming sensation of release and tension, spasms that rocked her body. And his.

A few minutes later, Edwyna still lay across Nick's body. He gently lifted her off him, toward her side of the bed. She turned toward him for one more kiss, a sweet kiss. He had already rolled over, his back toward her.

Edwyna fell asleep, both sated and unsatisfied.

CHAPTER 7

The Crystal Palace of Love

EDWYNA WONDERED WHY the tinkling bell over the door to The Crystal Palace of Love had not summoned a sales clerk, the seer—or whatever she was supposed to be—or anyone for that matter. She wandered among the displays that seemed haphazardly placed around the sales floor. There were cases of tarot cards and displays of earrings, brooches, and pendants that suggested the signs of the zodiac and other symbols that Edwyna didn't quite recognize. One case seemed to hold nothing but different size rocks. Edwyna spent as much time as she could—which was little time indeed—looking at the objects. And then her watch. She was on time. It was six. She'd rushed from her office, still in her office uniform of black suit, crisp white blouse, and low stacked black heels. Where was Howard? Giving up on the objects in the cases, Edwyna looked at the books displayed on shelves that lined one of the walls. *Know Your Sign: Know Your Self. Star Signs to Health. Use Your Chart to Chart Your Career. Crystals of Clarity.*

Really they were just another form of self-help book. Edwyna didn't know why she'd agreed to meet Howard here. It was not her thing, not her thing at all. And when Edwyna looked more closely, she saw that the glass cases were dull with generations of fingerprints. The books were slightly dusty or well-pawed. The shelves had long lost their paint or lacquer. They sagged under the weight of books that must have been there for decades. This place certainly smelled exotic, some mixture of incense and the oils lined up in dark bottles along one shelf. Where was Howard anyway?

As Howard had predicted, there was a velvet sofa—green, not red—facing the back wall of the store. On the wall was a large, lurid poster with a giant blue eye inside a red hexagon against a yellow background. Edwyna eyed the sofa suspiciously. It seemed clean enough. She sat tentatively on the edge of the seat. But facing that poster and sitting with her back to the empty store and its front door made her too anxious. As she stood, her hand brushed against a book someone had left on the sofa: *Moon Worship in the West.* The front doorbell sounded to announce Howard, and a door alongside the poster opened. A young woman came out through the door, a door Edwyna hadn't even seen before it opened.

They spoke at the same time.

"Sorry, sorry I'm late. Damned Muni." That was Howard.

And the woman who'd appeared from the recesses of the store held out her hand to Edwyna and said, "Hi, I'm . . ."

Howard and the woman looked at each other and laughed a bit. Edwyna was not amused.

"Let's start over," the woman said. "You must be Edwyna." She held out her hand again, and this time Edwyna took it. "And you, I gather, are Howard." Once more she held out her hand.

"Then you must be Tanya," Edwyna said as she shook the woman's hand.

"Almost right. It's Toni.

So her name wasn't Tanya. And she wasn't Russian. It was Tony or Toni, probably a shortened form of Antonia, maybe Italian. And she certainly didn't look like a tarot reader or anything Edwyna had imagined a tarot reader would look like. Her hair was short, not flowing. Not a really cute short cut, just short and held back behind her ears. A style you'd expect to see in a gym. And her clothes did not suggest any attraction to the occult. Just jeans like everyone else. Not even jeans with embroidered rear pockets. A turtleneck shirt of no particular distinction and one of those sweaters that seem to be made of undyed wool. In other words, she was plain.

All of this flashed through Edwyna's mind as she watched Howard shed his scarf and jacket.

"By the way, I spell it T-O-N-I," the woman said. "I'm named for my father, Anthony Antonioni, known by everyone as 'Tony.' Of course, he wanted a son to carry his name. Such an old-fashioned, Italian tradition. He waited through my three sisters—Lucia, Theresa, Gina—and when my mother told him I was the last one, no matter what, he decreed I'd be named for him. As the story goes, my mother agreed, but when she filled out the birth certificate, she accidentally or on purpose gave me a more feminine version. Now which of you is first?"

"Ladies first," Howard said.

Toni ushered Edwyna through the door in the wall into a small yet comfortable sitting space, gestured to one of the faded armchairs that faced a wooden table, and took the other herself. There was a small ink-black velvet pouch on the table, a cassette recorder, and nothing else. Edwyna had expected a crystal ball, some hanging bead curtains, new age music in the background. But there were just the two chairs and the simple wooden table, no different from a table she might see in someone's home. At least this room seemed less musty than the outer store, Edwyna thought, and settled back into the chair.

"We have an hour together," Toni said. "Would you like to start with your chart for the coming year or with a reading of the cards?"

"What does 'your chart' mean?" Edwyna asked.

"What most people would call your horoscope. We don't like to use that word because it suggests the glib snippets that you can find in the daily newspaper. Those are much too general to be of use. We could use your chart to look at the year ahead or to answer any particular question you have."

"What kind of questions?"

"Could be about career. Could be about money. With the markets so crazy, so many layoffs, Lehman going under, bailouts, TARP—many of my clients would rather think about their economic futures than anything else. Or your questions could be about relationships. Family. Health. Love." Although Toni smiled as she said each of the words, she looked directly at Edwyna.

"Yes, let's do the chart. The year chart." Edwyna thought about her desire for this year as she approached fifty, but she was not going to give anything away by letting Toni know what interested her. She'd seen the smile and the look and she'd read how charlatans work by worming information out of you and then feeding it back to you. Edwyna swallowed uncomfortably.

Almost as if she could read Edwyna's mind, Toni said, "That's fine. I like to begin with no information about my clients except for the essentials . . ."

Here it comes, Edwyna thought, the inquisition.

"So just tell me your birth date—just month and day—and the time of your birth if you know it."

Edwyna told Toni her birthday, then added, "Around five in the afternoon." That question didn't seem unreasonable. Even

she knew you could not do a horoscope—or chart if she preferred to call it that—without knowing someone's birth date.

Edwyna sat back and waited. Toni was looking at her. No,
staring at her. Was this some part of the entry into the supposed
occult?

"Are you . . . ," Toni began. Then shook her head. And started
again. "I know this is a strange question, but are you sure that's
your birth date?"

"Yes. As a matter of fact, as you can figure out, I recently celebrated my birthday and I've always turned the year, every year,
on this date. And I wasn't found under a tree or on a doorstep so
that my birth date would be uncertain. What a strange question
for you to ask. Is this some technique you're using to get me to
open up?"

"No, no. Forgive me. I just . . . Usually I have a reasonable
idea about someone's sign from how they look, the clothes they
choose, but . . . Never mind. Let's just do your chart. Would you
like me to record what I say so that you can listen to it later?"
Toni gestured to the tape recorder.

"Sure," Edwyna said, although she could not imagine she'd
want to have anything repeated since she didn't even want to
hear it for the first time.

"I see a good year ahead for you," Toni began. "Much that
you want will come to you although you will have to put forth
some effort to gain your desires."

Duh! Edwyna thought. I often have much that I want. I don't
have that one thing that I'm not even going to say in my head in
case she can read my face. Edwyna took a deep breath as if the long
thought itself was as difficult as saying it. And of course you have to
work for what you want.

As Toni went through the year, highlighting months of op-portunity and months of risk or danger, Edwyna felt her emo-tions lighten and darken in response to what was said. She tried to keep a poker face.

"Do you have any specific areas of life you'd like me to focus on?" Toni asked. "Or should we move to the cards?"

"Cards," answered Edwyna.

Toni picked up the velvet pouch and carefully drew the deck of cards from it. "Before you begin to shuffle the cards, think of a question you'd like to ask them."

"Ask it aloud or silently?" Edwyna thought she knew the an-swer to that one.

"Silently is usual better," Toni said, surprising Edwyna. "The deeper you go into yourself, the deeper the reading. So don't worry about the time. Think about how you want to phrase the question, and when you are ready, just say the words in your own mind as if you were speaking to the cards, and shuffle them three times as you would any deck."

Edwyna knew her question, and this time she decided she would say it to herself. And—if Toni were to be believed—the cards would hear her. "Will I find true love this year?" she asked, and asked again. And then again as she shuffled the cards three times.

"Now cut the deck into three and put each pile in front of me."

Edwyna did as she was told, momentarily caught up in the ritual. Toni picked up the middle pile and spread the cards, face down, in front of Edwyna. "Choose one," she said.

Toni turned up the card Edwyna had selected from the deck. "This card is the High Priestess," she said. "In the reading, it is your significator. In other words, it represents you." She then picked up the deck on the left and laid out ten cards in a pattern on the table. As she turned up each card, she explained its purpose. For the first card, she said, "This card represents the general atmosphere around you." As she turned up the second card, she said, "This card represents forces against your desires. This third card shows your hopes for the future."

By the fifth or sixth card, Edwyna had lost track of which cards showed the future and which the past and which showed good events and which bad. But she did get that the last card, the tenth card, showed the outcome of all the other cards. She sat through the reading, not paying much attention to what cards were major and which cards were minor, why that was important, or what they represented.

She did like the look of some of the cards that came up. There was a card for the moon, which showed a man playing a lute while a woman reached toward him from a balcony. The card for lovers showed a couple with cupid in a cloud above them. Edwyna liked that card too, although she wasn't sure what the old man leaning on a cane might stand for. She didn't like the card for death with its figure of a skeleton. It was really confusing that Toni said that "Death," which looked so ominous, could be beneficial, signifying "drastic change," and some of the prettier cards were malign. Edwyna waited impatiently for the outcome, the explanation of the last card, or as Toni said, "the culmination of all the forces as revealed through the final card."

"As you can see," Toni concluded, "the answer to your question may be positive, very positive indeed. But you must watch out for the forces aligned against you—some of which, as I said, may be within you, not outside you. And you must counter those forces with thoughts and actions that bring you to the conclusion you want."

Toni gathered the cards and slipped them back into the velvet back. She looked at her watch. "That's about it for now as far as our time goes. I'll send you the reading as an email attachment. Feel free to ask any questions once you get it. Do you have any questions I can answer right now?" She was already rising from her seat as she said this.

Edwyna knew a signal to leave when she saw one, and she had no questions anyway. The chart reading—as Toni had called it—told her to work for what she wanted. And the cards said things may go well or poorly. It's all up to you. So what else was new? This hadn't been as painful as she thought it would be. But it also didn't provide the help Howard had suggested it might. Although to be fair to Howard, he'd presented it as a lark, not a serious endeavor.

At the door, Toni turned toward Edwyna once more. "My dear Edwyna," she said, and she took Edwyna's hands in both of hers. "When I asked if you were sure of your birth date, I saw in my mind's eye that something about how you present yourself to the world doesn't jibe with your inner self. Call it intuition if you will, but I have learned to trust those feelings."

Edwyna's hands grew warm within Toni's. Toni looked up into Edwyna's eyes and held her gaze. Toni continued, "You too must trust whatever it is that you are now concealing. Whatever it is, know that this part of you must be freed for you to find all you seek. You have something very special. Don't fight it any longer." She gave Edwyna's hands a final squeeze, then dropped them and opened the door to Howard.

Edwyna sat on the green velvet couch. It was already past seven. She hoped she wouldn't be too hungry, too impatient while she waited for Howard to learn his fate. But before she knew it, there was Howard. She must have dozed off or something because an hour had disappeared.

She stood, stretched each arm over her head, and reached for her handbag. "How'd it go?" Edwyna asked Howard.

"To be truthful, I was hoping for something more after the way my friends raved about Toni. Of course they were mostly interested in last year's election. Obama or McCain? They think it will make a big difference to—you know—'Don't ask. Don't tell.' Etcetera. I wonder . . ."

"I can't believe it. Do you actually have friends who would go to a so-called psychic, a fortune teller, to learn the outcome of the election? Terrific. No more TV pundits, voting rights fiascos, endless snarky ads. Just a crystal ball, a fringed scarf, and *voilà*!"

"But tonight," Howard continued, "frankly I found her rather distracted. Two or three times she began a sentence and didn't finish it. Even stranger, she asked me something about you."

"About me?"

"Yes, she asked me if I knew when your birthday was. I told her. Then she said, 'Yes, that's what Edwyna said.'"

"She said something like that to me. Why'd she think I'd make up a birthday? Did you ask her why she asked you?"

"I did."

"And?"

"She sort of looked off into the distance and said something like, 'Her sign, her appearance, her cards.' Or maybe 'her chart.' Then she paused. Murmured some words under her breath, sounded like 'doesn't add up.' After that she was really apologetic about taking time from me. How was yours?" He asked as they began walking toward the door.

"I can see how this could take someone in, but it was a big nothing for me. She said I could have what I want if I work for it. That was the sum total of the chart—as she called it—and the reading. And I really got lost during the reading. Which card was the past, which the future. Edwyna paused for a moment as they put on their coats. You sound disappointed. What were you looking for?"

"I don't know. Some insight."

"Insight into what?"

"Nothing in particular. But it was all superficial." Howard shrugged his shoulders.

"Yes. What a lot of mumbo-jumbo," Edwyna agreed.

"Yet not even enough mumbo-jumbo to be good for a laugh."

Howard opened the door of The Crystal Palace of Love and ushered Edwyna into the chilly San Francisco night. She took his arm. "Let's have dinner," she said.

"That always cheers us up."

CHAPTER 8

Match Seeking

EDWYNA SAT AT her desk in front of her laptop, her head in her hands. Although she didn't think any of the so-called predictions of Toni had even a hint, a whisper, a breath of truth in them, she had heard the exhortation that she had to take action. That was how she'd built her career. She wouldn't have a successful accounting practice if she'd just stayed home and waited. In the beginning of her career, she had not been shy about speaking to friends and acquaintances—even her parents' friends—about becoming her clients. When she wanted something, she made a plan and she put that plan into action. Once she did, she always had success.

Now, the very next day after her visit to The Crystal Palace of Love, her plan was to use the Internet to find her one true love. That seemed an odd mismatch—love of the whole person divided into bits and bytes. Like everyone else, she used the Internet—to shop, check the weather, stay abreast of the news. But she realized she was not completely like everyone else. She had avoided Facebook. Yes, she knew she could stay in touch with friends from college or distant cousins, but she didn't trust the very openness that made it so popular. Why would she want all that info about herself out in the cloud, as they called it? The cloud was not the nebulous cumulus fluff one imagined. What a trick of marketing! All that information—personal, financial, medical, and more—was stored in huge hermetically sealed, security-patrolled, electricity-hungry data silos.

She was procrastinating, working herself up into a silent rant on tweeting and blogging, but this was her first attempt at computer-matching, at finding a . . . finding a what? A lover? A mate? A match. That was what they called it. Obedient to her plan, a few moments ago, she'd started to join RomeoandJulietMatch. com, advertised as the world's best, the world's biggest mate-matching site. As soon as she realized that she had to put in her email address, she had to backtrack. She was not going to give the world—or that part of the world—her usual email address. She didn't want to receive—she wasn't sure what she'd receive—anything mixed in with her business emails or the others she got from family, Howard, her book buddies. So back to the email drawing board. Her real email, or real as she thought of it, was one of the usual formations people used on Gmail, Yahoo, or any of the others. What could she do that was different? She thought of edie. glen. That felt too close to the real one and sounded old fashioned. Indeed her whole name sounded old fashioned, unattractive.

Edwyna had hated her first name since she was a child. It was unlike any of the names of her classmates or anyone else she met. They had good names, names like Lisa, Susan, Karen. She'd asked her mother and father over and over why that was her name. All they would ever tell her was that it was a family name "going way, way back." When she was six or seven, she thought that meant her family had been kings and queens and she was, of course, a princess. But when she was a little older she realized that it combined her father's name, Edward, with her mother's name, Winifred. How egotistical she'd thought them when she was in high school. She always wanted a nickname, but it couldn't be Eddie—that was her dad's. And it couldn't be Winnie. That was so Pooh. And then a brainstorm! If men called Edward could have the affectionate diminutive of Teddy, then why couldn't Edwyna also be nicknamed Teddy? But not that masculine, Teddy. Teddie? Teddi? Tedi? The last one was it. She would become Tedi in her match-seeking. Maybe if she'd always been Tedi, no one would have come up with that ridiculous idea that she had special powers. For a moment she pictured herself as a petite, yet cuddly, blonde called Tedi. Then she realized that even if she'd changed her name, she would still be tall, and she'd still have dark hair and fair skin.

She wrote "Tedi" down on the pad next to her computer and hoped she wouldn't inadvertently jot other notes on the paper and then discard or lose it. Although she was tightly organized in her work and her apartment was generally uncluttered, some- how she was always losing her user names and passwords, her identities. Where did lost identities go? Were they somewhere in the world of Peter Pan along with the Lost Boys?

Edwyna lifted her head and looked at the screen. Now that she had an identity, she was ready to face RomeoandJulietMatch. com. Her plan was to give only the most basic information about herself—her email address, her height, her age, where she lived—and even that in the most general terms so that she could see what was out there. Or who was out there. She went to the first screen. Okay. This was info she was willing to give—marital status, gender, age of men she was looking for. That gave pause. She decided to give it five years either way and entered 44 to 54. Then she paused. Which age should she use as the basis for her arithmetic? Her age now—49? Or her age when she hoped this search would be over—what she was quickly beginning to think of as "the dreaded five-o?" Should she enter 44 to 54 or 45 to 55? Still another question stopped her. Did she want to be with a man five years younger than she was? Carolyn, one of the Wise Women, was seven years older than her husband and that seemed to work for her.

She left the entry blank.

The next screen asked what country she'd grown up in. That seemed innocuous. And then her sign. Yuck! Shades of The Crystal Palace of Love. At least she could opt out from having her sign revealed. She clicked on to the next page. Page after page of questions followed. Edwyna barreled through them, ignoring question after question. She did pause on the page for movies she liked to select comedies, romances, and foreign films. For a moment she wondered how this would appeal to the man who would turn out to be the love of her life, but those were the movies she liked.

Then she was stymied. She had to enter a profile of herself. She had no idea of what to say.

She checked her email. Got up for a drink of water. Sat down. Got up. Watered the cactus. Sat down. Slid open the center door of her desk and pulled out a vaguely familiar dark blue folder. As she opened it, she realized that it was the folder she'd brought home from the book club. She could have sworn she'd left it in her tote. Happy to forget thinking about her profile for at least a few moments, she opened the folder again. Just as before, there was the news article on top, no further information. She skimmed the news article. Funny, she was sure the article had been from *The New York Times*. This was from Toronto.

Globe and Mail

January 24, 1971

Saved by a Stranger

Lucky Father and Son

Toronto—James Johansson, 39, of Berry Road, reported a stranger saved him and his son, James, Jr.14, from frostbite or worse during the heavy storm on Lake Simcoe yesterday.

The two drove to Lake Simcoe where, as Mr. Johansson said, "we thought we had a line on some fishing huts. I'd heard this lake is a really popular spot for ice fishing. I should have realized something was up when there were so few folks around. I don't know why I didn't listen to the weather report."

"I couldn't wait," Jimmy commented. "We piled our gear in the car and took off."

Unaware of the looming storm, they set up their tools and dropped their line. They felt the first flakes fall but thought nothing of them. By the time Mr. Johansson realized how heavily the snow was coming down and set out for shore, they were blinded by the intensity of the storm.

"Jimmy was very brave," Mr. Johansson said, "but I was shivering in my boots. And it wasn't just from the cold. I know what cold can do to a man. Frostbite. Hypothermia. We could have died out there."

Jimmy said, "Suddenly I felt a hand on my shoulder turning me a full ninety degrees to the right. It was weird."

Mr. Johansson added, "And I heard someone say, 'This way, gentlemen.' By now it was not only the snow but the evening that obscured our vision." Both Johanssons agreed that they never saw the person who saved their lives.

Johansson Senior said, "I don't know who he was or how he found us. I wish he would come forward so we could thank him. I don't know how he did it. It was a miracle."

Edwyna thought perhaps, after all, it was the same article she'd read the other day because she clearly remembered the last line, the one about a miracle. She lifted the article she'd just read, and there underneath it was the one from *The New York Times*. Miracle saves in New York and Toronto. How about San Francisco? She needed a miracle if she was going to complete this damned profile. She closed the folder firmly. Slid it into the drawer. Shut the drawer with a slam. Stared at the computer screen. RomeoandJulietMatch gave some suggestions about what to include, but none of them resonated with her. The site suggested: "How would your closest friends describe you?" Edwyna did not specialize in having close friends. But there was Howard. Should she call him? Could he be of help? Then she'd have to reveal to him what she was doing. Well, he should take some responsibility for this. After all, it was Howard who'd led her to admitting she had to do something, and this was the something that had emerged.

Howard answered on the first ring. "What's up, bubbelah?" he asked.

"I want you. I need you. Now. Right now. Please come here," Edwyna answered. "I'm doing this computer thing and I'm stuck. I can't do it."

"What computer thing? Fix your computer? I can help . . ."

"No. Remember Toni? Crystal Palace? What you said?"

"You've lost me," Howard answered.

Edwyna took a deep breath. "I agreed with you that I had to do something if I'm going to get what I want. The person I want. The love I want. So I tried . . . I'm trying to register for RomeoandJulietMatch.com and they want me to write a profile, tell them what I'm like, what I want, and I can't even get started. Please come up here and tell me what to write."

"I can't tell you what to write. It has to come from your heart."

"My heart?"

"Okay, your head," Howard said.

"At least come up and hold my hand while I work on this."

"How can you type if I'm holding your hand?"

"Very funny. You know what I mean, Howard." Edwyna hesitated. "I think I'm afraid I'll say the wrong thing. And then, I don't know. No one will ever write to that damn email account I had to set up. Or whoever writes will be like Vladimir."

"Ah yes. The now-famous Vladimir. Tempt me and I'll be there."

"Come up and I'll make you a cappuccino in my new Xpresso." Edwyna had recently acquired one of the popular machines that offered a dozen or so strengths of coffee—designer cups of espresso, cappuccino, or lattes—each in its own capsule.

"I'm yours. Give me ten."

Ten minutes later, Howard was at the door and Edwyna was in the kitchen. She offered Howard the glass candy jar that held the varied color capsules.

"I think I'll go blind," Howard said. And he shut his eyes as he reached into the jar. "Ah," he read the label, "Fortunato Intensenato. Sounds good, and maybe that means you'll have intense fortune today."

"Fortune can be good—or bad."

"Yes, but 'intensenato'—which is probably not a word in Italian or whatever language this coffee pretends to be—always means good."

As both of them sipped their coffees, Edwyna asked, "Do I really have to do this?"

"It's really your choice. But, *mein kind*, as my bubbe would have said, you have something you want in your life. Maybe this is not the way to go for it. So either bite the bullet—or your profile—or look for other ways."

"Maybe I could try a different website."

"You'll always have to reveal something about yourself."

"Yeah, but I can't write what I really want to say."

"What is that?"

"'I'm a forty-nine-year old woman. I've never lacked for men. But now I'm looking for true love.' I could never say that about myself."

"You just did."

"That was just to you," Edwyna said. "You know what I mean. Not to the world. I couldn't say that to the world."

"Even the world of RomeoandJulietMatch.com?" Howard asked.

"Especially the world of RJ," Edwyna affirmed, confirming her words with a sharp nod of her head. "And what if I'm too old?"

"Too old? Did you know that the fastest growing demographic of people using the Internet matching sites is people over fifty-five?"

"True?"

"True and verified by research. Research—we both like that."

"Maybe I'm too young," Edwyna countered.

"You are avoiding this."

"It's that damn profile. I just can't do it. At least not right now."

"Is that your final answer?"

Edwyna nodded again.

"Well, I'm not Regis. This isn't *Who Wants to Be a Millionaire*, and I'm not accepting that answer." With that, Howard moved to the desk and sat down in front of Edwyna's computer. "Do you want me to drive?"

"No. You win. Shove over." Edwyna pulled another chair next to the desk for Howard and sat in her newly vacated seat. "Now what?"

"You are really playing dumb. Open the site, and let's go through the questions, one by one."

"All of them?"

"Maybe you can skip some, but I'm staying here, holding your feet—or should I say fingers—to the fire until you are finished. What's the first part?"

"Physical appearance. Height and all that blah, blah, blah."

"Fill it out. You certainly want to put in your height and your hair, eyes—what's wrong with all those basics? Your basics are pretty far from basic, I might add."

Edwyna filled in the blanks dutifully, sighing in time to her keystrokes.

"You are one drama queen today. Is there any place to enter 'negative attitude to this whole enterprise'?"

"I'll fill in some of the checklist stuff on my own, but here's the hardest part. This is where I was when I phoned you: my profile—who I am, what I want."

"Just start typing." Howard waited. Edwyna's hands were poised over the keys. Nothing happened. "Or we could start with where you began before. You said something like you were forty-nine and looking for true love. What else would reveal the inner you?"

"Okay—here goes . . ." A long pause followed as Edwyna looked up at the ceiling. After a few moments she said, "How's this? 'I'm an accountant and I want a man I can count on.'?"

"I can see by your face that even you think this is not your best effort. Clever wording, but that's about it."

"Well, I am an accountant," Edwyna said defiantly. "But it does suck."

"Here's how I see you. You are so different from most other women. 'Exotic.' That's a word I would use."

Edwyna bristled. "How can I be exotic? I was born right here in the good old U S of A."

"You're not only tall, but you carry yourself so regally, as if you know something no one else can fathom. Your dark eyes and hair and your flowing clothes—when you aren't in accountant drag—make you seem special."

"You know, one of the ideas for writing the profile was to ask your best friend what she or he would say about you. I don't agree with what you've said, but it certainly sounds better than what I suggested. So—let's see—'In my daily life, I seem to be an ordinary working accountant, but my best friend tells me that I'm exotic because I have dark eyes and hair and wear flowing clothes. He thinks there's something special about me. How about you? Would you like to find the special in me?' I don't know, Howard, I don't think I could say that publicly. It's not the me I see."

"Wait a moment, Tedi. Maybe that's not the 'me' that Edwyna sees, but could it be the 'me' that Tedi sees?"

"Maybe."

"But your last sentence is too corny. Go back to what you said earlier for your ending."

"What did I say?"

"That you were forty-nine. That you've never experienced a shortage of men in your life—and as your upstairs neighbor, I can attest to that fact—but that now you are looking for true love."

Edwyna dutifully typed the words as Howard dictated them again—minus the comment on his testimony to her popularity. As she finished, she looked up at Howard. "Finished?" she asked.

"Finished," he said and leaned across her to click the "finish" button, the one that sent Edwyna to the final "submit" screen. Without clicking that ultimate button, she closed the lid of her laptop.

The next morning, Edwyna turned to her computer to check her email. As a lark, she switched to Tedi's account. She was confused at what she saw. It seemed almost a dream to see responses to her attempt to sign up for RJ in her inbox. There were more than ten names, and she could click on them and see a profile. The second profile she looked at appealed to her. The man answered most questions, "Tell you when we 'talk.'" And he gave the age range of women he preferred as forty-two to sixty-one and a half. For desired height, he'd said, at least four feet and no taller than eight. At least he had a sense of humor. Then she clicked through the other ten. She realized almost all of them had answered most of the questions the same way: "Tell you when we "'talk.'" And most of them had given their desired height for women as four to eight feet. She figured it out. Those answers—"Tell you when we 'talk,'" and desired height of "At least four feet and no taller than eight" were the ones the computer algorithm filled in when the match seeker did not answer. The match the computer had found between her and the men shown to her was that they had given the same answers she had. No answer at all. Edwyna was glad she had not completed the final step of submission. That meant she was not registered and no one would get her info.

She thought about cancelling the membership that hadn't even begun, but she decided to let it ride out there in the cloud.

A few days later, Edwyna was glad she'd left her unfinished application nestled in the cloud because every day or so she got more suggestions from RJ. One man's tag line had so intrigued her that she could not resist responding. He'd written: "Are you Scarlett looking for your Rhett? Can I be Bogey to your Bacall? Fred to your Wilma?" If she wanted to email him, she'd have to finish enough of her self-description to become a member. Instead of fussing over the details and trying to get it just right, she let herself say whatever came to mind. She didn't quite remember what she'd written and didn't want to look at it again, sure she'd cringe in embarrassment. This time she hit the "submit" button.

She couldn't resist the mix of references to film romance on both the big screen and the small one of her childhood, even though she knew she'd been snookered by movie references in the ill-fated response to *The New York Review of Books*, the response that had brought her Vlad. At least that had been good for a few laughs with Howard. She debated the wisdom of responding to movie references for a few moments but, she decided, if she wrote off everyone who said anything about movies, that might eliminate the very person who shared that interest—to be honest—that obsession of hers. And so she'd answered his mail. He'd answered hers. And now, after a few more email exchanges, she was about to meet Joel R. at the local Starbucks. It was Saturday, a sunny Saturday. Edwyna pulled on her jeans and then considered the rest. Saturday. Starbucks. Casual. Comfortable. But comfortable would not be, not be what? Alluring? Sexy? Edwyna avoided those thoughts. She pulled a favorite indigo sweater from the drawer, threw a matching scarf around her neck. Shoes? Boots? Flats? Heels? She definitely didn't like the look of tottering women in spikes with jeans. And he'd said—Joel R.

said—he was taller than she. "At least six feet tall and slim," he'd written. But why take a chance? She pulled on the tan leather boots. Good soft leather and almost flat.

Edwyna grabbed her handbag, looked in the mirror next to the front door, and ran back into her bedroom to put in a pair of dangling silver earrings, exchanged them for a pair of gold hoops. She looked in the mirror over her bureau. Put in one silver and one gold. Turned her head this way and that. Opted for the silver. She looked at her watch. Now she was going to be late. She hated being late.

Edwyna almost ran the few blocks to the Starbucks, but when she was one block away, she slowed herself to a businesslike walk. After all, she didn't want to appear to be too eager. Just as Edwyna reached the door, she realized a man behind her was opening it for her. She half-turned and realized that it was probably Joel R. At least it looked like the photo of Joel R. He was tall, at least as tall as she was, and he was slim. Maybe even too thin.

"Tedi?" he asked.

Edwyna almost didn't answer until she realized that was the name she'd given herself on RJ. "Hi. You must be Joel," Edwyna answered after what she hoped was not too long a pause.

Joel found a table for them and brought their coffee orders from the counter. Other than discussing what coffees or sweets they wanted, they had not said more than the initial hellos. Now Joel sat with his hands around the cardboard container and stared into the dark fluid. Edwyna just watched him. Was she supposed to start? What should she say?

And then he spoke. "Boy am I glad you're a brunette. After the last one, I swore off blondes. That's what I told my friend. I said to him, 'If this one doesn't work out, I'm switching to brunettes.' And here you are. A brunette."

Edwyna had no idea what to say next. Should she comment on the color of his hair? It was rather nice hair. Brown and curly. Not balding, just receding ever so little. It was her turn to stare into the murky depths of her cup. She found she was imitating his posture. "Why no blondes?" she asked.

"It's like this," Joel said. "After you're divorced, you think, 'I'm going to go for the gold. Find the perfect woman.' And you know—blondes—Marilyn—all of us guys—I guess we're jerks, we think it's got to be a blonde. And maybe the blondes just know they're every guy's dream. They don't treat you—let's just say, I didn't pick the right ones. And," he smiled at Edwyna, "you're one heck of a brunette."

"Thank you," Edwyna said. She guessed that was a compliment. "Might I point out that you are a brunette as well. Nice hair."

It was Joel's turn to smile. "I get these curls from my mom. When I was growing up, my family always said that my hair was wasted on a boy. I have two sisters and their hair is straight as sticks. What about you?"

"I have a brother, Donald. I guess his hair is kind of sandy looking." Their email conversations had been smoother than this. Edwyna could not imagine where to go next. But she didn't have to say any more.

"You got kids?" he asked.

Edwyna was sure she'd answered in the negative to that question on RJ, but anything was better than talking about hair color. "No. What about you?"

"Yeah. I have two. Terrific kids. Boy is all into sports, and the girl wants to go into modeling."

For a moment, Edwyna thought he meant that she wanted to create models, like the miniature three-dimensional plans for buildings that one saw when a museum or office building was in development.

But then he said, "She's only fifteen, but she sure has the looks for it. I just hope that jealous bitch doesn't ruin it all for her."

Again, Edwyna didn't know how to respond. But again, she didn't have to.

"That woman is some piece of work. Not that work is her thing. I make a good living. All I asked was for her to give me and the kids a good home. Make meals. Not clean. We have someone for that. Be there when they come home from school. But could she do even that? No. It was tennis, tennis, tennis, and more tennis."

Edwyna opened her mouth, but no words came out. It didn't matter.

"You know what she said?"

Edwyna shook her head. But she didn't even have to offer that minimal response as Joel just rolled on.

"This is what she said, 'Tennis is not a game. Tennis is like life. It's where I am most myself.' Couldn't she be herself making dinner or driving Jake to his games or Madison to her dancing lessons? Let me tell you, those dancing lessons are important. It helps Madison with her posture, grace, all that stuff. You know what I mean? Don't you think I'm right? When I'm right, I'm right."

Edwyna chose to answer the question about dancing lessons. "Yes, they are great for young girls. Gives them confidence. I took ballet when . . ."

"Instead she hired that no-good college dropout kid from around the corner to drive them. How did she even know he was safe? Not a dopehead or worse. Do you know what I mean?"

"Maybe she—I'm sure, she checked him . . ." Any attempt she made to stop the tirade failed.

"She didn't take the time to do anything like that. All of this so she could play tennis. At first I humored her, you know, paid for the tennis court time, the outfits, even got her a tennis brace-let. She was a decent player, I'll give her that. And she looked cute in her little tennis dresses and all. And then she decided she needed lessons. 'Lessons for what?' I asked her. 'You already tell me you win all the matches with your friends.' 'To move to the next level,' she says. Do you know what that means?" Joel stared at her.

Edwyna felt she had to answer. "Not really, no. I'm not much of a tennis player."

"No. You wouldn't know. The next level was played lying flat on her back. Catch my drift?" Joel didn't wait for an answer. "Flat on her back with her legs wrapped around him and . . ." Finally Joel seemed to have run out of steam.

Edwyna wasn't sure whether the wife or ex-wife was also the blonde who had ended it for all blondes, but she didn't care. She wanted to flee but felt she had some obligation to at least contribute to the conversation. Maybe if she redirected it, he would get over whatever anger was making him grip the cup so tightly that it was now crushed in his fist.

"I really loved what you said about movie romances in your RJ description."

"RJ? What's that?"

"Sorry, it's my nickname for RomeoandJulietMatch.com. Just shorter. Easier."

"Oh yeah. I get it. Cute. RJ. I'll have to remember that."

"Have you seen any good movies lately?" Edwyna felt lame even as she asked the question.

"You notice how all the movies these days are about bitchy women. Women who desert their men. Women who poison their men. Women who want to get the upper hand, never satisfied, like that one about the woman cop. Not enough she gets promoted, she has to lord it over all the men."

Edwyna had not noticed that. In fact she had no idea of what movies he was talking about. Maybe some of them were TV shows or even his own inventions. But she'd had enough.

And apparently so had Joel R., who looked at his watch and said, "Oh shit! The kids! I'm supposed to go see Madison at a dance recital in just an hour and I have to get over the bridge. I don't suppose you'd want to . . ."

"Thank you," Edwyna said, "that's so kind, but I'm sure your daughter will enjoy having you to herself."

They pushed back their chairs, almost bumped into each other in the doorway, and hesitated over that awkward moment of whether to hug or shake hands. Joel pushed the door open, hesitated, then turned to hold it for Edwyna.

"Bye," she said over her shoulder as she brushed past him.

Edwyna strolled home, laughing to herself as she thought of Howard's reactions to this meeting. Joel was marginally better than Vlad, but that was indeed a low bar.

CHAPTER 9

At the Ocean

ONE OF THE best things about living in San Francisco was its proximity to the ocean. Edwyna liked nothing better than to drive to Ocean Beach, just ten minutes from her home, turn into the Great Highway, park, and walk along the beach. Usually she didn't stay on the concrete walk but went down the few steps that led to the sand. The water itself was frigid. No one swam even on the sunniest of days. Brave surfers wore extra thick body suits. And most walkers even avoided any touch of the frigid water on their toes.

It was a drizzly Saturday morning. As usual, she stood at the top of the concrete steps, took off her tennis shoes, and tied the laces together so that she could carry them over her shoulder. She walked briskly across the sand, feeling the damp wind swirl around her. She headed right down to the ocean's edge and stopped. Edwyna looked out across the ocean and thought of the great distance between her and any other land. She wondered if she could squint and see Hawaii. She pictured the islands of Polynesia as bathed in sunlight, the so-absent San Francisco sunlight. And she thought of Australia, which would be moonlit night at this hour.

Edwyna hitched her tennies more firmly on her shoulders and walked as close as she could to the water. Every now and then, she jumped back to avoid the rivulets of water that resulted from waves that broke far from the shore. Edwyna got her best ideas when she was near water, almost any water, but especially the ocean. Even as a little girl, in Petaluma, one of her favorite activities was to walk along Dillon Beach with her parents. She'd loved looking out at the waters of Tomales Bay and back at the sand dunes that lined the beach.

Thoughts of those dunes brought a memory. She was walking at Dillon Beach with her parents and her younger brother, Donald. She thought she was probably about eight, which would have made him five. She couldn't have been much older because she was carrying her favorite doll, Inanna. That day, Donald had been such a pest.

First he ran way ahead, and her father ran after him, shouting, "Donald, Donny, come back here. You are too close to the water. Be careful. Slow down!" That was so unlike their father who was usually so calm.

Donald did come back and then deliberately went into slow motion, making each step slower and slower, picking up his leg and putting it down with exaggerated care until their mother lost her patience. "Donald, could you please stay with us? This is a family walk. Let's walk together as a family." And she turned back toward him and took his hand.

Donald opened his eyes as wide as possible, a face he obviously thought spoke of innocence. "Daddy told me to slow down, so I'm just being a good boy." And when their mother had turned away, he stuck his tongue out at Edwyna.

Edwyna ignored him. She concentrated on Inanna, who was still wearing the beautiful blue dress in which she'd come to Edwyna four years earlier. Donald was a brat. But she knew if she said something, her parents' annoyance would just spread to her.

So she murmured to Inanna, "Do something. Make Donald stop. Make him go away. Do something."

Edwyna wasn't even looking at Donald when she heard her father say, "Oh my God, now he's done it." She realized both her parents were running toward Donald, who once again had gotten ahead of them. He was lying face down in the sand.

Their father bent down quickly and turned Donald over.

"He's had the breath knocked out of him," their mother said as she bent over him. "Donny, are you okay? Tell me what hurts." And then she turned to Edward to say, "He's bleeding. Give me your handkerchief."

"What happened? How did he fall? There isn't even a root or rock to trip on." Winifred fired questions as Edward carried Donald to the car.

The day ended with a trip to the emergency room. Donald's face was badly scraped, and a piece of shell had cut deeply into his forehead. To this day, he had a small scar over his left eyebrow.

For a long time, Edwyna felt somehow responsible for what had happened. She remembered whispering to herself—or was it to Inanna. She'd wanted him to stop goofing around. She didn't think it would end with his bleeding. Going to a hospital. That wasn't what she had meant at all when she had told Inanna, "Make him go away." Over and over her parents told her, it was just an accident and it was Donny's own fault for running. To this day, she remembered Edward's words. He'd found her crying in her room more than a week after Donald's accident. After a hug, he sat back from Edwyna, reached for a tissue near her bed, and dried her eyes.

"It was all my fault," Edwyna said between the hiccups that followed a long cry. "Donny was all my fault. I wanted him to stop goofing around. I was really angry. And then . . ."

Edward held her by her shoulders, looked into her eyes, and said, "Even if you were annoyed with Donny, that did not make him fall. We were all annoyed at him that day, but none of us made him fall."

Now Donny was married to Angela. Had three kids. And sometimes when he still wanted to tease Edwyna, he would say. "You know my whole life is your fault. You made me fall that day back when we were kids and that scar over my eyebrow is just so sexy, it made me irresistible to girls. That's how I got my Angela, my angel."

Of course Edwyna did not believe she was any more responsible for his adult happiness than she now believed she was responsible for his childhood fall.

This Saturday on her beach walk, she just wanted to relax and let her mind take its own course. She'd tried responding to several other men from RomeoandJulietMatch.com, but nothing had jelled. She looked at other matching sites, but they all looked the same. That was not the way to go. She felt she had wasted a month wandering through cyberspace. On the one hand, she thought she should do something about finding her love. On the other hand, she thought, if this was really romance, he should just appear in her life. Like the guy in the soup aisle, although that entire romantic encounter had probably lasted something like three and a half minutes—or maybe 3.1 or 2.8 or only 2.4 . . . Edwyna realized the futility of her thinking. How could she begin to parse an encounter that wasn't an encounter, a something that was truly a nothing?

Edwyna continued to walk along the beach, heading south, away from the two big restaurants that offered stunning views of the ocean, the Beach Chalet on the other side of the Great Ocean Highway and the Cliff House up the hill on the same side as the beach. Both the beach and the concrete walk were almost deserted. The day was too nasty even for the intrepid dog walkers or the older Russian émigrés who could often be seen in groups of two or three, talking as fast as they walked. For a moment, she wished she was still a little girl with a doll as a confidant, a companion, a consultant. Ridiculous. Enough of this frigid solitude. Edwyna wheeled about and began walking toward the restaurants. The wind, which had been at her back, was now in her face. She bent her head and shaded her eyes as the windblown sand hit her face. She felt the salted sand on her lips, tasted it. Despite the overcast sky, she stopped to put on her sunglasses, hoping they'd keep the grit from her eyes. At least she could warm herself with a coffee or even a Bloody Mary at the bar of the Beach Chalet.

Edwyna climbed back from the beach to street level. She brushed the sand from her feet, donned her tennis shoes, and walked to the traffic light. While the Great Ocean Highway was not a limited access high-speed road, the four lanes of two-way traffic whizzed by quickly enough to deter her from simply running across the road. Edwyna tried to shake off the wind and cold as soon as she entered the spacious lobby of the building—the Golden Gate Park Visitor's Center—that housed the restaurant. She never went through the lobby without a mental salute to the 1930's frescoes of San Francisco life painted all around its walls. This Saturday—she was still so cold—she wished that she could simply slide into one of the scenes, particularly the picture of smiling people sunning themselves on the beach. Clearly not the same kind of beach day she was having. Edwyna climbed the imposing marble stairs to the restaurant. Her hand grazed the deco-carved wooden handrail.

A wall, about four feet high, divided the large restaurant into two distinct halves. On the left were glass-topped tables that provided an unimpeded view of the beach, the ocean, the sky through floor-to-ceiling windows. To the right was the long bar along with a number of small, dark wooden tables. Edwyna always thought it strange that patrons sat at the bar with their backs to the ocean. Sometimes it felt warm and cozy. Today just gloomy. Although she knew she could swivel on her bar stool to look out at the sea, she didn't.

There was certainly more life in the Beach Chalet than on the beach. Clearly she was not the only person who thought being indoors looking out was better than being outside on this cold Saturday. Edwyna grabbed a seat at the crowded bar and considered her options.

"Bloody Mary, please," she answered the bar tender's query. She figured she could eat the celery and olive, and the tomato juice must have some nutritional value as well.

She sipped her drink, still lost in thought, and didn't even realize that someone had taken the bar stool next to hers until he leaned toward her and asked, "Do they make a good one here?"

For a moment she had no idea of what he was talking about until she realized he had gestured toward her drink. "Yes, if you like them spicy."

"Spicy? Yes indeed I like them spicy. Do you? Like things spicy, that is?"

Edwyna didn't know if she wanted to be in this kind of flirty-flirty conversation on a Saturday morning. But then she thought if she wanted to meet someone serendipitously, she could hardly avoid talking to strangers. She smiled and said, "I like this Bloody Mary."

"I'll follow your lead," the man said and gestured to the bartender to give him the same. "I know this is a corny line," he turned back to Edwyna, "but do you come here often? Really,

I'm new to San Francisco and trying to figure out the lay of the land, as it were."

Edwyna softened. At least he had abandoned the spicy tack. "I often come for a walk on the beach. But today the weather drove me inside."

"Me too. I'm from the East Coast. Love the ocean. Swam all my life—all my summers—but this ocean. They call it 'Pacific,' but it's anything but peaceful to me. And cold—my oh my—I just put in one toe . . ." He mimed a shiver. "By the way, my name is Hank, Hank Morse." He held out his hand.

Edwyna shook his hand. It was even colder than hers had been. "I'm . . ." Edwyna hesitated between Tedi and her real name. What the heck, she thought. "I'm Tedi." Now there were two men who not only didn't know her, but didn't even know her real name.

"Hi, Tedi. Nice to meet you. You're my first new friend in this city." Hank swiveled his bar stool toward Edwyna's. "There's an empty table over there." Hank gestured to one of the bar's round tables. "Want to move? It's easier to talk face-to-face rather than side-by-side."

Edwyna nodded her agreement. They picked up their drinks and claimed one of the round tables across from the bar.

"Since you're my new friend, my only friend, therefore my best friend," Hank said, "how about some early lunch or late breakfast?"

As they walked to the table, Edwyna recognized that she and Hank were about the same height. Maybe this was a good sign. "Yes," Edwyna said. "But let's keep it Dutch treat." She didn't want any misunderstandings or awkwardness when the check came, as checks always did.

"Everything okay?" Hank asked.

"Oh fine," Edwyna said, "just for a moment I had a thought about work."

"Work? I thought you were a goddess beyond all that mundane stuff," Hank said. Then he laughed at his own words. "Gosh, first I start to rattle on about 'spicy,' then I ask you if you come here often. Now those corny words. Hope you forgive me. I'm just out of practice. Here's a better response: You said you were thinking of work. So I should say, 'Work? What do you do?'"

What had he meant by "out of practice?" Was it okay to ask him? Or should she just answer his question? "I'm in business," she said. And then she asked, "What do you mean 'out of practice'"?

"It's been a long time since I went to a bar and—picked up—no, not picked up—just started a conversation with a beautiful stranger. Or any stranger, for that matter. Or not just a bar, actually anyplace. I told you I was new to San Francisco. And that's true. I managed to move here from my firm in New York. I wanted to leave New York because of—just too many memories. Not to make it a sob story—let me just say—my wife died almost two years ago. And every place in New York spoke her name or called me. I don't believe in ghosts, but if I did . . ."

Edwyna instinctively reached across the table for his still-cold hand. "Sorry, I shouldn't have asked."

"Not at all. Fair game. I brought it up. I'm a lawyer, and once a topic is introduced, it's okay to ask about it."

"Even I know that from *Law and Order*," Edwyna said.

"Are you a fan? I know, as a lawyer, I should just laugh at it, but I watched it religiously when it was on the air, and now the reruns . . . I'm an addict."

That was enough to get the conversation going—and going. It was two drinks, an omelet, and several cups of coffee later that Edwyna looked at her watch. She suggested they get the check.

"This was really a nice beginning to my time in San Francisco," Hank said as the waiter brought the check and they both reached for credit cards. "Let me treat."

"No thanks," Edwyna said. "We agreed, and a deal is a deal."

"Then can I take you home? I have my car . . ."

"I have mine as well, thanks."

"Then, at least your phone number. Let me call you—see you again?"

Edwyna fished around in her handbag, as if she were searching for a pen, playing for time. This was just a bar pickup. All he knew at this point was her name, and not her real name at that.

"How about just your email address?" Hank said. "I'd give you my business card, but I haven't even gotten any with my new info on them."

He did seem nice enough. And this pickup—if that's what it was—was in broad daylight.

"Look. I'll understand if you don't want to . . ."

"Just looking for a pen," she said and brought her bag closer to her face. A movie she'd seen flashed through her mind. Gwyneth Paltrow—*Sliding Doors*—that was it. Showed how small changes at one moment could lead to big changes in her life. Wasn't that what she wanted—a big change in her life, in her luck?

"Try this one."

Edwyna looked up and saw that Hank was holding out a pen. She wondered how long he'd been standing there, waiting for her to make up her mind. He handed her the pen and a napkin. She wrote her phone number and thought of telling him her real name. She signed the napkin Tedi, with a firm dot over the "i."

CHAPTER 10

Finger Play

EDWYNA WAS CONSUMED with work in the week that followed her meeting Hank. Suddenly it seemed that all her clients needed attention, immediate attention. Obama's handling of the country's economic woes had exasperated fears of those who leaned politically right and done little to calm those who leaned left. All were worried, and rightly so, about their own investments and businesses. Edwyna herself had little time or energy to worry. If anything, the financial crisis, as it was now being called, had increased her billable hours. She was so tired from the clients' frequent calls and emails as well as her own need to focus clearly on close detail, that her eyes closed almost before she'd pulled her comforter over her shoulders and under her feet, making the nest that pulled her into the arms of Morpheus.

When she thought of Hank at all, it was just before falling asleep, and that moment was barely a few seconds long. So there was a feeling of the unexpected when he called a week later.

"Hi, Tedi. Hank here," he said. "Hope you remember me. We met at Ocean Beach. I'm the one who . . ."

"Of course. Of course I remember you," Edwyna said. "I only gave my phone number to a dozen or so men at the beach that day, but you stand out."

"I wouldn't be surprised if you attracted even more than that, but since I do stand out in the crowd of your beach suitors, would you like to meet again? Dinner?" And he proposed a restaurant, date, and time. "Would you like to meet at the restaurant, or should I pick you up at home?"

"No need. I'll meet you there." Edwyna wasn't sure why, but she wasn't ready to invite him to her home or even to reveal where she lived. And she was still Tedi.

Hank had chosen Bursa Kebab, a small Middle Eastern restaurant in West Portal, a cozy neighborhood of several blocks of shops, eateries, and a movie theater. It was barely five minutes by car from Edwyna's home. She had just arrived in front of the restaurant and was deciding whether to wait outside or inside when a car pulled out from the parking space that was dead center on the restaurant's door and, with a roar, a sports car zoomed into the space. The driver killed the engine and got out in a seamless series of moves. It was Hank.

"That was magic," Hank said. "Did you make that happen? I love this place. The only bad thing about it is finding parking. You have some special kind of parking karma?"

Edwyna was about to bristle with her "I have no special powers response," but he gave her no chance.

"Terrific. You're here on time too. You look terrific. This way . . ." And he used one hand at the small of her back to direct her the few steps to the entrance and the other to open the door.

"Mr. Hank, welcome," the host said. He led the way into the restaurant. "I think you'll like this table." He gestured and Hank nodded.

Edwyna was surprised that Hank and the restaurant host seemed to know each other, that Hank had been there enough times to be considered a regular. How was that possible, given Hank's self-declared status as a newcomer to San Francisco? As soon as Hank sat down, a bottle of wine appeared almost out of nowhere.

"I hope you like this place," he said. "I discovered it almost as soon as I moved here. The food is always fresh, well-seasoned without being spicy. And the noise level is lower than so many places."

"That's because it's not catering only to twenty-somethings," Edwyna said, looking around at other customers ranging from a tattooed young woman and man to several grey-haired couples and a family group of four.

Edwyna wondered if Hank lived in this area. It wasn't where she'd expect a single man to live. The homes were moderately large with well-tended lawns or landscaping. There didn't seem to be any apartment houses or even small multitenant buildings. She'd pictured him living in one of the newer high-rises that had grown up in several contiguous neighborhoods completely on the other side of the city. Near China Basin, Mission Bay, generally south of Market. In SOMA, as it was now being called, the buildings all promoted themselves as something special. "The greenest new development!" "Walking distance to the ball-park!" "Just a block from Whole Foods!" "Enjoy your dinners at Boulevard and other fine restaurants."

The meal was as Hank had described it. They'd lingered over wine long after their main entrées of rack of lamb and kafta kebab were finished. Their Turkish coffees and shared baklava were gone when Hank reached across the small table and played lightly with Edwyna's fingers. His touch sent an unexpected tingle through her body. Probably the wine, she thought, but she didn't move her hand. With his thumb and the first two fingers of his hand, he stroked each of the fingers on her right hand. Almost as if it had a mind of its own, her left hand moved to the table, as if it were jealous of the right. Hank smiled and moved his attention to her left hand. Then he stopped the gentle play and grasped her hand.

"Let's go, Tedi," he said, and pulled Edwyna to her feet. He helped her on with the cape she'd worn over her silk blouse, caressing her shoulders ever so lightly.

Edwyna didn't object, didn't ask any questions. With his hand on the small of her back, he ushered her through the doors of the restaurant. He opened the car door and helped her in, putting his hand on the top of her head to protect her from the roof of his low-slung Mercedes SLK250. Almost as if I were a perp captured by the cops, Edwyna thought, then settled into the rich red leather of the seat.

They sped across town, Hank's hand alternately on the gear shift and Edwyna's knee. Just as she'd supposed, he did live in a high-rise in Mission Bay, a few blocks from AT&T Park. At least that's where they were heading. He pulled into the garage and pulled her out of the car and against him. All in sure, swift moves.

They were not alone in the elevator to the top floor, so they had to be content with holding hands. Edwyna had never felt so much life in just one hand. She barely had time to look around the sparsely furnished apartment to note the city view before he once more took her hand and led her to the bedroom. There was nothing in the bedroom except the bed, a king-sized bed covered with a black silk comforter.

Hank did not give Edwyna the opportunity to choose whether or not she was interested. In fact, it was too late for the question. She was clearly interested, more than interested. But she was not going to make the first of the final set of moves. One part of her wanted only to make love, the other part wanted to see how the lovemaking would unfold. Would he wait for her to take off her clothes or move closer for a kiss? Up to this point— she realized—they hadn't even kissed. And no kiss followed. She stood facing him, just a few inches between them. Given the urgent clinch in the garage, she expected him to close that gap, maybe even push her down on the bed. Instead he reached over, took her cape, and hung it in the closet. He carefully lifted her silk shirt over her head and hung that in the closet as well. Her slacks followed.

As he removed each garment, he seemed careful not to touch her skin at all. Edwyna had never taken as much time as he did in hanging up her clothes. By the time he was up to her shoes—down to her panties and bra—she was starving for his touch. But she waited.

Edwyna stood naked in front of Hank, who still wore all his clothes. "Your turn," he said. "Undress me. Be careful. Don't mess my clothes. Or anything."

Edwyna had caught on to the game. Just as carefully as he'd removed her blouse and slacks, she removed his shirt and pants. Just as carefully as he'd hung up her clothing, she hung up each garment in his closet.

Of course there was one difference, one big difference, which she saw as soon as she unzipped his trousers. She ignored it and continued the obsessively neat, nontouching removal of his socks, his shoes, and then his boxers.

When they were both naked, Hank meticulously unfolded the comforter, revealing white silk sheets beneath its blackness. Once more he took Edwyna by the hand. This time he led her to the bed. She sat, then lay down. He laid down next to her. With his right hand, once more, he picked up the fingers of her left. Again he stroked her fingers. So lazy, slow were his motions that she had already begun to move from exited to relaxed, when he stopped. Suddenly he was on top of her, penetrating her. He leaned down and kissed her, pushing his tongue into her mouth even as his lips touched hers. One kiss, not even very long, and then he said, "Touch my chest, baby. Rub my chest. Like this." He grabbed one of her hands and showed her how to rub his chest in circles. "Do you like this? Do you like me inside you?"

Edwyna wasn't sure what to say. Everything had been so slow, and now she felt like she was on an express train to—she didn't know where. But then there was nothing left to say as Hank climaxed.

"Wow," he said when he could catch his breath. "Sorry, I'm not usually so fast. As I told you, it's been awhile."

"That's okay. It was fine," Edwyna lied.

"Really?"

"Yes, really?"

"Did you . . ."

Edwyna wasn't sure whether she wanted to lie this time. What would Tedi say? "Yes. I said it was fine."

"You said it was fine, but I don't know. Maybe it wasn't even okay." Hank's smile had turned to a pout.

"Besides we do have to get to know each other better, then . . ."

"I knew it. I knew it wasn't fine. It was a big nothing for you." Hank had been leaning over Edwyna as they spoke. Now he lay back down with a plunk. "I don't know if you'll even want a next time."

"The only way to find out is to ask me." Edwyna tried to be matter-of-fact.

Without a response or pause, Hank reached over to his iPhone, which he'd put on the floor near the bed. He squinted at the time. "It's getting late. I'd better get you back home for your beauty sleep."

What a corny line, Edwyna thought, and remembered back to the other corny lines when they'd met in the bar at Ocean Beach. She stood and went to the closet for her clothes. He had surprisingly little in the closet, she thought. Just the clothes he'd worn, another pair of slacks, a jacket, and two shirts.

"I know the cupboard looks bare," Hank said. "I'm still waiting for several boxes of my clothing and things from New York. I just have what I brought with me." Hank had moved back from pouting to smiling.

Hank drove Edwyna back to her car in West Portal without asking for a next time.

Well, that's that, she thought. Too bad. She'd enjoyed his company and the beginning of their lovemaking, but who knew what had really happened for him. In fact, who knew the answers to the many oddities she'd noticed. They made quite a list.

A week later, Hank had called and, once more, they'd made a date for dinner. This time he asked her to a restaurant closer to his apartment. She accepted his offer to pick her up. This time she was going to ask him the questions on her list. In fact, it was these very mysteries that drew her to him. As before, they lingered over dinner, seeming never to run out of conversation or laughter. And, as before, after coffee and dessert, he began to play with her fingers.

"Will you take another chance with me?" he asked.

"I'm here," Edwyna said. "Aren't I?"

"Do you want me?" Hank asked.

Edwyna nodded. Once again, his finger play had reached other parts of her body.

As they walked the two blocks to his apartment, he wound his arm through hers and put her hand into his pocket. "Don't want you to get chilled in this foggy night," he said. "And I have a surprise for you."

Edwyna felt the surprise in his pocket even before he said anything. How very Mae West! She thought of saying, "Is that a pistol in your pocket, or are you just happy to see me?" Instead, she simply allowed the side of her hand to brush up against his heat.

"Keeping your hand hot?" he asked. And then groaned.

Edwyna felt the warmth turn wet. Was that what he wanted?

"Don't worry. There's more where that came from."

In his apartment, he went through the same, careful undressing routine as the first time. He didn't seem the least bit embarrassed when Edwyna saw the damp circle on his boxers. Again, he pulled her into the bed, held her hand for a while, then climbed on top of her—jumped me—Edwyna thought. This time, without saying anything, he moved Edwyna's hand to his chest.

Edwyna's body had—in short order—accommodated itself to his routine so that this time when he climaxed, so did she. "Good girls," Edwyna wanted to whisper to her clitoris and G spot.

"Now that was better," Hank said. "I told you it would be." He patted her hand and stood, ready to dress and take her home.

On the way home, she thought of asking Hank the questions or at least some of them, but in her postcoital glow, she decided to let it all slide as she slid into the comfort of Hank's Mercedes.

CHAPTER 11

The Creep

THE FIRST TIME she'd heard the voice of The Creep—that was how she'd come to refer to that damned nuisance, in capital letters—he'd identified himself as conducting a survey for some health and nutrition magazine.

"I hope you can spare me just five minutes of your time. The information we are collecting from women like yourself may prove of help to others your age and younger."

He seemed so polite and she'd done some telephone survey work when she had a part-time job in college. Why not? she thought, and said, "But as soon as I think you are really selling something, I'm going to hang up."

"No problem. This is not a sales pitch."

Now she couldn't quite remember how the conversation had gone. At first, as she recalled, he asked her about her use of facial cleaning products, something about Retin-A and then about body washes, and before she realized what was happening, he said something like, "I know this is personal, but do you use any special feminine hygiene products to reduce odors?"

That was easy. She answered, "No."

And then he asked, "Do you think you have a small, medium, or large vagina?"

That had stopped her answering. Yet she hadn't hung up. She'd been silent for what seemed to her like forever, but had probably been only a few seconds because the next thing he said was, "I'm asking about your pussy. Don't you want to talk about your pussy?"

She slammed down the phone.

That call had been several weeks ago. She was shaken but then dismissed it and him from her mind. But The Creep had obviously not dismissed her. Just when she was lulled into thinking it was a one-off, that she'd never hear from him again, there he was.

The second time, there was no pretense. Edwyna had picked up the phone and he immediately began, "You didn't tell me the size of your pussy. I really need . . ."

She couldn't hang up fast enough. She dialed *67 to find the number The Creep had phoned from, but the impersonal answer was "Blocked ID."

The two calls had made her jumpy. The first time Joel called her she almost hung up before he said her name and began to talk.

"Hi, Tedi," he began. "I don't know if you remember me. We met through RomeoandJulietMatch at the coffee place."

Of course she remembered him, but she wasn't sure she wanted to talk to him. On the other hand, she didn't need to be as rude as he'd been.

"Hi," she answered. "I remember you." But she didn't say aloud what she was thinking about her memory of him. She couldn't believe he was calling her after their awkward meeting and his hurried departure.

"In case you don't remember, I was the really negative one."

Negative! First he'd blasted blondes and then ranted about his wife or ex-wife. She waited for him to continue.

"Listen, I was in a really bad place that day. Certain things happened with my ex-wife and I was upset for my kids." He took a deep breath. "That's not what I want to talk about today. While I was a total shmuck, you really handled it all so calmly. Any chance . . . Any chance you'd give me another chance?"

"I'm listening," Edwyna answered.

"I don't want to go into the stuff with my family again. We've really just met. Haven't really even met because I wasn't myself . . ."

Edwyna thought of asking who he'd been if not himself. But she kept silent, listening.

"What I mean is, I'm a basically happy guy. I feel I'm in a whole new phase of my life. I wake up excited to be alive. I'm like a teenager, just bursting with—with life."

Edwyna was a bit more interested, but not sure she wanted a teenager any more than she wanted that sour middle-aged man Joel had first presented. "I'm listening," she said.

"Let me make it up to you. What's your favorite restaurant?"

Edwyna did have favorite restaurants, but she hated that question, particularly when asked by a potential date. She never knew whether to say Boulevard, which was so expensive, or her neighborhood Chinese restaurant—inexpensive and busy and noisy—or something in between, which she didn't care about at all.

"What's yours?" seemed a safe enough reply.

"There's a small place I really like. Italian. How about dinner? Do you like Italian?"

"Sure. Who doesn't?" Edwyna said.

"Then will you let me make it up to you?" Joel repeated, this time as a question.

They went to a lovely bistro. It was up a flight of stairs in the Castro, and it was clear that someone took pride in every detail. Small floral arrangements dotted the bar and the tables, each one slightly different from the other, yet all sharing in a lovely mix of yellows and purple. Small candles on each table echoed the color scheme and cast a soft glow on the diners and the food. The owner of the restaurant himself came to take their order and to recommend that night's special—veal scarpariello—and a hearty reserve Chianti to accompany it. Joel had reserved a table in a back corner so that they could hear each other clearly—a rarity in San Francisco restaurants. Edwyna enjoyed herself. He's not so bad, she thought as the evening drew to a close. Maybe that first date was an aberration. She was glad she'd given him a second chance.

Although she continued to date Joel—along with Hank and Nick—she knew he was not the one. He'd kissed her and, as she might have said to a girlfriend if she had one, "He's a good kisser." But he hadn't taken her face in his hands. And he was a good lover too. Just good. No better than Nick. No worse. No better than Hank. And no worse. An expression she'd learned somewhere or other had come to mind after the first time they'd made love: "Same, same but different."

Nick had his book of routines that he followed religiously: kissing, lip stroking, lip sucking, breast nuzzling, body stroking, body licking, entering one way or another, climaxing. She had to admit that his routine was a good one. It was the rapid retreat that followed that always left her hanging. Hank always began by his playing with her fingers and ended with her rubbing his chest. Although each of them asked her how it had been for her, neither of them seemed particularly attuned to her desires during the act itself. Joel, on the other hand, was too solicitous. The first time they made love, he began with gentle kisses. Then he nibbled at her lips, kissed her harder, and gently probed her mouth with his tongue.

"What do you like, baby?" he asked as he moved from one kiss to another. "This one?" He kissed her slowly and softly. "This one?" He pressed his lips so firmly to hers that she feared for her teeth. "Or this?" He pushed his tongue around hers, around her teeth, around the inside of her cheeks.

"All of them," she answered.

"But which one best?" he asked.

"The combination," she said.

He moved to her breasts. He cupped them. He tantalized her nipples with his thumbs. "Do you like this?" Joel asked.

"Mmm," Edwyna said.

"How about this?" Joel asked. He moved his mouth down to her right breast. He sucked gently on the nipple, then ran his tongue around the nipple and the areola. He moved to her left breast. Then he looked up.

Edwyna realized he was waiting for an answer. "Yes."

"Which way do you like best?"

"All of them," she answered.

He moved down her belly. Licked her skin. Brushed it with the slight roughness of his chin. Once more he stopped and asked.

Once more Edwyna answered.

Joel took her hand and placed it on his pulsing penis. "Look what I have for you, baby. Are you ready for this?"

"Yes," Edwyna said. Indeed she was ready.

But again Joel paused. "Which way do you like it? Missionary? Side by side? From the back?"

Edwyna appreciated his concern, but she just wanted it. Any which way would be fine. "Any way you'd like," she said.

"But I want to know what you like," Joel insisted.

Edwyna pulled him on top of her and he slid in easily. The rhythm of the motions matched, first slow and then faster.

Edwyna was lost in the moment, moving toward climax, when Joel spoke again. "Remember who's your daddy. Remember who gives you what you want, what you need. Just tell me. Just tell me." And he shuddered in orgasm.

Distracted by his verbal interruptions to their rhythm, Edwyna had lost the way to her own orgasm. That's the problem, she thought. You aren't giving me what I want, what I need.

It was the first time, she thought. Joel knew all the right moves, and now that he knew what she wanted, things would go more smoothly. But the litany of questions continued each time they made love. Good enough, but not great. She couldn't get past that sticking point, the point of good enough. Maybe she should give them all up. What was the use of good enough when she wanted so much more? The so-much-more had nothing to do with technique and everything to do with emotion. Nothing to do with orgasms and everything to do with love.

And then there was The Creep. Again. The third call was just a few nights after the second one. She'd tried to pay attention to Caller ID before grabbing the phone, but somehow the number listed had not rung any alarm bells.

"Hello," he said, "I love watching you. Touch your pussy so I can . . ."

She hung up as quickly as she could. And then the phone rang again right away. It was a different number but she didn't pick up. There he was on her voice mail. "I can see you. I see your tits and your cunt. Yesterday I watched your ass move as you walked home. I'm gonna fuck that ass."

Edwyna felt frozen to the spot. She looked at her windows. All the blinds were down. No one could see her. She reached over to pick up the phone to erase the voice mail. But the phone rang again. Again she didn't pick up. The call went to answer and she waited, shivering, for The Creep's voice, but it was just an appeal from some charity collecting for the latest in disaster relief.

The charity collector was a woman. At least it sounded like a woman, but Edwyna's mind would not stay still. What if The Creep was able to disguise his voice? What if he had a woman accomplice? What if he really knew her and knew where she lived and would come to her home? Should she call the police? Should she tell Joel or Hank or Nick? How would any of them be of help? They were no knights in shining—or even dull and rusted—armor.

Edwyna sat in her big blue chair in front of the window with her head in her hands. Every now and then, unable to help herself, she looked at the blinds to be sure they were drawn. She felt tempted to raise the blinds to see if there was anyone lurking on the street, but then she knew she could be seen. Unless she also turned off all the lights in her home. But then she'd be in the dark. She could not free her mind from these wandering, scary thoughts. And she was not the kind of woman to be scared. Once in the book group, one of the women had described a friend of hers who kept all the lights on when she was home alone and who did a routine check of closets to be sure no one was hiding. How the other book group women had laughed at the story. Obviously none of them was afraid to be alone. And Edwyna could not remember ever being afraid. Before The Creep, that was.

"Get off the chair, drink some wine, forget this," she ordered herself.

But she didn't move. Vlad. Did Vlad even have her number? He was certainly strange. Maybe he was angry because of the nonexistent husband she'd threatened him with. But then, if he thought there was a husband, would he be calling?

Instead of sitting here waiting for the phone to ring again, she should call Howard. And then the phone rang again. Again she let it go to voice mail. If she wanted to erase the calls quickly, she feared she couldn't. In that moment, she could not remember the numeric key that erased calls from the system.

Again there was a message. "Pick up, pick up, sweet pussy. I know you're there. I can see you. Look outside. I have a big cock for your sweet pussy."

Edwyna waited, then picked up the phone as if the instrument itself were dangerous. She held it to her ear, fearing that somehow The Creep was still on the other end. She was so nervous that she misdialed Howard's number three times before getting it right. A quick review of the evening's calls brought Howard immediately to her door.

"First, we have to settle you down," he said. "What's it to be? Scotch? White wine? Chamomile tea?"

"I'll go middle of the road," Edwyna said. "Wine."

Howard knew Edwyna's kitchen as well as he knew his own. He disappeared for a moment and reappeared with two glasses of chardonnay in hand. "Let's hope he calls again this evening. If he does, let me answer the phone. How did this guy get your number?"

"I wish I knew. Maybe it's someone I hurt or insulted. I don't know. I just don't know."

"It might not be from anyone you know," Howard said. "It could just be some kinky guy, random dialing until he gets a woman's voice. Then he just keeps calling."

"I hadn't even thought of that. Every time he calls—I know this sounds nuts—but I feel guilty."

"Guilt is for my people," Howard said.

And he got the laugh from Edwyna that he'd hoped for just as the phone rang again.

Howard put his finger to his lips, lifted the receiver, and waited.

"Hi Pussy, my sweet . . ."

Howard assumed a voice at least an octave lower than his usual soft speech. "This is the police. Do not call this number again . . ."

Even before Howard had gotten to the word "again," The Creep hung up.

"He's gone," Howard said to Edwyna. "Now fill me in. Tell all on your swains. I haven't talked to you in days."

"Where did that voice come from?" Edwyna asked Howard.

"You may think of me as your friendly neighbor, occasional white knight, and friend—I hope. Remember in my other life, I'm the CTO of a major player down the peninsula. When I can't get my techies—or a vendor—to perform, after the usual cajoling, that's the voice that works."

"I love it. Your CTO voice. I'm just glad I've never been on the receiving end."

"Trust me. It works. Nine times out of ten, and I bet it worked again tonight."

"Then he might call again."

"But then again, he might not. Just wait and see."

For a moment there was only silence. The silence lengthened.

"Let's talk about something else. Your swains?" Howard said.

Edwyna smiled. She was grateful to Howard, but he was right. She was not at all sure his intervention was going to work.

"I think I'm beginning to like Joel," Howard said after all the tales were told. "Nick is a known quantity and it's not a very big number. Hank may be a bit too smooth. But Joel has a certain *je ne sais quoi*."

"Right!" Edwyna answered. "You know what *je ne sais quoi* means? It means: 'I don't know what.' And that's about the size of it."

"Well! If you want to talk about size . . ."

"Howard! Finish your wine and then it's bedtime."

"Seriously. Do you want me to sleep on the sofa? I'm happy to be your Sir Galahad for the night."

Edwyna put down her glass, took Howard's from his hand. She pulled him to his feet and into a big hug. "I'm okay now," she said. "You are this girl's BFF."

"Are you sure?" he asked again.

"I feel safer just knowing you are here, a stone's throw away."

"You mean 'a phone's throw away,'" Howard said.

"That did it. You're out of here." Edwyna walked down the stairs with Howard, gave him one more hug, and opened the door.

CHAPTER 12

Bibliophile

AFTER TELLING HOWARD the saga of her current prospects, Edwyna realized that she'd have to continue her search if she were to find what she really wanted. The man she really wanted. The man who really wanted her in the way she wanted to be wanted. Edwyna took a deep breath and sighed. She was reluctant to return to the games of RomeoandJulietMatch.com. Just reading the profiles of the men bored her. And although she continued her walks on the beach, she knew it was unlikely there would be another Hank.

Then, just a week ago, at a meeting of the Wise Women book club, Dorothy mentioned an article she'd seen in a library newsletter. It was for a speed-dating event at the main branch of the public library. After their jokes about the likelihood, or even desirability, of finding fourth husbands, Lila turned to Edwyna and said, "You should go."

"Yes, go," Carolyn urged.

While all of them nodded their agreement, Diane put her hand on Edwyna's and said, "Just try it." She said it quietly, yet definitely.

Now Edwyna was getting ready for "Biblio-Dating." She knew what she would wear—jeans, of course. That's what everyone wore. But she'd pair the jeans with one of her beautiful floaty blue tops. The real question was which book to carry.

Should she choose a book she loved, a book that would reveal something about her, or should she choose a book she thought the kind of man she was looking for might choose? If she wanted to reveal herself, and since she was looking for romance, should she carry one of the great romantic novels? *Wuthering Heights*? Probably not a good idea. Too classic. Too female. Too old. What about Dan Brown's *Da Vinci Code*? It appealed to men and women, but what was there to say about it? She and some imagined partner-in-conversation could talk about favorite scenes or great clues. But then what? No. Besides, it was already several years old and she'd have to reread it to get the many details straight. Maybe nonfiction was the way to go. Talk about facts. Be matter of fact. She liked Gladwell, *The Tipping Point*, but nonfiction seemed kind of cold. And then a stroke of genius—at least that's what she told herself—*The Maltese Falcon*. It was a classic mystery. A story everyone knew because of the film. And Hammett's writing was itself a gem. If everything else failed in the four minutes allotted with each person, she could just read sections aloud.

She went to her bookshelves happy that she kept her books in some order, all fiction on one set of shelves, arranged, more or less, alphabetically by author. She removed the book from its place just as the phone rang. She opened the book to the first page with one hand and reached for the phone with the other.

"Cunt. Suck my . . ." Damn him. She slammed down the phone. Howard's deep voice had not worked.

She read the first lines of the book to get back in the mood. What if someone had never seen the film? If she met such a strange being, he was definitely, most assuredly, certainly not the man for her.

Edwyna grabbed a jacket from the closet and her handbag from the top of her dresser. She slid the paperback into her bag, checked her image in the hall mirror, made one more adjustment to her long hair, and—the telephone rang. She'd already decided to screen all calls, let them go to voice mail, before picking up.

But there he was: The Creep. "I'm here. Let me lick your . . ."

Edwyna raced to the phone, lifted the receiver, and let it fall with a clang back into its cradle. She was shaken. Shaken and angry. "That fuck," she murmured under her breath, although there was no one there to hear her. "That fuck!" she said again, louder. She looked in the mirror once more, squared her shoulders, and—hesitated—did she dare to open her door? What if . . . She was not going to let The Creep rule her life, ruin her life. She marched down her stairs, opened the door, and left for Biblio-Dating.

She had to admit, she was eager to see what this was like. And maybe even who she'd meet. At the same time, she didn't have high expectations. She was pretty sure that this kind of event would draw far more women than men.

Edwyna walked through the Larkin Street doors of the library into the entry rotunda. She always meant to read the plaques of library history that lined the rotunda's walls, but not tonight. She strode across the interior bridge, barely glancing at the stacks below her, and took the staircase down to the lower level. Edwyna was surprised to find she was one of only two people on the staircase. She looked at her watch. Was she late? Too early? Or was this going to be one of those disastrous events where too few people made a large room seem even emptier than it was?

The room was decorated for the event. Tables for two ringed the space. On each table was a single rose in a bud vase, a small stack of plastic glasses, and a split of sparkling wine. About twenty people milled about in the large central space. Contrary to her expectations, there seemed to be about the same number of men as women. The women had gathered near the center of the circle in groups of two or three and were already displaying their books to each other. The men stood closer to the tables, almost encircling the women. One, then another, picked up the wine bottle from the table closest to him and read the label, studied the label. They seemed so ill at ease that Edwyna thought they might flee before the evening began. Then with a flurry of noise, about ten more people showed up. Their entrance broke up the isolated circles that had formed.

Before the attendees could regroup, a smiling man strode to the middle of the circle. "Welcome," he said, "to Biblio-Dating. I'm Ray, your friendly librarian. Tonight, instead of helping people find books that interest them, I'm hoping the books you brought help you find people that interest you." He smiled broadly and nodded, obviously pleased with his speech.

Everyone focused on Ray. It was almost as if they were playing a game, one in which they were not free even to look at one another until the rules of the evening were explained and a referee blew that starting whistle. Ray explained how each woman would sit at a table, with her book before her, and how the men would rotate around the tables. As in speed dating, each couple would have four minutes of conversation, after which he, Ray, would ring a bell—Edwyna was glad to hear there was no whistle-blowing—and the men would move to the next table, going clockwise.

"Here's the important part," Ray concluded. "At the end of the evening, you will open the bottles of wine. While you are sipping from California's best, I will collect all the books and place them on this table at the front of the room." He gestured toward the table. "If you would like to continue the conversation with someone, find his or her book, take one of the pieces of paper provided on the table, and leave a note with your name and contact information inside the front cover of the book you'd like to explore further." He grinned and then continued, "Of course, I mean the book that belongs to the person you'd like to get to know better. So be sure you know who's reading what before you leave a table."

With that explanation, the women settled themselves at tables, put their books down, and—with a little encouragement—each man sat at the first table of his circuit. Edwyna couldn't help remembering her high school dances, where the boys always seemed so shy of the girls at the beginning and then so intent at getting closer and closer by the end.

Maybe it was his shyness that kept the first man at Edwyna's table almost silent. He put his book on the table so that it was upside down, print toward him. The back cover, rather than the front, was on top. He picked up Edwyna's book, opened it, and began to read silently. Edwyna turned his book over and around. It was a brand new travel guide to Spain.

Silence ensued until Edwyna couldn't take it any longer. "I see you're interested in Spain. Have you been there recently?"

"No," he answered and continued to read *The Maltese Falcon*.

"Oh, are you planning a trip?"

"Not really." More reading.

"I love this book," Edwyna gestured toward *The Maltese Falcon*. "Hmm."

"Have you read it or seen the film?"

"Never heard of it."

At least he'd stopped reading. But just for a moment. Then he picked up his own book, seemed to open it at random, and began to read. Silently.

This was torture.

The next few men who followed Spanish Travel Book Guy were not of any interest to Edwyna, and she could tell they were not interested in her, either. But at least they carried on conversations about her book and theirs.

A loud thunk on the table drew Edwyna's flagging attention. A very tall man dressed in a blue jacket almost obscured by various pins and medals had plunked a thick volume on the desk. He sat down, but before he looked at Edwyna, he took a small mirror from his pocket and smoothed his few remaining white hairs even closer to his skull.

"This is the most important book you'll ever read," he said emphatically. He had a deep, loud voice which blurred the hum of conversation from the other tables.

Edwyna was willing to learn why this was the most important book she'd ever read, but at this moment he sat with his large hand obscuring the cover. All she could see was that the book was well-thumbed.

"Know what it is? Know why it is? Know how it's important—the most important book? The most important book you'll ever open?" He fired the questions at Edwyna.

She tried to speak, but he continued.

"Tells you how to get from here to there. Wouldn't you like to know that? Tells you when to leave there to come back here. Bet that's of interest to you. Right?" He took out his mirror once more and looked at his hair.

He must be satisfied, Edwyna thought, as he didn't smooth it again.

"Are you concerned about time? Do you like to be on time? Do you like to be in the right place at the right time? Did you know your life will be better if you can do that?"

Edwyna had become somewhat curious. Maybe the book was some mystical guide or a guru's self-help tome.

"When you are ready to answer my questions, I'll let you see the book. Think about my questions. Are you ready to answer them?" He glared at Edwyna.

Edwyna was about to say something, when he spoke again.

"Do you remember the order of the questions? Order is very important."

Edwyna shook her head.

"That's okay. Not everyone gets it right away. I'll ask you again. Know what it is? Know why it is?"

Indeed he'd gone back to what Edwyna thought had been the first question. He continued to fire them all at her again, every now and then taking out his mirror to check his hair.

The bell rang. Question-Man removed his hand from the book's cover. "Too late for you to get into this," he said. "Here's what you missed." The cover read: *Railroad Timetables of the World: 1950–1955.*

"I can see how that would be useful," Edwyna spoke her first words in four minutes.

"Useful? You don't know the half of it," he replied and moved on to the next table.

Somewhere around the fifth or sixth change, about a third of the way through the process, Edwyna saw a familiar-looking man at a table before hers. She couldn't quite place him, but she knew that they'd met somewhere. Or maybe she'd seen him somewhere—on the Muni, in a restaurant. She knew it wasn't someone she knew well, yet . . . She barely paid attention to the man at her table. He had a book about Rasta, and he was clearly an enthusiast. She wasn't sure if he loved the reggae music, admired Haile Selassie, or actually practiced the religion by smoking pot. However, she didn't have to exert herself much as he spoke, quite energetically, with many gestures, throughout the entire four minutes.

The bell rang and the familiar man moved forward. He carried *Flying Solo: The Cookbook for Single Men*. Of course, Edwyna knew the moment she saw the book, it was the man she'd met a while ago at the supermarket. Soup Guy! Would he remember her?

"Hi, I'm Bob." He held up his book. "Eating alone is really a bummer. But you don't look like you ever have to eat alone."

Obviously he didn't remember her, since those were almost the exact words he'd said in the supermarket. Should she mention that they'd met before? Would that make him think he was so hot? Unforgettable? Should she just follow his lead on eating? She decided she would just start talking and see what words emerged. Not her usual careful style, but . . .

"I agree about eating alone. But not if you have a good book to read." She held up *The Maltese Falcon*.

"That is one great book," he said. "Sam Spade. Effie. Brigid O'Shaughnessy. What great characters. And Joel Castro. But I must admit, the movie overlays the text. I can't read it without hearing Bogart and Greenstreet."

"And, of course, the great Peter Lorre as Joel Castro."

"What do you think about watching movies? Alone or together?"

"Together is definitely better." Edwyna was surprised he'd gone right back on track. "Because . . ."

"Because then you can talk about it, agree about what you like."

"Or argue." She wasn't sure why she'd put that in.

More conversation about *The Maltese Falcon* followed before Edwyna decided to mention their earlier meeting. "By the way," she began, "you know I think we . . ."

"Just what I was going to say. I think we should talk again. Be sure you remember my book. I want to impress the title on your memory so that you don't forget it when it's time to write our notes." Once again he held up his book. "And I will certainly remember you, Ms. Maltese Falcon. By the way, what's your name?"

"Tedi," Edwyna said. She was intrigued. Given their history—brief as it was—she didn't think she was the one who'd forget.

With that, the bell to rotate tables rang. Bob smiled, picked up his book, and moved on.

By the end of the evening, Edwyna realized that the only possibly interesting man was Bob, the Soup Man, as she couldn't help herself thinking about him. Ray gathered the books and signaled the group to open the wine bottles. People moved about more easily than at the beginning, and Edwyna saw there was a group of men—including Bob—around a pretty blonde woman. She was about her own age, Edwyna figured, but was dressed like someone much younger. Her jeans were skin tight and slung so low they barely covered the crack between her buttocks, which Edwyna had to admit, were nicely round. Her cleavage-revealing shirt, purple with teal spangles, was as much above her waist as her pants were below it. The effect was to bare her belly in the front and reveal a tattooed rose in the rear. A rose whose stem disappeared into the top of the jeans.

Edwyna stood at the back of the room, considering putting her name in Bob's book. She wondered if he'd do the same. Then she saw the blonde pied piper leading her troop to the table. The blonde held up her book, *The Dude Takes the Duchess*, and at the same time, gave out pieces of paper to the waiting crowd of admirers. From a distance she looked like a really hot kindergarten teacher distributing supplies to eager children. The book that she still held up showed a bald, bare-chested man, his hands encircling the woman's breasts, which of course bulged far beyond the restraints of whatever garment she was wearing. Edwyna looked from the book to the blonde and back again. She could swear that the woman on the cover was wearing the same blouse—if you could call it that—as the blonde herself. Edwyna decided to wait.

By the end of the evening, she was still uncertain, still standing back. She thought she saw one or two men, but not Bob, put slips of paper in her book. However, she couldn't be sure. As people had slipped their information beneath the covers, the books themselves had moved into disarray. Even as she drew closer to the table, she was still hesitant.

She wanted to peek inside her book to see if Bob had written anything, but Ray had been insistent that no one look into their books until they left the library. He had given several reasons for this and they'd made sense to Edwyna, so she resisted. What the heck. She picked up a slip of paper, wrote Tedi, and then hesitated. She would not give him her phone number. No more callers were needed. She wrote down her email address and slipped the paper into *Flying Solo*.

The crowd was dispersing. She picked up *The Maltese Falcon* and slipped it back into her bag. Time enough to look inside when she was home.

At home, she felt she had enough courage to tackle the multiplying voice mail messages. For each one, she played only a word or two before deleting them. They were all from The Creep. That chore finished, she sat down in front of her fireplace, withdrew the book from her handbag, and opened it. There was one note, and it was from Bob. Like her, he'd provided an email address. Still, she decided, she wouldn't contact him. She'd wait and see.

CHAPTER 13

The Creep Redux

THE NEXT MORNING, Edwyna awakened from a fitful night's sleep to the ringing of the phone.

"Hello," she answered in barely a murmur.

"Hi, Sweetie." It was her dad's voice. "Did I wake you? Sorry. Want me to call back later?"

"Hi, Dad. Yes and no. Yes, the phone did wake me up. And no, don't call later. Let's talk now." As she spoke, Edwyna moved to a semisitting position and pulled the comforter over her shoulders. "What time is it?"

"It's after nine. So I thought you'd be up. But I can call you . . ."

"It's fine, Dad, really fine. What's up with you and Mom?"

"That's my question. We haven't spoken in more than a week or so, and we were just wondering if you were all right. Wondering 'what's up with you?' as you'd say. I know . . . we know . . . you're really busy, so . . ."

Edwyna realized with a guilty start that she hadn't called her parents. And it might actually have been more than two weeks. It was that caller, that damn caller. His calls made her feel that the phone itself had some hidden malevolence. She didn't want to touch it. "I'm sorry. I should have called."

"I don't want you to feel you have an obligation. It's just . . . Are you . . . Is everything . . . ?"

"Things are pretty much the same. Nothing new to report. I'm . . . I don't know."

"You sound downhearted. Anything you want to share with your old dad?"

"I could use some advice. But I don't want to scare you."

"I don't scare easily. But your saying you don't want to scare me does raise my antennae."

"It's nothing, really. Really nothing."

"Then tell me the nothing and I'll give you advice on the nothing."

"I've been getting some phone calls," Edwyna began and then told her father the sequence and gist of them. It was difficult to do without using the actual language of The Creep.

But Edward got it. "I'm sure his words were even more shocking than the ones you've told me. Do you have any idea of who it is?"

"I've tried to guess. But no."

"Is the voice familiar?"

"Not at all. I even listened to one of the calls for a longer time, trying to see if it sounded like someone I know. I found myself searching for an accent or a way of speaking. But no. Except now the voice is familiar as his voice, The Creep's voice."

"Would you like me to come into the city? I could stay with you until he calls and tell that creep to disappear. In no uncertain terms."

"Sorry, Dad. I wish that would work. My friend Howard tried it. To no avail. And he sounded really convincing. But obviously not to The Creep."

"Have you called the police?"

"Hadn't thought of doing that. Aren't they too busy with serious crimes to care about crank calls?"

"I want you to call the police."

"What can they do?"

"I don't know for sure, but with computers and such, I bet they can figure out who's calling. Or block him. Or . . . Just call them."

"Don't tell Mom," Edwyna said, knowing it was a futile request.

"Will you call the police?"

"Okay. Okay. But remember, nothing to Mom."

At the end of the conversation, Edwyna slipped back into a sleeping position. She pulled the comforter not only over her shoulders, but over her head. She appreciated her father's advice. It was usually sound, but she wasn't ready to call the police. She wasn't ready to face their questions. She wasn't even ready to face the day. She'd almost fallen back to sleep when the phone rang again. It was probably her father checking to see if she'd called the police.

"Not yet," she answered.

"Not yet what?" It was a familiar woman's voice.

"Sorry. I thought it was my father checking up on me."

"Good morning, Edwyna. I wanted to find out how the Biblio-Dating worked out for you."

Edwyna realized it was Diane. "Thank you for suggesting that I go. I actually had a rather strange encounter. Maybe more odd than strange."

"Yes?" Diane prompted.

"This is a kind of weird story that actually began a couple of months ago. Do you have time to hear it?"

Diane said yes at the same time that Edwyna said, "Or do you want the bottom line?"

Diane laughed and said, "Sometimes I forget you're an accountant. I always want the whole story. That way I get to my own bottom line. But I do have an idea. Do you have time for a coffee this afternoon?"

"That would be lovely," Edwyna said.

"That will give us all the time we want for stories and ciphers and bottom lines."

Just before she left the house, Edwyna remembered the folder she'd found in her tote well more than a couple of months earlier. She looked in the desk drawer, sure that's where she'd last put it. It was no wonder she hadn't thought of it sooner. Out of sight. Out of mind. She opened and closed the desk drawer and reached into its recesses, although it was a rather shallow drawer, not many recesses. She realized she was going to be late if she kept up this futile search and slammed the drawer closed.

"This coffee is better than the best hot chocolate of my childhood," Edwyna said. She looked around the coffee shop that Diane had suggested. It was in the Richmond, a neighborhood due north across Golden Gate Park from Edwyna's home. This wasn't Starbucks or any other chain. It was a local place with a marvelous aroma of coffee and fresh pastries, and a warmth that came both from the several space heaters and the smile of the woman barista. The intricate oriental designs of the somewhat worn rugs seemed to hold memories of a time and place far distant from the Richmond. The fringes of the gold fabric window coverings moved with an unseen breeze. Around marble-topped tables, stained from long use, deep, well-cushioned upholstered chairs called for an unhurried settling in.

"I love the idea of all those mixed coffee drinks," Diane said, "but I still like a simple sugared coffee. In Russia, I would have had this coffee with a lump of sugar held in my mouth so that I could taste the coffee infusing the sugar."

"How long ago were you in Russia?" Edwyna asked.

"A long time and not so long a time," Diane answered. "Now back to the present. You are going to tell me your odd story or story of a strange encounter."

"Let me think of how to begin. Last evening, at the Biblio-Dating . . . No, wait a moment. This will be clearer. Several weeks ago . . . Maybe a month or so, I was at the supermarket. Just your ordinary supermarket, looking at cans of soup. Yes, I know. Canned soup is awful. But I digress."

Edwyna looked at Diane and realized she would patiently wait for the story as long as it took. It was so relaxing, so calming to feel she could just tell the whole story, with all her feelings about it, to Diane. So she did. She began with the supermarket meeting and finished with the notes in the books.

"Are there other men in your life besides Soup Guy, as you call him?"

Edwyna was not surprised by the question. In fact, she wanted to tell Diane more. She described Nick and his regularity, Joel's initial rant and subsequent apologetic lovemaking, and Hank's appearance at the beach.

"Many women would envy you all this attention, but you don't seem satisfied. I don't need to read your mind to see that. If you were satisfied, you wouldn't have gone to the library last night. What do you want?"

That cut right to the bone. "Wow!" she said. "I don't know if I can describe it to you. I'm not sure I can put it into words."

"Try," Diane said. "What about an image?"

"Here's the image," Edwyna said. "Don't laugh. I know you're experienced and . . . Anyway, you know in a movie, when a man— the hero—is kissing a woman for the first time, and he takes her face between his hands?"

"Yes, I understand completely. It's what all we women want. We want it at the beginning of a love affair and until the very end of a long marriage. The very end of our lives. That gesture, the feeling it evokes, goes right to our brains. Our endorphins flow."

"The endorphins, yes."

"I also understand it's none of these men. If you don't mind, I also feel that you are troubled today. Not troubled by the strange encounter. Something else. And this is not how you have seemed at our book club. I think something else is happening now. Something else?" Diane invited Edwyna to continue.

"There is something else. There is a man. A man I don't know at all. He has somehow found my phone number. And maybe I was stupid the first time I spoke to him . . ." Edwyna told the entire story, virtually call-by-call, to Diane.

"What have you done to stop him?"

"My friend, Howard, answered one of the calls. Pretended he was the police."

"And that didn't work, obviously."

"My father wants me to call the police."

"Call if you want to satisfy your father, but they won't do anything useful. They may suggest you change your number, but that creates its own problems, doesn't it?"

Edwyna nodded.

"Have you used your own power against him?"

"What do you mean?" Edwyna asked.

Diane looked up toward the ceiling and nodded as if discussing something with herself. Then she reached into the large, elaborately embroidered, canvas bag that hung from the back of her chair. "I want you to take this special charm."

Diane held her hand closed. She put her fist into Edwyna's palm. She opened her fist and let something fall into Edwyna's hand. "Close your hand and don't look yet," Diane commanded.

Edwyna obeyed.

"Keep this charm near your phone. The next time he calls, answer the phone. Hold the charm tight in a closed fist and say in the deepest voice you can, 'Go away. Go away now. Never again.' Let me hear you say it."

Edwyna was embarrassed. They were in a public place, a coffee shop. While all of the customers seemed involved in their own business—working on computers, reading, or talking—she felt these words could interrupt the entire room. "Go away. Go away now. Never again," she said quietly.

"You have to speak in a deeper voice. You don't have to be louder, just deeper. Listen to me." Diane lowered her voice, just as Howard had done, and said the phrase again. "Your turn."

Edwyna cleared her throat. "Go away. Go away now. Never again."

"Even deeper," Diane said. She repeated the phrase in what seemed to Edwyna to be a growl. And although Edwyna could recognize the phrase as a whole, it was almost as if the words had been turned into some other language.

Edwyna took a deep breath and repeated the phrase. It sounded the same, just deeper.

"Excellent," Diane said. Now put the charm in your handbag and take it out when you get home.

How strange, Edwyna thought as she walked home. She should call the police as her father suggested. That would certainly work better than a charm and a deep voice. But this was not a

911 matter. Maybe she'd just walk over to the precinct and see what whoever was there had to say. She didn't know exactly why she felt so reluctant to go to the police. Embarrassed even. This wasn't her fault.

"Going my way?" Edwyna heard Howard before she saw him as they both rounded the corner of their building.

"Yes. If you'll help me out once more. It's The Creep."

"My deep masculine threats did not work."

"No. At least, not yet. My dad wants me to go to the police. And . . ."

"And you want me to . . ."

"To go with?"

"Let's get it over with." Howard agreed and they changed direction to walk toward the police station at Taraval and 23rd.

Edwyna appreciated the traditional blue lantern that, along with the Romanesque solidity of the building, announced the identity of the police station. The brick face of the building held plaques commemorating those who'd been killed in the line of duty, a frieze celebrating law and order, and an incongruously large relief of children at play. Edwyna and Howard entered through the studded wooden door.

"Shades of the Tower of London," Howard whispered.

"Why are you whispering?" Edwyna answered in an equally soft voice.

"I don't know," Howard said in his usual speaking voice.

The exterior grandeur was not matched by the worn, serviceable furnishings of the room they entered. Faded beige office chairs sat on brown tiles. An unused L-shaped grey metal desk faced the waiting-room chairs, but no one sat behind the desk. The walls were covered with signs. Homemade flyers for missing cats and dogs shared space with wanted posters and directions for avoiding bicycle theft in English, Spanish, Chinese or Vietnamese, along with an exhortation to "Get Guns Off Our Streets."

Edwyna had expected to see a high desk separating the officers from the public. Instead, at the end of the waiting room, she found a thick glass wall with a telephone handset. And instead of a burly officer, complete with beer gut, she was facing a trim policewoman, her hair held back in a tight braid. Her name tag read Officer L. Leung.

The officer picked up her handset and gestured to Edwyna to use the one on her side of the glass. Leung may have looked young to Edwyna, but she was all business. Edwyna wasn't quite sure how to begin, but Officer Leung did know. She interrupted Edwyna's several false starts, saying, "Why don't we start at the beginning. First just tell me your name and address. And the identity of the gentleman with you."

Edwyna was happy to begin with the innocuous—her name, Howard's name, their relationship as friends and neighbors so that when she told Officer Leung about The Creep, the facts flowed smoothly.

"We're going to make a record of your report," Officer Leung said. "Once I get a few more details, there are some steps I might suggest. But before that, let me make sure that there is nothing more than the calls. Has the person on the phone threatened you? Has the person on the phone said anything to suggest that he knows where you are?"

Edwyna was more frightened by the scenarios Officer Leung's questions suggested than she had been before.

Edwyna hesitated. Then she shook her head and said, "No."

Officer Leung made a note and then said, "You seemed uncertain about whether he knows where you are."

"Well," Edwyna said, "he says he can see me, but he's never said anything to make me believe he actually can see me."

"What about his voice. Do you think you recognize the voice? Even if you are unsure."

Again Edwyna said, "No. Definitely not."

"Are there any patterns—days of the week, times of day, any seeming routine?"

Once more, Edwyna said, "No."

The next questions were harder to answer. "Is there anyone who might have an issue with you? Anyone who might want to make you feel bad?"

She wondered if she should mention Joel or Hank. Or Vlad. But why would any of them want to make her feel bad? She really felt good with them, at least good enough. Edwyna hesitated, but finally again said, "No."

"When you receive the calls, what do you do?"

"I try to screen them, but if I miss and he gets through, I just hang up. He also does sometimes reach my answering machine."

"Hanging up is the right thing to do. Your caller is a type of sex offender we are quite familiar with. He achieves his sexual satisfaction through the fantasies of the call. You were right in not engaging him in conversation since that whets his appetite. He's more of an annoyance than a danger."

"What do you mean? How is he more of an annoyance? I mean, what do you mean by 'more'? Could he become a danger? How would I know? How do you know?" Edwyna was glad she was sitting down. She could feel her knees shaking.

"Maybe I can help. I'm Inspector MacArthur."

Edwyna heard the deep voice before she saw the man to whom it belonged. Concentrating on her conversation with Leung, Edwyna had not seen anyone enter the police station.

Indeed the whole station behind her had dropped from her consciousness as she focused on Leung, behind the window, trying to communicate with her through the impersonal handset.

"May I?" he asked as he took the phone from Edwyna's hand and nodded at Officer Leung, who hung up hers.

"Come with me." He held out his hand to Edwyna and then Howard.

MacArthur entered a keypad code, then ushered Edwyna and Howard ahead of him into the room where Leung sat. He passed Officer Leung's desk, nodded to her again, took the notes she'd made, and said, "Thanks for getting it started."

Then once again to Edwyna and Howard, "Please come with me." He led the way to his office.

"I'm sorry I got so agitated," Edwyna said. "Just when the officer said something about his being less a danger than an annoyance, I got the idea that he could be some sort of danger."

"I saw you were getting more nervous," Inspector MacArthur said. "And since I'd just returned to the station, I thought I might help." He gestured to the notes he'd placed on his desk. "I have all the details we need for the record, but I would like to hear the events once more. Would you like some water before you begin?" He looked down. "Ms. Glendower and Mr. Rosen?" He continued reading for a moment. "This indicates that you are Ms. Glendower's friend and neighbor," he said to Howard. "Is that right?"

"Yes," they answered in unison.

"Good," he said.

"Edwyna, do you mind if I call you Edwyna? What is your complaint? Just tell it to me again."

Once Edwyna had finished the story, Inspector MacArthur leaned forward toward her, his hands on his knees. "I know this is upsetting to you, but I can assure you, the man calling you may be neurotic, but he is not psychotic. Unless you get some reason to believe he actually knows your name or who you are, I would suggest three possible actions. One would be to change your phone number."

Edwyna started to speak, but he cut her off. "I know what a pain in the neck that is. Your family, your friends, any business associates . . . But that's only one option. Another is to have the telephone company put a trap on your phone. I would arrange that. Then as soon as the individual phones, you call me and I have the phone company trace the number of the call."

"Don't I have to keep him on the phone for a while for that to happen?"

"You are remembering too many old movies or detective shows. That used to be true, but now with digitization, the number is known in a virtual instant. Even after you've hung up."

"But he seems to call from different numbers. That's why he sometimes gets through to me."

"Yes, but we—that is the telephone company and I—can be persistent, and eventually we can catch him. However, you realize that as important as this is to you, and therefore important to me, priorities for police resources may not always be available to you at the moment that he calls. I'd like to be, but . . ."

"Then, what do you suggest?"

"We have found that most of these individuals eventually stop. They may not stop entirely, but they stop after a while because they look for the sexual titillation from someone who does engage them in conversation."

"Just wait?"

"I know that's difficult. Yes. Just wait him out."

"I don't know," Edwyna said. "Maybe I didn't expect any more from the police, but my father told me I had to . . ."

"Your father was right. Now the record is on file. If he doesn't stop, or you get more upset, or if something changes that makes you feel at risk, please call. In fact, please call me." With that he handed his card to Edwyna.

"Douglas MacArthur?" Edwyna said.

"Please call me Doug. And my father was a World War II buff, so what can I say? I'm stuck with that moniker. And for you also, sir." He handed a card to Howard.

"I know what it's like to have a difficult name," Edwyna said.

"At least we have that in common. That's a start." Doug MacArthur held out his hand to Howard and then Edwyna.

At home, after the walk from the station house, Edwyna felt in her bag for the charm. When she saw it, she was more amused than amazed. It was an old rabbit's foot, complete with key chain and some other tiny object hanging from the chain alongside the foot. But she placed it near the phone.

"What's that?" Howard asked.

"Oh, just a good luck charm one of my book club ladies gave me."

"What did you think of Detective MacArthur?" Howard asked.

"He was considerate, but I'm not sure he'll be of any help."

"Handsome man, I meant. Are you interested?"

"Not what I was there for."

"I know. But, c'mon!" Howard insisted.

"Okay. He was handsome. And it's Inspector MacArthur."

"'Inspector?' How very British."

"Don't be a New York dork. That's what they call all detectives in San Francisco."

"But what did you think of the *inspector*?" Howard stressed inspector.

"But Howard, really! Focus!"

"I know this is serious stuff, but . . ."

"Anyway, why do you ask me? It's you who should be interested," Edwyna said.

"Moi? Baby, that guy was all hetero. Heterosexual. But I did like his jacket. A dark blue plaid with subtle stripes of a lighter blue and tan. And the way the back hugged his butt. No vent. Tailored perfectly for his body. Did you see that?"

"You saw all of that, and yet you deny he . . ."

"I didn't say that I didn't notice him. But I also saw that he couldn't take his eyes off you."

"He was only looking at me because I was the one doing the talking. And I'm the complainant. Or whatever. Didn't you see how he looked when he shook your hand?"

"No special way." Howard shook his head.

"Your gaydar was down. You'll see."

"No. You'll see. And now it's back home for this Sir Gay-la-had."

"That's awful," Edwyna groaned.

As she climbed the stairs to her flat, Edwyna wondered once again what had happened to the folder. Maybe it was back in her book tote and she'd forgotten placing it there. It couldn't be hiding in the desk drawer. There simply wasn't enough room. How annoying. She wanted to get it back to its owner, although no one from the book group had mentioned losing it. Maybe it wasn't all that important.

And there it was. Not in her desk drawer. Right on top of her desk. Hiding in plain sight, she thought. She opened it once more. Once again she saw a newspaper article.

The Times Picayune

August 18, 1969

Helicopter in Daring Rescue

Girl Saved

New Orleans—Roy Lee Boudreaux, 47, helicopter pilot and owner of Boudreaux Flights, saved young Susie Darling from the storm's fury yesterday.

Susie Darling, 12, owes her life to the quick thinking of Roy Lee Boudreaux, the helicopter pilot who rescued her yesterday. Susie was alone in her home when yesterday's furious storm hit.

Interviewed today, she said, "I heard the instructions on the radio, and I climbed out my window and shimmied up to the roof."

Winds reaching 100 MPH and heavy rain apparently ripped the house from its foundation and caused it to tilt forty-five degrees.

"I felt the house shake and shake, and then it was going onto its side. I began to slide off. I was so scared. I thought I was going to fall into the flood and die."

Boudreaux reported that his helicopter was blown off course as he was trying to land it in a nearby field. He saw the girl and was able to steady the craft long enough to drop a ladder to her. Susie grabbed the ladder and was saved.

When interviewed, Susie thanked Mr. Boudreaux, then said, "I don't know how it happened." Mr. Boudreaux echoed her words and added, "I've been flying helicopter rescue missions for more than a dozen years. I've never seen anything like this. It was a miracle."

Edwyna was positive this was not the article she'd read earlier. Could this be the kind of senior moment her parents and her parents' friends sometimes joked about, joked but always with a sigh?

"Get over it," she said to herself. "You aren't even fifty."

But if it wasn't her memory that was at fault, then what was going on? She was positive she'd last left the folder in her desk. Now she'd found it on top. She was sure she'd looked for the folder before she'd gone for coffee with Diane. Then it was gone. Now it wasn't. And the newspaper stories. So similar yet not quite the same. And the order of the stories. That was another weird thing. She started to remove the article from the folder, to look beneath it, when the telephone rang.

It was her father. She was glad to be able to tell him that she'd followed his advice and gone to the police. She was even happier that she'd done so when she heard the relief in his voice. She had enough to think about without worrying about a folder filled with some old papers.

It wasn't until several evenings later that The Creep called once more. Edwyna listened for a brief moment and picked up the charm. Should she listen to Doug or Diane? MacArthur had stressed not engaging, just waiting it out. Diane had given her a formula to end the torture immediately. But relying on a rabbit's foot and a deep voice seemed unrealistic. She put down the rabbit's foot, picked up the phone, and slammed it down. The phone rang again. She let it go to voice mail. Once more it rang. She picked up the rabbit's foot and drew herself up to her almost six feet. If she was going to use her power—whatever that meant—she could do it better when she was at her tallest. Some errant thought about making yourself as big as possible when facing a predatory animal ran through her mind. She held tight to the rabbit's foot, took a deep breath, then another, and said, "Go away. Go away now. Never again." She didn't know the source of the voice within her. It was almost as deep as Diane's. And

the sounds had become somewhat garbled—not exactly garbled—
more like a roar, like Diane's.

Edwyna was surprised to realize she was listening to the disembodied operator's voice saying, "If you want to make a call,
please hang up and dial again." She didn't know how long she'd
been holding the phone. But The Creep was gone.

CHAPTER 14

An Invitation

EDWYNA STOOD IN the doorway of her living room surveying the arrangement of chairs and tables. On small tables near the sofa and armchairs, she'd set small glass bowls. One held a mix of almonds, cashews, and raisins. Another had a cheery collection of small, licorice-filled, pastel-colored candies. A third had dried apricots. On the large glass coffee table in front of the sofa, she'd placed five wine glasses and a chilled chardonnay along with a bowl of green grapes, a stack of five small plates, and a low pile of beverage napkins. It pleased her that the single line that edged the plates was the same color as the grapes, and even the napkins were decorated, in one corner, with a small bunch of grapes that could have come from the bowl next to them. Most important, she'd placed the dark blue, ribbon-tied folder on the table. She would be sure to mention it tonight, find its owner, and return it to her.

Another month had passed. She looked at the clock. The Wise Women would be there for their meeting in about an hour. Her copy of this month's book, *Persuasion*, sat on the small table near her favorite blue velvet chair. She looked at the sky, or what she could see of it. Another cloudy San Francisco evening.

Thinking of the Wise Women brought Edwyna back to her conversation with Diane and the rabbit's foot Diane had given her. She kept it near the phone—ready to use again—although it had been a week since Edwyna had last heard from The Creep. In fact, the last call was the one she'd answered with that rabbit's foot in her hand. Still she jumped each time the phone rang. She wanted to be certain that The Creep was really gone from her life. Yet she continued to listen with suspicion each time she checked her voice mail. There were the usual annoying messages—the last one combined a so-called survey with the "opportunity for two free nights on a cruise to thank you for your participation." Right! But there had been nothing more from The Creep.

Only the evening before she and Howard had argued about The Creep. That argument was a first in their friendship. They'd been in his condo, seated at the round dining table, sipping wine—an excellent pinot noir from the Willamette Valley—when he'd asked her about The Creep.

"I hate to bring up unpleasant topics," he said, "but have you had any more of the calls that were driving you nuts?" Howard reached into the large, carved wooden bowl in the center of the table and removed two walnuts still in their shells.

"I wouldn't exactly say they were driving me crazy. Although they were annoying."

"Annoying? Is that all? Toots, you were scared out of your wits."

"Maybe I was somewhat anxious. But 'Toots?' 'Toots!' From what ancient hole did you dredge up . . . ?"

"Have we lived through the same moments in time? Did I or did I not try to get that creep to stop calling? Did I or did I not go with you to the police station where you almost fell apart talking to Leung and then the beautiful Dougie MacArthur?" Howard shifted the walnuts from his right hand to his left and back again.

"Aha! I told you that Inspector DM was for you."

"That's not the point I'm making. Forget the point I was making. Let's not argue about how upset you . . ."

"I wasn't all that upset."

"I'll buy it," Howard said. "Not all that upset. What I'm trying to . . ."

"Are you just saying 'not upset' or do you mean it?"

"Just answer me. Have you had any more calls?" Howard put the walnuts back into the bowl and dusted his hands against each other.

"The short answer is no. I hate to say so, but I think the magic worked."

"You're kidding. Right?" Howard reached into the bowl and retrieved the two walnuts, as well as the red and blue nutcracker that hung from the far edge.

"That call was the last. It worked." Edwyna wasn't sure why she was being so insistent since she'd assiduously denied any possibility of magic since she'd given up believing in her doll some time in high school around the same time she'd realized that her father's blue pencils held only the magic of her own intellectual gifts. And she wasn't even sure that the call the week earlier would truly turn out to be the last one.

"Have you considered any other possible explanations?"

"Other than . . ." Edwyna realized the nutcracker represented a drummer. She watched as Howard used a lever in the back of the nutcracker to open its mouth. He dropped a walnut into the drummer's mouth, moved the lever again, and extracted a perfectly cracked walnut.

"Other than magic." He shook the meat free of the shell and popped it into his own mouth.

"Why not magic?" Edwyna asked.

"I can't believe we're having this conversation. You've told me how tormented you felt as a kid when other people thought you had special powers."

"I'm not saying I have special powers, just . . ."

"Just what? Just the power of the foot of some poor, dead rodent?" Howard cracked another walnut.

"Not a rodent. A rabbit," Edwyna said.

"I think rabbits are rodents," Howard said through a mouth full of walnut meat.

"I happen to know that they are not rodents. Rabbits have more teeth than rodents."

"I yield. Let's get back to the real issue. First the calls seem to have stopped, which is great." Howard put the nutcracker back on the bowl.

"It is great."

"Another explanation. I think Leung said this. Or MacArthur. One of them. Often these callers move on to some other person if their sick needs are not being met by calling you."

"I'm happy to have him move on. But I do think it was the magic charm. And Diane. You should have heard her voice when she told me what to say. And my own voice. I have never heard anything like it. It was a roar from some primal space within me, yet somehow not of me."

"You are sounding too weird. And you're a rational person. An accountant."

"I thought you of all people would appreciate the idea of the magic."

"Why me? Because I'm gay? Does that make me a fool?" Howard cracked three walnuts in quick succession.

"Not a fool. Just open to more than meets the eye. I thought you . . ."

"You do remember that I work in Silicon Valley, CTO . . ."

"So?"

"My training is in science. In observing the observable. In measuring." Howard took five walnuts from the bowl. "In moving among facts." He lined the walnuts up carefully. "That's how I see life since college, probably even before college, MIT . . ."

"MIT? I thought you were from New York."

"Of course I'm from New York. Did you think New Yorkers were not allowed to cross the border into other states?"

"Massachusetts Institute of Technology? You?"

"Seven years at MIT—undergrad and graduate degrees." Howard added two more walnuts to the lineup.

"So what's with all the Brooklynese, your *bubbelukshen*?"

"I can't believe that on the one hand you suddenly believe in magic and on the other hand you can't picture that I both loved my granny and left New York and went to college."

"Can you prove it was not the rabbit's foot?" Edwyna tapped the table with her forefinger as she enunciated each syllable of each word.

Howard carefully straightened the line of walnuts which had jumped a bit with each tap of Edwyna's finger. "You can't prove a negative," he said matter-of-factly.

Edwyna sighed. "Why are we arguing? Give me some more wine, crack a walnut for me, and let's call it a draw. We've never argued before."

"If that will make you happy." Howard poured the wine and cracked a walnut for each of them.

Edwyna was about to say, "It's a matter of the truth, not my being happy." Instead she sipped her wine.

Although Edwyna and Howard had finally agreed to stop arguing and just drink their pinot noir, a day later the aftereffects of the argument still tinged her feelings with some regret. She didn't even know why she'd been so insistent on magic. She would call him as soon as the meeting of the Wise Women ended.

Carolyn and Lila arrived together, and Dorothy was right behind them. As Edwyna poured wine for each of the women, she thought she saw each of them glance at the folder. She wasn't sure, but she also thought Carolyn had run her hand across the cover, the way one fondles a long-cherished book. But no one moved to pick it up until Diane arrived.

Diane took the folder from the table. "What have we here?" she asked, then turned and handed it to Dorothy.

Dorothy looked at Diane and raised her eyebrows as if answering the question with a question. If Dorothy's eyebrow-question required an answer, none was forthcoming from Diane. Edwyna waited.

Dorothy undid the ribbon, lifted a piece of antique vellum, then looked at Diane again.

"Read it to us, dear," Diane said.

Dorothy read:

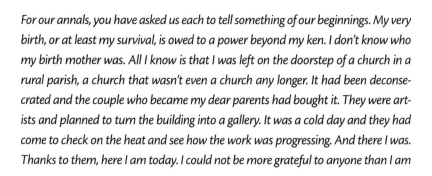

For our annals, you have asked us each to tell something of our beginnings. My very birth, or at least my survival, is owed to a power beyond my ken. I don't know who my birth mother was. All I know is that I was left on the doorstep of a church in a rural parish, a church that wasn't even a church any longer. It had been deconsecrated and the couple who became my dear parents had bought it. They were artists and planned to turn the building into a gallery. It was a cold day and they had come to check on the heat and see how the work was progressing. And there I was. Thanks to them, here I am today. I could not be more grateful to anyone than I am

to my dear parents who are now departed and buried in the St. Louis Cemetery #1. I don't need to remind you that it is also the final resting place of Marie Laveau. It is an honor to visit her when I return to pay my respects to them.

A collective sigh arose from all the women.

"That was beautiful," Edwyna said.

"Beautiful."

"Lovely."

"Thank you, Dorothy," the Wise Women echoed each other.

Edwyna was surprised. She'd seen only newspaper articles and assumed that's what the folder contained—newspaper articles about averted tragedies, unusual saves. She was trying to formulate a question, maybe ask who'd written the piece, when Diane put down her wine glass, picked up *Persuasion*, and said, "Let's get to tonight's lovely piece of writing. Edwyna?"

Edwyna, as host, was expected to lead the evening's discussion, but it wasn't long before all of the women were engaged in following up each other's ideas and introducing others.

"Without the friendship of women, where are we?" Carolyn asked.

"Better off!" Lila answered. "If it hadn't been for Lady Russell, Anne wouldn't have turned down Wentworth when she was nineteen."

"And she wouldn't be suffering the life of an unmarriageable spinster these seven years later," Dorothy agreed.

"But Lady Russell came around by the end of the book. Gave her blessing to Anne and Wentworth," Carolyn argued.

"Right," Lila said. "When he has the moola and the Elliot family is broke thanks to that shallow, spendthrift pomposity of a papa."

"You seem to like him even less than Austen did," Edwyna said.

"Not less than. The same as. I guess I've known too many of that type," Lila said.

"Any of them husbands?" Carolyn asked.

"Don't be catty. Just some narrow escapes. But I will agree that it is a woman, Mrs. Smith, who saves the day for Anne," Lila said.

"She is the true friend to Anne, but there are any number of women we wouldn't like to have as friends in *Persuasion*. Diane enumerated them: Mary, Anne's whining sister; Elizabeth, who takes after her father . . ."

"And the scheming Mrs. Clay," Edwyna picked up the thread. "Sorry if I interrupted," she turned to Diane.

Diane smiled at Edwyna.

"What I love about Austen is that the women come in all different shades of . . . ," Dorothy began.

"As do the men," Lila added.

"But I always feel it's the women I know best," Dorothy continued.

"Do you think that's because we are women and read more into them? Or because Austen had a better understanding of women?" Edwyna asked.

"Her understanding of human emotions and relationships is impeccable," Carolyn said. "Don't you agree?" She looked around the table, letting her gaze settle on Diane.

"I agree with all of you," Diane said, "if that's possible, but I want to come back to what Edwyna said. We do read books as women. In fact, we experience all of life as women. Simply put: We are women. And that gives me an idea. But first . . ." She reached for the wine bottle and turned to Edwyna. "May I?"

Edwyna nodded and Diane poured the wine into each of their glasses. "First," she continued, "a toast to womanhood." She raised her glass.

"To all women," Carolyn said.

"To women everywhere," Lila said.

"To Wise Women," Dorothy concluded the toasts as they drained their raised glasses.

"Now for my idea," Diane said. "I propose we spend an evening enjoying the infinite variety of women."

"Yes! The Baths!" Lila exclaimed.

Carolyn clapped her hands. "A field trip." Then she, too, subsided and looked at Diane.

Diane continued to smile. For a moment Edwyna thought she was going to propose they all go to Bath—Bath as in *Persuasion*—Bath as in England—and she began to consider the time and money that would be involved.

"The Baths," Diane said, "are a wonderful San Francisco institution, thanks to the Japanese heritage of our city. Three days a week, the Baths, which have communal pools and showers, are open to women only. There is a whirlpool, a cold dip, special showers, lounging chairs, and more. All of which are enjoyed by women, usually naked women. I propose an evening at the Baths."

"I'm in!" Dorothy said. "Who else?"

Carolyn and Lila nodded affirmatively with as much enthusiasm as each could put into her nod.

"Should we look for a date?" Edwyna asked. "Should I get a paper calendar?"

The other women were silent. They looked at Diane. "No need. Here's the next good date. She named a date two weeks later. The others looked at Edwyna and waited.

Edwyna was surprised that no one took out an iPhone or other calendar to check her availability. They just waited for her. She wanted to check her own calendar, but she figured if this was what group cohesion called for . . . "I'm in," she said.

The others leaned back in their chairs, sipped their wine, seemed even more relaxed than earlier.

"By the way," Carolyn said, "we saw a man just as we arrived. A short, pudgy guy. He really glared at us."

"Seemed angry. At us," Dorothy continued. "Do you think he might be . . . ?"

Diane interrupted. "Time to go, Wise Women."

The Wise Women stood. Amid a flurry of "thank you" "lovely wine" "great discussion," the women donned their wraps against the chill of the night. As Diane passed the telephone, she said, "I'm glad to see you have my gift near the phone. Has it worked?"

"So far, so good," Edwyna said.

Diane picked up the charm, caressed it, and put it down. "Keep it. Just in case," she said. And then, "See you at the Baths."

The Wise Women gone, Edwyna sat back in her chair, thinking of Jane Austen, thinking of the invitation to the Baths. Sounded like it would be an enjoyable evening. She rose to straighten the living room, and as she reached for the glasses and plates on the coffee table, she realized the folder was still there, still there on the coffee table, still there in her hands, not the hands of some other Wise Woman. Now she remembered that at the end of the meeting, she'd meant to ask about the story

Dorothy had read, but she'd forgotten to do that. She'd meant to ask whose folder it was, and that had slipped her mind too. Too much wine or too many conversations, she thought, as she moved the folder back to her desk.

She forgot to call Howard.

CHAPTER 15

The Bathhouse

IT WASN'T AT all what she had expected. Edwyna couldn't believe how beautiful all the women—all the naked women—looked to her. The soft lighting of the large bathing room enhanced rather than concealed the details of face and body of each woman. Edwyna didn't want to be seen staring, but she could not keep her eyes from the glistening, swelling belly of the pregnant woman who was dipping a foot into the warm whirlpool before she walked down the few steps to sit on one of the stone benches that encircled the water. Next to the pregnant woman was a girl, clearly her daughter, who sat, completely relaxed, her hand resting on her mother's belly. The gently moving water lapped at the girl's small breast buds and covered her tummy, which still retained the slight roundness of childhood. Across the bench, submerged in water to their shoulders, were two women—in their twenties, Edwyna surmised. Their bodies were perfectly formed, as were their faces. They sat turned slightly toward each other, as if ready to hear a secret or tell one. But they were silent, as relaxed as the pregnant mom and her child.

Edwyna sat on one of the lower benches near a jet. She moved slowly from her right buttock to her left so that the jet eased first one side of her back then the other. She shifted so that she was leaning on one arm and let the jet caress one foot and calf. And then she switched sides so that the other foot felt the loving warmth of the water. Finally she sat submerged to her chin. Her long hair was tied in a top knot. Only a few escaping tendrils were wet. She did not want to move—ever.

And the Wise Women. All of them were in the same state of satisfaction as Edwyna, lolling on the benches of the very large, perfectly warmed, gently moving whirlpool. It seemed that they had been sitting there forever, when Diane made the smallest of gestures with one hand. Dorothy, Lily, and Carolyn stood slowly. Carolyn held out her hand to Edwyna, who also stood. They climbed from the whirlpool and walked across the stone floor of the bath to the cold plunge. They walked up the few steps to the cold pool, and then plunged in and out of the icy water quickly. They were as vigorous in entering and leaving the cold pool as they had been languorous in the warm pool.

Following Diane, they removed their towels from the nearby hooks and rubbed their bodies vigorously. Each of them in turn rubbed the back of the Wise Woman nearest her. Their skins turned pink from the cold water and the rubbing.

Once more everyone but Edwyna seemed to see some signal from Diane and they all moved to a table that contained a pitcher of water, a pot of tea, glasses, and cups. Dorothy poured water for all of them, and each one drained her cup. The next stop was the steam room. Edwyna did not like steam rooms. Hot saunas were fine, but steam always made her nose and throat feel clogged, almost as if she were drowning. She held back when she saw the steam escape as Carolyn opened the door. This time Lila took her hand to coax her in. Obviously whatever one Wise Woman did, they were all required to do. How long were they going to be in the steam room? Would she be able to tolerate it? Soon the fog that obscured their bodies filled her mind, and she had relaxed into the steam when it was clear that the Wise Women were moving on.

They were back in the whirlpool and, with no one else to distract her, Edwyna looked at the bodies of her friends, for friends they were indeed becoming. Of course they showed their age. Skin was no longer taut. Puckers of fat graced thighs. Breasts sagged. And they were all beautiful. Edwyna didn't know if it was the lighting, the water, or something else, but she could not stop smiling at the marvel that was womanhood.

She remembered an earlier time. She'd been a member of a community pool and swam there several mornings a week. During one summer, the women's locker room was shared with a chattering group of girls, probably eight to ten years old, from a neighboring day camp. One day, a counselor announced just before the girls came down to the lockers, "Ladies, please cover up. The girls are coming, and we think it's not good for them to see adult women. Some of you don't have perfect figures, you know." Edwyna remembered her thoughts at that time—thoughts that were only reinforced by this evening's experience at the baths— that girls should see women of all body types and ages so they know how good it is to be a woman at any age. She was sorry she'd never said anything to that perfectly toned twenty-something counselor. She had simply ignored her request to cover up.

Once more the Wise Women rose as a group, but Edwyna did not need anyone to send her a special sign. She knew as they knew when it was time to move. They dried themselves once again and went back to the tea table. With towels wrapped around them, they each took a cup of tea and followed Diane to a door next to the steam room, a door that Edwyna hadn't even noticed earlier.

Unlike the grey stone surroundings of the cavernous water room, this room was richly decorated. A thick white rug with sinuous cobalt designs covered the entire floor. The walls were painted a glowing gold, as was the ceiling. Five high-backed armchairs, upholstered in white linen, formed a semicircle around a table on which there was a tall pillar of a purple candle sitting in a multicolored, multicurved glass candlestick. A white silk robe hung over the back of each chair. Following the actions of the other Wise Women, Edwyna hung her towel on a wooden hook on the back of the door and donned a white robe.

Dorothy walked to the wall that was at right angles to the door. She pulled a braided cord that hung on the wall and the golden wall seemed to break apart to reveal a window. Edwyna gasped. Perfectly centered in the window was the thin crescent new moon. It was so perfectly placed that Edwyna thought it might be a painting. The women stood in front of the window, their tea cups held on high.

Diane turned toward Edwyna and said, "Our prayer to the new moon."

Edwyna realized that these were the first words anyone had said since they'd shed their clothes in the locker room and entered the pools area.

Diane continued, "Blessed are you, moon of our foremothers, who brings us the start of all that is new and all that is renewed from month to month. Bring us a month of peace and love. And so may it be for all women—and their men—everywhere." She paused for a moment and then turned to Edwyna. "Would you like to recite it with us?"

Edwyna nodded, although she was concerned that she would not remember all of it.

"I'll say a phrase, and you repeat it after me," Diane instructed. And after she said each phrase, the four Wise Women, including Edwyna, repeated it. "Blessed are you, moon of our foremothers," Diane said.

And the women echoed, "Blessed are you, moon of our foremothers."

"Who brings us the start of all that is new" was recited twice.

"And all that is renewed from month to month" reverberated twice through the room.

"Bring us a month of peace and love." Edwyna realized that as the words were recited twice, she found herself as close to prayer as she had been since she was a child. Her family had not been particularly religious. Christmas-Easter Christians they called themselves. Those services and sporadic attendance at Sunday school were all that Edwyna remembered of any childhood praying.

"And so may it be for all women—and their men—everywhere." The final sounds of the prayer filled the room.

The Wise Women took their seats, which had been set so that they could continue to look at the moon through the window.

"Would you like to light the candle of the new moon?" Diane asked Edwyna.

"Do I need to do anything special or say a prayer?" Edwyna asked.

"There is no formula, but this is a very powerful time, so before you light the candle, you might want to think about what you want the spirit of the moon to manifest for you. Just sit back, look out at the new moon, and then close your eyes. Whenever you are ready, light the candle."

Edwyna was caught up in the spirit of the moment—or the spirit of the moon. She looked at the moon and felt what it would be like to have what she wanted. She felt the hands of a loving man on her two cheeks and almost felt a kiss when the feeling dissolved into acute discomfort.

Her white silk robe was sticking to her still damp thighs. The seat of her chair had too deep a depression, springs worn by over-use. Hardened pools of discolored candle wax marred the surface of the table. What was she doing here? Would it be too rude to refuse to light the candle now? Might someone else want to light it? She decided it was simpler to follow the directions even if they didn't mean anything to her. She'd already looked at the moon. No need to look again. She closed her eyes, counted to ten, then twenty, then picked up the matches and lit the candle. For a moment as she looked into the candle's flame, she thought she saw a face. Whose face? Then she realized it was just that kind of afterimage one always gets after looking too long at a light source.

The Wise Women were silent for a while as they sat looking out at the moon and in at the candle. Edwyna wondered what time it was, how much longer they'd stay, and what exactly she'd inadvertently become a part of.

"I guess you are wondering what's going on," Dorothy said. "The history of celebrating the new moon is a very ancient one. It goes all the way back to the ancient Israelites and Jewish rituals that many Jewish women are again celebrating today. They call it *Rosh Chodesh*, which means 'head of the month' or 'beginning of the month.' And it has always celebrated renewal. Did you notice when we made the date to meet here, we all knew ahead of time what date it would be? That's because we keep track of the date of the new moon each month."

Carolyn picked up the thread, "Originally it was a day of celebration when the whole community celebrated the new moon in their prayers and when women didn't have to work. They say that women didn't have to work as a reward from God because they refused to give up their jewelry to build the Golden Calf. So today some women do try to refrain from work that is particularly associated with women like sewing and weaving."

Lila chimed in with a typical Lila response. "Of course that wouldn't save most of us from much work since I haven't woven in quite awhile now. And the only one woman I know who does weave, does so as a very expensive hobby."

"Wait a minute," Edwyna said, unsure of how to ask the question. "Not that it matters, but are you all . . . are you Jewish?"

"I grew up Jewish," Lila said, "but my family was hardly observant, and once I left the nest, I was even less so."

"The rest of us aren't Jewish," Dorothy said, "but the tradition in Judaism is so strong and so important to all women that we use a prayer that is based, very loosely, on traditional prayers associated with the celebration of the new moon. So the foremothers in Jewish prayer mean the four matriarchs of the Old Testament: Sarah, Rebecca, Rachel, and Leah. But for us they mean literally our mothers and all the great women—women of power—who have preceded us."

"Helen of Troy."

"Cleopatra."

"Emily Dickinson."

"Golda Meier."

"Rosa Parks."

The group was off and running with a list of women. The list was governed by neither time nor place. Nor apparently by field of endeavor. Some names evoked nods. Others disagreement.

"Madame Chiang Kai-Shek."

"Not her—she was cruel."

"Sometimes great power includes cruelty."

"Sigrid Undset."

"Who?"

"Nobel Laureate for literature."

Edwyna listened to the list but did not find it clarified the evening's events—the baths, the nudity, the moon, the candle. The white robes. The names of the foremothers being added or challenged moved to the background as her own questions arose. She thought she'd heard someone say Tituba when Diane raised a hand and the listing stopped.

She turned to Edwyna. "Does that answer your questions?"

"Not really," Edwyna said. "I understand why Jewish women might celebrate the new moon today, but not why you all . . ."

"The spirit of the moon is very powerful," Diane said. "It can bring great healing if honored and great harm if it is not."

Edwyna had another thought about the group. This was worse than thinking they were all Jewish, not that that was bad at all, just different from her. But Howard was Jewish, and she couldn't imagine him at any moon-related celebration. Wait. Her mind was wandering. She wanted to hold on to this thought. Should she take the plunge? She'd already plunged into the cold pool and she'd done the steam room. This was a time to be brave, to screw her courage to the sticking point. "Then are you—I know this is going to sound crazy—I don't mean you'd be crazy if you are—but I mean the question could sound crazy."

"Spit it out, girl," Lila said.

"Are you, by any chance

. . . ? Is this a, some sort of a . . . coven?" There, she'd said it.

The group was silent. They looked at Diane, who looked into the candle. "Do you mean are we Wicca? Or witches, as Wicca used to be called?"

Edwyna didn't know if that was a rhetorical question or if she was supposed to answer. "Was that impolite of me?" she asked.

"No, no, not at all," the group answered all at the same time.

Again there was silence. "Here's an answer that might be more helpful than trying to find a label for us."

Edwyna cringed. She had put her foot in it.

"Not that there's anything wrong with labels, but they aren't as explanatory as the more complicated truth. As you know from our reading, we focus on the strength of women. In our book club, it's women writers. In our personal lives, it's ourselves we try to empower. We are aware of the moon as a symbol of female strength, lots of moon goddesses in many different cultures. So we like to get together at the new moon, relax, and consider our own force." Diane, who had been sitting forward in her chair, leaned back and looked at Edwyna. The other women nodded.

Edwyna guessed that was a good explanation. What was wrong with a little relaxation, tea, and candles? Goodness, she did as much by herself sometimes when she ran a warm bath, burned some incense and candles, and sipped red wine. Diane was right, why label what they were doing? Edwyna nodded too.

"By the way," Carolyn asked, "did you see anything special when you lit the candle? Sometimes when I have had the privilege of lighting the candle, I do see something I want to manifest—or even something I didn't know I wanted until that very moment."

Edwyna wasn't sure whether she'd seen something or someone or not. And she was even less sure that she wanted to say what she might—or might not—have seen.

"That's how I first saw Stephen," Dorothy said, naming her husband.

"That was the first time I saw my daughter's face," Lila said, "her face just as it was the day she was born. It was odd. I didn't even know, at that moment, that I was pregnant."

"I just saw the moon and then the candle," Edwyna said. "I wish I had seen the future and someone who will love me as I want to be loved." She didn't know why she had revealed even that much about herself. And she was dying to get out of the wet white robe. It had gone from sticky to chilling. Shivers were moving from her back and thighs down to her feet.

"Time to go," Diane said rising. "Time to blow out the candle. With one last prayer. Edwyna, you can just listen this time, but we do like to hold hands. So . . ."

With that, everyone rose and held hands as all of them but Edwyna said, "As the moon brings the tides, as the tides bring the waters, so may we be. Until the next moon."

For the next few days Edwyna asked herself if it had been Nick or even Joel she'd seen in that momentary flash of something. Maybe it wasn't even a flash of something, just the nothingness of smoke.

She made up her mind to watch for any signs when she was with either of them, signs that they really loved her and she loved them. As soon as she had that thought, she dismissed it.

The idea came and went repeatedly. As her next Saturday night date moved closer, the idea of observing her relationship with Nick more closely resurfaced until the actual date was upon her. It was that night.

CHAPTER 16

Confluence

EDWYNA WAS REACHING into a cupboard for a wine glass when she heard Nick behind her, then felt him behind her. He reached around her and squeezed her breasts. Hard. Almost too hard. As he pressed himself against her, Edwyna realized he had taken off his clothes. She moved away slightly and let her dark blue silk gown slip off her shoulders to the floor. As she did this, Nick released one of her breasts and with his right hand he cupped her vagina, rubbed her clitoris, and then pushed a finger into her. Just like that she was ready for him. Half carrying her, half walking behind her, Nick led her into the bedroom. He pushed her down on the bed with her back to him. He wasn't rough but he was very definite. He raised her hips, then rubbed his aroused penis against her buttocks. Edwyna shook her head. She did not want anal sex. She'd tried it once and it hurt too damned much.

Nick used one hand to still her head, almost patting it. "Don't worry," he said. "I know what I'm doing."

"I don't like . . ."

"I won't hurt you. I promise."

Edwyna didn't know how much that promise was worth. But as Nick caressed her breasts, cupping them, teasing them, tweaking her nipples, she found herself giving in to the moment. Once again he reached down to torment her clitoris. He seemed to know just how much she could take before she would cry out. Cry out to stop or cry out for more.

Then he lifted her hips and entered her. Not her anus but the place where she wanted him. Wanted him so badly. This time, Nick drove to his own pace. She didn't know if she could keep up or even what keeping up meant. Then the feelings consumed her, all thoughts subsumed, she was with him on the glorious ride. She cried out. Wordlessly.

They both collapsed onto the bed, Nick still on top of Edwyna's back. Only for a few minutes, maybe seconds, before he rolled off her. She turned over toward him.

"Whew!" he said. He patted her hip. "That was something else." He settled onto his back.

That had been last night. Now, as Nick gave her an efficient kiss good-bye, she thought, another efficient Sunday morning. Another efficient Nick fuck! These dates with Nick were not getting her any closer to what she wanted. Maybe she should just chuck him. Chuck all of them. But then what? Stare at the moon? Light purple candles? The date she would turn fifty was drawing closer. Of course, she thought, it could never get further away. Surely she was too young to give up on love. Although those awful articles on the difficulties of women finding husbands in their thirties came back to mind—their thirties! Howard had denied the reliability of those studies. Still! But then look at the Wise Women. They had clearly found their final—their current— husbands when they were well past their thirties.

Why was she putting up with Nick? He was a nice guy, but that was all. She could even live without the sex. She would drop him. It wouldn't be easy. After all, they'd been in this relationship—or whatever you'd call it—for—she couldn't believe it—for more than a year. Enough!

Maybe hearing the names of all those powerful women through the centuries had had some effect on her thinking. She was still feeling the afterglow of her time at the Baths even though it had been almost a week earlier. It was a marvelous sense that combined relaxation with extraordinary energy. She thought it probably came from the combination of hot whirlpool and cold plunge, certainly not from the pseudo-religious, magical-mystical stuff around the moon. She didn't need magic to break up with Nick, just a strong will. And, she added, a gentle touch. After all, he didn't even know that she was dissatisfied. She would call him that evening. That would give her time to plan what she would say.

Now the rest of a beautiful June Sunday stretched enticingly before her. She wondered where Howard was. She hadn't seen him or heard from him since their argument. She'd meant to call him, to smooth things over, but then the Wise Women book club meeting, the Baths, her own work. Something seemed to interfere. And then, as if she could manifest appearances, she heard Howard's unmistakable ring on her doorbell.

"Hi," Edwyna greeted him. "I was just thinking of you."

"Good thoughts, I hope. I was afraid you were still annoyed at me because we had that stupid argument."

"Me? At you? I was afraid you were annoyed at me."

"Since we've resolved that and Sunday Nick is gone, how about a walk? Brunch?"

"Perfect," Edwyna said. "One moment and I'll be ready."

They left their building together and walked north to the park. It was indeed a beautiful San Francisco day, the kind of day that made others envy the climate. San Francisco days such as this made people forget what season it was. The sun warmed the air and a breeze cooled it. Sixty-three degrees Fahrenheit was often the high whether the date was in February or July.

"I'm really sorry I got on your case about how you stopped The Creep," Howard said as they strolled through the Japanese Gardens.

"Forget it. I don't know why I so insisted it had to be magic. You're probably right. I don't believe in special powers."

"No, it was my fault for not being open."

"Forget it. Let's not go back there. Although my memory of you cracking and eating those walnuts is very clear. At one point you were shoveling them in so quickly, I thought you might choke."

Howard cleared his throat. Then cleared it again.

"Still stuck on walnuts?" Edwyna asked.

"Not exactly."

"Not exactly stuck?"

"Not exactly walnuts," Howard answered.

"You've lost me."

"I've been avoiding telling you something. Something important."

"Is it bad? If it's bad, say it very fast."

"Not bad at all. Good. Very good. At least I hope you'll think it's good. I think . . ."

"Now! Tell me now," Edwyna demanded.

"I've met someone. A really nice man. Gregory. Greg."

"Someone you like? I mean, like in the special way?"

"I like him in all ways."

"Why wouldn't you want to tell me? Why wouldn't I think it was good?"

"You wanted to meet someone so badly. And I did. I thought you might be envious. I didn't want it—him—Greg to come between us. It's really because of you that I met him. After I tried to help you with your profile on RomeoandJulietMatch.com, I started looking around on the Internet and other matching sites. I was really looking for another opportunity for you, and then I came across RomeoMeetsRomeo.com. Well, the rest, as they say . . ."

"Is history." Edwyna completed the sentence. "Now you have to tell me that history."

Howard and Edwyna strolled through the park as he told her the details of his email, texting, and phone exchanges with Greg, about their first date and all that followed.

"I was actually afraid to bring him home," Howard concluded. "For fear that we'd run into you on the landing or in the street before I had a chance to tell you. But chances to tell you kept slipping by. Now I can't wait for you to meet him."

Edwyna was happy for Howard. She listened as he extolled the wonders of Greg—ten years younger, a lawyer, loves jazz, "balding just like me"—as they continued to wander until they exited where they had entered, on Ninth Avenue.

"Park Chow?" Edwyna asked as they came to a familiar neighborhood stop. "My treat to celebrate."

"Sure," Howard said.

Park Chow was a casual restaurant. The ground floor included several cozy—or call it crowded—groups of tables and a fireplace that was lit throughout the year. Highly varnished wood tables, not covered with cloths or place mats, held glass jars with individual sets of utensils wrapped in brown paper napkins. Howard and Edwyna were offered a table on the second floor. There was no roof, but they were partially shielded from the breeze by a canvas awning and warmed with an overhead heater. No matter how warm it was in San Francisco, the winds usually blew in from the west, carrying a reminder of how close the city was to the Pacific Ocean.

As they sipped their Bloody Marys, Howard said, "I don't want to start another argument, but I really am a New Yorker and I've gotta call 'em as I see 'em."

"Uh oh," Edwyna said. "Danger lurks. Whenever men rely on sports metaphors, you know something unpleasant is coming. Just say it."

"A few evenings ago, maybe a couple of weeks ago, in fact the night after our little tiff, I was just coming home when I saw several women—three or four—going to your apartment. I don't know what it was about them, but they gave me the willies."

"The willies? You were scared of four women."

"Not scared. I just felt there was something off about them. They didn't look right. One of them, I guess the oldest, really gave me a strange feeling."

"As a matter of fact, one or two of them said they saw some man glaring at them when they arrived that evening." Edwyna left out the description of the man as short and pudgy.

"I didn't glare at them. *Au contraire.* One of them gave me one of those 'if looks could kill' looks."

"Howie, as your *bubbe* would call you, I don't know what you saw or what they saw, but let's just forget it." Edwyna was not about to tell Howard about the experience at the Baths. "They are my friends. Or they're becoming my friends. You are—will always be—my true friend. Let's forget it," she repeated.

Their conversation shifted to current events in the city— possible corruption of a local official, a marital scandal of another, and efforts to expand some development with the usual kerfuffle around it.

After their brunch they walked slowly back to the house in which they both lived. Just as they were parting, Howie to go to the door on the left, Edwyna to the right, they heard someone call and saw a familiar figure coming toward them.

"Ms. Glendower, Mr. Rosen." He caught up with them. "I thought I'd stop by and see how you were doing. Have you had any relief?"

Edwyna looked at MacArthur. He was dressed much more casually than at the station—a dark blue pullover whose V-neck revealed the lighter blue collar of a knit shirt, neatly pressed jeans, soft buck half boots.

"How thoughtful of you to come here to ask," Howard said, then paused. When Edwyna did not chime in, "Inspector MacArthur," he added.

"I was in the neighborhood, just walking around on this terrific Sunday, and I realized I was near your home. You know, policeman's mind. As soon as I saw the address, the whole interview popped into my mind."

Edwyna wasn't sure what to say. "Thank you" seemed a good beginning. "So thoughtful of you." She looked at Howard.

Howard began, "Why don't you tell Inspector MacArthur . . ."

"Please call me Doug," he interrupted, "since this is my day off."

"What happened with the calls?" Howard completed.

"Yes," Edwyna said, "they have stopped just as you suggested they would."

"That's great," MacArthur said. He seemed to be waiting for something else.

"Would you like to come up for a coffee?" Howard asked. "We could go to my place." He gestured to the door on the left.

"Or mine," Edwyna awakened to the social niceties and gestured to the door on the right. "The scene of the crime, as it were."

"Coffee would be terrific. Either place. That's very generous." He turned to the right.

Edwyna led the way up the stairs into her flat. She wasn't quite sure what was up with Inspector MacArthur, probably after Howard as she'd first surmised. She wondered if Howard would still be interested, now that Greg was on the scene. Or was it too late for MacArthur? Go with the flow, she thought. She'd make some coffee. Even as she was turning the key into her flat, she was considering what biscotti or other coffee-accompanying goodies she had in the pantry.

"What a beautiful home you have." MacArthur walked to Edwyna's favorite windowside chair. "May I sit here?"

For a split second Edwyna wanted to say that he couldn't sit there. It was her chair. His sitting there seemed almost too personal, almost as if he were touching her. An unwanted, half-formed image flitted across her mind before she said, "Of course. Make yourself comfortable. Let me just get the coffee going. Any preference?"

"Edwyna has a wonderful coffee maker, an Xpresso—*molto Italiano*. You can have an espresso, a cappuccino, a latte, a long black—what does the company call that—a continuato?" Howard turned to Edwyna, who was ready to strangle him. She'd planned to make a simple pot of dripped coffee, put out the few biscotti she'd finally remembered, and let the two of them disappear into what was left of the afternoon.

"I'll play barista," she said. "Howard's given you the menu. Your choices?"

"I'll help," MacArthur said.

"That's okay," Edwyna answered, "I'll . . ."

But he was already out of the chair, her chair. "Let me see this wonder of wonders."

"C'mon, Howard," Edwyna said. "Join the fun." She wanted to add that he'd started the project.

"That's okay," Howard echoed Edwyna's words. "I'll just read the funnies." He opened the Sunday *Chronicle* that had been lying on the coffee table.

"Nice kitchen too, Ms. Glendower. Great combo of high tech and homey," MacArthur said as he followed Edwyna into the kitchen.

"Please call me Edwyna. I thought we'd already gotten to first names at the station."

"I didn't want to presume. That was then and there. This is now. And if I recall, you still called me 'Inspector MacArthur.' So let's be fair. If you're Edwyna, I'm Doug." And he held out his hand.

Edwyna smiled and reached out to shake his hand. He seemed to hold her hand a little longer than the usual handshake. Maybe that's the policemen's way, she thought. Helps them size up the suspect.

"Okay, Doug. It's a deal." With her hand, still warm from his, she reached into a cabinet for the jar of Xpresso capsules. The phone rang.

"Excuse me," Edwyna said and reached around Doug for the phone.

It was Dorothy. After the usual greetings, Dorothy said, "I'm calling to find out if you enjoyed the Baths and our greeting the moon."

"It was lovely," Edwyna said, "but I'm with some friends now. Can I call you back later?"

"Of course, I understand," Dorothy said. "Just one more thing. When we talk later. The problem. You know. The calls. How's that going?"

"Talk to you later. Bye," Edwyna said. That was peculiar. Having Doug here in the kitchen at the same time as she got a call about The Creep. And how did Dorothy know anyway? She'd only told Diane. Edwyna hoped she wasn't going to be a source of gossip.

Doug leaned against the counter, watching Edwyna. "Didn't know if I should give you privacy," he said.

"No problem. Just a friend. I'll get back to her later."

Coffee making completed, Edwyna and Doug joined Howard at the coffee table in the living room. Steaming cappuccinos and biscotti in hand, they had just settled into a conversation when the phone rang again.

Edwyna excused herself to take the call in the kitchen. It was Hank. She had more trouble getting off the call than she'd had with Diane. Hank insisted on knowing what she was doing that made her unavailable when he wanted to talk to her. Then he wanted to know with whom she was doing whatever she was doing. Edwyna was vague, evasive. It wasn't that drinking coffee was some secret sin or that having an afternoon's conversation with Howard and Doug was somehow off limits. It was simply none of Hank's business.

"Listen," she finally said. "I told you I have company and I can't talk now. I'll call you later, or if you prefer, call me when you'd like."

"I will call you," Hank said. "I'll call you in exactly two hours." And he gave the time to the precise minute.

Back in the living room Edwyna said, "I'm so sorry." And she meant it. She'd been enjoying the easy give and take of their conversation.

"I have to get going. I can see you're one busy person," Doug said.

Edwyna didn't want to break up the party. "Why don't you stay a little longer?"

But Doug was already on his feet.

"I'm really sorry. This is unusual. Just two friends—out of the blue—I hardly ever get calls. Well, you know now that I don't get the other calls. The Creep's calls, I mean. These were just . . ." She realized she was jabbering on.

Doug smiled. "Don't be upset on my account. After all, I was an unexpected, uninvited guest."

"But not unwelcome," Edwyna said as Doug and Howard walked to the door. Not unwelcome at all. She wished he'd shake her hand good-bye so that she could feel his warmth again. She hoped Doug and Howard would become friends or more than friends. Then she'd see more of him.

True to his word, Hank called at exactly 5:17 p.m. "Is there anyone with you now?" he asked without even saying hello or his name as if he expected Edwyna to know his voice.

Although she did know it was Hank, she replied, "Who's calling?"

"I asked what you were doing. I asked who you are with," Hank said. "Just answer me. You know full well who this is."

"I think you mean who is with me?"

"Answer me," Hank demanded but didn't wait for an answer. "I want to see you and I want to be sure you're alone."

This conversation was no longer fun, Edwyna thought. In fact it was downright annoying. "Sorry, I'm busy for the rest of the day," she said.

"That wasn't what I asked you. I asked you what you were doing. You didn't answer. I asked you who was there. You didn't answer. Now none of that matters. What you are doing right now doesn't matter. And whoever is there doesn't matter. Get rid of him."

"Why do you think . . . ?" Edwyna began.

"I want whoever it is to be gone in thirty minutes. I'm coming to see you. I'll be there at precisely 5:47."

"Wait a minute," Edwyna said and then realized the phone line was dead. It took no more than a few seconds for her to realize as well that she was not going to wait around for Hank. His compulsive sexual routines were one thing. Trying to compel her to see him tonight, to the minute, was another. She started to straighten the living room, picking up the cups and crumbs, and then decided that could wait. She did not want to be at home when Hank arrived. She grabbed her bag and headed down the stairs to the outside landing she shared with Howard. She hoped he'd be home. And she hoped that if he were with Doug, their friendship had not yet progressed to anything more. She'd just have to take that chance. It was better than the chance of being at home when Hank arrived. And she had her keys in her bag. If Howard was not home or if he was otherwise engaged, she'd just get in her car and figure out where she would go from there. She could always drive to Petaluma to her parents', although her unexpected arrival on a Sunday evening might alarm more than please them.

At the landing, she had just turned from locking her front door, was ready to ring Howard's bell, when she caught a glimpse of something, someone that made her turn to the street. There was Hank, leaning against his Mercedes.

"Going somewhere?" he asked. "Hope you are planning to return home"—he paused to look at his watch—"in seventeen minutes. That's when it will be 5:47."

"You're early," she said, although that wasn't what she wanted to say. She wanted to say something that would convey both her annoyance at his demands and an internal shiver of something that was almost fear.

"I'm ready now. Are you?" Hank continued to lean against the car.

"Sorry, I told you I have other plans. I can't see you this evening."

"You are going to see me. You are going to see all of me. And you are going to like what you see." As he spoke, Hank moved quickly from the car, up the steps to the landing. "Come with me. Now!" He grabbed Edwyna's hand.

"Let go of me," Edwyna said. "Your hand is cold."

"It will soon be warm. All of me will be warm. And you will be hot."

"I said let go of me." Edwyna tried to shake her hand free of his, but he held fast and just smiled.

"Let me go, you bastard."

"Stick and stones . . . But I still have you. Let's go upstairs now. Be a good girl."

"We are not going upstairs. For the last time, let go of my hand," Edwyna demanded.

"Or what?"

"Or this." Edwyna swung her handbag which she'd been holding at her side and hit Hank a glancing blow on the side of his head. It wasn't hard enough to do damage, but it was hard enough to startle him and make him relinquish her hand.

"You bitch, you'll be sorry for this."

"I am sorry."

"I don't want your apologies."

"I'm not apologizing. I'm sorry that I met you, that I ever went out with you."

"Don't be like that." Hank rubbed his ear where the handbag had landed. "We do have good times, don't we?" Hank's tone had become wheedling.

"Not really," Edwyna said. She hadn't enjoyed the times they were together except for the very first dinner at Bursa. It was all downhill after that. "Look. Let's just call it quits. No hard feelings."

"Maybe none on your part, but this is not the last you'll see of me. I don't like being disobeyed. I don't like being turned down. Most of all, I don't like being attacked. Maybe you get turned on that way. But not me."

Edwyna could not believe that he thought her attempt to free herself had been part of some sex play. "Clearly we're on separate wavelengths. So let's call it a day."

Hank got up close to Edwyna, so close that she could feel his breath on her face as he spoke. "You can call it what you want. I call it disobedience. Remember, I don't like being turned down. I don't like a disobedient woman. I know how to get to you. If I don't get to you, someone else I know will. You will think you are safe, then you'll feel you are being followed. And you'll never know. You'll never know what I can do or when I might do it. Have you ever been frightened?" He didn't wait for an answer but turned away and ran down the few stairs. Just as he got to the car, he turned back and shouted, "I know that you know what I mean."

Edwyna was surprised that all the noise had not brought Howard to the door. No sooner had Hank left than Edwyna rang Howard's bell, a long, insistent ring. No answer. No wonder he had not come to her rescue.

Edwyna went back to her flat, making sure her front door was double locked behind her. She was well rid of that creep. My God, she thought, was he The Creep? But what would have been his motivation before today to torment her with those ugly calls? Back in her chair, staring out at fog beginning to roll in, Edwyna looked back on the day. She'd begun the day by deciding to drop Nick. But Nick was at least pleasant to be with, always mellow. And now she had dropped Hank, dropped him with a swing of her handbag, and good riddance it was.

Edwyna reached for the phone to return Dorothy's call. Her hand was shaking. She sat back, took deep breaths, and tried to hold her hands still on her lap, one hand on each thigh. That felt a little better, but when she lifted a hand, either hand, it still shook.

She thought of calling Diane and telling her what had just happened. After that time in the coffee shop, she felt closer to Diane than to any of the other women. But then Diane had talked to Dorothy about her and she didn't want to be any more grist for a gossip mill. Thinking about the gossip was, in fact, making her even more upset.

Edwyna knew how to handle her own emotions. She'd make a list. Put down what she had to do on paper. That always worked. She got up from the couch to move to her desk and realized that her legs were as wobbly as her hands. She wished Howard was home. He'd make her some tea, even run a bath for her, say something—even a joke—to put the whole event in perspective.

That's what she'd do. Take a bath. Make a list, take a bath, and then return Dorothy's call. She stood again and wobbled to her desk, took a blue pencil in hand and a sheet of paper from her desk.

1. Hank
   She couldn't think of what to write after his name. Be thankful he was gone? She was still too angry to be thankful. And scared.
2. Diane. Call to find out what she said to Dorothy that made Dorothy ask her about . . .
   Edwyna hated "he said, she said" conversations. They were never satisfactory and only led to worse feelings than those that had begun the conversations. That was her experience anyway.
3. Dorothy. Call and find out . . .
   Find out what? What had Diane said about her to Dorothy? There she was back in "he said, she said."
4. Nick
   She'd think about Nick tomorrow.

Edwyna crumpled the paper and threw it in the wastebasket. "Useless," she muttered to herself, then realized the list-making had not been useless. Although there was no list, her hands were no longer shaking. She stood. Her legs were steady.

Edwyna ran a warm bath, sprinkling it with lavender bath salts. She pulled her hair to the top of her head, just as she'd done in the bathhouse, and sank into the water. She moved her hands to create ripples of lavendered water over her breasts and belly. She stretched her legs and wiggled her toes. Every now and then she used her right foot to move the handle that let more hot water join her in the tub.

After her bath, wrapped in a warm, terry-lined robe, she was ready to call Dorothy. They chatted a bit about their experience at the Baths. After some of Dorothy's probing, she admitted that she'd had mixed reactions to the new moon rituals, how she'd found them moving, even inspiring, to begin with, and then a little strange.

"All of us felt that way the first time," Dorothy reassured her. "Would you do it again next month?" she asked.

"I'll think about it," Edwyna said. "I don't know." And after a pause. "Maybe."

"Why not mark it in your calendar so that you can decide as the date comes around?" Dorothy suggested.

"By the way," Edwyna said, "when I spoke to you earlier, you asked about the phone calls that I'd been receiving. I wonder how you knew about them. I only told Diane."

"I thought I might have slipped when I asked you," Dorothy said. "But Diane was so worried about you, and one day I saw how distracted she was, so I asked her what was going on, and she told me. I hope I didn't ruin anything between you and Diane."

"It is disturbing to find out people are talking about me."

"I understand, but please know it was all out of friendship. I don't know if you realize that the Wise Women all knew each other before the book club ever began. We so cherish having you as a new friend. Please don't let my indiscretion . . ."

"But still, to think of people gossiping . . ."

"No, no, no! Not gossiping. Caring. That's how it is. We all care for you."

"All? I thought just you and Diane talked about the calls, The Creep."

"Do you remember when we formed the book club and said we wanted you as our little sister? Any concern one of us has, all of us have. Do you remember? Little sister?"

Little sister. There was an idea Edwyna liked. She could not resist the idea of being little. Because she'd always been tall for her age, she was the one who was always chosen to be in charge. And 'little sister.' Once Donny's big sister, always the big sister.

"I get it," she said.

"And will you come to our next new moon?" Dorothy asked.

Edwyna laughed and said, "Don't push your luck. Let me think about that."

Edwyna was about to hang up when Dorothy said, "One more thing. I don't want to pry, but you seem a little different tonight. Worried? Or anxious? Perhaps sad."

"Not at all. Just the end of the weekend," Edwyna answered.

"I was worried you had heard from your caller again."

"No. All solved." At least she hoped it remained solved.

"Then I'll see you at our next book club meeting, and maybe by then . . ."

Just as Edwyna and Dorothy were saying their good-byes, Edwyna heard the call waiting signal. Probably Hank, she thought and ignored it.

CHAPTER 17

Police Matters

THE MORE EDWYNA thought about Hank's final words to her, the more threatening they seemed. Was he saying that he was The Creep or that he had sent The Creep to her? And not only his words, but his actions—demanding he see her at a precise time, waiting outside her home, grabbing her hand. Holding her hand. Tight. Too tight. She hadn't told Howard because that might lead her to talk about how compulsive Hank had been in his lovemaking. She wasn't going to tell either of her parents, who would go ballistic. She never told them more than the barest details, if that, of anyone she was seeing. What would be the point when none of her relationships were serious? The only other person she might tell was Diane. But Edwyna still resented Diane's breaking her confidence, telling the other Wise Women about the obscene calls.

These thoughts went round and round Edwyna's mind as she waited for the other shoe to drop. Hank's other shoe. When nothing happened for a few days, she began to relax. Then early one evening when she came home from her office, she heard the voice of The Creep on her voice mail.

"Wait until you see the big cock I have for you. A special treat for girls who've been nice. Even better if you've been naughty."

It must be Hank. The Creep always talked about his body parts or hers, but she didn't remember his ever having said anything about her being naughty or nice. At least not that she could remember. She almost wished she had kept all the recordings so that she could listen to them. She thought she still had an old, unerased message from Hank. An innocuous one confirming a time. She pressed the telephone key for "play old messages" and listened. There it was, the old message from Hank. "Let's meet at eight," was the gist of it. Then, one by one, she erased all the messages between Hank's "let's meet at eight" to the new one from The Creep. Back and forth she went between the messages. Not the same voice. Not unless he was really good at changing the sound. Weren't there analytic techniques that could compare voices just as one could compare handwriting? Maybe she should call Doug after all. Or maybe she should use the rabbit's foot once again. Where was the rabbit's foot? She was sure she'd left it right next to the phone. She scrabbled around looking for it and finally found it on the floor under a chair. It was already gathering dust. Maybe that's how The Creep got through. The rabbit's foot had lost its power—too far from the phone, too dirty. She was being ridiculous. She had to get a grip on herself. Nevertheless she dusted the rabbit's foot with her hand, careful to get every scrap of lint from between its tiny claws. She put it next to the phone.

As if the rabbit's foot had summoned some external force, the phone rang again. She waited. Let it go to voice mail.

"Look outside. Here I am. Ready to stick my . . ."

Edwyna put her hands over her ears. She didn't want to hear the rest of the message and she didn't want to pick up the phone. Then The Creep would know she was home. If he didn't know already.

As soon as she was sure the phone had clicked off, she pulled Doug's card from the drawer beneath the phone and dialed his number. She prepared herself to leave a message, not sure if she'd get someone at the desk who screened his calls or his voice mail. She didn't even know what hours he worked. It was past six in the evening.

"Hello, MacArthur here."

"Hello." She hesitated for a moment, not sure what to say next.

"MacArthur here," he repeated. "Can I help you?"

"Hi. Hello. It's Edwyna. Edwyna Glendower."

"Good to hear your voice."

"I'm calling . . . Here's why . . ." Edwyna wasn't sure where to begin.

"Or maybe not so good." Doug's voice changed from cheerful to businesslike. "Have you heard from the obscene caller again?"

"I have and—and I'm frightened. This time more frightened than annoyed. I might have a clue who it is—"

"Why don't we talk about what's happening in person. Would you have time to come to the station? I'd be happy to come to your house, but that would have to be much later this evening and it sounds like you want some help now."

"Yes. Now. I can be there in about twenty minutes. Is that okay?"

"Fine."

"Oh yes. When I'm there, can we listen to my voice mail? It has the messages and something else."

"Of course."

"Do you want me to ask Howard to come with me?"

"Only if that makes you more comfortable."

As soon as she hung up the phone, Edwyna was out the door, in her car, and at the police station. She was seated at Doug's desk in less than her estimated twenty minutes.

"Do you want to hear the message first?" Edwyna asked Doug.

"Why don't we start with what makes you so much more frightened this time. I sensed from our phone conversation that something else has happened."

Edwyna was torn. She wanted to tell Inspector MacArthur all that had happened with Hank, but she didn't want to reveal anything about her relationship with another man to Doug. "I'd rather start with the two most recent phone calls, if you don't mind." Edwyna figured that would give her time to figure out how to explain why she thought the caller might be Hank.

Doug handed Edwyna the phone. "Dial your number and answering pin," he said. At the same time he kept his steady gaze on Edwyna. "Are these the most recent messages?"

She felt uncomfortable, as if he already knew some secret about her. Some dirty secret. "Yes, the last two."

Doug played the messages. They brought back the same rush of fear that she'd felt when she first heard them.

She had to tell him the rest. Even if he thought less of her. Indeed she thought less of herself. In her bones, she'd known there was something strange—wrong—weird about Hank from the very first time they'd made love. All that neat folding of clothes. The empty closet. She couldn't even explain to herself why she'd ignored all those signs.

As soon as the messages stopped, she said, "I think it's someone I know, although the two voices are not the same. I mean the last two messages are from one voice, but the other message, the older one . . . I thought maybe you could have someone analyze the two voices to see if they are really from the same person, someone who can alter his voice."

"Before we get to that point, tell me why you think it might be this man you know?"

Edwyna took a deep breath. She felt it shudder in her chest and throat. That shudder reminded her of how her breath felt when she was a child, the first breath after a long cry about some denied pleasure or some rare punishment she felt was undeserved. Now she had to tell Doug more of those circumstances. "There's a man I dated a few times. He called me on Sunday. In fact, you were there when he called. Remember I got a call?"

Doug nodded.

"Then he called back. Later. He was a bit odd. More than a little bit. He told me exactly when he was going to call back—to the minute—and he did. In the second call, the one after you left . . ." Edwyna looked at MacArthur to see if he'd understood the sequence.

"I get it," Doug said.

". . . he put me through the third degree—I guess that's not a good expression to use here."

Edwyna paused, looked at Doug, who continued to listen.

"Asked what I was doing. Who I was with. Seemed to assume I was with another man. Of course, earlier, I had been with another two men—you and Howard." She tried to smile at Doug but her face was frozen. "Then he said he was going to come to my home in thirty minutes. Again he gave me this crazily precise time." She paused. Tried another deep breath, felt another shuddering breath.

"What happened when he got there?" Doug asked.

"I decided I wasn't going to wait for him. It was all too bizarre and annoying. And he had other—other strange—let's just say strangely compulsive behaviors. I'd had enough. So I left almost immediately to go to Howard's. You remember we live in the same building?"

Doug nodded.

"He was waiting outside. He ran up the stairs to the landing between my door and Howard's and he grabbed my hand and wouldn't let go of it."

Doug continued to nod and made some notes on the pad he had in front of him.

"Then what happened?"

"I argued and tried to pull my hand away, but he was too strong. So I hit him on the head with my handbag." Edwyna felt an unwanted giggle escape her throat as she said this. "Am I in trouble for hitting him?"

"Sounds to me like that was a good idea. He was assaulting you and you defended yourself. Do you think you hurt him?"

"Just enough to make him let go of me. I think it was more surprise than injury."

"Too bad!" Doug said. "Not very professional of me, but I wish you'd given him a really good blow. What happened next?"

"This is the part that gets really scary. He said I was 'disobedient'—I remember that was exactly the word he used. Then he said something like he or someone else would get to me. That they would follow me and I would never feel safe. Never be safe. He said, 'You'll always be frightened.' And he said something else that seemed to show he knew I was already scared."

Edwyna felt the tears well up. She hadn't cried when it happened, but now telling it to Doug, seeing how concerned he looked, how angry he looked—she could see how taut the muscles in his neck had become—made the horror of that moment more real. She let herself go, put her face in her hands, and cried.

Softly Doug asked, "Do you want to take a break?" He handed her a tissue from a box on his desk. When she moved her hands from her face, he put more tissues near her hands and waited—just waited—for the crying to stop.

"The early message . . . ," Edwyna said between the gulps of subsiding sobs. "The early message is from the man, not the man who made the calls, but the man I'd been—I'd dated . . . I thought maybe you—or some expert in voices—could see if they are one and the same."

"I'll listen again in a moment, but I'd like to know more about the man who assaulted you."

Edwyna told Doug Hank's name and address, even his make of car, but that was all.

"Was there anything about him before the event you described, anything you found odd?"

"Here's one thing. He told me he'd just moved here from New York, and maybe that explained why his apartment was barely furnished, but the odd part was that he had almost no clothes in his closet, just another pair of pants, a shirt, maybe a jacket."

"Anything else?"

"He took me to a restaurant in West Portal, although as I said, he lived on the other side of the city, and the host seemed to know him as a longtime customer. Greeted him warmly. Gave us a bottle of wine without asking. That kind of thing."

"How did you happen to see what was in his closet?"

That was the question Edwyna did not want to answer. "Umm, well—let's just say he was very neat in whatever he did. Liked to hang up his clothes as soon as he took them off. Anything off." She felt herself blushing. God! Crying, now blushing. Was she reverting to her childhood?

"I get the picture," Doug said.

Edwyna feared that he did.

"Let's listen to the messages again," he suggested. After listening, he said, "You're right. They don't sound alike. I can have a copy made of the recordings. And we can have them analyzed. But even if they aren't the same person, Hank—that's his name, right—might have someone who makes the calls for him. He may even be there with the other person."

"That's even creepier." Edwyna pictured Hank and another man making the calls and then . . . She tried to erase the image of what they might be doing to each other from her mind.

Doug continued, "However, the phone calls are not my main concern. My concern is the threatening nature of his remarks to you and his assault on you, his grabbing your hand and not letting it go. I'm more concerned about protecting you than punishing him, although they might go together. I could bring him into the station, but even if I charged him with assault, the district attorney may not charge him. The DA would likely see it as a 'she said, he said' case."

"I forgot to tell you. He's a lawyer. Or so he said when I met him. Now I don't know what to believe."

"Did he tell you anything else?"

"That he'd moved from New York but was working for the same firm. That his wife had recently died—about two years ago—and that's why he left New York."

"Do you have a photo of him? Maybe in your phone?"

Edwyna shook her head.

"Did you by chance get the license plate on the car?"

Again Edwyna shook her head.

"Here's the plan. I'm going to check him out the best I can. See if he is who he says he is and if there's anything more in his past that would interest us, that would concern you. And I'll get back to you with what I find. Meanwhile I'll arrange with the phone company to put a trap on your phone and we'll see what that yields. I'll let you know as soon as I've done that. Here's another card with my number. It rings here and on my cell. Call me anytime. Day or night."

Edwyna held the card to her heart and smiled. It was the first time she'd smiled in the several days since her encounter with Hank. "You have no idea how grateful I am for your help."

"I'm happy to help you. How are you getting home? It's dark out there."

"I have my car, and I got a spot right in front."

"I wish I could go with you myself. I'm going to have a squad car follow you for now and make sure you get home safely."

"Are you suggesting I can't go out by myself or can't go out at night? That's pretty scary in itself."

"Just be careful."

Edwyna didn't have to be told to be careful. She was spooked. She looked around her car when she got in and out of it, made sure the outside landing light was on before she left the house even if she expected to return while it was still light, and she finally told Howard all that had happened. Like Doug, he was aghast. He promised to watch the street and keep an eye on her front door whenever he was around. She was glad that he didn't make any derogatory comments about Hank or her choice of men. He must have sensed that she was in no mood to be teased.

With each passing day, her vigilance increased. Although she had not received another call, she was as fearful as she'd been right after Hank's threats. She'd feel that roller coaster effect in her stomach each time she replayed the moments on the landing. She didn't want to forget what had happened. That might mean letting down her guard. On the other hand, she wanted to forget what had happened, put it in the past, chalk it up to another aborted relationship. She'd had her share of those and had barely remembered them as she moved on to other men or other interests. But all the others had ended happily as if both she and the man had just decided it was time to call it quits. Just as she'd done in high school and college, when she got bored with a man or didn't want to be with him for one reason or another, she'd think about their friendship being over. And somehow as if she could make the man read her mind, the next time they were together, he'd say exactly what she'd been thinking. It was as if she could magically write the script for them. But she couldn't figure out the script that might make Hank—and The Creep—simply disappear.

Doug called ten days after Edwyna had seen him and made her report at the station. "How have you been?" he asked.

"Okay. No more calls. But still scared," Edwyna said.

"I have some information about Hank for you," Doug said, paused, then added, "I have a couple of days off. Would you meet me for coffee and I can tell you what I found?"

They agreed to meet at Roasters, a coffee shop only a few blocks from Edwyna's home. Like most small coffee shops, it was crammed with small tables set close to each other, often at odd angles to make use of every inch of space. When Edwyna arrived, she saw that Doug had snagged a corner table. No one was on one side of them, and the bearded, youngish man to the other side was not only staring at his laptop screen but was wearing the ubiquitous earbuds. They settled into their corner facing each other over a table just big enough to hold two cups of coffee and two small, muffin-sized plates.

"I have some news you aren't going to be happy to hear," Doug began. "And I find it's best to tell it to you right away, rather than beginning with polite chitchat."

Edwyna gripped her cup of coffee and leaned forward.

"There is no Hank Morse. No Henry Morse. At least not here in San Francisco. There is a Henry Morse who is an attorney. He is with a law firm in New York City. But he is still there, not here in San Francisco. And, as far as I can see, his wife is very much alive. By the way, I think you said your Hank Morse is in his early fifties."

"I don't like thinking of him as 'my' Hank Morse."

"Fair enough. The San Francisco Hank Morse is in his early fifties. The Henry Morse in New York is thirty-eight."

"No way they're the same person."

"That's what I thought. The law firm that Henry Morse in New York works for does have a branch in San Francisco, but they have not had anyone named Morse working for them in any capacity. In fact, they haven't even had anyone named Henry or Hank working for them as a lawyer, a clerk, an administrator— or even as far as they know—as a maintenance man in San Francisco. On a hunch, I went so far as to check with the company that has the maintenance contract for the building and they have not had any workers named Morse or Henry. They do have a worker named Henrique who's been with them for more than ten years, but he is Mexican-American, about five foot five, and speaks English with a distinctly Spanish accent.

"Not the same person. Not at all. Maybe he could fake a Spanish accent, but he couldn't shrink. Or grow."

"So much for my hunch. That's what I thought when the manager described him. I then looked into the address you gave me. I'm afraid I have more bad news. The apartment is owned by a management company, a company that buys apartments in luxury buildings planning either to flip them or rent them. The apartment number you gave me is vacant. It hasn't had an owner or a renter since the last family moved out almost a year ago.

So Hank, or whoever he is, has mastered the art of high-end squatting."

"But he did have some furniture, a bed. I think there was a chair in the living room. How did he do that?"

"There aren't many who do this, but those types of squatters just buy some stuff and abandon it when they think they are about to be caught. Or he might have several such places around the city or elsewhere. It's easy to move around the Bay Area or anywhere in the world if you have some money and identification. And it's identification we are looking for. Of course, there is no one with his name, no one anywhere near the right age registered with the DMV in California or I would have started with that as a source."

"So what next?"

"The only area of exploration still open is his car. A black Mercedes SLK250 is neither a common car nor a rarity. We've started a search of owners—you don't by chance know the year, do you?"

"Sorry," Edwyna said.

"But I don't expect the search to yield much since we don't know if Hank or Henry Morse is even his real name. And given his apartment and other clues, he may not even be the owner of the car he drove. He might have 'borrowed it,' as they say. If we're lucky, we may find enough details to discover his real name."

"That's an awful lot to take in. Well, who is he?"

"That's what we don't know."

"What should I do?"

"I've had the trap put on your phone. Here's what you must do," Doug spoke emphatically. "As soon as you get a call from your caller—what do you call him? The Creep—hang up and call me. If and when Hank calls you again, you can hang up or talk to him. Just be cool. Don't reveal any of your fears or thoughts. As soon as you hang up, call me."

"I don't know if I could talk to Hank and play it cool. I guess I could just seem distant and not say why or how angry I am or ask him who he really is."

"Then just hang up on him too. He probably won't be surprised, given the way your last encounter ended."

"You said 'if and when he calls.' Do you think he might call? Or might not call?"

"I'm not sure. But under any circumstances, do not agree to see him. He may apologize and beg forgiveness. Just refuse."

"Are you kidding? There's no way I would ever agree to see him again."

"And should you actually see him—near your home or office or anywhere—get to a safe place and call me."

"I guess I should say thank you, but you have me scared out of my wits."

"Stop and think for a moment. Nothing I told you changes what happened already. You already went out with him and—other than the last episode when he was angry—you did not feel you were in any danger. Nothing I told you puts you in danger then, in the past. As to the future, you were already afraid of him—that's why you came to my office. For what might happen now or some time from now."

"That's true."

As Doug looked steadily at her, Edwyna felt her fear dissipate. She picked up the wooden stirrer and moved it purposelessly through her black coffee. "You know," she said, "it's hard being a single person. You have a choice of just being alone or with friends, not seeking anything more, not seeking love, or you have to take a chance that you're going to meet some nut job.

Let's face it, whether you pick someone up at the beach—and that's how I met Hank—or you go online or to a bar or to the library . . ."

"The library? I never heard of that as a hot pickup spot."

"The library actually held a speed-dating evening. You know what speed-dating is?"

"Unfortunately I do. Been there. Done that. But not at the library," Doug said.

"So you know. You know that you never really know who you're meeting. Hank could just as easily have been at the library or someone I met online or . . ."

"Sometimes you just get lucky." Doug looked down into his now-empty cup. "You meet someone through your work. Get to know them a little that way." Doug stopped for a moment and looked up, directly at Edwyna. "Or this way."

Edwyna felt a shift as if the air in the coffee shop had suddenly been stirred by a giant spoon. The whirring coffee grinder, hissing steam maker, and clattering silverware all fell silent.

"I don't want you to think I'm taking advantage of your vulnerability. Or my pursuing your case will change based on your answer to my next question."

Edwyna did not think he was going to ask her again about Hank's license plate or birth date.

"From the first moment I saw you in the station house, I was attracted to you. That's why I told Leung I'd take over. And because you seemed so upset. For a moment I was worried that Howard was your husband or special friend, but I could see I was wrong about that right away. Last Sunday I walked by your house on purpose. I didn't expect to see you in the street, but I did have more than half a mind to ring your bell. I was not ashamed to use the excuse of seeing if your calls had stopped. But I was also hoping something, some conversation, would let me get to know you better. When we went up for coffee, I thought this was my opportunity, but then your phone kept ringing and ringing. I figured the best way to reach you was by phone. I even tried calling you later that evening, but I guess you were already out."

Edwyna remembered the unanswered call that she'd thought was Hank.

"So here's my question. I'd like to see more of you. Are you interested?"

"You don't think I came to you because . . ."

"No. Of course not. You were assaulted and frightened and you did the right thing. Does that mean that you don't want to . . . ?"

"Everything is so confused for me now. I really appreciate all you've done. But I don't think I can move ahead in any direction. Time to hunker down. In fact, all I want to do when I get home is get into bed and pull the covers over my head. I've got to get Hank out of my life, out of my mind."

"I'll keep working on the case. I'm dogged, if nothing else. You can count on that."

CHAPTER 18

Bye Bye Baby

FOR A FEW days after her meeting with Doug, Edwyna was very much aware of her surroundings. She looked up and down the block whenever she got into her car, made sure the front-door light was on before she left her house, and could barely resist the urge to turn and look over her shoulder every few minutes. Gradually, after a couple of weeks, the feelings of fear eased as she heard neither from Hank—or whoever Hank really was—nor from The Creep—who might be Hank or his surrogate.

Saturday evening came, and she felt almost herself. She'd spent the day catching up with office work. While the losses in the stock market had all of her clients worried about pensions and their 401K retirement accounts, for most those were future problems. What concerned Edwyna was how to help her clients suffering the immediate credit crunch. That crunch kept them from their regular routine of short-term borrowing, a routine that allowed for the cash flow to purchase inventory in order to sell it. For now, the work was complete, the books were closed until Monday, and she had changed from her jeans and shirt into her long, luxurious blue and silver silk robe. She sat in front of her living room window with her knees drawn up so that even her feet were covered in silk. Edwyna looked through the window into an exceptionally clear night sky. The stars seemed closer, more numerous than ever. She was happy to have the evening, the night, the rest of the weekend to herself. No obligations, not even any social obligations. And no Nick. This was not one of his every-other-Saturday nights.

The very thought of Nick disturbed her rest. She shifted her legs, moved them from one side to the other. She really had to find a way to tell him that their romance—or friendship with benefits—or whatever he might call it—was over. How would she do it? She remembered a long-ago episode of *Sex and the City* in which Carrie's boyfriend had broken up with her using a Post-it. Nick deserved more than a Post-it. But she couldn't picture telling him during one of their dates. When would she do it? When he picked her up? During the restaurant meal? After they'd made love or after dinner before making love? Various scenarios ran through her mind, but as quickly as they appeared, they were rejected as awkward at best and cruel at worst.

Edwyna restlessly got up, took a glass of wine, and sat down again. The night was so clear. And the moon looked huge. It was a full moon. The biggest full moon she could remember seeing. If only she had a candle, she thought, or some full-moon ritual that could simply make Nick disappear. Not really disappear. Just disappear from her life. The easy way, the way boyfriends seemed to slip away in high school and college. Slip away as soon as she realized that she'd lost interest. Like Scott, her first boyfriend. High school, sophomore year. She wanted a boyfriend because all her friends had them. And Scott—a much sought-after senior, handsome, smart, popular—called her out of the blue. It was fun being with Scott, being part of his crowd, but then he began to want more and more of her time, more of her. She remembered wishing he would just back off, go back to one of the cheerleaders who swooned over him. Edwyna smiled as she remembered telling Inanna her problems. She no longer believed Inanna solved her problems, but talking to her had become an ingrained habit. Then one day, he did just that. He didn't invite Edwyna to the prom. He and the captain of the cheerleaders went together and were declared king and queen of the seniors. Her friends thought she was putting on an act when she said she was happy for Scott and his queen— Elizabeth, that was her name. King Scott and Queen Elizabeth. But it hadn't been an act. She realized, in retrospect, that she hadn't had much emotional investment in Scott. And now, the same was true of her feelings for Nick.

Memories of Scott and thoughts of Nick faded as she continued to look at the moon. The moon mesmerized her. She sat, sipped, and stared. No thoughts. No plans. Just sitting and staring. Almost in a trance.

Until the phone rang. She jumped up, heart pounding, waited a few rings to catch her breath, and answered. It was Nick.

"Hello, Edwyna," he said. And then after a few polite preliminaries, "I wonder if you'd have time to meet me for coffee tomorrow morning or sometime tomorrow that would work for you. I have something important I want to tell you, ask you."

This was so very un-Nick, suggesting getting together in his sacrosanct morning gym time, suggesting anything other than their routine, that all Edwyna could think of saying was, "Sure. How about ten tomorrow morning?"

Nick named a local diner. The date was made.

Edwyna went to sleep with her mind strangely at ease. She didn't know what Nick wanted to talk about, but she was going to use this opportunity to gently sever her ties to him. Whatever it was, he seemed eager to talk to her, but his voice didn't suggest concern. This was going to be fine.

The restaurant was busy at ten on a Sunday morning. Edwyna looked around and saw that Nick was waving to her from one of the red vinyl booths.

Once again, Nick began their conversation with pleasantries, asking how she was, how her work was going, and what seemed like a million other hows of this and that. Just as Edwyna thought the polite preliminaries were drawing to a close, the waiter appeared at their table ready to take their orders. Edwyna realized she was hungry and ordered Breakfast Special #3—scrambled eggs, bacon, the works.

Edwyna was eager to hear what he had to say so that she could fit her own agenda into the conversation. Maybe he was going to have to travel. That would give her a chance to suggest they needed a breather. Or if he had a new job, she could use the same tactic. The only nagging fear she had was that he was going to ask more of her than they now had. But she hadn't had any signals that he was leaning in that direction.

Finally, Nick said, "Edwyna, I know it's unusual for us to get together like this on a Sunday morning. That is, without a Saturday night date, but . . ." He stopped in midsentence. The pause drew on.

"It's okay," Edwyna reassured him.

He took a deep breath. "But," he continued, "I need a change in our relationship." He sat back and looked at Edwyna as though he had asked a question. Or said something she could respond to.

Edwyna waited.

Another deep breath. "Look," he said. "I mean, listen. I really like you. And I enjoy our times together." More breathing. "I wanted to say something about this last time we were together, but I wasn't sure." Again he seemed to be waiting for an answer from Edwyna.

She had none.

"Here's the thing of it. I really like you."

That's the second time he said that, thought Edwyna. What's next?

"I really like you. But I've . . . Things have changed for me. I respect you too much to . . ."

Nick inhaled more deeply than Edwyna had ever seen anyone do.

Then in one long exhale, he said, "I've met someone else. Someone who has just changed my entire life."

Edwyna smiled.

Nick, breathing more normally, said, "I have enjoyed all our time together. But this other person. Gloria. Somehow I want to spend all my time with her. Gloria's just wonderful. Makes me feel like a different person. You know, Edwyna, you'll understand. When I'm with her, with Gloria, time just disappears. I forget all about my routines. Gloria understands me in a way no one ever has. Gloria has the most amazing . . ."

Edwyna was relieved. She did not have to break up with Nick. He was breaking up with her. On the other hand, she'd had enough of his recitation of Gloria. Of the glories of Gloria. She reached across the table and took Nick's hands in hers. "Nick," she said, "you don't have to say anything more. I understand. I really do."

"No hard feelings?"

"None at all. We both knew that what we had was limited. And I'm happy for you that you've found something more. Someone who can give you more." She thought about telling him that she was going to break it off as well, but there he was a grown man, grinning like a boy. She had no need to say anything negative. Instead she looked at her watch and said, "I'm happy for you, but I realized I have some accounts to review for a meeting early tomorrow. So I'm off, back to the salt mines. Congratulations."

"Thank you, Edwyna. Thank you for your understanding. And for the congratulations. I didn't want to tell you all at once, but I think Gloria and I are going to marry. And very soon. I want to spend every minute of my time with her. And she wants to be with me."

Edwyna listened to more of Nick's paean to Gloria. She couldn't believe that this was the same rigid man she knew. Just goes to show what love could do. Maybe it would happen to her.

"But you have to leave," Nick said. "And I'm keeping you here. Thank you again, Edwyna." He pushed back his chair, came around the table, and gave her a hug. It was one of those awkward hugs, no longer a hug of lovers, a hug in which the hugger and huggee both managed to hold each other and yet keep all their intimate parts from touching.

She didn't really have any work to do at home. She thought about how she would spend her free time, time and mind that were even more free than they'd felt the evening before. Her relief at Nick's announcement was combined with a premature nostalgia as she already remembered her times with Nick as if they belonged to some distant past.

This would be a great day to guiltlessly stay home and watch one movie favorite after another. *Sabrina*, or any of the Hepburn-Tracy films. *Desk Set* was the best. Librarians, early computers, a soused Katherine Hepburn, Spencer in Katherine's bathrobe. She laughed to herself as she played the film in her mind. Maybe she'd call Howard and ask him if he felt like watching too.

Probably not. She saw less of him now that Greg was on the scene. She missed Howard's easy availability, but she was happy for him. At least when she was in a good mood. She wondered whether any of the Wise Women liked to fritter time away watching and rewatching old films. There was plenty of time in the day and evening to watch a flick or two or more. She'd send an email to the group. See if—on the spur of the moment—she could lure one of them to her ritual.

Edwyna was surprised when her email did get a response from both Lila and Carolyn. And it was a quick response. Each of them said they were free, that there was nothing they'd like better than to watch a movie or two with Edwyna.

Carolyn arrived carrying a bag that could only hold a bottle of wine. Lila followed soon after.

"My contribution," Lila said, and removed a box of gourmet chocolates from her bag. "And one more thing. I almost forgot. This is one of my favorites. Set in New York City, of course. I'm hoping we can watch it." She rummaged in her bag and pulled out a DVD of *Moonstruck*. "You must know it," she said to Edwyna.

Edwyna felt a frisson of wariness. Not more moon stuff.

As if she could read her mind, Lila said, "Don't worry. No candles. No ceremonies. Just a terrific flick. So romantic. Yet real."

Edwyna was not going to resist the wine, the chocolates, or the movie, which truth to tell was also a favorite of hers. Before they began, however, she wanted one more chance to find out about the folder or return it to one of them. She'd put it on the coffee table before they'd arrived and now she picked it up.

"You know this folder that I found after one of our meetings months ago. I'm still not sure what it is or who it belongs to. Take a look at it," she said and handed it to Carolyn.

Carolyn opened the folder. Then closed it. "You do the honors," she said and passed it to Lila.

Lila opened the folder and looked quickly at the piece of fine linen paper on top. She closed the folder, patted its cover, opened it again, and began to read.

I guess it's my turn to tell the beginnings of my story. It is so much more prosaic than any of yours. I was born in Brooklyn, New York (that's almost a joke in itself), but the Brooklyn of the fifties, the Brooklyn I grew up in, was a magical place. Big leafy maples and oaks cast giant shadows on the sidewalk in summer and became spectral sights covered in winter's ice and snow. There seemed to be a grand synagogue or small shul not only on every corner but in the middle of blocks as well so that in early fall the sound of the ram's horn could be heard throughout the streets in early morning and at dusk. My parents were ordinary, neither too strict nor particularly lax, but it was my grandmother to whom I clung. When my grandmother entered the kitchen, wonderful layer cakes, light-as-feather pastries, perfectly cooked chickens, and succulent meats would appear without her seeming to do more than whirl around the kitchen while murmuring from what I took to be her recipe book. Then she would sit with some beautiful velvet, exquisite lace, spools of many-hued threads, and garments would pour forth from her Singer sewing machine. I no longer have her machine, but I do have the recipe book.

Lila did not close the folder when she finished reading. Instead she leafed through the other papers. "Look, Carolyn," Lila said, "here's the story of your ice rescue . . ."

"More wine? Let's watch the movie." Carolyn cut off whatever Lila had been about to say. She refilled their glasses and asked Edwyna to start the DVD.

But Edwyna was not ready to start the DVD just yet. "Look," she said, and patted the folder just as Lila had done. I don't know how I got this folder. I'm not sure who it belongs to, and every time I open it, there seems to be stuff I didn't see before."

"Really?" Carolyn answered. "It's all there for you—or for that matter for any of us—to see whenever we want."

"Well, whose is it?" Edwyna asked point blank.

"It's all of ours. It's for us."

"Who 'us'?" Edwyna realized she was barely speaking English in her attempt to finally straighten out the mystery of the folder. "I mean who is the 'us'?

"It's just us—you know—the Wise Women. But if it's bothering you . . . If you don't want it here . . . If it's in your way, then I'll just take it when I leave." Carolyn's tone had moved from matter of fact to somewhat offended.

Edwyna was embarrassed. She felt she had made a mistake in asking the questions, although they were questions she wanted answered. She was undecided. She would be happy to have the folder out of her home, but she certainly didn't want to offend her new friends.

"Whatever," she said and started the DVD.

The movie ended just as the women finished the last of the wine. They each reached for a chocolate and sat back, satisfied with the romantic outcomes and all those outcomes said about the possibilities of life. This despite their actual experiences.

"Here's what we learn from this movie," Carolyn said.

"Oh no," Lila groaned. "Not a lesson. Another chocolate instead?" She held the box out to Carolyn. "She always likes to do this." She turned with the box to Edwyna. "It can be the silliest film ever, but Carolyn always says there is a lesson to be learned. Even when we went—for some obscure reason—to see the movie about the animals who run away from the Central Park Zoo."

"This lesson is important," Carolyn continued as if Lila had not spoken. "It's about the space between. You need the space between to find your true love."

"The space between what and what?" Edwyna asked.

"Look at the movie. Cher, aka Loretta, is stuck in a relationship with Mr. Johnny, who can't give her what she wants. He says it's because of his mother. But we know that kind of man. A no-commitment kind of guy. It's only when he leaves that Loretta is in the space between. She is then able to meet Ronny—Nicholas Cage in a wonderful romantic role—and fall in love with a man who loves her back. She was in the space between."

"That opera scene." Lila nodded in agreement. "I feel like crying every time I see Loretta cry. But it's a movie. What about real life? Wait a minute. As soon as I said 'real life,' I realized you're right about the space between. Listen to this story. The space between. I have a friend who was dithering between two guys. Although it was clear to me that neither was going to give her what she wanted—minimally a committed monogamous relationship. One was married."

"That's a pretty big clue that he's not going to commit to her," Edwyna said.

"No matter what he says otherwise," Carolyn agreed.

"And the other was talking about leaving New York, and spoke only in the first person singular. You know what I mean? 'I'll move to Philly,' he'd say. 'I'll buy a condo.' Never a 'we' passed his lips."

Edwyna was caught up in the story but still didn't see the connection to the film or to the idea. "And the space between?" she asked.

"I'm getting there. So she was supposed to go on vacation—skiing if I remember right—with married guy and he backed out. His wife was sick. If you can believe it. Annoyed, she went anyway. She was in a space between. The spot that was supposed to be occupied—in time and in her romantic imagination—by married guy was empty and first-person-single guy was not on the horizon. On that ski trip she met her husband. And—ta da—they've been married for thirty years."

"Funny," Edwyna said, "that we should be talking about this now. I just broke up with someone I've been seeing earlier today. And it does leave a space. Maybe I'm in the space between."

"Is there anyone else in your love life?" Carolyn asked bluntly.

"There was another. But he turned out to be a horror."

"A horror?" Lila echoed.

"In what way?" Carolyn asked.

"I don't even want to talk about him. Let's just say he's gone for good. Hank. A liar. A guy who scared me. Just say he's gone. And good riddance. A mistake from the start." Edwyna paused, took a breath. "But Nick, he was nice enough, but not right, not what I want. Nick's the guy I ended it with today. Or oddly enough he ended it with me."

"Why 'oddly enough'?" Carolyn asked.

"Last night, I was just wishing I could find a way to end it, and then he called and—presto—this morning, he told me he'd found someone he was really in love with."

"Last night—by the way—did you see the moon?" Carolyn asked.

"It seemed enormous," Edwyna said. "Did it look bigger than usual to you?"

"That's because it was a super moon. A full moon that's also closest to the earth in its orbit," Lila explained.

"A super moon," Edwyna repeated. "I almost felt I should have one of your rituals." She smiled.

"You might be right," Carolyn said. "A super moon is very powerful. But back to the space between. So you got rid of Nick—I think that's what you said his name was—and 'the horror.' Is there anyone else?"

Edwyna was embarrassed to reveal that she'd been juggling three lovers. But what the heck. "There's Joel. He's okay."

"Just okay?" This time Lila asked the question.

"You know. Nice enough. Good date. Okay in the bedroom."

"You've just used two of the deadliest words: 'nice' and 'okay,'" Carolyn spoke emphatically. "Ditch him."

"Just like that?"

"You already dropped Nick for the same reason," Carolyn said. "You know what you want. You can have what you want. But you must be clear."

"You need both. Clarity of mind and clear space around you," Lila emphasized.

Edwyna was afraid one of them was going to say aura. But no one did.

"Cut Joel away. Get into the space between. You say he's a nice guy. So do it nicely."

"You're probably right. I don't know. Maybe I could just wish him away."

"You could," Carolyn said. "This is a good time for wishing, now and the next couple of weeks. Do it now. Otherwise it will be another month."

Farewells were said, and Edwyna was alone when she realized that she had no idea why Carolyn had said this was a good time for wishing. It didn't coincide with the next New Moon ritual at the Baths. Whatever! She'd just call Joel and get it over with. After all, that relationship was not nearly as long-lived as hers and Nick's. She wasn't sure about all the moon stuff, but having a clear space—a space between—seemed more and more attractive to her.

CHAPTER 19

Russian Tea

EDWYNA WAS NOT the least bit surprised when Diane called her a few days later to suggest they meet for coffee in the same place as they'd met before: Diane's favorite, the coffee shop in the Richmond. Edwyna knew how the group worked. Lila and Carolyn had undoubtedly told Diane about Nick and Joel and all the rest of the conversation. She'd meet Diane, but if she wanted to pry further into her affairs, that would spell the end of her friendship with the Wise Women. She could drop them as easily as she'd gotten rid of Nick. That would make even more space in her life. No Hank. No Nick. No Joel. No women friends. Just begin again. She'd done it before, going way back to high school days, and she could do it again. Dropped friends who were getting too much into . . . into her feelings . . . her mind. Were getting just too close for comfort.

"Hey, watch out!" Howard said as they almost collided on the sidewalk in front of their building. "You look ready for a fight."

"Sorry. I was so caught up in my thoughts, I didn't look where I was going."

"You seem determined, angry even. What's up?" he asked.

"I guess I am annoyed, but it's not about that. Yesterday I invited two of my book club buddies to watch a film . . ."

"Without me?"

"And then we got to talking."

"Which one?"

"*Moonstruck*. Do you want to know why I'm angry or not?"

Howard nodded.

"And the talk turned to my love life—such as it is—I'd just broken up with Nick—or he broke up with me. Anyway, that doesn't matter. And now I've gotten a call from Diane, who wasn't there, who wants to get together. And once before when I told Diane something, everybody knew. Now I just bet that Lila and Carolyn . . . Well, you get the picture."

"I told you I didn't have a good feeling about those women."

"You did. But you didn't have any reason."

"I had a reason. Just didn't know what it was."

"What happened to 'I'm a scientist? I observe and yadda, yadda, yadda.'"

"They're gossips. That's the worst. Maybe I couldn't express it before. Nevertheless I appear to be correct," Howard said.

"Maybe. If I'm right and Diane wants to rehash what happened yesterday . . . Let's just say you won't see them on our front steps anymore."

On her drive across the park to the coffee shop, Edwyna let her anger grow. There was no way she was going to be the subject of gossip. This had gone too far. She was in the process of constructing a speech telling Diane just how she felt, when the car behind hers blared its horn. She realized that she'd failed to move forward on a green light. She took a few deep breaths and decided to let the situation develop in the moment.

Again, as soon as Edwyna entered the coffee shop, she was struck by its warmth, its faded luxury. Even the pleasantly perfumed air seemed to emanate a scent of faraway places and times gone by. Diane, who was standing at the counter, waved Edwyna over to a table and then joined her carrying a tray with two tea-pots, two glasses in what looked like silver holders, a pot of jam, and two spoons.

"Today we are going to have tea the Russian way," Diane said. She set a glass in front of each of them. "This pot has very strong tea," she said, pouring a small amount into each of their glasses. "And this is hot water to dilute it." She gave Edwyna one of the spoons. "Do what I'm doing," she said and dipped her spoon into the jam, stirred the jam into the tea, tasted the combination on her spoon, and put the spoon into the cup. Leaving the spoon in the cup, she began to sip the tea.

"Does this have some special meaning?" Edwyna asked.

"Only the meaning of delicious tea and, for me, memories of Russia. Try it."

Edwyna tentatively dipped her spoon into the jam, the tea, her mouth, and the tea again. It tasted like strong tea with jam. There must be something she wasn't getting. "I mean is there something beyond the tea and the taste? Some other . . . ?"

"You're right. Tea drinking in Russia is always a social occasion. A chance for good conversation. Is that what you meant?"

"Interesting glasses," Edwyna said. "Beautiful metal carving."

"Filigree. They're mine. I brought them back from Russia. They have great sentimental value. Nowadays in Russia, you don't even get this. Just plastic like everywhere else." Diane sighed. "Does it seem strange for me to bring my own glasses to a coffee shop? I guess so," she answered herself. "But this shop knows how to serve Russian tea, and I wanted to share my feelings for it with you. Have one of these cookies." She moved a plate of sugared cookies toward Edwyna.

"Jam and cookies and sugar. Isn't everyone in Russia fat?"

"Not to mention *wodka*," Diane said, with a slight emphasis on the *w*. "You need all those calories to withstand the cold Russian winters."

"Like bears," Edwyna said.

The tea drinking had done its work. She was relaxed, feeling sociable, no longer as wary of Diane and company, maybe not even ready to push them out of her life until Diane began speaking again.

"I spoke to Carolyn last night . . ."

"I know the group shares everything, but if this is about Nick or Joel and what . . ."

"Not really. She had an idea I want to propose to you."

"What?" Edwyna felt prickles of suspicion on her neck.

"She had an idea that seems perfect to me. I know all the Wise Women, not only Carolyn but Lila and Dorothy, agree that we would like to extend an invitation to you."

Edwyna hoped it was not another invitation to the bathhouse.

"We are traveling to China and we would like you, our little sister, to join us on this two-week trip."

"A trip? To China?"

"Yes." Again Diane poured tea and hot water into her cup, dipped her spoon into the jam, gave a leisurely stir of the jam and tea mixture, raised the cup to her lips, and sipped.

Edwyna followed suit. The rhythms of the conversation, indeed of the day, were slowed to match the rhythm of the tea-drinking rituals.

"Let me back up a bit," Edwyna said. "You are all going to China. And you'd like me to come with you. Is that what you said?"

"Yes," Diane repeated.

"I don't know what to say. Just questions. Why me? Why China?"

"First of all, why you. I think that should be obvious. We've only known each other for about a year . . ."

"Really less than a year."

"Not if you count the time when we met in the bookstore, but let's not quibble over time. The important part of what I want to say is how dear you've become to all of us. We are so impressed by your life, how you're handling your life. All you accomplish. Maybe we feel like you're a younger version of each of us."

"Impressed by how I handle my life? Right now all I have is a mess. I have what I don't want and I don't have what I do want. If you know what I mean."

"I do. That's just it. It's easy to handle life when all is going well. It's when it's a 'mess,' as you call it, that true grace emerges. That's what we've seen. That's why we'd like to have you on our trip to China."

"How long have you been planning this? Why are you asking me now?"

"Maybe we should have asked you sooner, but for a while we only knew each other through the book club, and we didn't know if you'd be amenable, be . . ."

"Compatible?"

"Partly that," Diane answered. "Travel is exhilarating, but also trying. We like to know we can count on each other."

"And now you feel you can count on me? Why? Why now?" Edwyna could not think how she had impressed the group when all she had in our life was one problem after another.

"Just getting to know you. Seeing how you live. Hearing that you too have some problems—as we all do—but you cope with them."

"So I passed the test?"

"Actually, yes." Diane answered.

"Was the moon ritual in the Baths part of the test?"

"No. I wanted you there. But I did like that you were open to being there, watching. Maybe even feeling part of it."

"I didn't really go along with all of it," Edwyna confessed. "First I felt caught up, and then, the feeling of something special just left me."

"We all question what we are doing sometimes and we experience the same moment differently. That's part of the fun of traveling with others, with people you like."

"But not necessarily people who are exactly like you," Edwyna added.

"Precisely.

"Let's put my wonderfulness aside. Why China?"

"Why not China? We like to travel. This isn't our first trip together. We've been to Turkey, Italy, Greece, Germany. China has so much to offer. The very ancient bumping up against the newness of its growing economy."

"I've heard that there's so much building going on that the national bird of China is the crane," Edwyna added with a straight face.

After a pause, Diane laughed and said, "I just got it! We're going to combine that newness and the old in our travels. Beijing . . ."

"Oh yes. The Forbidden City," Edwyna said.

"The Great Wall," Diane continued. "Shanghai."

Edwyna sighed as she pictured herself in these places she'd always wanted to see.

"Guilin, a marvelous city on the Li River. We'll take a boat trip on the Li, which is absolutely magical."

"Magical? How is it magical?" Edwyna did not want a repeat of the bathhouse experience.

"'Magical' in the sense that most people use the term. When the ordinary or expected seems special, seems to have occurred in some extraordinary way. Puts you in touch with something bigger than yourself. Like rainbows. Or a particularly spectacular sunset over the ocean. Our minds know that sunset occurs every day, but sometimes a sunset, or a rainbow, touches something in our hearts. Maybe spiritual is a better word for what I'm trying to describe. That's what it's like in Guilin. As the boat floats along, limestone cliffs arise through the mist, seeming to appear out of nowhere."

Edwyna wanted to put the question more clearly, and she was still thinking of how to phrase it when Diane spoke.

"We're also going to Xi'an where, in the third century BCE, the emperor commissioned a huge army of terracotta warriors complete with . . ."

"Yes," Edwyna said, "I've read about that army. Complete with horses, chariots, soldiers of every rank. And it was all buried until a farmer digging a well in the 1970s came across the first pieces. Can you imagine how that farmer must have felt? How staggering the experience must have been!"

"You've got it. That enthusiasm you just expressed is why we people who like to travel enjoy it so much. The thrill of our own discoveries. The ability to share that thrill with people we like. And that's where you come in, dear Edwyna."

Edwyna took a few more sips of her cooling tea, then refreshed it from the pot of hot water.

"There's so much more I need to know before I take the trip—consider taking the trip."

Diane smiled. "I like that slip of the tongue," she said. "Of course there's more to know. I have some papers that include the itinerary and all the details of flights and hotels. I remember that you are an accountant and need all the details. It's another aspect of you that I admire."

"What about your husbands?" Edwyna had a sudden feeling that she might be the fifth wheel—or it would be the ninth wheel—on an excursion of couples.

"They're used to our taking some time just to be with each other, to go someplace special. Maybe once a year, sometimes less often, sometimes more."

Edwyna and Diane stopped talking and sipped their tea. They dipped their spoons into the apricot jam, and nibbled at cookies. The barista left her stand behind the counter to refill the pot that held the hot water. She poured some more tea and then some water into each of their cups. She brought another plate of small pastries, crescent shaped, with nuts and cinnamon.

"*Spacibo,*" Diane murmured.

"*Ne za shto,*" the barista replied.

Each time Edwyna looked up from her tea, she saw Diane apparently engrossed in the tea-jam-spoon-mouth sequence. After one more sip of tea and another bite of a delicious crescent cookie, Edwyna asked, "When do you plan to go?"

That question not only broke the silence but also interrupted Diane's tea-drinking sequence as she reached into her capacious handbag and pulled out a sheaf of papers. "We leave in a month—five weeks to be exact—and we'll be traveling for two weeks. Here's the itinerary." She handed the papers to Edwyna.

"A month! I don't know if I can get all the work done for my clients in a month."

"It's actually five weeks," Diane said after looking at the papers once more.

"You know my clients are mostly professionals with their own individual practices and small business people. This recession has really thrown some for a loop followed by or caused by—who knows—the drop in real estate value. And then the Madoff scandal made them even more uneasy even though none of them had invested with him." Edwyna took a breath. "And I have clients who filed tax extensions. I have to have them ready for the October 15th filing deadline. I don't know. I just . . ."

"I know you feel responsible to your clients. See what you can do. Please."

"If I'm interested, what next?"

"I've checked with our travel agent and there will be no problem adding you. We're not going on a group tour. It's all self-arranged, our own drivers and such. Of course, you'll need to call her if you want to go, to give her your details."

"And credit card. What do you think the cost will be?"

"That's all in the papers, almost down to every meal."

The whole thing was too weird. No comments on the events of the previous evening. No advice on getting into the space beyond or whatever it was called. Now an invitation to go to China. For a moment she thought of her first visit to Hank and how she'd ignored all her initial suspicions. Maybe she should ask Doug to check out the Wise Women. Or maybe that was just another thought about getting in touch with Doug, whose image and voice had stayed with her since the last time she'd seen him.

"Let me think about it." Edwyna put the papers into her own handbag. "I don't want to seem ungrateful, but this is a lot to take in at once. And I have to see if I can clear my calendar at the time you're going." Edwyna realized, as she spoke, that she was already juggling client needs in her mind. She knew what that meant. The trip was a real possibility.

"Call me in a day or two, when you've made up your mind. Or even if you haven't decided," Diane said and reached across the table to take both of Edwyna's hands in hers. "I know you'll figure out whether this is right for you."

Edwyna sat at her desk a few hours later, her laptop in front of her, the itinerary to one side. Beijing, Shanghai, Xi'an, Guilin. There was nothing unusual about the itinerary. It echoed what many tours included in about the same amount of time. And except for Guilin, all were places she'd long planned on visiting.

But since her suspicions had been raised, she then googled everyone in the Wise Women. Everything she thought she knew about them checked out. The only surprises were where some had gone to college or honors they'd won at points in their lives. Nothing she saw raised a red flag. She felt herself leaning toward accepting the invitation, even began to think about how to get her clients' work in order.

Still, she thought she should confirm her perceptions with someone. Not Doug. This wasn't a police matter and she didn't want him to ask her out again. Maybe some other time. Not now. Howard would be good because he was thorough and he didn't like them. That would make him ask all the right questions.

She'd sleep on the invitation—metaphorically—not like pieces of wedding cake that some girls put under their pillows.

The next evening, she presented the idea to Howard. They sat at his dining table, the pages of the itinerary in a neat pile, the laptop open and ready. Greg was somewhere else in the flat. He'd greeted Edwyna when she arrived but had obviously been clued in by Howard that he and Edwyna had some work to do. Edwyna had met Greg a few times, and each time she'd been more impressed by him. He was easy to be with, clearly very fond of Howard, and immediately accepting of Edwyna as Howard's friend. Now his ability to disappear into another room in the flat to give her time alone with Howard was another mark in his favor. Not that she actually had a vote in the matter.

At first Howard was incredulous. "They are inviting you to China? Maybe this is a hoax."

Then he was suspicious as she hoped he would be. "Are they going to say you're going to China and then sell you? I don't know. Where would they sell you? Who would buy you?" Howard asked.

"Just because you don't find me attractive . . ."

"Maybe for your organs," Howard said. "Let's look at this realistically. First, how will you be flying? Scheduled flight? Charter?"

"The itinerary gives Cathay Pacific dates, times, and flight numbers. I looked them up and there they are on the Cathay Pacific website. The flights look genuine."

"Where will you be staying?"

"All at major hotels. Some part of chains we're familiar with, others not. But again I looked them all up and the hotels all check out. Never in someone's home or a hostel or anything strange."

"Will you be rooming with them? How many to a room?

"Single rooms all the way."

"How about within China?" Howard zeroed in on more details.

"We do take private cars in the cities, but we fly between cities on Chinese airline flights."

"And they're scheduled flights?"

"Check and double check. What's more, the travel agent they recommended has an office in the financial district. I know that

Internet reviews have to be taken with a grain of salt because anyone can write them, but all of hers are reasonably positive."

"Better Business Bureau?"

"Forgot to check that." Edwyna went to the laptop. After a few moments, she said, "An 'A' rating."

"That takes care of all the obvious details. But how well do you know these women? Do you really want to take a chance on going with them?"

"What could go wrong?"

"What if you find you just don't get along? You might feel trapped in a really uncomfortable situation."

"I have my credit card. It would be awkward, but I could fly home or go off by myself. It's not as if we're going to the ends of the earth, trekking in the Himalayas or anyplace like that."

"What about the gossip factor? That really bothered you the other day. My people—that is the Hebrews, not the gays—consider gossip one of the worst offenses. It's called *lashon hara*."

"What does that mean, sounds like some version of your bubbe's favorite dish—but not a good version—, 'horrid noodles'?"

"Literally, 'evil tongue.'"

"The answers to all your other questions were a piece of cake, but I guess I could find out I just don't like these women. China is far ahead of the United State in bringing cell phone reception virtually anywhere. So I can call you to rescue me."

"If I were you, I wouldn't call me. I'd call United Airlines and get myself out of there. But then if it was me, I wouldn't go. They wouldn't ask me, and I wouldn't go. Last question—at least for now," Howard said. "Why China?"

"I asked that question and Diane described the itinerary. I got really excited about the trip when she described it. Lots of people go to China. Tourists, I mean. Do you see anything suspicious about going to China? China in and of itself?"

"I guess not. You usually like these women, right?"

"Right. Sometimes too nosy or bossy. Fine. They're usually fine."

"And when not 'fine'? There's something you're not saying. I can see it in your face."

"Well," Edwyna drew out the word, then said it again. "Well. There are just two strange things. Not exactly things. One was an event. The other a thing."

"Um hmm?"

Edwyna had not told Howard anything about the moon evening. She paused, trying to figure out how to describe the evening succinctly. Just get to the bottom line, she thought, and began. "One night, a couple of months ago, they invited me to meet them at a bathhouse."

"Bathhouse! You're kidding. That's for my people—this time I mean the gays, not the Hebrews.

"Not that kind of bathhouse. The Japanese bathhouse. At first it was lovely, all women, relaxing in warm water, drinking tea."

"Naked?"

"Of course."

"Did someone make a pass at you?"

"I told you. Not that kind of bathhouse."

"Get to the strange event."

"We went into a private room, put on some white robes, looked at the moon, lit a candle, said some prayers."

Although Edwyna recited the events as quickly as she could, she had not finished before Howard was choking with laughter.

When he gained control of his voice, he said, "You put on some white shmata with a bunch of witches who brayed at the moon, and now you're going off to China with them?"

"Prayed. Not brayed. But when you put it that way, it does seem foolhardy to . . ."

"No. You have to go. I can't wait to hear the stories when you return."

"Don't be like that. I already asked. Diane said there are no bathhouses on this trip. Look at the itinerary."

"You said there were two things. What's the other?"

"Wait here. I have to get something upstairs."

"With bated breath as they say," Howard answered and leaned back in his chair.

Edwyna ran up the stairs to her flat and took the folder from its place on the coffee table. She was glad this was not one of the times it seemed to disappear. She ran back down the stairs and into Howard's flat.

Greg had joined Howard at the table. "I thought you were finished," he said. "I still have some work to do in the other room." And he got up to leave.

"Please stay," Edwyna said. "I'm trying to figure out whether to join some friends on a trip to China."

"Some friends," Howard said and wiggled his eyebrows.

"What does he mean?" Greg asked Edwyna.

"He's just being Howard. He doesn't particularly like these women. But I do have reservations, too, so it would be great if both of you looked at the papers in this folder."

Howard reached toward the folder which Edwyna still held. "Wait a minute," she said, clutching it more firmly, pressing it against her chest. "Let me just tell you that the folder appeared in my bag after I went to a meeting of the Wise Women."

"The Wise Women?" Greg asked.

"My book club," Edwyna said. "And every time I try to return it to one of them, I still have it. And the pages seem to change order of their own accord. Sometimes one is on top, then another."

Howard was again convulsed with laughter. "Give it here," he said between guffaws.

Edwyna released the folder into his waiting hands. He opened it and riffled through the pages.

"Just some newspaper clippings. What's the big deal?"

"Okay," Edwyna said. "Close the folder."

Howard closed the folder.

"Now open it again."

Howard opened the folder.

"Oh my God!" he exclaimed.

"What's there?" Edwyna felt her breath quicken.

"Chicken feathers. Bloody splotches. Eye of Newt."

"Howard. Be real." Edwyna laughed in relief.

"Exactly the same clippings," he said. "Greg, you take a look."

"May I?" Greg asked Edwyna.

She nodded.

Greg looked at the pages more carefully than Howard had. "Just newspaper articles," he said, "from different cities—Toronto, New York, New Orleans. Maybe the cities themselves have some meaning. I don't see anything strange. Do you want me to close the folder and then open it again?"

Again Edwyna nodded.

"Nothing different," Greg affirmed and handed the folder back to Edwyna.

"I think I'm going to go to China with the Wise Women," Edwyna said. "If nothing else, in addition to the rice there'll be lots of *bubbelukshen*."

Greg got up from the table. "I'll make some green tea to celebrate your coming trip." He walked past Howard toward the kitchen, putting his hand on Howard's shoulder for just an instant.

That gesture and Howard's smiling response told Edwyna that Howard would be fine without her whether or not she'd be fine on the trip.

"Just remember to take your credit card and my phone number," Howard said as they waited for the tea.

The following day, Edwyna called Diane. "I'm seriously thinking of going with you all to China, but I do have a few questions." Edwyna was a little reluctant to ask the question. "I know you're all into rituals. The new moon. Candles. I wonder . . ."

"Let me reassure you. I can't imagine anything on this trip that will make you uncomfortable."

"Just one more thing. You know the folder that was left in my house. I keep wondering what it's about. Whose it is. I know that question is not about the trip. But . . ."

"Why don't you bring the folder with you? That is, if you want to go with us. We can talk about it on the flight or we'll have lots of other free time. In fact, this trip is the perfect time for us all to get to know each other better. You will find so many of your questions answered. Travel does that."

Edwyna still felt hesitant.

"Do come," Diane said. Her voice sounded as warm as her hands always felt. "It will be a lovely trip. And lovely to have you, our little sister, with us."

CHAPTER 20

In China

THE WEEKS BETWEEN the invitation to travel with the Wise Women to China and the actual departure date seemed to fly by in a flurry of activity—going to the Chinese consulate for a visa, buying good walking shoes, stacking up guide books she was too busy to read, and reassuring her clients that they would not need her for the two weeks at the end of September during which she'd be gone. In the crazy months that began in 2008 and continued into 2009, she'd held their hands through the AIG debacle, the government takeover of General Motors and Chrysler, and the persistent unemployment numbers. But, in truth, there was little she was able to do except listen. Sometimes she felt she'd become more a therapist than an accountant. If nothing else, it was time she took a vacation.

She'd successfully ended her relationship with Joel, although he had briefly returned to the petulant man she'd seen at their first meeting. She tried to escape gracefully and easily, using the kind of line she'd heard from men in the past. "It's not you. It's me. I'm just not ready for a relationship right now."

First Joel had whined. "I thought you liked me. I tried so hard to do everything you wanted."

She offered a few words of reassurance. "I know you did. It's not your fault."

"Didn't I always ask you if you liked what I was doing to you? What we were doing together? You certainly seemed to like how I touched you. There was plenty of moving and moaning." He became petulant. "Don't tell me you're one of those women who's learned to fake orgasms. If you're one of them, let's just say it's your loss, sister."

Edwyna waited for his anger to subside.

Instead it surfaced, full blown. "When I met you, I told you I was off blondes. Now you've ruined it for me with brunettes. I might as well go back to the bitch. At least she's a redhead."

Edwyna struggled to suppress the giggles that his final response evoked. She wanted to be nice to him, as difficult as it was. She reached out to pat his arm as they said good-bye, but he pulled it away from her roughly, running his hand down his sleeve to wipe away her final touch.

All that was behind her. China and two weeks with the Wise Women lay ahead. She settled back into her aisle seat on the upper deck of the 747 jet to Beijing. Carolyn was at the window to her left, Lila across the aisle, Diane and Dorothy behind her. Edwyna had planned to read at least one of the guide books, or at a minimum a description of Beijing, their first stop. But she barely turned the pages, staring instead at the clouds passing the window, sipping the offered champagne and chatting occasionally with Carolyn and Lila when none of them were dozing, or even sleeping cocooned in the isolating luxury of the business class sleeping-seat. The flight from San Francisco to Beijing was uneventful, which was the best, Edwyna thought, one could want from a flight.

Mr. Lee, who was to be their guide throughout their trip, met them in the airport, and helped them get luggage and sort their way through immigration and passport control. Finally Edwyna was in Beijing. She was struck immediately by the sheer number of people and vehicles. Bicycles, bicycles, and more bicycles. Motorbikes roared around the bikes. Cars passed the motorbikes. And everyone simply surged forward. She was happy for the respite of the hotel.

At the sumptuous buffet breakfast, Mr. Lee gave them their marching orders for the day. "Today, it's Tiananmen Square to start, then the Forbidden City, and on to the Bell Tower."

Obediently they all met in the lobby. Impatiently Edwyna trekked from one site to another. Of course she was aware of the political significance of Tiananmen Square, but it was the Forbidden City that she was eager to see.

"Did you see Bertolucci's *The Last Emperor*?" Edwyna asked Carolyn, who happened to be walking alongside her.

"Was that the one about Rome?" Carolyn asked.

"No. China. Right here. Part of it is set here." Edwyna pointed around her, wordlessly. She couldn't share how what she was seeing made her feel, not with someone who didn't even know the film. That film had made her feel that she was living the imperial life and then, sadly, its demise. As she walked through the Forbidden City, the seemingly endless succession of courtyards, doorways, and chambers was the same as in the film. And the ornate carvings and sculptures of dragons or snakes and lions were all perfectly correct—merging her memories of the film with the current reality. But instead of palanquins filled with nobles and mandarins clad in silk, the courtyards were filled with tourists, most being led by their guides who held flags to signal their charges, the charges themselves identified by matching baseball caps—a group in yellow caps, another in red, a third in white. The guides had devised their flags so their groups could easily spot them. Some flags matched the colors of their groups' baseball caps. Others were three-dimensional stuffed animals. Edwyna saw a panda, a lion, a carp.

Suddenly Edwyna realized that while she'd been watching the other groups of tourists, she'd lost sight of her own. No one she knew was anywhere near her. A slightly nauseous feeling rose from her stomach to her throat. There were hundreds, no thousands of people around her and she didn't know anyone. She was breathing too quickly. Then she felt a hand on her shoulder and she whirled around. It was Mr. Lee.

"Don't lose sight of our rabbit," he said, smiling. He raised the flag, a slightly flat but undeniably three-dimensional green rabbit, a bit higher and, as if summoned by some royal decree, Diane and the others gathered around him.

Tucked in alongside the magnificent buildings were stalls which sold the usual tourist trivia. Edwyna could not help the burst of laughter that exploded from her.

"What? You okay? Edwyna?" The group stopped and turned to Edwyna who, absorbed in her surroundings, had again fallen quite a ways behind them. When she could stop laughing, she pointed to the sign on one of the stalls. "Starbucks," it read. And it was indeed a Starbucks.

"No escaping our fine American culture," Lila said. "What next? Bloomingdales?"

"More likely Walmart," Dorothy answered.

Throughout the day, Edwyna found herself always lagging behind the group of four women who stayed together in tight formation. What captured her attention eluded theirs, and when they stopped to exclaim over some sight, Edwyna heard what they said but never quite got what intrigued them. But always there was Mr. Lee with his rabbit flag, making sure she did not stray too far.

Edwyna's feelings of loneliness grew throughout the next several days, although like everyone else she climbed a small part of and marveled at the greatness of the Great Wall. Like the others, she enjoyed the trip to the Summer Palace and, like the others, she had her photo taken near the animal and mythological creature statues of the Ming Tombs and Sacred Way.

Her loneliness was particularly acute at night. As the detailed itinerary had stated, each of the women had her own room in the hotel. However, on the third night, after climbing the Great Wall, she was sure she had heard the voices of the four other women in a nearby room. At first she wasn't sure that it was her group that she heard, but then she heard Lila's unmistakable laugh and someone saying, "Shh." After that, there was quiet, then the voices as they grew louder until, apparently, someone remembered to quiet them again. Hearing one more burst of laughter, Edwyna was tempted to go into the hall, to sneak down the hall, listening at doors until she found the one that led to the voices. Maybe it wasn't the Wise Women at all, but some other group of women. How embarrassing that would prove to be, knocking at some door, demanding to be let in, only to find a group of strangers. And if it were the Wise Women, wouldn't that be more embarrassing, to find that they had gathered without her? Didn't want her or didn't remember she was there or were talking about her. Gossiping. What had Howard called it? Evil tongues! Besides, she was already in her nightgown. Edwyna got into bed, turned off the light, and tried to sleep.

Every lunch and dinner the group gathered at a round table where a seemingly endless array of steamed, fried, and stewed vegetables, seafood, chicken, and meat dishes were served by a wait staff that seldom understood any more English than the request for Diet Coke. Neither Edwyna nor any of the other women could discern an order to the dishes. On the first day, when soup arrived after seven or so other dishes, they agreed this was probably the last course. But then other dishes continued to arrive. Edwyna joined in the discussion of which dishes they liked and which they disliked. That was the only time Edwyna truly felt included. They easily reached consensus that the vegetables were the best part of their meals.

However, at this particular lunch, Edwyna didn't particularly want to talk about the wonderful freshness of the vegetables or their amazing variety. Her mind was on the conversation she'd heard the night before. Or thought she'd overheard. She wanted to ask if all the women had gathered in one room, and if they had, why they hadn't invited her. But no, she cautioned herself, girls learned in junior high school or even earlier that no matter how bad they felt about being left out of some pajama party or roller rink birthday celebration, they couldn't ask why. Asking allowed those who'd been included to offer a saccharin sweet apology or smirk or both. Fortunately she'd been one of the popular girls ever since she'd decided she wanted friends in junior high school. As soon as she'd wanted to be included, she was in. Strange to be the one who was outside. But there was nothing to be done about it, nothing to be said. Edwyna reached her chopsticks across to the best green beans she'd ever tasted and added another serving of them to her plate.

Their last day in Beijing ended with a rickshaw ride into a hutang, a neighborhood of narrow, winding streets with traditional houses clustered behind walls. Each rickshaw, really a pedicab with a red and gold canopy, could carry two passengers. With no conversation, they paired off—Dorothy and Diane in one, Carolyn and Lila in the second, and Edwyna by herself.

Edwyna tried to pay attention to the houses and markets around her, but instead she anxiously looked around, trying to keep the other two rickshaws in view. When she did catch sight of one of them, she craned her neck to see what her travel companions were viewing. They were never looking at her. Or for her. For all they cared, she could disappear into the narrow streets never to be seen again.

"Get a grip!" she said to herself. That alleviated neither her anxiety nor her loneliness.

After awhile, they left their rickshaws to wander through the streets and thriving markets.

"So different from the Forbidden City," Carolyn said.

"Yet they are both walled off, rich and poor walled off," Lila answered.

Edwyna realized that she herself felt walled off, walled off from the other members of the group. They seemed to move so effortlessly from one site to another, taking in everything, not saying much to each other, but in an easy companionship. She didn't think they were deliberately doing anything to exclude her. She just didn't feel with them, with it—whatever the "it" was. Maybe it had been a mistake to come on this trip with women who'd been friends with each other for a long time, had traveled together before. She was definitely the newby. She tried to dismiss her discomfort. Maybe it was jet lag, but she couldn't erase the memory of their voices behind a closed door somewhere in the same corridor as her hotel room.

Their last evening in Beijing, Mr. Lee took them to a Chinese opera. Before the opera began, a guide explained the long history of opera in China, the nature of the stories, and the symbolic meaning of the face paint and costumes. All of this went over Edwyna's head as she remained lost in thought about her own discomfort on the trip. The costumes were indeed lavish, as the guide had promised, and the music was as unusual to Edwyna's Western-trained hearing as expected. But while the others seemed to have caught on to the story since they all laughed or gasped at the same times, Edwyna was unmoved.

That night, in her own room again, Edwyna was restless. She did her nightly ablutions, creamed her face and arms. She put on her nightgown and robe and turned on the TV. The only English show was a cable news channel, and she could not concentrate, did not want to concentrate, on whatever was happening back in America or, for that matter, elsewhere. She clicked off the TV and sat in the quiet. She strained to hear any voices coming from other rooms. All she heard was the hotel hum of air conditioners. She reached into her bag for a guide book. The next day they were going on to Shanghai. She'd read again what she was going to see. Instead she took out the folder. Diane had told her to bring it on the trip, and obediently she'd done so. Of course, the newspaper articles that Howard and Greg had seen were no longer on top. Instead there was another piece of fine letterhead. This one had a large embossed many-curlicued C in the upper left-hand corner. Edwyna read:

⬥⬥⬥

First a thank you to Dorothy for taking the start in telling of your birth circumstance. My story could not be more different. This time I was born into a very strict Lutheran family, in Minneapolis. My parents were always present, always watching over me, or at any rate, always watching me. There was nothing I could do that didn't have a rule. And none of the rules allowed any fun at all.

By the time I was ten, I knew I had to get away from these people who could not be more different from me. As soon as I graduated from high school, I left Minneapolis and roamed around a bit. That's how I met my first husband, the Canadian, and ended up in Toronto. It was in Toronto that I saw how my particular skills could best be used as a biologist. I realized that any unusual laboratory events would be explained by my research.

Edwyna read through the brief bio. Then read the beginning again. The third sentence. "This time I was born . . ." Too much. Moon worship or whatever. Was Carolyn also suggesting that she'd been reincarnated? Did these women really believe in the stuff that the folder suggested? Maybe this was some exercise in fiction or fictional memoirs. She did not want to discuss what she had just read with any of the Wise Women, not while there was still so much trip ahead of them. She'd give it another couple of days. She didn't want to get any closer to them. Right this moment, Edwyna was glad to be alone. However, she did want to see Shanghai, and then she just might exercise her credit card home option.

Four days after their arrival in China, Mr. Lee ushered them out of Beijing to the airport for the flight to Shanghai, and then out of the airport into Shanghai. The traffic in Shanghai, if possible, was even more congested than in Beijing. Edwyna found herself holding her breath as their car swerved around motorcycles and came perilously close to a bus on one side and a bike on the other.

Their first stop was the Bund, a paved embankment along the Huangpu River. Edwyna remembered a novel she'd read, set in Shanghai before World War II. *The Distant Land of My Father.*

There was such a moving scene early in the novel, when the young girl stands with her father in his office overlooking the Bund and reads the names on the buildings to him. That was when the Bund was the commercial center of a thriving international community. Now thriving once more, it nevertheless did not have any of the romance—the elegance—that the novel evoked. Now there was the noise and site of construction mixed with the chatter of more tourists.

"I read a terrific book that starts right here, almost where we are standing." She named the book and looked at the others. They waited for her to say more. She tried to explain how beautiful the life in Shanghai seemed to the young girl, how important impressing her father with her ability to read was to the daughter, how Edwyna herself had identified with the girl. They nodded and moved on.

In the Shanghai Museum, there were several bodhisattvas that Edwyna wanted to share, to tell someone how peaceful the sitting figure made her feel, but each time she looked around, the others had moved on. In the painting gallery, a long scroll showing a young girl reading in the mountains in springtime almost brought her to tears. She saw the girl's youth and the passing of time to come—the young girl's imagined time, the painting's time of centuries, the time of her own life going by. Edwyna remembered how Diane had defined magic as seeing the extraordinary in the expected. Her experience with the painting "Reading in the Spring" was magical in that sense. She stared at the painting for a long time, again wanting to share her experience with someone, but the others were already exclaiming over elaborately carved and decorated chairs and screens in the furniture galleries.

The following day, in the Jade Buddha Temple, as Edwyna watched monks in yellow and brown robes walk from the courtyard into the open chamber of the temple, she felt someone take her hand. It was Dorothy. An enormous gong signaled the start of their prayers. In unison, deep male voices began. The high roof both held and echoed back their chanting voices as if a pedal on a giant piano kept each note reverberating on the note that followed it, and then both joined the notes that followed them. All the Wise Women were silent. In fact, most of the tourists were quieter than usual, and when a tourist's voice rose above the monks' voices, you could feel the crowd turn as one, not even needing to utter a word of hush.

A second sounding of the gong ended the prayers and, in stately procession, the monks left.

"Did you feel that?" Carolyn asked.

"Yes," Diane said. "That's what we travel so far to experience."

"Not the tchotchkes or even the silks, as beautiful as they are," Lila agreed.

Dorothy turned to Edwyna. "And you?" she asked.

"I was moved," Edwyna said, "very moved. It was beautiful."

"Beautiful," Carolyn echoed.

Everyone seemed to be nodding in agreement, not seeking words, just feeling as she was feeling, Edwyna thought.

The trip changed for Edwyna from that moment. The next day they visited the Children's Palace, a Saturday school for the arts. They peeked in at a group of six- or seven-year-old ballerinas, all wearing pink leotards and lighter pink tights. Diane nudged Dorothy, who tapped Carolyn on the shoulder, who touched Lila's arm and pulled on Edwyna's hand—all to point out a little girl who had defied the pinkness by wearing four red barrettes, one on each side of her hair and another pair on her braids. They smiled in recognition as they passed a practice room of somewhat older boys and girls learning the piano, creating multiple, cacophonous versions of "Fur Elise," a standard of their own childhood piano lessons.

Edwyna's sense that a barrier had come down increased as another flight took them to Xi'an where they marveled at the ranks of terracotta warriors and considered whether they wanted to order any reproductions from miniature statues that could be held in one hand to colossal figures that would require a truck for transport from SFO to one's home. As her friends debated the merits of ordering souvenirs for their husbands, Edwyna considered sending one to her dad, her brother Donald, even Howard. She realized that at this moment there was no love interest in her life, no man she yearned to be with. She was truly free of Nick and Joel. And certainly of Hank. For a moment she wondered whether there were any nasty messages from The Creep silently awaiting her on her voice mail. She'd just begun to think about that when Diane interrupted her thoughts.

"Tomorrow we begin the most important part of our journey," Diane said. "We leave for Guilin on an early morning flight. It's a quick one, so we will have no trouble meeting our boat for the afternoon and evening sailing on the Li River. Mr. Lee has arranged for an early check-in, so we can change our clothes and prepare all we need for the boat ride."

Edwyna wondered why Diane was suddenly giving such precise information. Up to this point, they had all relied on Mr. Lee and simply followed his directions. She'd said this was the most important part of the trip. Her specificity reinforced that notion. But no one had said anything about Guilin before this, other than to note its dates on the itinerary.

As if sensing Edwyna's rising discomfort, Dorothy took Edwyna's arm to walk companionably with her. "It's just Diane being Diane. Don't let her bossiness throw you off. She really has been looking forward to this river cruise."

"What did she mean 'prepare all we need'?" Edwyna asked.

"Probably it will be warm in the afternoon and cool at night, so take a sweater or a shawl."

Edwyna was not convinced. She started to ask, "Is this anything like . . . ," but then wasn't sure if she wanted to finish her question.

"I don't expect it to be like anything you've seen before." Dorothy picked up on the beginning of Edwyna's question. "The Li River, I've read, is fabulous, with limestone cliffs often shrouded in mist."

"Boring! You sound like the guide book." Carolyn had come up alongside them.

"Right," Lila said. "Here's a more accurate description. The Li River, polluted, fetid stream nevertheless attracts unknowing visitors who breathe in its unhealthy miasma."

"Not even vaguely funny," Dorothy said.

The inane conversation had not really satisfied Edwyna. But this was their last stop in China before flying home. In for a penny, etc., she thought. She'd just wait and see what the next day would bring. If she hadn't exercised her credit card ticket home option earlier, she wasn't going to do so now with just this one more day to the trip.

The next day, in the hotel lobby in Guilin, Edwyna waited for the other women, her suspicions about the day intact. She watched the other women as they arrived, looked for unexplained packages or extra bulky bags, but everyone seemed to have their usual array of layered clothing, cameras, and the handbags of stuff each one could not do without—tissues, hand sanitizer, lipstick, sunscreen, allergy or stomach tablets, and more.

The afternoon sun played hide and seek with the water as clouds made their way between the tops of the limestone cliffs. Their boat—which they had to themselves—shared the river with other excursion craft and working boats—fishermen, two men poling a raft ferrying boxes from one side to another, another two pulling alongside a larger excursion boat offering the guests carved souvenirs. Small islands here and there were covered with green leaves and small trees. Cormorants flew overhead, occasionally swooping down on an unsuspecting fish. But it was the limestone cliffs, one behind the other, rising up straight from the river that were the stars of the show. Edwyna and the Wise Women watched them from the top open deck of their boat for the hours of the afternoon, through sunset, until the start of the evening.

Some words from a boatman led them to know that they should return to the lower deck where the crew of three served soup and dinner that they had cooked on the small rear deck of the boat. Carolyn tasted the soup as they all watched.

"Surprisingly good," she said.

"Nice and warming," Dorothy echoed as the evening chill had set in.

Some rice and seafood, Chinese beer and tea, and repeated comments on the wonders of the cliffs filled the early evening until Diane said, "It's time now." She pulled aside the curtains that somehow had been drawn across the boat's windows without Edwyna even noticing. The river was alive with boats all bobbing with colored lanterns. In a town on the shore, people were gathered, also carrying the festive lanterns. Edwyna could hear singing from that not-so-distant shore.

Dorothy reached into a space beneath the seat and took out five white robes. Without explanation, she handed one to each of the women. Edwyna saw these were the same robes as in the Baths. Or if they weren't the same ones, they were identical to them. How had they been smuggled aboard? Without speaking, Diane signaled that they should don their robes and return to the open top deck of the ship. On the deck, Dorothy touched Edwyna's shoulder and pointed to the sky. Edwyna was not surprised to see the moon. But where she'd expected to see the crescent of a new moon, this moon was almost full. She was not surprised but somewhat annoyed. Diane had obviously avoided her questions about the moon rituals. Now Edwyna could not remember exactly how she asked Diane about the rituals, nor could she remember precisely what Diane had answered. But certainly Diane had assured her . . .

The women joined hands and Diane took hers. Together, as they had done in the Baths, they recited, "Blessed are you, moon of our foremothers, who brings us the start of all that is new and all that is renewed from month to month. Bring us a month of peace and love. And so may it be for all women—and their men—everywhere." Edwyna had no trouble remembering the words that she'd only recited once before.

"Now you see why I said this is the most important part of our trip," Diane said.

Ah ha! Edwyna thought. Finally—as they say—all will be revealed.

"We are participating in the Moon Festival, a holiday that celebrates the moon goddess Chang'e, the goddess of autumn and winter, of water, of calm. She is the female essence, the Yin."

"Do you mean we came all this way—halfway around the world—for one evening of celebration?" Edwyna asked.

"I guess you could say so," Dorothy answered. She gestured at all the boats and floats on the river and all the people on the river bank. "But what a celebration! Look at how many others are joining in our celebration."

"Or you—or we—in theirs," Edwyna replied. "We are the interlopers, the foreigners."

"No," Diane answered. "All who celebrate the moon are one."

"Yes, one," Carolyn and Lila said in unison.

"We are one," Dorothy said, "but we have two moons." She pointed at the river. There was the moon above them in the sky and below them in the water.

"Having sight of the moon and her reflection is very powerful," Diane said. "It is a double opportunity to bring about any change we want. That is why, dear little sister, we wanted you with us on this journey."

That might have been why Diane wanted her, but not what Edwyna wanted for herself. What had begun as an unformed question had morphed into outright annoyance. Edwyna felt she'd been tricked into another moon celebration. She turned from Diane and started to move toward the stairs down to the lower deck. Diane took her hand and pulled her around into a hug. She patted Edwyna's back as if Edwyna were her child. She whispered in Edwyna's ear, "You are seeking but you look in the wrong places. You do not use the power that you have. Stay with us. Stay with me a little longer and you will have all that you want before this moon festival next year." Diane continued to hold Edwyna, continued to soothe her back, began to sing a soft wordless tune. The other Wise Women joined the quiet melody.

Edwyna felt her annoyance subside, realized her breathing had become slow, deep, regular. She felt at peace. Whether it was Diane's soft tones, the patting on her back, the melody, or the rocking of the boat on the Li River, she did not know. Nor did she know how much time had passed—several minutes or a few hours—staring at the moon in the sky and the moon in the river, before she once again found herself one of the Wise Women in a circle, chanting their concluding prayer. "As the moon brings the tides, as the tides bring the waters, so may we be. Until the next moon."

The following day was filled with the bustle of the flight back to San Francisco. Edwyna had no time or energy to think about all that had happened on the Li River, although every now and then Diane's words did return to her. Would she really have what she wanted by this time next year?

Their flight from Guilin to SFO took them first to Hong Kong, where they waited in the business class lounge for a several-hour layover. The walls of the lounge were decorated with giant photographic murals depicting the wonders of China, the wonders they'd so recently visited. Terracotta warriors were frozen, half in and half out of the ground. The Great Wall's expanse stretched before the travelers. The cliffs of the Li River rose in a motionless mist. Large plinths placed carefully around the lounge held replicas of blue and white Ming dynasty porcelain. All of the Wise Women seemed to have melted away, all but Diane, who sat side-by-side with Edwyna, their two armchairs touching.

"I hope you can remember how you felt last night," Diane said.

"Confused," Edwyna answered.

"I think you were annoyed, then confused, then at peace," Diane said. "In fact, I know that's how you felt. And I am so glad you moved to the place of peace."

"You're right," Edwyna said and sighed.

"Take three more deep breaths and let them out. That is what you need to do," Diane continued. "With each exhalation you must get rid of the false front you have assumed for yourself. Even more important, with each inhalation, you must reassume the powers you had as a child."

"What powers?" Edwyna asked, although she had a suspicion of what Diane might say next.

But Diane did not go where Edwyna expected. "You know that we worship the moon, that we get our powers from the moon. And we do have extraordinary powers, as do you. Last night we gave obeisance to the moon goddess in her Chinese name of Chang'e. You know who I am, who I am named for—Diana."

Of course, Edwyna thought. Dummy! I should have picked up on that sooner.

"In Turkey and Greece, we worshipped at temples for Artemis, the Greek name for the same moon goddess."

Now Edwyna did not know where the conversation was going. Did Diane think she was a goddess? Did all the Wise Women think they were goddesses?

"Of course you remember your special doll. Her name was . . ." Diane waited for Edwyna to answer.

"Inanna," Edwyna said, then repeated, "Inanna."

"How did you get that name?"

"I don't know. I was a kid. It just came to me. Maybe I was thinking of Nana, you know, the dog in . . ."

"Really?"

"Or Nana. That's what many kids call their granny. Or, I don't know. As soon as I saw that doll, I knew I had to have her. And when she arrived so unexpectedly after my mother had said

I couldn't have her, her name just came to me, as if the name came from the box at the same time as I lifted the doll."

"And did you talk to the doll?"

"That's funny. I used to tell her my problems. All kids do that with a doll or a made-up friend. When I was little I thought she was the one who solved them." Edwyna attempted a laugh.

"Exactly. You were right. Then. You were right then. Now you are wrong to deny her, to deny her power, your power. Inanna is one of the oldest names of the moon goddess, going back to— but you don't need to know all of that."

"I don't want to seem rude," Edwyna interrupted, "but are you telling me you are a goddess, and my doll is—or I am . . ."

"A goddess? Consider us acolytes, women who have a special relationship with the goddess. We worship the goddess, and the goddess responds to us. What you need to know is that you have the power of the moon, and the strongest times for you are at the new moon and the full moon. Watch the moon when you seek what you want. Wear your special moon-worship clothes, the blue robe with the stars and moon on it."

"How did you know about the robe?" Edwyna asked.

"Because you are truly one of us, no matter what you deny to the outer world, and we each have a garment just like the one I described. You were drawn to your true nature from earliest childhood, then denied it as irrational, and you have waited too long to reclaim it."

Edwyna wanted to protest, but all that Diane had said seemed true, impossible but true. Or although possible, clearly untrue. Clearly crazy. Yet oddly familiar. She looked down at her hands, lost in thought. When she looked up, the other women had gathered in nearby chairs.

"We have a gift for you," Dorothy said. "A gift from all of us." She handed a small jewelry box to Edwyna.

Edwyna opened the box slowly. In it was the most beautifully carved jade brooch in the shape of a rabbit. "I cannot take this," she said. "It's too much. Why? I have nothing for any of you."

"You have given us the gift of returning a Wise Woman to the moon. This is to remind you of our time together last evening," Dorothy said.

"The Jade Rabbit lives on the moon with Chang'e," Carolyn explained. "When you doubt yourself or start to forget all that happened last night, wear the Jade Rabbit."

"Yes," Lila added. "When you want to wear your outer clothing, your concealing clothing, pin this innocent Jade Rabbit to your shoulder. Everyone else will think you are Accountant Edwyna. Only you will know who you really are."

"Inside," Diane concluded.

CHAPTER 21

Home Again

THE FIRST THING Edwyna did when she got home was to fire up her computer and google "Inanna." Just as Diane—or Diana—had said, Inanna was a name for the moon goddess. That part was true. Edwyna read on. She was worshipped in ancient Mesopotamia, dating at least back to 2000 BCE, maybe even 3100 BCE. A priestess, Enheduanna, composed long verses in Inanna's praise. All very interesting, Edwyna thought, but just a coincidence, until she read two more facts. The first was that Inanna was the goddess of love, but also a fickle goddess, one who attracted men, then rejected them. That sounded too close to home, too close at least to recent events. The next fact—at least on the website Edwyna was reading—was that the eight-pointed star was a symbol of Inanna. Edwyna rushed to her closet, although she was fairly certain of what she would see. Indeed, her favorite blue robe was decorated not only with symbols of the moon in all its phases but with stars—eight-pointed stars. She remembered how odd she'd thought the stars were when she had gotten the gown. Five-pointed stars and six-pointed stars were familiar. She hadn't thought anything more of the difference at the time except to note it.

The second thing Edwyna did was to check her voice mail. No call from The Creep. That was good. No personal calls from anyone else. She didn't know who she'd wanted to hear from, but whoever it was, neither he nor she had called. Of course, she reasoned, everyone in her life knew she'd be gone those two weeks, so there was no reason for her to have expected a call, still . . .

Finally she unpacked and fell gratefully into her own bed.

The next morning, Edwyna awakened with that sudden awareness of real time as opposed to vacation time. She'd missed her regular chats with her parents while she was traveling. After a quick call to them, she was on the road to Petaluma. She was struck by the beauties of the drive despite their familiarity. Or maybe because of their familiarity. She admired the towers of the Golden Gate Bridge as she approached it and then smiled at the throng of tourists on the walkway. So many were dressed for summer—October being one of the warmest months in San Francisco—but not for the ever-present chill winds from the Bay. She listened for the tooting horns as she drove through the Waldo Tunnel and remembered how she and Donald would hold their breath when they were children. There was some myth about wishes coming true if you could hold your breath for the entire length of the tunnel. As Edwyna drove north, the busy-ness of southern Marin yielded to the brown hills of Sonoma County. Edwyna exited at San Antonio Road, taking the back way past a combination of pasture and suburban development to her parents' home.

Her father was firing up the barbecue as she arrived, and her mom had prepared Edwyna's favorite accompanying dishes—no-mayo potato salad, sliced tomatoes with olive oil and chopped fresh basil, and a warmed crusty bread. When the food was ready, they all sat at the green wooden picnic table that had been in the yard for as long as Edwyna could remember. The red-checked napkin she spread on her lap was soft with years of use. And the plates were the same green melamine she and Donald had failed to break throughout their childhood.

Edwyna spent several hours describing the many sights to her parents, interrupted frequently by either Edward or Winifred chiming in on their experiences when they'd visited China at least ten years earlier. She'd decided to keep her feelings of loneliness on the first part of the trip to herself and the experiences in Guilin as well.

Then—seemingly out of the blue—Edward asked, "Weren't you in China right at the time of the Moon Festival? Did you see any of the celebrations?"

"I hadn't gotten to that part," Edwyna backpedaled. "We were in Guilin just at the time of the festival. In fact, we were on the Li River."

"Right, the limestone cliffs," Winifred said.

"Lots of boats, lanterns, singing," Edwyna continued.

"How did you feel?" Winifred asked.

"It was interesting. Someone else's holiday. You know what I mean. You watch it, but you aren't part of it." Edwyna realized she was lying to her parents. She got up from the table. "Let me help you clear, Mom," she said and began picking up plates to carry them into the house.

"Not so fast," Edward said.

She wondered if they were going to quiz her further, but then realized her mother had reached behind her, into the cooler, and brought out Edwyna's favorite dessert: lemon meringue pie.

"Welcome home," her mother said.

"Welcome home, darling girl," her dad echoed.

After lunch, Edwyna was in the kitchen with the dishes and her mother. "Mom," she said, "do you remember the doll I had? I got it when I was very young, and . . ."

"Of course I do. You got that doll when you were just four. You wanted it so badly, but I'd said no because you'd gotten another doll for your birthday. You were so angry at me. And then it came in the mail."

"That's just how I remember it," Edwyna said. "I had that doll with me all through college."

"I still have it," Winifred said.

"Excuse me?"

"I still have it. Remember you came home for a few weeks after college, before you moved into your own place? You took your clothes and books, but then you asked me to throw away 'the rest of the junk,' was how you put it. I did throw away most of it. But then I found your doll mixed in a bundle of your papers. I just couldn't throw Inanna away."

"You remember her name," Edwyna said to her mother as the memory of why she'd thrown Inanna into the depths of the mess in her college room closet came back to her.

"How could I forget?" her mother answered. "You opened the box, took one look at the doll, and said, 'Inanna.' You hadn't even named the doll you'd gotten for your birthday, but this one was Inanna, and Inanna she still is." Winifred put the pot she'd washed on the stove to dry and said, "Wait here."

In a few minutes, she returned. She held Inanna on her shoulder, almost like a baby, and patted the doll's back before handing her to Edwyna.

"She looks brand new," Edwyna said. "I remember her as kind of grubby by the time I left school."

"Just the other day, I saw her sitting on a shelf, and I took off all her little clothes and . . ."

"And you washed them?"

"And ironed them. She looks like new. I remember how you used to talk to that doll all the time."

"I never knew you heard me."

"It was so sweet. Your little voice speaking so seriously to the doll. One day I realized . . ."

"Realized what?"

"You used to think that Inanna made things happen for you. And I tried to talk you out of it. To pooh-pooh any ideas of magical thinking."

"That was what I thought. I mean, that's what I thought then. Then, when I was little, that Inanna made things happen for me. But all little kids believe in magic, and I grew out of it."

"That's just the thing," Edwyna's mother said. "Sometimes I think you were right and I was wrong."

"Who was right and who was wrong when?" Edwyna asked.

"I think you have special strengths that you don't use."

"Mom . . . ," Edwyna interrupted, a familiar warning in her mind, probably in her voice.

"Maybe Inanna helped you realize those strengths when you were young," Freddy continued as if Edwyna had not spoken. "I've tried to talk to you about those strengths for the past few years, even recently."

"Really, Mom . . ."

"You always stopped me before I've said all I want to say. You won't let me go there in our conversations. Don't stop me now. You can still have those powers if you choose to use them." Winifred stopped speaking and looked directly at Edwyna. "You've tried living a rational life, living without those powers. You've had a lot of success in your career—and I'm very proud of you—but I know you aren't happy in your . . . your personal life . . . your love life. Why not give this a try?"

Edwyna looked at her mother, then at Inanna still in her mother's arms, then back to her mother. "Does Daddy agree?" Edwyna asked, surprising herself by using her childhood name for her father.

"It's the one thing, maybe the only thing in our long life together, that I have never discussed with him. Remember he's a dyed-in-the-wool skeptic. I think he'd just laugh me out of the house and over the hills."

"I'm not laughing," Edwyna said.

Winifred silently held Inanna out to Edwyna.

Edwyna took the doll from her mother. "I just wish I knew what I thought now."

Back in her flat, Edwyna tried putting Inanna on her bed resting against the pillows. That looked too sappy, so childlike. She tried putting Inanna on the bookshelf next to her desk, but Inanna looked lost among the volumes of tax code. She carried the doll into the living room and looked around. She pulled a small semilunette table from one side of the room to the other and placed it between her chair and the window. It was the perfect size and place for Inanna. A Goldilocks moment, thought Edwyna. Just right.

She hadn't seen Howard since she'd returned, so she wasn't surprised when she heard his special ring on her doorbell.

"Welcome home, welcome home," he said and enfolded her in a giant hug. "Spill all. How was the trip? And the ladies? Did you get along with the ladies? Any woo-woo stuff? Any men?"

"Slow down," Edwyna said. "I'll tell you all if you pour me a glass of wine."

"Your wish, my command, etc. and so on and so forth," Howard said. "Red or white?"

"Your choice. You know where everything is." Edwyna settled into her chair, then popped up again to get a small box from her bedroom.

Howard returned with two goblets of deep red wine. "For you, Madame," he said. "Madame Bubbelah."

"And this is for you," Edwyna said. She handed Howard a box, about six inches long by four inches wide.

"Pour moi?" Howard opened the box which held a replica of a terracotta archer. "Magnificent detail," he exclaimed. "I've read about these, all buried underground. Right?"

Edwyna told him then about X'ian, the Great Wall constructed by the same emperor, and most of what she'd seen and done. She was candid with Howard, her best friend, about her initial feelings of loneliness, but she said nothing about the experiences on the river. She skipped all of what he would have called the "woo-woo stuff."

She was glad he had not spotted Inanna, had not said a word about her.

The next few days were filled with attention to clients and overcoming jet lag. She was tired when she needed to be alert and wide awake when she wanted to be sleeping, but by the following Friday, she felt very much herself. She had worked with every one of her clients who'd filed for extensions, taking the information they provided and adding it to the already substantial files for their 2008 taxes. She had little problem, as these were longtime clients and she'd trained them well, had them storing and sorting their records optimally so that the pain of tax time came only from paying taxes, not from the collecting and computing itself.

That afternoon she'd heard from one of her least favorite clients, a perpetually demanding woman. The client had wanted a forecast of her potential cash flow for the next several months. That wasn't an unreasonable request. It was the tone that was annoying. "I can't rely on luck," the client said. "Or go to some fortune teller to read the stars." Edwyna had laughed to herself at the same time as she'd assured the client she'd be available to see her early on Monday.

She was happy to be home, yet the weekend seemed to stretch empty before her. She wandered between her bedroom and living room, dried a glass and plate that had been sitting on her kitchen counter, picked up the day's *San Francisco Chronicle* which she'd already read from cover to cover, and put it down again. She sat on her sofa, then got up, got a glass of wine, and returned to the sofa. She swirled the glass of wine, then looked into it as if its pattern of moving liquid could yield some answers. She sighed, drank the wine, and returned to the kitchen to refill the glass. Again ensconced on the sofa, she drank some more, swirled some more, and then putting the glass down, she leaned back on the sofa. Out of the corner of her eye she saw Inanna.

Edwyna leaned over the arm of the sofa but, from that position, she could not reach the table that held Inanna. She stood, picked up Inanna, and brought her to the sofa.

"Inanna, why am I so blue?" Edwyna stared at the doll, although she knew the doll could no more answer her than the swirling wine could tell her fortune.

"Inanna, tell me what's going to happen to me. Where am I going? How should I get there?" Inanna stared back at her, her blue eyes unblinking, her arms still, her body held upright only through Edwyna's efforts.

"Inanna, I wish . . . I wish . . ." Edwyna did not let her words complete the thought. What was she doing? Had she slipped back into some childhood pattern so easily? Maybe the second glass of wine was one too many. Maybe . . .

The phone rang. Its bell seemed more jarring than she'd remembered it. It rang again. Edwyna looked at Inanna, put her down, and picked up the phone.

"Hello," she answered with the rising inflection that suggested a question.

"Edwyna, hi. It's me, Nick. Don't hang up please."

"Why would I hang up?"

"I felt I really wasn't very easy to be with when we met last time. I'm afraid I hurt your feelings. I think I made a bit of a fool—well maybe more than a bit—I made quite a fool of myself when we met. You remember when . . ."

"Of course, I remember. But don't worry. You weren't a fool." Edwyna waited to hear why Nick was calling. Was he going to invite her to his wedding?

"Here's the thing of it," Nick said, then hesitated. "Here's why . . . Here's what I mean . . ."

Edwyna had never heard Nick speak in such a disjointed manner. He'd always been as clear and precise in his diction as he was in his dating. Orderly. That was the word that always described Nick. Or at least had described him until he fell heels over head for Gloria. Edwyna wanted to giggle. Heels over head. Head over heels. Boy that wine was working.

"Here's why I'm calling," Nick began again. "I made a big mistake. I know I sounded like a fool—well, what is it they say? 'Only fools fall in love.' I see why. Let's just say I'm over my temporary insanity."

"Are you trying to tell me something about you and Gloria?" Edwyna thought someone had to chase to the cut. She giggled at her reversal. Obviously the wine was muddling her tongue or at least her head.

"Exactly!" There was a note of relief in Nick's voice. "Exactly," he repeated. "There is no more Gloria. That is, there is no more Gloria in my life. And I want to tell you that was a narrow escape."

Edwyna hoped that he didn't really want to tell her the details of the ending, of his "narrow escape."

"But that's not why I'm calling. I know you probably felt let down by me, but I'd really like to see you again. We had a good thing going. We like each other. We have fun together and we're good with each other. You know what I mean?"

Edwyna did know what he meant. And she was tempted. It would be easy to go back to seeing Nick every other week. He satisfied her sexual needs—almost satisfied with his every other week lovemaking—and he didn't demand much of her at all. It was all so regular. They could probably go on as they were for months or even years. Maybe decades.

"Edwyna? Are you there?"

Edwyna realized that her silence had slipped beyond the customary break between the give and take of telephone rhythms. "I'm here," she answered.

"Will you go out with me tomorrow? Or if that's too soon, maybe we could just meet on Sunday in the diner we went to last time. No," Nick answered himself. "Not a good memory. Or maybe you want to wait until next weekend. Go out on Saturday night next weekend, just like we used to do. What do you think? Are you still angry at me for our last conversation? You name the place. You name the date. You name the time. You can count on me. I'll be there."

As alone as she felt in that moment, Edwyna knew that returning to the routine she'd shared with Nick was not what she wanted. Nick might be ready to "be there," as he'd said. The problem was that the connection was no longer there for Edwyna.

"Nick, don't take this the wrong way. I'm not angry with you. I was never angry with you. I just think our time together is over. In fact, I didn't say anything when we last met, but I had been thinking about how I could end our affair."

"I'm afraid you're saying that because I hurt you. I never meant to hurt you. I hope you can forgive me. Consider it temporary insanity."

"I know you may not believe me, but you never hurt me. I wished you the best with Gloria."

"But there is no more Gloria."

"I understand that. And now I wish you the best without Gloria. Maybe, Nick, what each of us wants is what you described as your temporary insanity with Gloria. I think I'm looking for that kind of emotion."

"It hurts. It's great when it's happening, but then it hurts."

"I appreciate that and I'm sorry you're hurting." Edwyna wasn't sure that was quite the truth. "But seeing me or our being together just isn't in the cards. I think it's time we said good-bye. Good-bye, Nick. I hope you find what you want."

"I guess that's it, then," Nick said, and Edwyna heard the click of his disconnect.

Edwyna moved restlessly about the house for the rest of the weekend. She was certain that returning to her affair with Nick would have been the wrong thing for her. But she didn't know what the right thing was. "What am I mooning about?" she asked herself. Or rather, she thought, she wasn't "mooning," whatever that would mean to the Wise Women. They'd said she was now one of them, but she certainly didn't feel very wise. She'd emptied her life of lovers, sex partners, whatever one would call Nick and Joel, made the space between. She'd gone to the women's moon festival. She had her doll and the jade rabbit brooch. What was she supposed to do with all of it? Every now and then, she thought of calling one of them for advice, but they all had their own lives—their own men—and this was the weekend. She didn't want to disturb them. Even more than that, she didn't want to come across as needy.

But she was needy, and by Sunday evening, as she paced around her living room, she finally decided to call Diane. Maybe Diane would have time to see her in the next day or so. Diane must have heard something in her voice, because despite Edwyna's demurrals, she suggested—in fact insisted—that Edwyna come to her home right then and there.

Diane opened her door and her arms, welcoming Edwyna with an embracing hug. Edwyna felt the tension leave her body just as it had the evening of the Chang'e celebration on the Li River.

Diane was the first to speak. "Sit down. Drink some tea. Tell me what's on your mind."

Edwyna told Diane how she felt, how at odds with herself. She told her about Nick's phone call and sticking to her decision to break up with him. "Maybe I was too hasty," Edwyna concluded. "He's a nice enough guy, and maybe I should have someone in my life. I have no one."

"First of all, let's look at where you are now," Diane said. "You don't have 'no one.' You have your Wise Women friends, your family, and your friend, the man who lives in your building. What you mean is that you have no lovers. Right?"

Edwyna nodded.

"That is exactly where you need to be. You no longer want 'lovers'—in the plural. You want a 'love'—in the singular. This is where being a Wise Woman is going to help."

Edwyna thought Diane was going to suggest that the other women or their husbands would provide introductions to so-called suitable candidates. Or that they would come up with a program of strategies and events, like the library speed dating. She'd barely begun to speak, when Diane put her finger over Edwyna's lips.

"You will use your power as an acolyte of the moon goddess to achieve your goal." Diane paused. "Instead of your accounting style of lists and plans, you will pay attention to who you really are."

Diane stopped speaking and looked directly into Edwyna's eyes. As the silence lengthened, Edwyna felt she should say some-thing, offer some response. Just as she was about speak, Diane stopped her with another gentle touch to Edwyna's lips.

"I'll say it once more: You will use your power as an acolyte of the moon goddess to get what you want and what you deserve."

Again Diane was silent. Edwyna recognized some gesture that let her know it was now time for her to speak. "I know you all go to the ceremonies at the start of each month, at each new moon, but I don't know what I'm supposed to do. Am I just sup-posed to wait? To wait from month to month?"

"Nothing as passive as waiting," Diane responded. "You will pay attention. Having awareness is far different from waiting. At all times, you need to know what phase the moon is in. Your most powerful times, you already know, are the new moon and the full moon. Every night and every day, always know the phase of the moon for that specific date. Be ready to look for opportunities during your times of power. Be ready to ask for more during your times of power."

"How do I . . . ?"

"Here's a gift to help you with awareness." Diane reached into a drawer in the end table near the couch where they were sitting. "This is a calendar, organized by the phases of the moon. Look at today's date. You can see the symbol shows a moon waning from fullness. That is always a time to let go. You knew that instinctively. Look back to Friday, when Nick called. Also a time of the waning moon."

"I don't think I knew that," Edwyna said. "It was just a coincidence."

"Perhaps. I don't think so, but you may. Eventually you'll see how coincidence is really synchronicity. What were you doing when Nick called?"

"Just sitting around. I'd had some wine, and . . . I forgot to tell you. When I visited my parents last weekend, my mother still had that doll. Inanna. Remember we talked . . ."

"Of course. But why are you thinking of Inanna now, while we are talking about Nick's phone call?"

Edwyna didn't want to answer, but the truth was there. "Just before he called, I picked up Inanna and . . ." Even more, Edwyna didn't want to say she'd talked to the doll.

"And you began to speak to her," Diane completed her thought.

Edwyna nodded.

"If you really want what you have told me you want, and if you are not afraid to have it, you will talk to the moon goddess at the start of every new moon and at the height of the full moon. I would suggest you address her as Inanna, as that is the name you've always known. But the goddess will answer to Diana, Chang'e, Artemis—any of her names. Tell her what you want. Speak to her as you did when you were a child, with the innocence of childhood."

All Edwyna could think of asking was, "What if it's foggy? And there is no moon?"

"There is always a moon even if you can't see it. That's why you carefully keep the calendar. Be sure to come to our celebrations of the moon at the Baths. That will strengthen your powers. It is difficult to do this alone. Remember you are not alone. You are one of us."

Something about Diane saying "You are one of us" made Edwyna think of the mysterious folder with its ever-changing contents. "One more thing," Edwyna said. "Do you mind if I ask you about one more thing?"

"Not at all. Everything should be open between us, among all of us."

"The folder." Edwyna wasn't sure how to continue. What she was going to say sounded so weird. "There's the folder," she began again. "There's the folder I accidentally picked up at one of our Wise Women meetings or someone gave me. It's really strange."

"Yes," Diane answered without a question in her voice. "We did give it to you. It's meant to help you know us, and through us, yourself."

"I can see what it's about. But here's the strange part. Sometimes the pages seem to rearrange themselves. What was on top one day is no longer there. Something else is in its place." Edwyna felt she was blushing. She hadn't had this feeling of extreme embarrassment since she was a child. "I know that sounds like I'm crazy. But have you . . . has someone . . . come to my home and . . ."

"Crazy? Not at all. Let me see if I can explain. The folder is part of a larger work, *The Book of Moon Energy*. As such, it has an energy of its own, an energy that works with the life force of those reading it. Does this make sense so far?"

Edwyna nodded yes, then shook her head no.

"Let me explain it another way. Have you heard of Heisenberg's uncertainty principle"?

"I think so. It has something to do with physics." Edwyna remembered reading articles in popular magazines, probably in the dentist's office. "Right?"

"Yes. The principle is that an observer is not a being apart from her experiment. The observer affects the behavior of the very thing she is observing."

"I do remember reading that. It seemed bizarre. Almost like . . ."

"'Like magic' is what I think you were about to say." Diane continued, "Why not? Scientists are looking for a particle they call the God Particle. It's all connected."

"Are you saying I somehow made the pages move in the folder?"

"Maybe sometimes you did shuffle them without being aware of it, and sometimes the moon energy was at work with you. Your looking into the folder brought about changes. That is the uncertainty principle at work."

"I get it. Sort of," Edwyna said.

"All of our work is based on our observing and then manifesting. That is why I've urged you to watch the phases of the moon, to continue to talk to Inanna, to look into the candle at our new moon ceremony."

After a pause, Edwyna said, "This is a lot to take in."

"I know, my dear. But you don't have to understand it all. Just remember to concentrate your awareness on the moon, to speak to Inanna, to accept and trust your own powers."

Edwyna thanked Diane and rose to leave.

"Before you go," Diane said, "think about this. You have had success using your rational mind, success in your career. For this other side of your life, your intimate life, you need the powers you've denied. Why not try them and see what happens?"

For a moment, Edwyna wanted to ask Diane if she'd been talking to her mother. They had used almost the same words in urging her to put her old—or rather newfound—powers to work. She wished she could ask her father what he thought.

"One more thing," Diane said as she walked Edwyna to the door, "the man you are seeking is someone you already know."

"How do you . . . ? Who is . . . ?" Questions flooded Edwyna's mind, but she could not articulate them.

"I saw him in the candlelight, but I don't know any more than I already told you," Diane replied to the half-spoken questions.

Edwyna mused about the ideas of power and knowledge, of certainty and uncertainty, as she drove home. She thought about the kachina dolls, which she'd again noticed on Diane's walls. How could you help but notice? she thought. She wondered if Diane also used those figures in some ceremony. The thought made her feel squeamish. They were so strange with their feathers, flat bodies, and featureless faces. Edwyna shook her shoulders as if that would rid her of her thoughts. The idea of using the phases of the moon and of talking to Inanna were strange enough. Too strange. She didn't need to add anything more to the menu of weird.

Back in her living room, she knew right away where she would put the calendar of moon phases. She picked up the folder and opened it to slip in the pages of the calendar. On top of the pile of pages, she did not see any of the women's birth stories nor any of the newspaper articles. Instead there appeared to be a series of email messages printed out on ordinary paper. The first was from Lila to Diane. Edwyna read:

————— ✺✺✺ —————

Dear Diane,

Thank you for your invitation to San Francisco. I'm very glad to hear that we may all gather there before long. I have some things I need to clear up with my work before I can move because, as you know, New York City provides many opportunities for women with our abilities, but you will certainly hear from me before the appointed date.

Yours in Sisterhood,

Lila

————— ✺✺✺ —————

The second was from Carolyn to Lila.

————— ✺✺✺ —————

Dear Lila,

This is to introduce myself—Carolyn—as I think we've both heard from Diane in San Francisco. I am seriously thinking of taking her up on her invitation. I was settling in very nicely here in Toronto and it will not surprise you to hear I have recently adopted a beautiful tabby, but Diane's invitation for all of us to gather in San Francisco is irresistible.

Yours in Sisterhood,

Carolyn

————— ✺✺✺ —————

The last was also from Lila, this time to Dorothy.

Dear Dorothy,
I am looking forward to meeting you when we are all in San Francisco. While New York City provides plenty of opportunities for me, I can only imagine the riches you must experience in New Orleans. Please let me know when you'll arrive and how I might be of help.
  Yours in Sisterhood,
  Lila

Of all the papers and pages in the folder, this was the most interesting to Edwyna. It was clear, even from this scattered email correspondence, that Diane had invited all the women to San Francisco and they had all accepted her invitation. While the intent of the emails was clear, what Edwyna found intriguing was the idea that these three women, with established lives, had picked up and moved to San Francisco at Diane's invitation. Three women and their husbands! She remembered Lila saying that it was her grandsons being in San Francisco that had made her decide to move. Perhaps there were no grandsons; the grandsons were just a fiction. On the other hand, maybe the story of the grandsons was true and all of this folder stuff was just some form of fiction, a grand tale that the women enjoyed creating. Talk about uncertainty!

Edwyna put the calendar into the folder and enclosed both in her desk drawer. She wandered over to her window to look out at the waning moon.

Inanna sat on her semilunette table. Silent.

"Do you have anything to say about all of this?" Edwyna asked her.

Inanna did not answer.

CHAPTER 22

Casting About

EDWYNA KNEW THAT Diane had told her not to make lists, to wait, watch, and then act. But her list-making habit was so firmly ingrained that she could not resist trying. She took the calendar that Diane had given her out of the folder, picked up a blue pencil, and tried to translate her new instructions into a list.

1. Watch the phases of the moon
   New Moon to Full Moon=Waxing Moon: Time for Gains
   Full Moon to New Moon=Waning Moon. Time for Loss
2. Talk to Inanna about what I want
3. Wear the jade brooch

This was not even a vaguely satisfying list. There was nothing on it she could actually do. Even if she did sometimes speak to Inanna, it was more like thinking aloud. She could not see herself actually speaking to the doll. Perhaps what Diane had meant was that she should pray to Inanna. Praying was even less likely. She turned away from her desk to face Inanna sitting on her table. "Give me a break!" Edwyna said to the doll. Edwyna looked at the list again. She did like the idea of the moon as a sort of bookkeeping device, a means to keep track of gains and losses. The only action she could take would be to go to the new moon bath celebrations with the Wise Women. She added that as Number 4 to her list.

While Edwyna was sitting at her desk glumly contemplating her list, or rather her nonlist, the phone rang. She recognized the number. It was the one Inspector MacArthur—Doug—had given her.

After initial greetings and the usual question about whether this was a good time, Doug said, "I have some news for you about Hank. And about the caller who bothered you."

Maybe something was going to happen in her life after all. "Yes. What?"

"First, I can tell you that Hank's real name is Herman Karlinsky. And he is wanted in California and several other Western states for abusing women, particularly older women."

"Older women?" was all Edwyna could say.

"Don't get caught up in that detail. The important thing is that we now have him and he is in custody awaiting trial. And you have nothing more to fear from him. I am really grateful for that. If he ever . . ."

"Was he the caller?"

"Yes. In an odd way. On his computer, he had recordings of several different male voices. All making threats, suggestive comments, or expressing obscenities. We are still trying to find out if he had a willing accomplice in recording these or got them in some other way."

"How else might he have gotten them?"

"This is just a guess, but as you know, he can be quite persuasive. He might have tricked someone or ones into thinking it was a prank or even an audition for something. We don't know, but we hope to find out. In any event, once we arrested Mr. Karlinsky, all calls stopped."

"How did you find him?"

"Remember I told you about putting a trap on a phone? We had enough complaints that we encouraged two other women to put traps on theirs. And they both led us to Karlinsky's setup. Which, by the way, was hardly the luxury apartment you visited. It was little more than a rat hole. A small room in a deserted factory. He was squatting there, squatting with a computer and other electronics."

Edwyna wanted to ask about the other women. Were they her age? Did Doug find one—or both—of them attractive? She didn't know why she cared, as she'd already turned him down for a date. And now he was winding down the conversation without another hint of anything personal. Just asking her if she had any questions about Karlinsky or the case.

"Thank you for letting me know," Edwyna said. "It will be a relief to answer the phone without that shiver of suspicion."

"There's one more thing," Doug said. "If the case comes to court, you may have to testify. Can we count on you for your testimony?"

Edwyna assured him that he could and the call ended. That conversation was completely impersonal, Edwyna thought, after she'd hung up the phone. Of course, that was as it should be. She was actually glad she didn't have to turn Doug down again. He was a nice man, for someone else, but not for her. Besides, this was the waning time of the month, the time for separating, not connecting, if she believed in any of that stuff about the phases of the moon.

A few days later, Edwyna was as restless as she'd been on the weekend, before she'd visited Diane. She sat at her dining table, cursorily turning the pages of the *San Francisco Chronicle*. She was so bored, she read the Dear Abby column, grimacing at the thought of the lives the questions suggested. Her eyes drifted across the page onto the horoscopes. Hers read:

Looking for love in all the wrong places? Today is your day. If you are wired into the universe, you will find your one and only. A good day to shop for electronics. Enough said.

How ridiculous, Edwyna thought. Why would anyone use their horoscope for direction? But lots of people did, didn't they? She remembered something about Nancy Reagan directing Ronald's decisions based on the stars. Look how that had worked out! But hadn't Diane said something about accepting all sources of knowledge? Surely she hadn't meant the newspaper horoscope. Edwyna looked at the clock. Enough of this nonsense. She brought her coffee cup and cereal bowl into the kitchen, brushed imaginary crumbs from her pants suit, pinned the jade rabbit to her jacket, and left for work.

The work day ended in what appeared to be the start of a lovely warm evening. Edwyna had taken the Muni to her office and, leaving it, she decided to stroll for a few blocks, from the Montgomery to the Powell station, before boarding the N-Judah for the ride home. She was about halfway between her office and Powell Street when she realized she was in front of True Buys, probably the largest electronics chain in the area. She looked at the sign, smiled to herself, and continued on. As she walked, she found herself mentally rehearsing what she would ask for if she were to go back to the store. After all, she couldn't say, "I've come to meet my one and only. Or, she pictured herself saying, "Where is the one true love department?" Almost two blocks later, she realized she needed a new wireless keyboard and mouse. Not that she really needed one, but maybe she wanted one. Or she'd just look at them to see what was new. She turned back to the store.

Blinking from the setting sun, Edwyna entered the store. She paused a moment to let her eyes adjust to the interior light. If everyone who'd read the horoscope had gone to an electronics store to find true love, surely the store would be crowded. It would seem more like a bar scene on a Friday evening than an electronics store. Hundreds of people would be flooding every TV and computer store in the land. True Buys was fairly quiet with a few customers clearly intent on the merchandise, not on each other.

"Can I help you?" A uniformed young woman stood ready to direct customers to the departments they wanted.

"Just browsing," Edwyna said.

"Yeah, browsing for a man," she thought she heard the young woman say until she realized the words were her own, not uttered except in her mind.

Edwyna wandered through telephones, televisions, and sound systems into the huge computer department. Large sections of shelves displayed monitors, computers, routers, and more. Other shelves held covers for notebooks and e-readers, covers that ranged from bright dayglow neoprene to dark leather, from covers that shouted, *Look at me, look at what I have,* to covers that murmured, in a proper British accent, *I am here for a serious business purpose.*

She'd just picked up an elegant leather Kindle cover—although she didn't own a Kindle—when she heard a voice behind her say, "May I help you?"

She was ready with her line about wireless keyboards. As she turned, she started to say, "I was just browsing . . ." when she realized the salesman she was looking at was Bob, Biblio-Dating Bob, Soup Man Bob. She was sure it was him.

"Hi," Edwyna said.

"Hello," Bob said and repeated, "may I help you?"

"I'm looking . . . I'm interested in a wireless keyboard," Edwyna said.

"Right this way." Bob pointed in a generally leftish direction. "Follow me."

Edwyna followed Bob. So much for scoffing at horoscopes, she thought.

Bob pointed to an array of keyboards on a shelf. "The most popular brands are . . ."

Edwyna barely listened. She was thinking of how to ask Bob if he . . .

"Of course if you want an ergonomic keyboard, then you would want to consider this one." Bob pointed to a strangely curved model. "Do you spend a lot of time keyboarding? May I ask you a personal question?"

This was it. Now he was going to ask if she remembered him. Edwyna nodded. "Sure," she said.

"Do you find your wrists hurt at the end of the day or even bother you at night, disturbing your sleep?" Bob didn't wait for an answer, but continued, "Because if you do have that problem, you may want to switch to this ergonomic model. It makes a big difference, especially for more mature people."

"More mature?" This was just like Doug's talking about older women. Edwyna didn't realize she'd asked the question aloud until Bob answered.

"I mean the kids—the school kids—they don't seem bothered at all about how they misuse their bodies. But we adults have learned to pay attention. This model is somewhat pricey, but definitely worth it." Bob was deep into selling the curved keyboard.

"Do you mind if I ask you a personal question?" This time it was Edwyna who asked.

"Not at all," Bob said, although his face did not register welcome, his salesman's smile having faded.

"Not actually a question," Edwyna said. "I think we've met before."

"Have you shopped at True Buys before? Did I help you? I'm sorry that I didn't recognize you. Please forgive me. There are just so many customers I see in a day. Not that your needs aren't important."

Edwyna was afraid Bob was going to collapse in his paroxysms of apologies. "No, I didn't mean here." She was about to ask him about the meeting in the supermarket, but then realized that if he hadn't remembered their meeting in the supermarket when they met at Biblio-Dating, he was surely not going to remember it now. "I think we may have met in the library. At the Main Branch?" She finished her sentence as a question.

"I don't think so," Bob said. "I read e-books."

"Of course. That makes sense. I mean working here. And all," Edwyna said. She was sure she was blushing. Maybe this wasn't Soup Man. But he looked just like him. And sounded like him too. Not only was her face on fire, but she felt rivulets of sweat draining from her armpits toward her waist. She could not resist asking one more question. It wasn't that she wanted him to acknowledge having met her or even to pin him to the truth. Her embarrassment was like a toothache, the kind of toothache that makes you want to keep biting down, just to be sure it still hurts. "I went to a special event at the library. About three months ago. It wasn't just about books. Might you have been there?"

"I'm sorry," Bob said. "I really don't know why I would have been in the library if it wasn't about books and, as I said, I don't even go there for books. But I do like to read. You may be surprised," he said, "but my favorites are cookbooks. I've recently started cooking for myself, and . . ."

"Sorry, I have to run," Edwyna said, looking at her watch.

"This keyboard . . . ," Bob began.

But Edwyna had stopped metaphorically gritting her teeth and turned her back on Soup Man, Biblio-Dating, Bullshitting Bob. She was only sorry that she had even used the word "sorry."

Diane was right. Waning moon.

Although Edwyna didn't have to hurry home, she picked up her pace as she walked toward the Powell Street Station. It was rush hour and the streetcar, which ran underground at this point, was full, almost too full. Edwyna let the force of the crowd behind her push her into the car. She grabbed an overhead bar to steady herself as the streetcar began to move. Edwyna's height let her see over the heads of the other passengers. She liked that. There was no need to avoid eye contact, as few people were at eye level with her.

As she stared straight ahead into the crowd, she saw a familiar face. At least she thought it was a familiar face. Doug. At the other end of the car. She was wiggling her arm loose from the press of people around her, about to wave to Doug, when she realized he was not alone. His head was bent in apparent conversation with a blonde woman, a woman almost as tall as he was, almost as tall as Edwyna. She wished she could hear what they were saying. She couldn't hear a word, but she did see the blonde throw back her head—seemingly oblivious to others around her—in what could only be a hearty laugh. Or maybe it was that flirtatious move women use where they let their hair fall forward over their foreheads and then fling it back. Maybe it wasn't Doug. After all, she'd only seen the man in profile, but then the streetcar lurched a bit and everyone's position shifted slightly. It was Doug. Or not. Maybe the woman was just a business acquaintance. Or his neighbor.

The rest of the ride home Edwyna mused about the coincidence of meeting Bob and seeing Doug on the same day. Indeed within the same hour. San Francisco was a small town masquerading as a big city. Lila often marveled at how many friends and acquaintances she'd meet by chance in San Francisco comparing that to New York City where she knew many more people but rarely saw any of them without planning. Edwyna decided the coincidence was just that. It didn't mean a thing.

It certainly wasn't a coincidence that she met Howard in front of their building. This was the end of a work day. She was happy to return to the reality of life's routines, a reality that needed no exploration.

"What a gorgeous evening," Howard said. "How's work?"

"Work is fine, but . . ."

"Uh oh. Wherein, fair maiden, lies the 'but'? Come up for a glass of wine and tell all."

When Edwyna and Howard were settled on his sofa, a bottle of Sonoma-Cutrer on the table in front of them, glasses in hand, Howard said, "Sooo . . ."

"You won't believe what a strange afternoon I had. I saw Soup Man Bob again. This is the third time. The first time . . ."

"I remember. First the supermarket. Second the speed-dating time at the library. Where did you see him? Were you haunting the soup aisles of grocery stores in the vain hope . . . well clearly no longer a vain . . . ?"

"He's a salesman at True Buys."

"What were you shopping for? You didn't tell me you were in the market for any electronics. You know I can help you . . ."

"Never mind. I just wandered in. Let's get back to seeing Soup Man."

"I know there's more to the story than that, but what's bugging you?" Howard asked.

"Remember that very first time I saw him and you laughed at my saying I thought I'd see him again?"

"Sure. So what?"

Edwyna swirled the wine in her glass, then looked at the ripples. "Don't you think it's strange that I keep meeting him? In odd places?"

"San Francisco is a small city. Surely you have heard of coincidence." Howard took a long sip of his wine. "This is good stuff, I've got to say."

"Here's another one. Also today. Right after I left True Buys I got on the N-Judah and who was there? In the same car?"

"I give up. Nick? Joel? The prophet Elijah?"

"Doug!"

"Now that's interesting. Did you speak to him?" Howard looked at Edwyna over the rim of his glass.

"He was too far away. The other end of a crowded car. Besides, he looked like he was with someone, a tall blonde woman."

"Who?"

"How should I know?" Edwyna knew her annoyance was with the situation, not with Howard, but she could not keep her feelings out of her voice.

Howard poured some more chardonnay into Edwyna's glass. "Calm down. Drink up. I thought you didn't like him."

"I never said I didn't like him. I guess I'm confused," Edwyna said and followed Howard's orders to drink. "Speaking of confused," she continued, "have you ever heard of the uncertainty principle?"

"Sure. You must be talking about Heisenberg's uncertainty principle," Howard answered.

"It means scientists who conduct experiments influence the outcomes. Is that true?"

"Where did you get that interpretation?"

"I was asking Diane about the folder. Remember I showed it to you before I went to China and talked about how the pages seemed to change places within it? Diane suggested that my thinking of what was in the folder, somehow . . ."

"Good grief! Spare me your pop-physics. If you want to become all moony, go ahead. But don't—please don't—pretend there is some scientific basis behind your thinking."

"You don't have to get all huffy about it!"

Howard drained his glass, refilled it, and took several more swallows before he spoke again. "Yeah. Sorry. You pushed one of my buttons. It's just when serious scientific discoveries are popularized so that they lose all meaning, that I—never mind. It's not your fault. Do you want me to explain the uncertainty principle? Will that make up for my anger?"

"No," Edwyna said. "But another glass of wine will do it."

They relaxed against the cushions of the couch. Edwyna, sipping her wine, thought about Doug and the blonde.

Edwyna waited impatiently for the day of the New Moon. She was determined to take advantage of what she thought of as "The Good Days."

On the night of the new moon, she met the Wise Women at the Baths. Once more, they went through the calming rituals of bathing, steaming, and tea drinking. Again they retired to their private room and donned their white robes. This time Edwyna felt completely with it. She recited the opening verse. She was shivering as they moved toward the moment of lighting the candle. She expected Diane to hold the candle to her for lighting and was disappointed when it was Carolyn who was asked.

"Before we begin," Diane said, "I sense some tension in the room. Too much expectation. Remember our goddess asks us to be patient, to remember that there is an endless repetition of new moons. The moon is as old as the earth. It was here long before any of us, long before humans, and it will be here for each of us for as long as we live. Let us each take some deep breaths before we begin the candle lighting." After a few moments of quiet and deep breathing, Diane said, "Remember to look at the moon once more. Remember to think about what you want the moon to manifest for you. Then close your eyes."

As before, the tall purple candle sat on the table, waiting to be lit. Edwyna and the others sat in their linen chairs, their eyes closed. Edwyna felt the rustle of Carolyn's robe as she rose to light the candle. She heard the match strike the flint. She kept her eyes closed and held her hands over her eyes. Once again, as she had the first time in the Baths, she felt warmth on each of her cheeks. And once again, there was a fleeting image of a man. As she heard the murmur of her friends' voices, Edwyna opened her eyes.

Edwyna was about to ask Diane whether her sensation of warmth had come from the candle or some other source, to ask her if the shadowy man in both her visions had been the same man, and to ask her how she might find that man or even just find out who he was—when Diane put her finger across Edwyna's lips, silencing her. Edwyna wavered between resenting this repeated silent admonition and savoring the warmth of Diane's finger on her lips.

In the changing room, as the women shed their white robes and reached into lockers for their slacks, shirts, and sweaters, Edwyna remembered her questions about the email invitations, the invitations that had brought Carolyn, Lila, and Dorothy from their homes to San Francisco.

On their way back to their cars, Edwyna found herself walking alone with Lila. This was her opportunity. "I was thinking about all of us, about how everyone but me comes from someplace else. That is not from California." Edwyna thought her own words sounded awkward, as awkward as she felt in asking the question.

"Right," Lila said. And kept walking. Her car keys were out in her hand and Edwyna feared the moment was about to disappear.

"I was just wondering how you all, how you, for instance, managed to just pick up, leave what you'd been doing. Leave New York, for instance. And your husband?"

"I hear a question in your voice. But I'm not sure what you're asking. I didn't leave my husband."

They were at Lila's car.

"I don't mean leave your husband. I meant how did you and your husband manage to leave your careers, just pick up and come to California when Diane asked you to?"

"Well, it wasn't as simple as you make it sound. It took some doing, a couple of years, but we were both—in our own way—ready to make some changes. California beckoned anyway. Remember, our grandchildren are here."

Edwyna was about to try to dig deeper when Lila opened her car door.

"Speaking of grandchildren," Lila said, "I've got to run. They're sleeping over. I'd better get home and rescue Alan."

Lila was already in the car, the motor running, when she rolled down the window. "I guess by now you have experienced that when Diana calls, there's no resisting her. She knows where we are needed."

Lila had already driven off when something she said echoed in Edwyna's mind. Hadn't Lila said "Diana," not "Diane?" Probably a slip of the tongue. What difference would it make? It was true that Diane—or Diana—was always able to persuade Edwyna to do what she wanted. She was irresistible. Edwyna thought of asking the other women, but she knew in her heart they would have the same matter-of-fact answers. Whatever mystery there was would remain mysterious. If she was going to accept that she herself had powers, powers that came from the moon, then why shouldn't she accept the fact that three powerful women could find a way to make the move, with their willing husbands, from New York, New Orleans, or Toronto to San Francisco?

Despite Diane's promise—as Edwyna now saw it—that there would be some event, some change in her life, in her status during the first two weeks of the month, nothing happened. Every evening she dutifully sat in front of her window, holding Inanna. Although she was alone, she whispered her thoughts. "I wish, I wish I could find the man who will truly love me." As she whispered the words, she looked at the night sky, from the sky to Inanna and then back again to the sky. She leaned back in her chair, holding Inanna to her heart, and pictured the feeling of a man's lips on her, his hands cradling her face. Nothing else happened.

Winter had set in early, one of those San Francisco winters that brought rain and clouds every day and evening. The El Niño, it was called. El Boring was what Edwyna called it. Damp shoes, dripping rain coat, umbrella drying in the tub or on the office floor. If there was much more rain, she thought she'd turn green with mold.

Not only was she disappointed as each day passed without a sign from the moon goddess or any one at all, but her encounter with Soup Man Bob had left her more morose than she'd expected. At first, she'd found it amusing. He was so much the same in each encounter—self-absorbed, to put it mildly. Then he joined the pantheon of losers and weirdoes she'd met in the past several months, from Vlad, the imposter-not-the-impaler, to Hank (aka Herman), whom she felt lucky to have escaped.

Seeing Doug—if it was Doug—with another woman continued to bother her. She couldn't write Doug off as another loser-weirdo, nor could she consign him to the Joel-Nick group of those she'd rejected as unsuitable. He'd been a possibility that never had a chance. Now she'd never know what might have been. At some point, one of her clients had said in acceptance of his current financial status, "It is what it is." She hadn't understood what he meant. But now she got it. There were just some circumstances over which she had no control. Doug. It is what it is. Or it was what it was.

The rest of the month went by the same way. Edwyna tried to forget about the whole moon goddess thing. Every now and then, as she passed Inanna, she'd pat her head, as if Inanna were an old dog that had given up the chase and lay around each day.

She only realized she'd missed a new moon celebration when Dorothy called to ask where she'd been. Edwyna sloughed the call off with excuses of work and family stuff. She knew she'd been unconvincing but she didn't really care. In fact, she hadn't even bothered to incorporate the symbols for the phases of the moon into what she thought of as her "real calendar."

She rationalized her lack of interest in the new moon celebration. After all, she hadn't seen the moon in what felt like weeks.

CHAPTER 23

If Wishing Could Make It So

EDWYNA FLIPPED THROUGH the local evening news programs—CBS, NBC, ABC—hoping to hear there was going to be a change in the weather. But they all told the same story. As happened every time there was an El Niño winter, hillsides in the Bay Area became unstable, endangering homes perched at their tops. Another neighborhood under stress was identified. There were the now-too-familiar pictures of people hurriedly packing their cars with a combination of necessities and precious items— wedding, baby, and graduation photos. Whole lives—and their pets—were jammed into the family car or truck. Edwyna knew she should feel grateful that what she was experiencing was minor compared to the people she was watching. But it was ennui not gratitude that she felt as the phone rang. Slumped on the couch, she almost didn't answer it. But then she experienced the premature annoyance that would come if it were a call she had to return. She reached for the phone on the fourth ring and answered in a voice that did not conceal her overall malaise.

"I wasn't sure you'd be happy to hear from me, but I didn't think I'd actually hear such sadness in your voice," a man said.

"Who is this?" Edwyna answered with more than a hint of annoyance.

"Sorry. Maybe I'd better start over. Hi, it's Doug."

"Doug?"

"Douglas. Douglas MacArthur."

"Now I'm sorry," Edwyna answered. "Sorry I didn't recognize your voice right away. My mind was elsewhere."

"I heard that in your voice. Is something the matter?"

"Not really. Just the weather. That damned rain . . ."

"I'm glad it's not me."

"Not you at all." Edwyna had no idea of where this conversation was going.

"I hope you remember that awhile ago I said I'd like to see more of you."

"Yes, I remember," Edwyna said.

"I also said I was dogged."

"I thought you meant in looking for Hank or The Creep."

"I did mean that as well. But I wanted you to know that I wasn't going to give up on seeing you. Just to be clear—seeing you with no connection to work. Have you had enough time?"

"What do you mean?"

"You said you needed time. 'To hunker down,' was the expression you used. I'm asking if you've finished hunkering."

"Yes," Edwyna said. "I'm finished hunkering. Now I'm into simple sitting. Sitting and staring at the rain."

"We can't have that. It's obviously my job to get you out of the house. Into the sunshine. Would you accompany me tomorrow for a walk on sunny Ocean Beach?"

"I'm happy to go somewhere with you." Edwyna realized that what had started as a polite response was actually the truth.

"Great! It will be our first date. I'll pick you up at eleven in the morning. Is that time okay?"

"The time is fine. But how do you plan to arrange for sunshine? Is a walk on the beach a wise choice for our first date—as you called it—in this weather?"

"Trust me. I'll see you tomorrow morning."

When Edwyna fell asleep that night, she could still hear the rain hitting her roof. The first thing she did as she awakened was to listen. She heard no rain. She got out of bed, went to the window, opened the blinds. Sunshine. Maybe this was a good omen for the day, although she was sure the beach would be too soggy and the sidewalk alongside the beach would be full of puddles, muddy puddles of sand that the wind had blown beyond the sea wall.

Exactly at eleven, Edwyna's doorbell rang.

"See. Just as I promised," Doug greeted her and gestured toward the sky.

"You are a man of your word," Edwyna said, then felt a frisson of embarrassment as she thought not only of Hank the liar but of Doug's knowing all about Hank.

"Right this way," Doug said and held open the door of his black Prius.

A short ride later, they were parked in an almost empty parking lot off the Great Highway, and they began their walk along the sidewalk. Storms were still at play somewhere over the ocean, and they stopped frequently to watch the breakers heave their way on shore. They leaned on the parapet of the sea wall, raising one arm, then another, to point out gulls and other sea birds gliding overhead and swooping in for whatever delicacies they had spotted in the sand or at the edge of the beach where sand and water met.

"I always love it here," Edwyna said. "A great way to begin the day."

"Did you say 'to begin our date'?"

"I could have, but . . ." Edwyna realized that Doug was laughing. Obviously he'd heard her correctly. She turned back to look at the water. After a few moments she said, "I have such great memories of my childhood times at the beach with my parents and my brother Donald. One time," she began. Then she realized she was about to tell Doug the story of Donald's fall and how, at the time, she'd thought it was her fault. She wasn't sure she wanted to let him into . . . into what? Into her family? Into an idea of how she thought then? Into . . ."

"You started to tell me about another time here."

"Not here. At another beach. Dillon Beach. Do you know it?"

"Sure. Near Tomales Bay."

Edwyna realized Doug was waiting for her to go on. She continued to look out over the beach and ocean as she told him the story of Donald's misadventure, Inanna, and her feelings of guilt that day.

Doug was quiet for a while after the story. Then he took Edwyna's hand to continue their walk. They had walked almost all the way from the southernmost beginning of the walk to its northern end and were part way up the hill, in front of the giant camera, the "Camera Obscura," when the sky suddenly grew dark, let loose a few fat drops of rain, and then a torrent of water. Doug tightened his grip on Edwyna's hand and they ran farther up the hill into the shelter of the Cliff House, a combination bistro-bar-restaurant.

"You promised sunshine," Edwyna said as she shook her wet hair back off her face.

"Never said how much or for how long," Doug said. He lifted one wet lock that had remained draped over her eye and put it back in its rightful place. "I was going to suggest brunch after our walk. Is this okay?"

"Lovely," Edwyna said, relieved they had not run for shelter at the Beach Chalet, the restaurant on the other side of the road, the restaurant where she'd first encountered Hank. She kept those thoughts to herself.

Mimosas and lunch went down easily, as did the conversation. Edwyna's story about Donald had opened the way for each of them to talk about their childhood. She learned that Doug was also a native Californian. He'd grown up right in San Francisco, came from a long line of policemen. He'd gone to local Catholic elementary and high schools. He hadn't even left the city for college, attended the University of San Francisco. "After two years of living on campus," he said, "I was ready to branch out some more. Rented a house with a few other guys—and girls—and I've essentially been on my own since then. I live almost directly across the park from you, in the Richmond."

By the time they'd finished their meal, the sun was out again. They walked slowly back to Doug's car, still telling stories of their childhood. When they reached her house, Edwyna didn't want the day to end.

"Would you like to come up?"

"Of course. You have that magic coffee maker."

"Make yourself comfortable," Edwyna said. "I want to get out of these clothes." As soon as she was in her bedroom, pulling her wet sweater over her head, she felt self-conscious undressing with Doug right there, on the other side of the wall. "They're still damp. How about you? Are you okay?" She called through the closed door.

"I've taken off my shoes. But that's as far as I intend to go," Doug called back.

Edwyna sped up her undressing and dressing.

"Is this a new addition?" Doug asked, pointing to Inanna.

"Do you remember everything? Notice everything?" Edwyna asked.

"I do have a good memory. As for noticing, I can't help it. That's my cop training—especially when it's something or someone important to me."

"That's the doll that was in the story. Inanna."

"You still have it?"

"As it happens, my mother discovered it a few weeks ago and gave it back to me. Coffee. Decaf or caf? Espresso or Americano?"

Doug did not leave until early in the evening and not before he'd asked her to dinner the next night. At some point during the day, Edwyna had thought of asking Doug about the blonde she'd seen him with on the Muni. But the question had slipped away as quickly as it had intruded itself on a lovely moment. She'd ask him another time. If she felt like it.

The morning after the second date, Edwyna left her home humming. She stopped to watch her two elderly Chinese neighbors performing their morning tai chi in front on the landings of the building next to hers. She'd seen them many times, but today they looked incredibly beautiful and coordinated in their balletlike movements, bending at the knees, stretching an arm, turning into a new pose. She watched them for a few minutes and was about to walk on to the Muni stop when Howard stepped out of his door.

Howard gave Edwyna a mock toe-to-head stare. "Must be a good morning," he said. "You are indeed very mellow yellow."

"You mean my new raincoat?" Edwyna was wearing a new yellow slicker that she'd bought in an attempt to shed the seemingly endless rainy day blues.

"That's the 'yellow' part," Howard answered. "The mellow part comes from something else, I think. Or I should say

I know. Didn't I see a certain someone leaving your apartment yesterday?"

"Don't be coy. Doug was here."

"Something new in your Creep case?"

"No. That's all over with. I told you what he'd found and that Hank-Herman was gone."

"That's what I thought. I told you he liked you. I told you. Bubbe's boy is never wrong when it comes to matchmaking."

"It was just two dates."

"Aha! The plot thickens. I only knew about one." Howard's voice took on a different tone as he began to sing, "Edwyna's got . . ."

"If you start chanting 'Edwyna's got a boyfriend,' your bubbe will never see you again."

"Bubbe's in a place where she sees all, knows all."

"I know that. I'm saying . . . Oh just cut it out."

"Tell all and I'll be quiet."

"Truly nothing to tell but two dates."

"Did you have a good time? Did you, you know?" Howard wiggled his eyebrows.

"The answer to both is none of your business, and yes and no. And that's all I have to say. I feel like we are in junior high school."

"Junior high school is just a state of mind. C'mon, I'll walk you to the Muni."

Edwyna and Howard waved at the two women who smiled and continued their routine.

That evening, as Edwyna got dressed for another date with Doug, she giggled to herself. If Howard had known about the third date for the third day in a row, he would have been irrepressible.

He'd probably have been at her door with Greg. Both of them checking on how she looked, what she'd say. Right now she really wanted to hug her growing—growing friendship—growing relationship—growing whatever—to her heart. "Slow down," she said to herself. "Slow down." She didn't feel rushed by Doug. He was easy to be with. But his easiness with her and her ease with him made her feel she'd known him forever.

Maybe there was danger in that sense of ease. Look how she'd been taken in by Hank-Herman. But she hadn't felt easy with him. Maybe Doug was just a smoother type of . . . She couldn't finish the sentence for herself. Surely he was not going to abuse her unless building her up and then dropping her down was his particular form of abuse. Edwyna continued to fix her hair, ready herself for her date, but the seed of suspicion she'd planted had not died.

That evening after a long, conversation-filled dinner, Doug and Edwyna came back to her apartment as had already become their habit. Edwyna went into the kitchen to start the Xpresso and Doug followed her.

"What style?" she asked him. "Intensenato or Delicato?"

"Both," he answered and slipped his arms around her. He hugged her back against his chest, then turned her around.

He was right. The first kiss started as delicato and then turned quickly into intensenato.

Still kissing, they walked from the kitchen, through the living room, and into her bedroom.

Somehow they managed to shed their clothes without letting go of each other. They made love with the excitement of new lovers, the excitement that comes with anticipation released. At the same time, there was none of the awkwardness of a couple unused to each other's bodies. Their breath mingled sweetly.

Their sweat felt as perfumed as the oils of Arabia. Their parts fit together seamlessly—her breasts against his chest, his arms supporting them, her legs around his backside.

When they had both climaxed and lay satisfied in each other's arms, Edwyna said, "Yes. Delicato and so very, very intensenato." She looked away from Doug's eyes for a moment. "Look at our clothes. Helter skelter. All over the room." She leaned down from the bed to pick up a stray garment. Doug pulled her back to him.

"Not yet," he said. "Not yet." The kissing began again.

The next evening, Edwyna and Doug stayed at home, her home. She cooked a roast chicken with potatoes, stuffing, and gravy, served with a green salad and a crisp pinot gris. They didn't even make it to the peach cobbler he'd brought for dessert before their clothes were once more helter skelter.

After making love, without any discussion, they both moved toward the bathroom and the shower. They stood under the warm spray of water, soaping each other back into desire.

Doug took Edwyna's hand, stopping her. "I have something I want to say. I can't believe this is only our fourth date. I don't even feel we are dating anymore. I feel each of our times together really represents a week or even more of our being a couple. Don't think I'm crazy." For the first time Doug sounded uncertain. "But I bought you an anniversary present. It's our fourth date equals one month anniversary."

Edwyna had been so caught up in what Doug was saying that she hardly realized they were still under the shower until he reached around and turned off the spigots. He handed her a towel and took one for himself.

"Wait here," he said. Only partially dried, he went back into the bedroom.

Edwyna could tell by the jingle of his belt buckle that he was moving his slacks.

He returned with a small white cardboard box that he handed to Edwyna. She opened it and saw a dark blue velvet box.

Doug put his hand on hers. "Wait," he said as he'd done a few minutes earlier. "I'm not asking for anything in return for this. But I want you to know that I hope this is the first of many of its kind."

Edwyna opened the box. There was a silver ring. In the center of the ring was a small ivory sphere carved with the image of the man in the moon. Around the moon there were three small amethysts set in silver bezels. She was overcome by the gift, by what Doug had said, and by the coincidence of the moon image. Of all the things she had told him, she'd never mentioned what she thought of as the nonsense about the moon and the moon festivals.

"This is too much," she said as she felt tears well up.

"Too much? Do you mean too soon?" Doug asked.

"No. I don't know what I mean. Too much to take in suddenly. No. It's perfect. You're perfect." She put the ring on the ring finger of her right hand. "Look. It fits perfectly."

Doug took her hand to his lips, kissed her hand above the ring. Then he lifted her left hand and kissed that ring finger.

The next day, Edwyna got no work done. She had two postures. In one she stared at the ring, the moon ring, and relived every wonderful moment with Doug. In the other she stared at the home screen of her computer and let the seeds of doubt continue to send questioning sprouts into her mind.

"To google or not to google," she said to herself. Finally she gave in to the impulse. No good can come of this, she thought even as she entered Doug's name and prepared herself for his Facebook page and whatever other information emerged. The first was his official police bio. Everything he'd told her about his work and education was there. Then the Facebook page. Pictures of men who had to be his cousins or brothers they looked so like him. Then, there she was, the blonde from the Muni. No caption, a photo of Doug, some of the other guys, and Blondie. Edwyna felt her stomach lurch. But she continued her search. Maybe she should have asked him about Blondie when they first started dating. And what if it was some woman who had been in his life? He certainly wasn't inexperienced. "Had been." Those were the key words. The desired verb tense. But what if she were in his life right now? A powerful girlfriend, a fiancée, even a wife. Edwyna continued to roam around his Facebook photos and entries. There was Blondie in one scene after another, but never with a notation of date or event.

Edwyna thought she would have to ask Doug about her after all. But that could destroy the mood they were in.

That evening, instead of calling Doug to ask about Blondie, Edwyna sat in her favorite chair, staring at a new moon, holding Inanna and silently wishing for all to be well.

Days and nights sped by. Doug and Edwyna spent so much time together that Doug moved in a toothbrush, razor, and several changes of shirts and underclothes. Those were not the only things he moved in. At the start of his moving things to her apartment, Doug asked Edwyna if she was sure she wanted to move that close to each other so quickly.

Edwyna nodded, then remained speechless as he sealed her lips to his and enveloped her in his arms.

As their bodies began to heat up, Doug pulled away. "Sit down," he said, leading Edwyna to her favorite chair. "Please sit down. I have something important to discuss with you."

Edwyna's heart pounded. Was this the moment when it would all end?

"You know that I'm an inspector in the San Francisco Police Department."

Of course she knew that.

"When I'm on duty, I have to carry a gun. I have that gun with me now. If I'm going to stay here or if you're going to stay at my home, you need to know that I have a gun." Doug reached down to the briefcase he'd carried with him. He drew a key chain from his pocket and unlocked the case. He took out a gun and laid it on the table. "This is the gun," he said, "a Sig Sauer semiautomatic."

Edwyna knew that what she was seeing was a gun. She didn't care about its precise name. The thought of a gun was frightening enough. The presence of the gun was downright scary.

"When I'm here, I need a safe place to store the gun, preferably one I can lock. If you don't want the gun here, then I'll have to make other arrangements—stay at my home—on the days when I have shifts."

"No. I want you to stay here, or if you're there, I want to be with you there. I guess the gun will be . . . I don't know . . . just with us."

"Do you want to see how it works?"

"No. I've seen enough TV and movies. Bullets go in and you pull a trigger and bullets come out and . . ." Edwyna did not want to follow her own train of thought.

"Do you have any questions about it? About the gun?"

Of course Edwyna had questions. But she couldn't put them into words. All she could do was shake her head and say, "I have a place that might be good. In the bedroom. One of the night table drawers locks. I'll clear it out and you'll have the key."

"Are you sure it's okay with you that the gun is here? This is your home. Remember, there are other options."

"But if we want to be together . . . I mean as long as we're together . . ."

"Which I hope will be a very long time."

"I'm going to have to get used to it. Sooner or later."

"I could arrange for you to go to the firing range and learn how . . ."

"No. No!" Edwyna held up her hand in the universal symbol for stop. She walked into the bedroom and returned with the small key that fit the night table drawer. She held it out to Doug.

"Do you have another copy of the key?" Doug asked as he added it to his key chain.

"No." Edwyna shook her head.

"Or should I have one made for you?"

"Why would I . . . ?"

"Just in case you wanted to . . ."

Edwyna did not want to pursue the "just in case" thought and shook her head again.

Several weeks later, which was as many wonderful days, evenings, and nights together later, Edwyna called her parents for what she thought, at first, would be one of her routine Sunday calls.

Sometime during those weeks, at his invitation, Edwyna had gone with him to his condo in the Richmond. She knew he was thinking of Hank's apartment when he said, "I just want you to see how ordinary—even boring—my apartment is." He was right. It was refreshingly ordinary, but far from boring. His book-shelves gave her insight into how deep his interest in American history and government went. His collection of lead soldiers ar-rayed in battle formation on a coffee table spoke to a boyhood hobby that endured. In front of the books on one shelf, Edwyna saw a collection of photos. All those guys she'd seen on Facebook were there along with Blondie.

"This is it," Doug said. "I've been afraid to reveal my one deep, dark secret."

"You're married," Edwyna blurted out without thinking.

"Married. Not at all. Never," Doug said. "Maybe this is worse than being married."

Edwyna was afraid some story about a child or children, his children was about to emerge. But he was laughing, so that was hardly likely to be it. That would have called for a more serious mien.

Doug continued, "While I'm an only child, my dad was one of six, and I have a collection of cousins who can make your life delightful or unbearable. You're going to have to meet them, but be ready. They are going to tease the dickens out of you. No mercy will be shown. No holds barred." And he named them: "Jamie, Artie, Clarke, Chuck . . ." The names seemed to go on forever and some of them were duplicates, a Jamie and a James, an Art, an Artie, and an Arthur. Doug continued, ". . . and the baby of the family—but the worst of the bunch—Catherine." He pointed at the blonde. "Who insists upon being known only as 'Mac.'"

Now as Edwyna waited for one of her parents to pick up the phone, she was happy she'd never given into the impulse to ask Doug about the blonde on the Muni. After all, it was reasonable to expect that he'd had as many relationships—she didn't even want to think the word "lover"—as she. She did know he'd never been married before, as he knew that about her.

"Something is different," Edward said as soon as he heard her voice.

"Yes," Winifred echoed. "You sound so . . ."

"Happy," Edwyna supplied. She had no reluctance to tell her parents about Doug, but she wanted to stretch the telling out. Savor the telling. She waited for the questions that she knew would follow.

"Happy?" her father and mother echoed in unison.

"Yes. Happy. Very happy," Edwyna replied.

"How should I put this?" Edward said. "What is the source of your happiness? C'mon, tell your Dad. What's brought about this change in my girl?"

Edwyna could not resist. She never could when he talked to her in that familiar way. "I've met someone. We've been seeing a lot of each other. And . . ."

"And?" Winifred asked.

"I think he may be, you know, may be more than any others have been." That was all Edwyna could get out.

"How long have you known him?" Winifred asked.

"Well, quite a while. He is . . . He was the detective who solved the case of those awful phone calls."

"Aha!" Edward said. "I get all the credit. I told you to go to the police."

"Yes, Dad. The credit is yours."

"How did he move from detective to . . . ?" Winifred began.

"Instead of filling you in, I'd like you to make your own judgments. Would you like to meet him?"

"When?" Again Edwyna's parents spoke in unison.

"Next Sunday?"

"Next Sunday."

The following Sunday, when Edwyna and Doug drove to Petaluma, the rains had stopped and the sun shone brightly on their day. If Doug had been nervous about meeting her parents, any anxiety quickly dissipated in their warm greetings. If her parents had held any suspicions about Doug's feelings for Edwyna, they, too, evaporated quickly. The time the four of them spent together reflected the sunshine from above.

After one of Winifred's excellent lunches, the four went for a walk in Shollenberger Park. Edwyna found herself walking on the path alongside the wetlands with her mother, quietly holding hands as they had not done since she was a little girl. Her mother said little, just squeezing Edwyna's hand in happiness from time to time. Edwyna wondered what her father and Doug were talking about. They seemed content to walk along together. Somewhere along the way, each had acquired a long cattail, which they swished back and forth in unison as they walked. Every now and then, Edwyna saw her father gesture with his cattail. He was probably pointing out a snowy egret, telling Doug about all the wildlife. Or maybe he was reciting the history of the park, starting with its volcanic beginnings or the settlements of Coastal Miwoks. Her father was an eager supporter of the park. She hoped he wasn't being too enthusiastic this time, not letting Doug get a word in edgewise. Meanwhile Athena bounded back and forth between the two pairs of walkers, her ears flopping with exertion and excitement. Every now and then she stopped to sniff avidly at one spot. Edwyna could not see what had intrigued Athena. Had she picked up the trace of a squirrel or a gopher? Maybe she was thinking of the dog park over on Casa Grande, probably her favorite place on earth.

About halfway through the two-mile loop, Athena stood panting, looking from one couple to the other. She commanded the four of them to come together to see what she was seeing, to praise her for seeing it. They each petted her and said, "Good dog, good girl," and she smiled her goofy dog smile.

When they continued their walk, somehow the foursome had switched walking partners. Winifred walked with Doug, Edwyna with her father.

"Do you really care for this man?" Edward asked in a low voice when some space had been created between the two couples.

"Don't you like him?"

"That's not the point. I'm asking you."

"I do, Dad. I more than like him. What do you think?"

"I don't want to jump to judgment," Edward said.

Edwyna worried what would follow. She felt a sudden hollow in her chest. If her father really didn't like Doug, she'd have to take that into consideration even though she felt sure of herself. After all, she was no kid; she was going to turn fifty. But her father was still her father.

Edward continued, "I've only met him today. But I like him. He seems solid."

"Solid" was one of the most approving things her father could say about any person. It meant he found them of sound values, consistent, someone you could rely on.

"Edwyna, I think he's going to ask you to marry him. I want you to be sure of how you feel."

"Really! Really? How do you know that?" Edwyna realized she was squealing like a teenager. Not at all like herself. She didn't even think she'd squealed when she was a teenager.

"Just say I have a father's intuition."

"Did he say something?"

"Not exactly."

"What did he say?"

"He said that you were too independent for a man to ask your father for permission to marry you, but if you weren't so independent, then he might have asked me that question."

"You're kidding. You just made that up."

"I didn't."

"What did you say?"

"I answered as carefully as he asked. I said something like, 'If a man like you asked me about my independent daughter, I would advise him to ask her, but I would appreciate—greatly appreciate—the respect such a question would hold.' Something like that."

"Are you kidding? Did the two of you plan this ahead of time or suddenly go to Toastmaster's or whatever? You know, the club where people learn to give speeches."

"Just two guys musing," Edward said as the two couples caught up with each other.

Doug spent most of the drive back to the city whistling. Edwyna tried to make out a recognizable tune but failed. She was about to ask him but then retreated to her own golden thoughts as the sun sank over the Pacific horizon.

The golden glow of Sunday faded into the reality of the work-week. Edwyna was back in her office and into the pleasant routine of accounting and client conversations, but one thought kept returning to her mind. What if now, now when she was so happy, something happened to spoil it all?

That morning, she'd looked at the lunar calendar. This was the period of letting go. Did that mean something would happen to take Doug from her? She found herself whispering to Inanna, whispering almost prayers that she and Doug would stay together. Continue in their happiness. Maybe what she had to let go of were her irrational fears. There was one element of her fears that was not irrational. Doug's work put him in danger. She didn't want to talk to him about how she felt, almost as if that could make something happen.

Now it was evening and, as if to hold all thoughts and fears at bay, Edwyna made Doug his favorite dinner of shrimp in green sauce with saffron rice. It was a delicate Spanish dish in which the green in the sauce came from peas and finely minced parsley. Mincing the parsley was therapeutic. She had to keep her mind on the greenery, the board, the knife, and her fingers. She made a salad and chilled an Albariño, a Spanish white—citrusy, light, dry—a wine that would complement the shrimp.

All was finished in time for Doug's arrival. But Doug did not arrive. Edwyna understood that Doug was a police officer, not an accountant, and he could not always predict when he would be home. While it was true that he worked specific shift hours, sometimes a case held him long beyond the planned shift. But he'd always called her when he was going to be late. This time, no Doug, and no call.

Edwyna had long ago turned off the flame under the pots of rice and shrimp. She went into the kitchen and emptied the pots into plastic containers for refrigeration. Doug was now more than two hours late. She certainly did not want to eat without him. In fact, she did not want to eat anything. Anything at all. Maybe not ever again. She wandered over to the living room window and looked out into the street below. No Doug. She lifted the receiver of the phone to check the dial tone. The phone was working. Besides, she'd already checked her cell for calls, emails, or texts. She'd texted him with a simple, "You ok?" But she had received no response.

"*Nada*," she murmured, the Spanish echoing the hopes she'd had for their meal together, their evening together. She picked up Inanna and sat in her blue chair waiting, just waiting. The blue of her beautiful new robe flowed into the blue of the chair.

Edwyna thought of getting a glass of wine, but she wanted to have all her wits about her to deal with whatever was going to happen next. She thought of making herself an espresso, but she was already too wound up to want any coffee. She hadn't felt this sensation of jumping out of her skin since she'd been in college. How foolish she'd been then, worrying about a so-called friend stealing her boyfriend. No one could steal someone from you. No one but someone with a gun. That was not a thought she wanted.

Edwyna got up, walked into the bedroom, and smoothed the duvet on the bed she shared with Doug, went into the bathroom, washed her face, and returned to the living room window, to her chair, to Inanna.

In the early hours of the morning, Edwyna, still wide awake, heard Doug's footsteps on the stairs. She waited until the door was open and she saw it was Doug before bursting into tears. He rushed to her and took her in his arms.

"I must stink," he said as he released her. "What a night."

"I was really scared," Edwyna said.

"I thought you might be worried, but there was nothing I could do. We were in the middle of it. There was no way I could break away, not even for an instant, to call you. I'm sorry. Really sorry."

"You don't have to be sorry for doing your work. I was just so scared. I kept thinking about your gun. And other people having guns. And guns kill. I don't mean the police."

"You mean the bad guys."

"Yeah, the bad guys," Edwyna said. "You're a cop. And cops get shot by bad guys. Every day."

"First, not all bad guys have guns. There are other kinds of criminals, other ways to break the law. Second, very few cops get shot and killed in San Francisco."

"How many?"

"Do you really want to know?"

"Since 1980, only five."

"But to their families . . ."

"I know, but people also die in car accidents and other ways. I'm sorry I put you through this. I'll try to call you when I'm going to be late, but . . ."

"I understand," Edwyna said. "Still, I was so scared."

"Of course you were scared. Next time, I'll try to call."

"But I know you can't always call. Don't take that on yourself."

"You're right," Doug said. "I did want to call tonight, did look for a moment to try. It just didn't . . ."

"I know. I really do. The last thing I want is for you to be worrying about me." She sighed, then said, "You must be hungry."

"You must be right," Doug said. "Donuts can only go so far. But let me tell you about tonight. Then you'll see . . ."

"Only if you want to."

Doug took Edwyna by the hand and led her to the sofa. "I was servicing a warrant for a sexual assault case. It was urgent. A juvenile."

"A juvenile victim or a juvenile assailant?"

"In this particular case, unfortunately, both. The girl—not even a teen—just eleven, and the man, the young man, the boy"—Doug ran his hand across his face as if that could erase the images of the night—"seventeen."

"Was it random? I mean, did he just see her somewhere and—I don't know—pounce on her?"

"Not random at all. It was grim. He was her cousin."

"Her cousin?"

"Her cousin! Most cases of sexual assault involve family members or those close to the family. In this case, very close."

"Didn't anyone in the family know? Couldn't they stop it?"

"Denial is alive and well. The two families—that is, the family of the victim and that of the perpetrator—could not have been closer. The father of the girl was the brother of the young man's mother. They were hardworking. Had saved and scraped together enough money to buy a house big enough for both families."

"Were they too close? I mean, maybe if each family had had enough room . . ."

"We really don't know why this abuse takes place. They did have enough room, had divided the one family house into two units. There was privacy. Just know that sexual assault is no respecter of race, ethnicity, religion, or social class."

"Was it hard to arrest him? I mean, did he have a weapon or hold someone hostage?"

"Actually, in this case, it was easy. If something so unpleasant can be easy. He was in his house, on his computer, playing a game."

"One of those violent games?"

"No. You won't believe this. He was playing old-fashioned solitaire. The kind you or I or our parents would play with a deck of cards, just to wile away the time. What was hard was dealing with the families. They didn't want to believe us, despite all the evidence. And the parents were beside themselves. The parents of the girl went from shock at what had happened to their daughter, to anger at the boy's parents for not keeping him in line, to fear for the boy who was, after all, their nephew. And the parents of the boy went through similar stages of grief and anger. It was painful to watch, painful to be a part of. And it was all hands-on."

"How awful." Edwyna put her hand on Doug's.

"Some of us were with the boy trying to get him to give a coherent statement. He started out sullen and silent but then began to cry so bitterly, he was incomprehensible. You know those good guy–bad guy cop shows? They couldn't be more wrong. We spent as much time comforting or consoling the guy as we did processing him." Doug stopped and stared into the room.

Edwyna got up from the sofa, poured two glasses of wine, and put them on the table in front of the sofa. She sat back down next to him.

Doug took a long drink of the wine and continued, "Several of the policewomen were with the girl, first at the hospital, then with social services. They had their hands full as well. I can't imagine how those families will heal. Where they will live. Can they ever again live together in the same innocent way?"

"'Innocent' is an interesting word," Edwyna said. "We usually use it to mean the opposite of guilty, but the word really means not having knowledge of good and evil."

"I wish I could be innocent again," Doug said. He leaned forward, his elbows on his knees, his head in his hands.

Edwyna rubbed his back in gentle circles. After a few moments, almost in a whisper, she asked, "Eggs and a bagel?"

"Perfect. A quick shower and I'll be there."

The next evening, Edwyna resurrected the shrimp and rice and chilled the Albariño once more. As they cleaned the kitchen together, Edwyna felt closer to Doug than ever before. As he passed each washed glass into the towel she held, he stroked her hands. She felt so much love from those small gestures, she couldn't stop the tears from forming and slipping down her cheeks.

"I know," Doug said. "You were scared."

"That's not why I'm crying. I'm crying because I love you so and I feel your love for me."

"That's what I want you to feel. Still, I think we should talk a little more about the gun. About guns."

"That's okay. We don't have to if you don't want to," Edwyna said as she polished the stainless steel edge of the stove.

"I do want to because I want you to know that I know how hard it is to get used to." Doug took another towel and rubbed the handles of the refrigerator. "When I was a young cop, a rookie as they say, and I got my first gun, I seemed fine, but my dreams told me otherwise."

Cloth still in hand, she waited for Doug to continue.

Doug continued his polishing as he spoke. "I had horrible dreams, repeated dreams, despite my excellent scores on the range and my feeling of control during the day."

"In one of the dreams, I'm with other cops and I'm facing a really bad guy. He's armed. I fire my gun. The bullet comes out very slowly. It moves through the air even more slowly and then drops to the ground. Not only am I unable to protect myself, but I'm responsible for all those around me."

Edwyna put down her cloth and came up behind Doug who was still assiduously rubbing at the spotless refrigerator. She put her arms around him and held him tight.

He continued to speak. "The other dream was sort of the opposite. I'm facing someone. I have a gun, but I haven't taken it out of its holster. I keep looking at the other person who seems to be shrouded in some mist—maybe a San Francisco fog—so that I can't see him clearly. I don't know if he's the one. If he's armed. I'm paralyzed. I cannot take out my gun. I don't know what to do."

Doug turned around within Edwyna's arms. They held each other tight, standing tight together in the kitchen.

CHAPTER 24

True Love

A FEW DAYS earlier Edwyna had looked at an email from Diane. It was a reminder that the Wise Women book club was meeting at her house later in the week. Edwyna wasn't sure she wanted to attend. She and Doug had spent every evening together—except when he had to work—for a few weeks. But she remembered how she'd always disapproved of women who dropped all their female friends when they had a man in their lives. She really didn't want to be part of the moon cabal, but did that mean she had to drop out of the group completely, suddenly, without explanation? Surely that was too rude. Besides, she'd read the book they had chosen for this meeting, *Cat's Eye* by Margaret Atwood. That seemed a good enough reason to go. And she still had the folder, another good reason to see the Wise Women once more. She wanted to be sure to return it.

She was now in Diane's house, once more looking around at the kachina dolls and listening to the women discuss the novel. Atwood's depiction of the effect childhood friends had on the main character, Elaine Risley's, life led them all to memories of other cruel and kind girls that had been part of their early lives. Edwyna mostly listened. She'd enjoyed the book, but she was more concerned with what she might talk about later with the Wise Women. She wondered how she could stay part of the book group, maybe even remain friends, without participating in—or even believing in—what she thought of as "all that moon gobbeldy-gook."

The discussion of the book had ended, glasses of wine had been poured, and the women were unusually silent. Dorothy, Lila, and Carolyn looked at one another, then at Edwyna, and finally at Diane. They seemed to be waiting for something, some signal.

What now? Edwyna thought but did not say aloud. Castigation for not attending the monthly ritual? Invitation to another trip? Maybe she was going to be dismissed from the group. That would not be a bad thing. Get her out of her dilemma. Get her out of whatever this was without her having to do anything. Oh God! She'd forgotten the folder again. Well, she could always mail it to Diane, or she could meet Diane at the lovely coffee shop. Sip some more tea the Russian way. Settle in for a good chat. Maybe she'd even introduce Doug to Diane, there in that coffee shop which was not too far from where he lived. Edwyna's wandering mind was brought back to the present when Dorothy began speaking.

"We want to congratulate you on the success of your goddess worship and wishing."

"Excuse me?" Edwyna said.

"Yes. Heartfelt congratulations, dear sister," Carolyn said. "You are successful."

"And so quickly," Lila continued. "Quicker than a New York minute, as they say everywhere but in New York."

"I'm not sure what you mean, what you're talking about," Edwyna answered.

"Of course you do know," Diane said. "You know and we know that you have now found the one person you've been looking for. And we know and you know that you succeeded by appealing to the moon goddess, looking for her image, speaking to her through Inanna."

"How do you know this?" Edwyna asked even as she felt pursuing the conversation was ridiculous.

"Even though you weren't with us at the recent new moon, I saw it in the candle," Dorothy said.

"So did I," Carolyn said.

"And I," Lila said.

"Not only did we all see your happiness at the candle ceremony, we can all see it in your face now," Diane said in a voice that brooked no argument.

"I do think I've met the right person for me," Edwyna said. "And I bet you can see it in my face, but my dear friends—I hope you'll forgive me—I had stopped wishing on the moon. I don't think it had anything to do with the moon or with my having any special powers."

The four other women looked at one another again. They smiled knowingly. They nodded, not in agreement with Edwyna, but in agreement with each other. She felt they were looking at her as you'd look at a child who couldn't believe that two plus two equaled four.

"Let's look at the details for the proof," Dorothy said. "What phase was the moon in when you met him?"

"I don't have any idea," Edwyna said. "I met him long before we began . . . before you introduced me to any of the moon ideas. As a matter of fact, I met him at the police station when I went to get help with the obscene caller."

"Did you know right away he was the one?" Carolyn asked.

"Not at all," Edwyna said, remembering how she'd thought Doug was interested romantically in Howard.

"Didn't there come a time when he made his intentions known?" Lila asked. "What was the moon phase on that day?"

"You sound like a character in *Law and Order,*" Edwyna said. "Again, I tell you I have no idea of the phases or when any events in my life might or might not line up with them."

"Didn't I give you the moon calendar?" Diane sounded disappointed. "You know you can use it retrospectively as well as for the future. You can see how events lined up in the past."

"I understand what you mean by retrospectively, but with all due respect, this just isn't how I see things."

There was a pause. Carolyn poured more wine into the five glasses. Each woman seemed more interested in precisely sipping the wine than in continuing the conversation. Every now and then one would look up, almost furtively, at Diane. Appearing, again, to be waiting for a signal.

Diane moved from her chair to an empty space on the sofa next to Edwyna. "I understand," she said softly. "You have spent almost all of your life denying your powers. It is enough right now to have those powers work for you. You don't even have to see that they are working or how they work." She took Edwyna's hand in hers. "How lovely," she said, caressing Edwyna's ring, the ring that Doug had given her. "How lovely to wear a ring with a moon goddess in it."

Edwyna opened her mouth to explain the coincidence of the ring, and Doug, and how he knew nothing of her forays into moon goddessing, but she closed her mouth, smiled, and squeezed Diane's warm hand in return.

"It is a lovely ring," Edwyna agreed.

That evening, she drove home musing about her friends. They were so kind, had accepted her readily into their group. But they were also mistaken about how the world worked. All that moon and wishing stuff.

She walked into her apartment quietly. Doug was probably sleeping, as he'd come home after a long shift. He didn't tell her much about his cases, but she already was aware of how some of them took much more energy from him, a lot out of him. She turned the living room lamp on to its lowest setting, preparing to divest herself of handbag and shoes before she entered the bedroom. Then her eye spotted a figurine next to Inanna on the semilunette table. It was a -small jade rabbit. Next to it, a note: *Came across this in Chinatown. Looks like a cousin to the jade rabbit pin you always wear. Hope you like it. Love xxx.*

Of course she liked the rabbit. She picked it up, fondled it for a moment, and put it back next to Inanna, whom she patted on the head. Ready for bed, she slipped in next to Doug. Still asleep, he reached out and pulled her close to him. In the moments before she was fully asleep, those moments of almost dreaming-almost awake, her thoughts tumbled around images of a crescent moon, a jade rabbit, and Inanna standing tall, smiling down on her.

The next day, at work, she could not get those images out of her mind. She knew that everyone had that kind of semi-dreaming experience. It didn't mean anything. There was even a name for it, the hypnagogic state. Sometimes people even heard voices in that state. She was glad that Inanna had not spoken to her! Still . . .

That evening she decided that she had to put the whole moon theory to rest—or did she mean to the test? Just a small test to be sure. She sat at her desk. If she was going to do this, she'd be professional, orderly about it. Edwyna lined up her supplies. Doug was out on a case, and she'd have plenty of time. She took out the calendar of moon phases and opened her computer to her personal calendar. She sharpened a blue pencil.

She took out a pad of yellow lined paper and, using a rule, created three columns. The first column was headed "Event." The second was headed "Phase of the Moon." She hesitated over the heading for the third column and then wrote "Evaluation," although she had not yet created a numeric scheme for matches and nonmatches. Although it disturbed her training as an accountant, she thought she could use a plus sign for a match and a minus for a nonmatch.

Under events, she listed:

1. Meeting Doug at the police station
2. Doug's first invitation to go out (rejected)
3. Doug's second invitation to go out (accepted)
4. First date
5. Receiving moon ring from Doug

She checked them out. Each of them had occurred between the new moon and the full moon, during the period of gain. The evaluation column was filled with a series of pluses.

Edwyna remembered the day she'd seen Doug on the Muni, seen him with the blonde woman, and she remembered also that she'd already noted, at the time, that it was during the waning period between the full and new moons.

Still, she thought, there were a limited number of data points. She wasn't convinced. But she was no longer certain that nothing depended on . . . that she could—or could not—influence . . . that she didn't have the powers she had so long scoffed at.

What about Hank? she thought. What kind of moon was it when she'd met him? She thought she might be able to reconstruct the date they'd met by counting back from their first date. Sure enough, they'd met on the date of a full moon, and their first date had been in the waning time. Joel—he certainly wasn't as toxic as Hank, nor was he the right one. She hadn't found anything like love with him, just some not-too-bad dinners and not-too-bad sex. When had she met him? Edwyna turned on her computer and went back to the exchange of emails with Joel, all the way back to the first time she encountered him on RomeoandJulietMatch.com. She pulled a piece of paper from her desk drawer, scribbled the dates on it, and then calculated the lunar phases. Working backward in time was a challenge, but she was pretty sure she'd met him for the first time during the waning moon. She should never have connected with him, just let him go. Just let them all go.

Whether she had special powers or not, Edwyna could not understand how she had let herself spend all that time, precious time, with men who were wrong for her. Even Nick, who was nice enough, had never been the kind of man she wanted. Edwyna got up from her desk, moved to her favorite blue chair, and picked up Inanna. "Can you tell me why I was so blind?" She looked into the enigmatic face of the doll. "If it's you I have to thank for all this good luck, I do. Thank you, Inanna." She held Inanna to her heart and sat back in her chair. She must have dozed off. The next thing she knew, Doug was standing next to her, smiling down at her.

"Come here, my love," he said, and lifted her into his warm embrace.

Two months to the day after their first date, Doug proposed that they repeat the day.

"It's our two-month anniversary," he said. "Let's do everything we did on our first date—walk on Ocean Beach, look at the ocean and the birds, end up at the Cliff House for brunch."

Doug's romantic nature was just one of the many things that Edwyna loved about him.

"Great idea," she said. "I hope we don't have to get caught in a sudden downpour just to repeat everything the same way."

"Unlikely," he said. "The rains are probably over by now."

As they walked, Edwyna remembered telling him about Donald's fall and Inanna. It was time to tell him what she thought of as her deep, dark secret, her slip into the fantasy that she actually did have powers. She wasn't sure how to begin until she looked at the ring he had given her.

"You know, I love my ring," Edwyna said, "but it's quite a coincidence that you gave me a ring with an image of the moon. I'm a little embarrassed to tell you this, but sometimes I think the moon played a big part in my life."

Doug listened as Edwyna repeated the whole saga beginning with the Wise Women, the first trip to the Baths, going through the trip to China, and ending with the recent book club meetings. The only part she left out was the image of a man cradling her face. Doug had given her his love in so many ways, but she realized he had never done that. That particular gesture no longer held any meaning for her.

"Do you believe in any of it?" he asked.

"What do you think?" Edwyna asked in response.

"It is a lovely idea. That you wished for me and just wished me into being in your life. Are you sure you don't have the powers? If you do, what could we wish for together?"

"I have everything I could wish for, right now," Edwyna said.

"I have almost everything," Doug said.

"Almost?" Edwyna asked.

"I think in about a half hour or so I may have everything," he answered enigmatically, "or maybe not."

"What's going to happen in a half hour?"

"Can't tell you yet. Keep walking and it may be sooner."

Edwyna picked up her pace, and Doug encouraged her by pressing his hand against the back of her waist as they walked up the last bit of hill to the Cliff House.

In the Cliff House, he led her to a table in the bar and set their two chairs so that they were side-by-side looking out at the water. He signaled to a waiter, who appeared with a bottle of *Veuve Clicquot* and a bowl of strawberries. The waiter uncorked the wine perfectly and poured it into their glasses without wasting a drop.

Doug offered the bowl of strawberries to Edwyna. She took one and it was then that she saw a blue velvet box sitting atop the remainder. She wasn't sure if she should take the box or wait. Nothing in her previous fifty years had prepared her for this moment, or for what she thought this moment was or was going to be. Her mind rattled on.

Unexpectedly Doug took the box. He slipped from his chair, got down on one knee, and opened the box.

"Edwyna Glendower, love of my life, will you marry me?"

Edwyna slipped from her chair to kneel beside him. She took his face in her two hands, kissed him, and said, "Yes, my own true love, I will."

The other patrons in the bar, all of whom, up to this point, had been invisible to Edwyna and Doug applauded. Laughing, Edwyna and Doug got up and bowed.

"I have never felt as loved as I do right now," Doug said. "When you held my face as you did, I felt infinitely connected to you. You do have power, the power over my heart. And if you have any special powers, I'll cherish them as I cherish all there is about you."

Edwyna looked down at the solitaire diamond on her left hand, at the moon ring on her right hand, and then up at Doug. She smiled.

That night, after making love, as they lay in bed, Doug said, "I know you aren't asleep. I can hear your wheels turning. If I know my Edwyna, then I know you are making a list. What is it this time?" He gave a mock sigh.

"We haven't talked about what kind of wedding we'll have. City Hall. Church. Big. Small. But you're right. I just started the guest list."

"Parents, sibs, maybe my cousins, Howard and Greg, of course," Doug used Edwyna's fingers to count off the people.

"I'm thinking of the Wise Women—you know—my book club."

"Right. Your coven."

"Don't even kid around about that. Maybe I should just forget about them."

"Now you stop kidding. They're your friends."

"They are," she said, and used his fingers to count, "Diane, Dorothy, Lila, Carolyn. And if we have a big wedding, they can all be my attendants."

Holding hands, they fell asleep.

Two months later, Edwyna and Douglas were married on a moon-swept terrace at a Bay-side restaurant in Sausalito. The night was clear. Edwyna and Doug, her Wise Women attendants, and all the guests could see the night sky clearly above and below them as the stars and the new moon were reflected in the waters of the Bay.

For Edwyna, the best moment in the wedding came after the judge, a friend of Doug's, pronounced them husband and wife.

"You may kiss the bride, your beautiful bride," the judge said.

Doug moved into the small space between them. He took Edwyna's face between his hands, looked deeply into her eyes, and kissed her. It was such a long, deep kiss that the gathered guests could not stop themselves from applauding, even whistling. Edwyna heard them as if they were in some distant background. She was, instead, fully focused on Doug's lips on hers, Doug's warm hands on her face.

The morning after the wedding, Edwyna and Doug faced the array of gifts they'd received the evening before.

"Where to begin?" Edwyna sighed. "Biggest first or last? Best wrapping first or last?"

She sat on her living room floor, resting on her heels. Doug sat cross-legged next to her.

"Blind man's bluff," he answered. "I'll close my eyes. You'll turn me around a few times and the first package I touch is the first one we'll open."

"Not very practical. You'll probably step on them before we can see what's inside. Besides, we'd have to stand, and I like sitting here."

"Good points. This is it. I'm closing my eyes and just leaning forward. Whatever I touch with any part of my body will be *numero uno*." Doug closed his eyes, stretched out his arm, and leaned forward. His hand landed on a flat package, about two feet long and half as wide. It was wrapped in gold foil and tied with blue and gold ribbons. He opened his eyes and handed the package to Edwyna.

Before she opened it, she said, "There is so much we don't know about each other. Are you a paper and ribbon saver or a ripper opener?"

In answer, Doug took the package back, tore away the ribbons, and ripped open the paper. Somewhat more carefully, he opened the gold box that he'd unwrapped. Even more slowly he folded aside several layers of white tissue paper. "What a beautiful book!" he caressed the dark blue, soft leather cover and the indentations of the gold lettering.

The Book of Moon Energy.

Do you want to open it?" He held the book out to Edwyna.

She shook her head. She knew what was in it—newspaper articles, stories of childhood beginnings, email invitations to San Francisco. She no longer thought she'd know what would appear first, but that no longer bothered her.

On the other hand, she was sure she'd left the folder in her desk. The last time she'd seen it was when she'd examined her recent life events in light of the phases of the moon. She hoped she hadn't left that in the folder.

"Hold on a moment," Edwyna said. She scrambled to her feet and went to her desk. Of course, the folder was not on her desk or in it, although the calendar of moon phases was there, along with her evaluation. Even its reappearance as a gift, surely a gift from the Wise Women, caused only a momentary ripple of surprise. She didn't know if the Wise Women had spirited the folder out of the house with Doug's help or had truly spirited it out of the house. She didn't care. She sat back down on the floor. "Please open it," she said.

Doug opened the cover. "It's not exactly a book. More like a folio. The pages are not bound." He riffled the pages. "It starts with a poem." Doug was quiet for a moment as he read to himself. Then, "Listen to this," he said and read aloud to Edwyna.

Inanna's Hymn

A Translation and Adaptation from the Writings of Enheduanna
High Priestess and Poet circa 2500 BCE

I am the moon's and
The moon is mine

All day my sun-sister pours her light onto me
So I may float among my star-sisters for all to see.

The earth spins on its axis
Giving sight of me to sighing lovers
Giving strength from me to doubting lovers
Giving love from me to all.

In my first crescent women see
The seeds of birth.
My fullness
Is reflected in
Their rotund bellies
Which empty fruit
As I wane.

Diana
Hecate
Chang'e
I am the moon
All three.

Acknowledgments

Thank you to the members of my writing group, CC Hart, John Talaga, and Maggie Tokuda-Hall, who offered detailed chapter-by-chapter critiques of *Blue Magic* during many of our working sessions. I look forward to continuing our support of each other's work

I appreciate the insights of my early readers who gave me invaluable feedback. You always wanted more than I had written. Thank you Jon Benjamin, Sasha Borenstein, Lillian Falese, Joan Green, Jill Kneeter, and Susan Roudebush for helping me uncover aspects of *Blue Magic* that had been hidden from me.

Special notes of appreciation go to two people who shared their expertise with me. Thank you to Elise Stupi, an accountant, who provided me with details of the relevant college courses and accounting practice. And thank you Daniel L. Lawson, Senior Director Public Safety at the University of San Francisco and Retired Captain, San Francisco Police Department. Dan not only checked and corrected my facts of police procedure but also enabled me to feel his personal experience in having the responsibility of carrying a weapon.

Of course, any errors in accounting, police procedure, or elsewhere in *Blue Magic* are mine alone.

To my entire staff—Martin Bloch—reader, editor, cheering squad, cook, and husband, thank you forever.

About the Author

Debby Bloch understands the journeys so many women undertake to seek love, friendship, purpose, and acceptance. She made a series of life-changing decisions that moved her to an entirely different path.

After a fulfilling professional career, Bloch enrolled in the University of San Francisco MFA program and became a novelist.

Bloch has published the novel *That Old Song and Dance* and a series of nonfiction guides about professional skills and career choices.

Bloch and her husband, Martin, split their time between San Francisco and Ashland, Oregon. She was inspired to write her latest novel, *Blue Magic*, while attending the Oregon Shakespeare Festival in Ashland.